The

SISTERS
of
VERSAILLES

The

SISTERS

of

VERSAILLES

A NOVEL

SALLY CHRISTIE

ATRIA PAPERBACK

New York   London   Toronto   Sydney   New Delhi

ATRIA PAPERBACK

An Imprint of Simon & Schuster, Inc.
1230 Avenue of the Americas
New York, NY 10020

First Atria Paperback edition September 2015

ATRIA PAPERBACK and colophon are trademarks of Simon & Schuster, Inc.

For information about special discounts for bulk purchases, please contact Simon & Schuster Special Sales at 1-866-506-1949 or business@simonandschuster.com.

The Simon & Schuster Speakers Bureau can bring authors to your live event. For more information or to book an event contact the Simon & Schuster Speakers Bureau at 1-866-248-3049 or visit our website at www.simonspeakers.com.

Interior design by Kyoko Watanabe

Manufactured in the United States of America

10 9 8 7 6 5 4 3 2

Library of Congress Cataloging-in-Publication Data has been applied for.

ISBN 978-1-5011-0296-7
ISBN 978-1-5011-0298-1 (ebook)

To John & Sylvia: Simply the Best

The

SISTERS

of

VERSAILLES

Hortense

We were five sisters and four became mistresses of our king. Only I escaped his arms but that was my choice: I may be eighty-four years old, and all that I speak of may have happened in the far distance of the past, but in a woman vanity is eternal. So I need to tell you: I could have. Had I wanted. Because he—the king—he certainly wanted.

I'm not speaking of the last king, our sixteenth Louis, poor hapless man dead these six years on the guillotine, followed by his Austrian wife. No, here I talk of the fifteenth Louis, a magnificent king. I knew him when he was fresh and young, no hint of the debauched libertine that he would become in his later years, with his drooping eyes and sallow skin, his lips wet with lust.

The story of my sisters and Louis XV is today mostly forgotten, their memory eclipsed by more famous and more scandalous mistresses, and by the upheaval of the last decade. I too am forgetful now, my memory faded and worn as my sisters slip in and out of the shadows in my mind. I spend my hours immersed in a sea of their old letters; reading them, then rereading them, is both my comfort and my sorrow. Is anything more bittersweet than the pull of past memories? These letters, a portrait of one sister that hangs above the fireplace, and a faded sketch of another pressed between the pages of a Bible, are all that remain to me now.

It was years ago that it all began: 1729, almost three-quarters of a century past. It was such a different time then, a completely different world. We were secure and arrogant in our privilege, never suspecting that things might change, that the accident of birth might not always be the promise it once was. We were born daughters of a *marquis*; titles and courtesy and the perquisites of the nobility were all that we ever knew, but now, what do those things matter? Well, they still matter a lot, though all we *citoyens* must pretend they do not.

The world—our world—was softer then; those who could afford to do so buttered and feathered themselves until they were insulated from all of the unpleasant realities of life. We never dreamed—ever—that a horror like the Terror could happen.

We were five sisters in our childhood home on the Quai des Théatins. Our home was in the center of Paris on a road by the Seine, lined with the houses of the rich and powerful. The house still stands on that street, now renamed the Quai Voltaire to honor that great man. I shudder to think who may live there now.

It was a grand house, an elegant house, a reminder to all of our place in the world. I remember well my mother's golden bedroom on the second floor, opulent and resplendent, the awe we felt when summoned for a visit. Of course, the nursery was not so grand; children in those days were mostly ignored, and so why waste money on things, or children, that were so rarely seen? Up in the aerie of our nursery on the fourth floor, the rooms were cold and bare, but comfortable, our haven in a heartless world.

We had no education to speak of; the aim was not an educated daughter, but a mannered daughter, one who knew her way through the intricate maze of politeness and social graces that governed our world. In truth, even with the wisdom that is supposed to come with age, I can't say that more education would have served me better in my life.

We were five sisters and we had no brothers; my mother sometimes remarked, when she was happy on champagne, the misfortune that had cursed her so.

Though we sprang from the same parents, we were all so

different. Oh, how different! Louise was the eldest, charming and somewhat pretty, nineteen when she was first presented at Court. She was a dreamer, always with stars in her eyes when she thought of her future and the happiness that would surely come for her.

Then there was Pauline, fierce with no softness in her body and a character to make a pirate proud. She was as headstrong as a horse and ruled the nursery; she towered over us, both in height and in strength. Even at seventeen, Pauline knew she would be powerful and important. How she knew that, I know not. But she knew.

Our next sister was Diane, fifteen then and always jolly, lax and lazy. She avoided conflict and only wanted to giggle and laugh and dream of becoming a duchess. Physically she reminded everyone of our sister Pauline, but without the force of personality. I suppose that was both a curse and a blessing.

Then there was I, only fourteen when everything changed. All called me the prettiest of the family and many commented on my likeness to my namesake, my famous great-grandmother Hortense Mancini, who in her time bewitched more than one king.

Finally there was little Marie-Anne, though it seems strange now to speak of her last. She was twelve and also very pretty, but hidden beneath her angel face was a sharp and shearing mind that emerged occasionally to astound our nursemaids.

I remember our years on the fourth floor of the Quai des Théatins as happy ones, years of light and love. Certainly, there were small differences, the usual squabbles and petty fights, but overall harmony reigned, a harmony that was all too precious and absent later in our lives. Perhaps there were signs, but they were faint and thin, mere whispers of the callousness and suffering to come. No, my memory is of a happy time, before the harsh world of adults caught us and covered us with its disappointments and cruelties, before we lost the closeness of our younger years and before Louise became broken, Pauline mean, Diane fat and lazy, and Marie-Anne manipulative and hard.

But through it all, through the good, the bad, the sin and the scandal, the heartbreak and the joy, the exiles and the deaths, through it all, they were my sisters. And now I am all that is left. I sit in my darkened rooms, an old woman, passing my days rustling through their letters and my memories. If I am careful, and still, I can hear their voices once again.

Part I

One in Love

Louise

VERSAILLES

1730

Versailles. Vastness and grandeur and echoes; the chatter of a hundred persons murmuring in polite whispers, the sound overwhelming though each speaks so softly; the smell of a thousand scents mingling; a great crush of people like a painting come to life.

Everything is gilt in richness and the walls are hung with enormous mirrors that lie like lakes against the marble and reflect your life back at you, magnified many times over. Everywhere are candelabras and chandeliers, some with two hundred candles, and at night the palace sparkles as though lit by the sun itself.

The endless corridors are lined with statues of kings and gods, enormous in bronze, marble, and stone. The ceilings are so high they reach the heavens and they are painted like the heavens too, only you can't twist to admire them, for one must always appear very sophisticated and disinterested.

In this vast palace it is hard to find one's way; traps and trickery are everywhere and life is rich in rules that everyone seems to know but myself. The palace is like a treacherous flower I once heard about, beautiful and lush, that eats the flies that dare to land on its lips.

I have been here for several months already, in the exalted position of lady-in-waiting to the queen, yet still every day I wake up and wonder: Is this the day that something dreadful happens? Will I fall when I curtsy? Slip on the orange-waxed floors?

Speak at the wrong time? Offend the right person with the wrong words?

My rooms are up three flights of stairs, not far from the great staterooms but not so near either. I have memorized the route from my apartment to the queen's, but today after Mass I was bidden to deliver a pot of mushroom pâté to the Duchesse de Luynes, a favorite of the queen who finds herself ill and in bed with fever. I make the delivery in the company of a Luynes maid but on the way back I find myself alone and in an unfamiliar part of the palace. It is dreadfully confusing: Is it possible Versailles was designed by a madman? Who else could create such a serene and uniform exterior hiding this jumble of rooms, passageways, and stairs?

I am far from the magnificence of the public halls, the grand rooms where the king and the queen and the royal family live and sleep; those rooms are only a small part of the palace, a little flourish on top of a great gesture. Back here, opulence is out of reach and there are no orange trees in great gilded pots to sweeten the air. The floors are dirty, the dizzying parquet of the great rooms replaced by flagstones and uneven oak.

A woman in a mask, her pink skirt slick with mud and sin, pushes rudely past me. I stop; surely I am not going where she goes? All is unfamiliar, and dread tightens my throat. Before I can decide which way to turn, six wolfhounds race past me, giant gray beasts smelling of wet fur and sticky rabbit blood, followed by two pages trotting. The road to the stables must be ahead, so I change direction.

"Going somewhere, little one?" It is the Comtesse d'Hauteville and a companion. I want to ask her help but she doesn't stop, just sweeps past as the dogs did and I don't have the courage to call out.

"Armande's daughter," I hear her say to her companion.

A tinkle of laughter. "Let's hope she doesn't take after her mother, poor lamb," says the other, and then they are gone down the corridor, their heels clacking on the stone floors.

I come upon another narrow corridor, where I am leered at

by men with no livery, jostled by servants carrying great barrels of water on their backs. I look out a window onto an interior courtyard. I am in the South Wing; do I need to go north to find the main palace? But I don't know where north is. We didn't receive much education in the schoolroom in our childhood home in Paris. Our governess, Zélie, was a distant relation of ours, and while I loved her dearly, sometimes her lessons were wanting. She would spin the globe and tell us about the world . . . I remember north was up. Or was that the sun? I find a staircase and climb.

At the top is a large square room hung with crimson drapes. A group of men in dark coats talk with animation in a corner and I daren't interrupt them. I move toward two men sitting by a window, but as I approach I see their coats are worn and their breeches stained. "Sirs," I start, then realize in horror they are drunk. One smiles at me and reaches out a dirty hand.

No, no, no. I stumble down a small flight of stairs only to find myself faced with another back corridor of whitewashed walls and stone floors. This one is quiet and it is hard to believe that elsewhere in the vast palace there is life and laughter. This part of the building feels older, lost, away from the comfort of the familiar and the opulent, and the mold of centuries soaks through the thin soles of my shoes. At the end of the corridor is a small door nestled in a panel. I open it, thinking to find another passage, but before me is a room. Two men standing too close, and a woman sitting watching. I freeze.

"Announce yourself!" roars the woman on the sofa in a voice of fury. She is wearing a fur wrap and holding a cup in her hand, her skin as shiny as pearls against the deep mink. I don't recognize her, but the luxury of her clothes and the room signal she is someone important. The two men are in front of her, one finely dressed and the other in the costume of the Swiss Guard, his shirt open. The noble doesn't remove his hand from the guard's breeches but just smiles at me in a wide vacant way, his rouge orange on his cheeks, his face disdainful, and his eyes dead. I shiver, snared by the dreadful tableau before me.

"Get out, get out, get out!" A woman in brown comes barreling toward me, summoned by her mistress's roar. Before she can physically push me, I back out and scatter down the corridor. At the end I sink to the ground, inhaling the sharp stench of piss, ignoring something sticky on the floor. I can't stop trembling. Nothing is what it seems here, and that, that was . . . what was that?

What am I doing here? A man runs past, a footman too important to stop, followed by two men bearing a great quantity of firewood. Faintly I hear bells chiming noon. The queen dines soon and I need to find my rooms, clean my hands and my dress. But I don't know how. I don't belong here, I think, gazing in defeat at the floor, still trembling. I want to go back to Paris, back to the safety and security of my childhood home. I want my mother.

๛

I had a happy childhood, safe and secure in our rooms on the fourth floor of our home in Paris. But no matter how content one is as a child, one cannot help but wonder what lies beyond the walls of the nursery, out in the wide world.

My sixteenth birthday was the beginning. I remember my mother that day in her gold-gilt bedroom, lounging on a sofa next to her friend, the Comtesse de Rupelmonde. Mama lived a glamorous life, often away at Versailles, often entertaining in Paris, often in the company of great men. A Mazarin by birth, she had the large ebony eyes of her famous grandmother Hortense. I did not inherit her exotic looks, and though I am often called pretty, no one ever says I am beautiful. That is a good thing; too much beauty would make me proud and I wish nothing more than to be humble. And beloved by God.

"You look very well, dearest," Mama murmured, and pushed me away to examine me. I was crushed into my best gown, my hair dressed back and my face heavy with unfamiliar powder.

I curtsied and thanked her. She raised her hand and motioned to one of her women. "The *caramelos*," she called, and a plate was brought over. "Here, child, have a *caramelo*."

I took one eagerly. There were two worlds in this house: my mother's world of luxury and indulgence and our children's world of austerity. I was eager to join the adult world and I hoped that she had news for me. I wanted to get married, leave the nursery behind and go to Court; fall in love with my husband, and have pretty little children.

"We have talked with Louis-Alexandre and his parents," my mother said.

As is often the case in families like ours, I had known for a long time that I would marry my cousin. I didn't know Louis-Alexandre very well—he was almost twenty years older than me—but at least he was no stranger. When I was a little girl he came once to visit us, and after our meeting I rushed upstairs to draw a picture that I might remember him by. All these years later I still have that drawing, tucked at the bottom of a small chest beneath my ribbons and gloves. When I was young I used to take out the creased picture and dream about our life together.

"Does May please you?"

I clapped my hands. "So soon! That is wonderful."

My mother took another candy and picked out a nut. In a petulant voice she said, "Rose, you know I can't abide cashews—what is it doing in the *caramelo*?" She dropped the offending nut on the floor.

"So eager to marry?" asked Madame de Rupelmonde. I nodded cautiously. In truth, Madame de Rupelmonde was not my favorite person; her languid manner and curled lips made me uneasy. She always seemed to imply something other than what she said.

"Of course she is eager to marry!" exclaimed my mother. "Who doesn't want to escape the nursery? And she'll be the Comtesse de Mailly—she'll hardly even change her name. And such a fine groom, such a fine groom. It is all very satisfactory."

"The finest groom in the land," drawled Madame de Rupelmonde, and they both laughed. I was not included in their laughter. "He adores swords, yes, and weapons of all types."

"No mind," said my mother quickly, and I knew I had missed something. "She'll be a wife and at Court." She turned to me. "Louise, Madame de Rupelmonde and I have been working on a little project."

"A big project," interjected Madame de Rupelmonde. Her lips were thin and dark, a leech on her white-leaded face. It's not polite to comment unfavorably on another's appearance, but I didn't like hers at all.

"We have been working . . ." My mother took another *caramelo* and her words hung in the air. I almost popped with anticipation, for I could guess what she would say next. She chewed carefully awhile then continued: "We have been working on a place for you in the queen's household."

I jumped and clapped in glee.

"Louise-Julie!" reproved Madame de Rupelmonde. "Such displays are unseemly. You must contain yourself." This time there was no hidden meaning.

"Oh, Marguerite, let the girl be happy," said my mother. "She's so very natural. It's sweet. Besides, the queen is also . . . natural. Who knows? Simplicity may one day be the fashion."

"Like a cow," said Madame de Rupelmonde lightly. "Natural, placid, like a well-natured cow. The queen, I mean, not you, dear Louise-Julie."

෫৽

I stand up, brushing away memories and determined to find my way. The queen. I must find her. I walk unsteadily down the corridor, not opening any more doors for fear of what I might find.

Ahead I see a footman in the livery colors of the powerful Noailles family.

"Noailles!" I call, panic making my voice imperious.

The man turns, appraises me, notices the sticky mess on my skirt, makes the faintest of bows.

"I am lost," I say, trying to keep my voice even and cool. "I need the Queen's Apartments."

The man smirks subtly and bows again, even slighter this

time. At Versailles gossip curls up like smoke and fans out to reach the farthest corners of the palace, and I know by tomorrow this story will be all over Court.

"Follow me, madame." He leads me down two corridors then opens a door and ushers me through to the Princes' Courtyard. I know my way from here. I want to thank him for his service, but to show me I am nothing he disappears without a word. Back in the familiar opulence of the main rooms, I trot as quickly as my heels allow to the Queen's Apartments. I rush in and almost collide with a footman carrying a large platter of purple aubergines, glistening in oil.

"Oooh, sweat!" shrieks my friend Gilette, the Duchesse d'Antin, and another of the queen's ladies. She pushes me toward a window. "Hold your cheeks here and cool down." She fans me vigorously. "Her Majesty is with the *dauphin* and will eat within the hour. Some powder! We need some powder!"

The staunch Duchesse de Boufflers, the most formidable and ancient of the queen's ladies, narrows her eyes as she takes a pot from one of the maids. "Put some on when you have stopped perspiring. And mind you don't get any on the napkins." She looks at me in distaste, as though she would like to pick something off me. "And what is that mess on your skirt?"

I flush miserably and keep my cheeks pressed against the cool of the window.

"How does one get lost here?" I hear her mutter as she turns back to the table to direct the placing of the plates. "The fish here. You, put the duck stew there. Where are the plum profiteroles?"

How does one *not* get lost in this place, I think miserably.

Too soon the doors are flung open and the queen wobbles in. We curtsy low and take our places behind and beside her chair, ready to serve. Twenty-six plates gleam on the table.

"Your napkin, madame," says the Duchesse de Boufflers in a voice as oily as the eggplant. The meal begins.

I stand at attention, trying to control my breathing that is still coming in ragged waves. That man had his hand in the other

man's breeches, on his . . . on his . . . oh. Will I ever fit in here?
Will I ever understand this world? Why did I ever long to come
here?

☙

I had thought that after my marriage I would go straight to Versailles, but then I learned that I would only enter the queen's
service once my mother-in-law, Anne-Marie-Françoise, the Dowager Comtesse de Mailly, retired or died. I could not wish her to
fall ill, or die, but sometimes I did hope. She was over sixty and
had lived a full life, hadn't she? When I thought such wicked
thoughts, I would spend the next day on my knees to pray away
my guilt.

After the wedding ceremony I traveled with Louis-Alexandre
to my new home. It would be impractical and scandalous, he advised me, for a young wife to stay alone in Paris. There were too
many temptations and people would talk. It was decided it would
be best for me to stay at a small family château in the country,
until the time came for me to go to Court. I was not asked if I
thought this would be best for me.

The village was not that far from my childhood home in Paris,
but it felt many, many miles away. The house was ancient: thousands of years old with sloping roofs, and even though the fire-
places were enormous—large enough to sit inside—the rooms
were always cold. When it rained, mildew grew behind the hanging tapestries and everything reeked of mold. It was as different
from our lovely house on the Quai des Théatins as a hunting
lodge is to a château.

No one talked to me in that house, not even the servants. Not
that I would confide in them, but still. The cook rebuffed my attempts to join him in planning the menus and the steward made
it clear I had nothing of value to contribute to his important business. Even the maids were unfriendly and never smiled back.

Occasionally, the local magistrate's wife came to visit and ca-
joled me into meeting with the ladies of the neighborhood. They
always asked me what news of Court, and when I dutifully passed

along what little information I had, those provincial bureaucrats' wives nodded and murmured as though I was simply confirming what they already knew.

When my mother-in-law learned of these little meetings, she forbade me to attend further. Some of the ladies, she warned me with lowered breath, are *bourgeoise* and you cannot be seen to have such acquaintances. She said *bourgeoise* in a horrified whisper, as though talking of lice on a houseguest. Every time I saw my mother-in-law, all I could think was: You are the only thing that is keeping me here.

I was eager to be a good wife to Louis-Alexandre but he was cold, even surly, with me, and only visited when he came to hunt in the forest bordering the château. On those visits he brought friends and together they hunted all day then drank too much at night. At the table they rambled about the day's kill and the gossip, big and small, of Versailles. I only truly listened when they talked of our young king and of his devotion to his Polish bride. What does she look like? I asked once, but the men just sniffed and glanced at each other.

"Like a cow," said Louis-Alexandre. "Plump and dull. Thick lips and quickly getting fat from all the daughters she keeps producing."

"She must use magic," one of his friends added. "Why else would the young king remain devoted to such small charms? They say he rode her seven times on the wedding night—that must be witchery."

"Pah!" spluttered Louis-Alexandre scornfully, spitting out his mouthful of wine. "She is not smart enough to employ such wiles—I'd wager my chestnut horse that she wouldn't know a love charm if it slipped up behind her and smacked her on her ample ass."

I was appalled to hear them talk of the queen in such a manner. She may be Polish but she is still our queen and I thought it so romantic that the king loved his wife and was devoted to none but her. It is the king who sets the fashion at Versailles, so why are the men of the Court not rushing to be with their wives? Our Polish queen, I decided, was the luckiest woman in the world.

Louis-Alexandre would come to me at night during those visits, slurring his words and reeking of brandy. As soon as he was done he left to sleep in another chamber. It was then that I truly felt the sad sting of loneliness. On the fourth floor in the schoolroom, with my four little sisters, I don't think I knew what loneliness was. And I didn't think marriage would be this. When I was young I thought that all husbands loved their wives, and that kissing would be delightful. But after Louis-Alexandre would leave me I would lie awake listening to the drip of the rain from the leaking roofs, the clack of oak branches against the windows, and the distant howl of wolves in the forest. The house was filled with people and my husband slept in the next room, yet I felt as though I were the only woman in the world.

Why wouldn't he spend the night with me? Why wouldn't he love me? He was not handsome—he is short and has a pitted face like an omelet—but he was my husband and I wished to love him as I wished he would love me.

"Won't you stay?" I asked timidly one night after he was finished. I never asked anything of him.

"Why?" he demanded, wiping himself with a cloth. He threw it on the floor and reached for his nightshirt.

I started to cry. I looked at him through my tears, pleading silently for him to return to bed and hold me. He paused in astonishment, then said coldly and firmly, "Control yourself, madame."

He left, and when he shut the door it was as if he shut my heart. In desperation, I broached the subject with the priest from the village. Once a month he came to the château to celebrate a private Mass with me and I took that opportunity to ask him what I should do to make my husband love me. He shifted uncomfortably and I regretted the question; I should have waited for the grille of the confessional to separate us.

The priest asked for no details but just cleared his throat and looked out the window. "You must give it time," he said finally. "At the moment the *comte* is very busy. He has his duties with his regiment and . . . and other things, I am sure, and he cannot be here very often."

"But even when he is here, he ignores me." I started crying and the priest looked down as though he would like to disappear through the flagstones. He took out a green handkerchief from his pocket and I thought he was going to offer it to me, but instead he twisted it in his hands then stretched it out to examine it with great intent. Finally he asked, in a higher voice than usual: "Do you share the bed?"

I shook my head.

"Has he not . . . has he not . . ." The priest looked up at the ceiling as though the painted beams held the words he sought. "Has he . . . he is not able . . ."

"Oh no." I was mortified when I realized what the priest understood. "He has . . . we have . . . consummated our marriage."

The priest relaxed visibly and blew his nose with the tortured handkerchief.

"But he does not stay . . . after. We—consummate—then he leaves to sleep alone in his own bed."

The priest looked me in the eye for the first time since the uncomfortable conversation began.

"But I fail to see the problem, madame? Many men prefer the comfort of their own beds. And you cannot say he is not doing his duty by you?" His voice was accusatory, as though I had deliberately misled him.

I flushed miserably.

"You cannot say he is not doing his duty by you?" he repeated.

"No, I cannot," I admitted miserably.

I wrote to my mother and begged her to let me come back to live with my sisters again at the Quai des Théatins. She told me to stop feeling sorry for myself and not to worry that my husband was a boor. She wrote: "It does not matter if you are not compatible; do not try to force your love on him. He has his life, and you have yours."

But what is my life? I would wonder in despair. Endless days spent in this lonely house married to a man who does not love me? The rest of her letter detailed the glitter and shine of her life at Versailles. How I longed to be there.

When my mother-in-law was not on duty with the queen she would sometimes drive over for the day, to visit and supervise my housekeeping skills. I could not say I disliked Anne-Marie-Françoise, for that would be disloyal to my husband and to my father; to my whole family in fact (for as well as my mother-in-law, she is also my great-aunt), but I found her visits tedious and irritating. If the candles were too low in their sconces or the soup served bland and cold, she was sure to let me know. Anne-Marie-Françoise was a relation of the last king's wife, Madame de Maintenon, but only a poor one. When her criticisms were especially harsh I would think: You are the daughter of a country squire, a nobody! But then if she was just a country squire's daughter, what did that make me, married as I was to her son?

One fine spring day she arrived without sending a note; her face was grimmer than usual. "Are you ill?" I cried, then caught myself, for my voice held more hope than concern.

"No, silly child, I am not ill. I am very rarely ill, praise be to God. Never a sick day in my life. I shall talk without waste. Do you know what today is?"

"Thursday," I said, then instantly I was unsure. My mother-in-law always made me nervous. Perhaps it was Friday? No, I was sure it was Thursday and not Friday; we had dined on rabbit. I then realized it was my wedding anniversary.

"It is my wedding anniversary," I said in surprise. "Two years exactly."

I was confused, for surely a husband should visit his wife on their anniversary. Why had my mother-in-law come?

"Louise-Julie. You have not even suffered a miscarriage, if I am correct?"

In one miserable instant I saw the reason for her visit.

"You should be ashamed of yourself. Louis-Alex assures me he has done his duty by you, yet still, nothing."

"But Louis-Alexandre is rarely here," I said in a small voice. I knew how one becomes pregnant, and surely if he wanted a child Louis-Alexandre should visit more?

"That is a lie!" cried my mother-in-law. "Louis-Alex said you would try to blame him. He comes as often as he is able, what with his duties with his regiment, and at great personal expense to himself. The ride is a long one, but he knows his duty. He comes here at least twice a month. You must not lie about your husband."

I protested the injustice of what she was saying. "He visits perhaps once or twice a *season*, and only for the hunt. And when he is here he does not . . . I do not always see him in my bed."

"Are you calling your husband, my son, a liar?"

Suddenly I hated her rather viciously. Zélie, our wise governess, always told us that we must never say we *hate* someone. *Hate* is a very strong word, Zélie warned us; the most we were permitted was to *dislike*. But suddenly I did not dislike my mother-in-law; I hated her. "He is a liar," I said, more forcefully than I intended, perhaps more forcefully than I had ever said anything in my life. "He never comes here! I am all alone here in this horrible house, and how may I be blessed if my husband is never here?"

Anne-Marie-Françoise regarded me with disdain. "I knew this would be a waste of time. You call my son a liar and insult this house." She rose stiffly. "You must watch yourself, madame," she hissed as she turned to leave. "I should tell you the story of my great-aunt de Villette. After too many barren years her husband had had enough and he put her in a convent. My sister at Poissy would be more than happy to welcome you, if married life does not suit. Convents are not only for nuns and pockmarked girls, you know."

I sat in horror after she left. I was sorry to disappoint Zélie, but I realized I truly hated my mother-in-law. *I hate her.* I said the words out loud to the walls and the fire screen and the candlesticks and the two stuffed chairs: I hate her. I hate her and I wish she would die. And then I could leave this place and finally start living.

The next day I didn't even do penance in the chapel.

It was a year later that everything changed. I was at work on a new set of covers for the twenty-four uncomfortable chairs that lined the massive old dining table. Beside me was my maid, Jacobs, the only one of the village girls I could abide. She had a calming presence and a clever turn with the needle, which I did not; we never learned much needlework in the nursery.

I grimaced as I saw the carriage pull up—my husband. But then I saw the horses were banded in black, as was the carriage, and a sudden hope leapt in my heart. My mother-in-law? But God knows when we think evil thoughts and does not hesitate to punish, for it was not my hated mother-in-law that had passed away and freed me from my prison. It was my poor Mama.

I traveled back to Paris in the carriage, my husband complaining all the way that to be pulled from his duties thus to attend to his wife was a great inconvenience and misfortune, and one he had not anticipated, for Conti was giving a dinner that night that he was loath to miss, yet he had to be here, with me.

I cried silently beside him in the carriage, my face buried in my hands to shut out his voice and the guilt that threatened to choke me. My head ached and I wondered if I too should die like my mother. They said she complained of an immense headache then died within hours. Would I die like that too, God punishing me for my wicked thoughts?

In Paris, my husband deposited me at my childhood home and disappeared, muttering something about a horse he had to buy.

My four younger sisters gathered to greet me. I hugged them and held them close; we were five black starlings huddled together in our misery. I found Pauline, two years my junior, surly and angry, with nary an apology for the mountains of unanswered letters. Diane was jolly, even in sorrow. And perhaps a little chubbier than I remembered. The two youngest, Hortense and Marie-Anne, at fourteen and twelve, had changed the most and had grown into poised young ladies, albeit ones with the red eyes of mourning.

"I'm almost fifteen," Hortense reminded me primly, and then told me she had prayed seven hours yesterday for our mother's soul. Hortense is very devout and puts us all to shame.

"I only prayed for an hour," piped in Marie-Anne, "but it is as Zélie says: quality is more important than quantity."

"Never in the eyes of the Lord," concluded Hortense, and there was no arguing with that.

Tante Mazarin, a stern-faced relative and the Dowager Duchesse de Mazarin, fussed around us and fitted us with veils, the thin lace like black spider's webbing. We were summoned to see our father in our mother's gold bed chamber, where already gray-frocked men with no wigs were measuring and inspecting her possessions. This beautiful room was where we would visit when Mama was at home; we would play on her bed and she would comb our hair and point out any new freckles, then powder us and sometimes allow us to practice with her rouge. Once she let us each have a beauty patch from her box; I chose one shaped like a little bird. I touched my cheek and stared at her portrait on the wall—how could she be *gone*?

My father was sitting on the bed, his face heavy with grief and his words slurred with sorrow and drink. He was magnificently dressed, as always, in black satin stitched with black pearls; only the buckles on his shoes were gold, not black. I thought he was about to gather us to him on the bed, but instead he ordered us to line up, in order of our ages—myself, then Pauline, then Diane and Hortense, and little Marie-Anne at the end.

"Her hair . . ." He started to speak. "Her hair . . ." Two men carrying an enormous gilded clock stumbled and dropped it with a clatter. My father roared his disapproval and flailed around for his sword to strike them with. We stood silent and fearful; our father was very inconstant and we never knew where his temper or drink might lead him. Our governess, Zélie, watched over us, rigid and tense.

When we were younger, Father would sometimes come up to the nursery, often when the rabble of creditors in the courtyard became too much for him. He would lounge around and flick through our books and abuse Zélie for educating us in matters that women didn't need to know. Then he would make us sing for him, then make Marguerite, our prettiest maid, sing for him, and then he would finally stumble back down the stairs and we would all breathe a sigh of relief.

"Her hair, her hair," he repeated as he lolled unsteadily on Mama's bed, the broken clock forgotten. "I must remember to get her hair."

He stared at us, his eyes blurry and his face high red. "I loved her, you know. Loved her! She was a fine woman. Even if she did only have daughters. Five daughters—a basket of rotten apples. What, I ask you, was God punishing me for?"

Then he broke down and cried and I too started to sob, and soon we all were crying, even Pauline, who is generally very unsentimental. Papa stood up, whether to silence us or embrace us I know not, for his feet were unsteady and he fell back on the bed again.

"You look like crows!" he cried. "Bad luck! Always my bad luck!" And then he ordered us all out, yelling that only Marguerite should stay, for she was the only one who could comfort him.

We traipsed slowly back up to the fourth floor, all of us still sobbing. The nursery seemed smaller and shabbier than I remembered, the tapestries more moth-eaten, the floors more uneven and the rooms colder.

"Agathe doesn't have any mourning clothes!" wailed Marie-Anne, flinging her doll on the floor. Sometimes I would forget that Marie-Anne was the youngest, for she was often very quick and sure of herself, and never afraid. But she was only twelve and still a baby at heart. I hugged her to me, her little body stiff in her black mourning gown, shaking with sobs.

"We can make her some out of our veils," said Diane helpfully, pulling hers off and jabbing it with a hearth poker to rip it.

"Oh! Tante Mazarin will be very angry," breathed Hortense, forgetting to sob.

"That's a good idea," said Pauline, taking her veil off as well and ripping it with her teeth. "No one will say anything, because everyone is sad for us. We are *orphans*."

"Not orphans!" I declared. "Our father still lives."

There was an uncomfortable silence.

"Perhaps she will come back," whispered Marie-Anne to me, Agathe now safely and properly wrapped in the black lace. Pauline snorted.

"Pauline!" I admonished. "Don't be so cruel." I wouldn't usually confront Pauline, but I was a married woman and felt a sudden responsibility for my little sisters. Whatever happened, I would take care of them. I gathered them all to me, even Pauline, who squawked in protest, and we embraced and cried again.

After the funeral everything changed. Pauline and Diane entered the convent at Port-Royal on the outskirts of Paris, and Hortense and Marie-Anne were sent to live with Tante Mazarin.

And I? Out of sorrow came my fortune, for my mother's death meant her position at Court was secured upon me. I was finally to go to Versailles. It was not the way that I had wished or wanted, but that is how it happened.

And now I am here in the center of the world, both hating it and loving it.

From Louise de Mailly
Château de Versailles
June 2, 1730

Dear Pauline and Diane,

Greetings, sisters! I trust you are well and enjoying life at the convent. I am sure the nuns are taking good care of you. Pauline, I hope that you are finally getting the education you always so desired.

I received a letter from Zélie; she is now in Picardy and writes that she misses us most terribly. It is so sad she is not able to be with us. Do you remember her exciting stories of China and Québec?

Life here at Versailles is wonderful. Yesterday I met the Turkish ambassador and last night the queen hosted a concert in her rooms—Couperin! Everything is very glamorous and exciting. The queen is a wonderful mistress and the other ladies are very kind and caring. My husband, Louis-Alexandre, is so attentive; it is wonderful to be together with him all the time, though he does not sleep at the palace but prefers his house in town. He says the dust in the palace causes him to sneeze too much.

Diane, I will try to send the ribbons that you asked for, but money is very tight here. My dear husband gives so much to charity that there is little left over for trifles! I must be very inventive with my clothes. Do you remember our everyday yellow muslin dresses we all wore in the nursery? I made mine into an underskirt and on my days off duty I wear it with my blue flowered chintz. All the other ladies admire it very much.

Pauline, please write to me! I would love to hear your news. Diane, thank you for your letter, but unfortunately the ink was smeared and I could not understand much of it. You must write to Tante Mazarin and thank her for taking care of Hortense and Marie-Anne. Do not be sad about Mama and remember to pray for her soul.

Your loving sister,
Louise

From Louise de Mailly
Château de Versailles
June 12, 1730

Dear Marie-Anne and Hortense,

My darling sisters! I trust you are well in Tante Mazarin's care. I saw her yesterday and she told me you are happy in your new home and that Hortense, you have stopped having nightmares about the rats living beneath your bed. Don't forget, bad dreams are caused by Satan, so if you fear nightmares, wear your crucifix to bed and He will protect you.

I received a letter from darling Zélie, she is now living in Picardy and says she misses us most terribly. It is so sad she is not able to still be with us. I will miss her dreadfully. Do you remember how she used to sing to us at night, whenever there was a thunderstorm? How sweet she was.

Life is wonderful here at Versailles. Everything is very glamorous and the people are very grand but very kind. My husband is very attentive and it is wonderful to be so close to him and not constantly separated as we were before. I hope when the time comes for you to be married, you will have as wonderful a husband as mine.

I will give Tante Mazarin a pot of fig jam for her to bring to Paris when she next goes; it is a gift to me from my friend the Duchesse d'Antin. I thought to share it with you as I know how much you love figs. Please don't write to Diane and tell her about it; she would be very jealous but I only have one pot left.

Do not forget to pray for our mother's soul.

Love,
Louise

Marie-Anne

If I had a diamond ring I would scratch it on the windowpane of my room and write: *Here Marie-Anne de Mailly-Nesle died of boredom, February 15, 1731.* Marie of Scotland, imprisoned in an English castle, engraved a sad poem on a window glass to prove she once lived, though she knew she would die soon.

Our governess, Zélie, told us that story, so it might not be true.

But even if it's untrue, I still feel some affinity for poor, doomed Marie. I have no diamond but one day I slipped a small sharp knife under my sleeve after dinner. I tried to scratch out my despair on the windowpane, but my sister Hortense heard the housekeeper yelling at the servant girls about the missing knife. She made me feel guilty enough to relinquish it to her superior person. She put it on a side table where a footman found it, then informed me she would pray away my wickedness.

After our mother died, our Tante Mazarin embraced us and said we must make a home with her, and consider all she had to be ours. Tante is a pious old bat. She's only just past forty and still quite beautiful, but she wears dark old-fashioned clothes that make her look like an ancient widow, and her lips are thin from a lifetime of disapproval.

I don't like our new home. I miss the fourth floor on the Quai des Théatins and all that was familiar. I wish our mother never had to die; she was too young and it all happened so suddenly. I wish our father was . . . well, not like our father is, and that we could have stayed in our house, instead of it being rented out to horrid strangers that Tante Mazarin doesn't even know. She says the new tenants might be *bourgeois*, and when she says that word she lowers her voice as if talking of the contents of a close stool.

I miss our old life. We were all together and it was fun and interesting. Lessons in the morning were useless—I often suspected Zélie, our governess, of invention—but in the afternoons we were free to play and do as we wished. I was very young, but by the time I was ten I had already decided that I wanted to be a scientist, if a woman was allowed such a thing. I carried out many interesting experiments: I gathered mice from the jaws of the cats and kept them in a box to see how long they would last before starving to death, and I liked to pull the legs off spiders to see how many they could lose before they lost the ability to walk. Five. And we had our toys—dolls, a perfect miniature crockery set to feed them, and a wonderful Noah's Ark with thirty-two pairs of animals.

Then my eldest sister, Louise, left the nursery to get married, and everything changed. I missed Louise, even though she was a bit soft and foolish. Zélie used to say that Louise viewed the world through a bouquet of flowers, which meant she only saw the good in everything.

Once Louise left, my older sister Pauline became insufferable. Pauline was always very nasty and she was jealous of Louise, because Louise got married while she was still stuck in the nursery. She often said that Louise didn't deserve to be married first, because even though she was the eldest, she was a ninny and a fool. My sister Diane, who worshiped Pauline, agreed with her, but Hortense, who was always so good, opened her eyes wide—she has very big eyes and is very pretty—and said we must not talk about our sister like that, for it was not very *sisterly*.

"Sororal," elucidated Zélie. "Not very *sororal*."

Sororal—it's a good word, but I think I am also guilty of not being sororal because I hate my sister too. Not Louise, but Pauline. She is tall and ugly, and once Louise left to get married she reigned over our nursery in complete tyranny, throwing spiders on us and forcing us to climb inside the chimneys.

Pauline took to gathering our toys and keeping them locked in an oak cupboard. She wore the key tied securely around her waist like a jailer or a housekeeper, and told us she would not open the cupboard and release the toys unless we offered her gifts. Sometimes it was food and we had to save our buns from breakfast and give them to her! And she already so big and fat!

I urged my sisters not to return their toys when Pauline demanded. In retaliation, Pauline announced that anyone who did not return their toy by the time appointed would not be able to play with it for two days.

I protested, hanging on to my doll Agathe. "You are not in charge here! You cannot make up these stupid rules."

Pauline's face darkened at my resistance. "Return the doll," she commanded.

Zélie said nothing against our tormentress—she said her duties were done when our lesson books closed at noon. There was no one in higher authority to stop the tyranny, so I plotted to use whatever means necessary to ensure Pauline's downfall. Just like the Roundheads did when they executed King Charles I in England. (Zélie says the English never executed their king, but I found a book in the library that says they did just that.)

I decided that instead of becoming a scientist, I would become a revolutionary. Or a rebel. What is the difference? Regardless, I decided to launch a revolution, or a rebellion, and burn down the prison-cupboard.

I waited until the toys were safely out of their jail. It was a drizzly afternoon and we would not be going out for a walk. I asked permission from Zélie to go down to the library and left my sisters playing in the schoolroom: Pauline reading a book, Diane and Hortense carefully feeding all the animals before they had to go back into the ark.

The sconces in the dark stairwell were lit and I took a candle and crept back into our bedroom. I held the candle to the oak closet but it just singed the wood and refused to catch. I considered calling one of the maids, for they had great experience in lighting fires, where I had none, but decided they might inform Zélie. Instead, I took a pillow from Diane's bed, lit it, and threw it inside the cupboard. I closed the door, snuffed out the candle and returned to the schoolroom.

"Where's your book?" asked Pauline suspiciously.

"I found nothing to interest me."

Soon there was a smell of smoke and Zélie leapt up in alarm as a maid came running to say there was a fire in the bedroom. In the bedroom? I only wanted to burn down the cupboard! There was great screaming and running and breathless servants as pails of water were hauled from the courtyard well four flights below.

We were hustled down to the rainy courtyard and the scene was quite dramatic: smoke was billowing from the windows and the servants were alerting the neighbors behind with great cries of "Fire ho! Fire ho!"

The fire was finally contained, at the loss of the cupboard, some linen from Diane's bed, and two old tapestries that were used to smother the flames. There was a full investigation and the house steward even climbed up to our nursery. To our eyes, Monsieur Bertrand was grander and even more important than our father, for it was he who dispensed money for clothes and toys and additions to the menu.

The final verdict: one of the maids neglected a live ember from the night fire. Little Claude, with pockmarked skin and a slight limp, was dismissed. It was unfortunate but in every war there must be some casualties.

That night the air smelled charred and we all coughed dreadfully. There was no closet to put our toys into, so we kept them at the foot of our beds. Pauline demanded to know where I had been when the fire started. Instead of denying, I simply said: "Next time, it will not be the cupboard. It will be you."

After that she left me alone and did not reinstate her control of the toys. It was all very satisfying. I thought, when I am older, instead of marrying and having children perhaps I will run away and foment revolution in strange lands. I seem to have quite the talent for it. And besides, there is hardly any money left for our dowries—apparently it has all been spent in an "orgy of dissipation," as I once overheard a footman saying. I'm not sure what an orgy is—it must be very expensive—but all I know is that it means we are now poor.

Shortly after the fire my mother died, and we had to leave our house and come and live with Tante Mazarin. Hortense is happy here; she likes the rigid order more than the mess and neglect at the Quai des Théatins. But I do not. Tante's house is dark and gloomy; crammed with misplaced statues and tables and mirrors. She has started renovating but it will be a long time before the changes reach our rooms on the third floor. The house is set back from the road by a large courtyard and behind lies a long, formal garden, hidden from the house by a solid wall of yews.

I feel as though I am in a crypt.

Entombed.

We pass our days with Tante or her women, reading scriptures and memorizing births and deaths from the *Genealogical History of the Royal Family and Peers*, which I suppose is also a sacred text. Tante insists on a great deal of needlework and we are never permitted to sit in chairs with backs—imagine if we slouched! And what a scandal that we weren't wearing stays before we came to live with her! In this house, girls are forbidden to run, skip, or even ask questions.

One of her waiting women is responsible for our manners and instructs us on the twelve steps required to take snuff elegantly and how to eat an egg properly. I am not sure this is very important, but Tante proclaims that thanks to her and the education she is providing, we *might* make better marriages than our dowries would normally predict.

I think our education is ridiculous—why should my future husband care if I crack my egg with a fork, or with a knife? And surely I'll never meet *all* the people we have to learn about?

"But it is important," Hortense protests when I mock our lessons. "It is important to know who is who in our world. In the future we may go to Court and meet these people. And imagine how awful it would be if you did not know how to address them properly, or know who their parents were? You would bring shame upon Tante and she would be accused of neglecting our education."

Hortense is two years older than me. Still, I do not believe that gives her the right to treat me as though I am her child.

"Oui, maman," I say in my most exaggerated voice, then regret it as Hortense flinches; our mother is dead only just over a year.

We are sitting in Tante's library, practicing "families" from the *Genealogical History*. I think the sun is shining outside behind the thick trees, but we must stay inside. I throw my sister what I hope is a difficult one: "Conti."

"Prince of Conti, title created 1597 and revived 1629. Current head, Louis François de Bourbon, born in 1717. Like you, Marie-Anne! Succeeded his father in 1727."

"Wife?"

"Marie . . . no, Louise Diane d'Orléans, Mademoiselle de Chartres."

"Children?"

"None, he only married this year!"

"Other titles?"

"Comte d'Alais, Comte de Beaumont-sur-Oise and of . . . Pézenas, also Duc de . . . Mérode?"

"Wrong!" I cry triumphantly, consulting the appropriate page. "Duc de *Mercoeur*, not Mérode."

"You're right, Duc de Mercoeur." Hortense frowns. "Mercoeur: title raised to a ducal peerage in 1569."

"Correct." I sigh.

Hortense is too perfect.

From Hortense de Mailly-Nesle
Hôtel de Mazarin, Paris
March 5, 1731

Dearest Louise,

Thank you for your letter and the pot of fig jam. One of the maids here was dreadfully sick with fever, so I gave her most of it for comfort. But then she died and Tante said we mustn't eat what was left.

Thank you for your news of your exciting life at Versailles! I am glad you and your husband are now able to be close again, and I pray that you will soon be blessed with a son.

Tante Mazarin says that Versailles is a cauldron of sin, and that one must be very careful to guard against temptation. Every night I pray for your soul and ask God to guide you on the good path. At least you have Tante watching over: you must heed what she says, for she is very wise and very good.

She is like a mother to us and takes great care of us. When she is in Paris she sees us every day and we even dine with her on occasion. Her women are very kind. We are learning a lot here, more than at the Quai des Théatins, though I do not want to insult dear Zélie.

Marie-Anne sends her love and this handkerchief that we sewed for you. Tante insists on much needlework and that is a good thing: she was very disappointed with our sewing skills when we arrived. Now we spend many hours a day practicing. I hope you like the handkerchief; please excuse the drops of dried blood next to the pansy—that was where Marie-Anne pricked her finger. She is still learning, though I find it very easy—look at the petals of the flower, how fine they are. Tante always praises my delicate fingers.

My love to you and your husband,
Hortense

Louise

VERSAILLES

1731

Finally I am beginning to find my way and my feet—in all ways, for I no longer topple over when I curtsy. At Court one must wear dreadfully high-heeled shoes: at first I was wobbly, but now I can walk with delicate gliding steps and in entire confidence.

Everything at Versailles is very fine: I used to think my mother's gold-paneled bedroom so opulent, but now I realize it was nothing. Amid all this luxury the queen lives a very simple life. She is pious and enjoys reading the Bible and the long religious tracts her confessor supplies. The queen has fifteen ladies in her service: the *surintendante,* a *dame d'atour,* a *dame d'honneur,* and twelve ladies of the palace. The younger ladies—there are a few of my age, including my friend Gilette and the very beautiful Princesse de Montauban—declare their lives insufferably dull, but I cannot see how anyone could be bored here. The formidable Mademoiselle de Clermont, a granddaughter of the last king and a cold, sour woman, is the *surintendante.* Her husband disappeared one day while hunting in a forest and was never found again! Gilette tells me the Court wishes it were she that disappeared, and not her luckless husband.

Tante Mazarin is also one of the ladies-in-waiting. My hated mother-in-law retired just a few months after I arrived at Versailles, and Tante took her place. Tante takes care of my two youngest sisters, Hortense and Marie-Anne, and declared upon her arrival that she would also take care of me. She has instructed me to be careful in my choice of friends and warns me there are some very bad moral examples amongst the other ladies. Pincushions, she calls them, because they are full of pricks. Tante is one of a group of ladies known as the Pious Pack, ladies who love to judge those they judge impious.

The queen's French is not very good and her accent is thick even after more than five years in France. She is a devoted mother and sees her children every day—three little princesses and two boys: our beloved *dauphin* and the little Duc d'Anjou, just a baby.

We spend most afternoons in the queen's private apartments, doing needlework, reading aloud, or listening to the queen play the harp. We also have French lessons to help her improve her vocabulary.

"Lackluster," suggests the Princesse de Montauban. She is very young and very charming and usually very annoyed with the queen, though she hides this behind bright eyes and dimpled smiles. "Try *lackluster*. It means dull and boring."

It still shocks me, even though I have been here almost a year, to hear the courtiers disrespect the queen. Never the king, but the queen . . . she is frequently the butt of their caustic comments and laughter.

"Lackluster," repeats the queen, pronouncing it *lohk-lohster*. "A very *goot* word, let me make a sentence with it." She pauses and looks around at her ladies, who all smile back. I smile with sincerity; I like the queen and dislike the way many are false with her. She considers awhile and the clocks on the mantelpiece tick on. Montauban widens her eyes and holds them open as though she were about to burst. Finally the queen says: "The boring play was very *lohk-lohster*."

We all nod in praise and encouragement.

"Or," says the Comtesse de Rupelmonde, shifting in her chair and rearranging the fine-filigreed lace that shields her large breasts from impropriety, "you could use it to describe people, or even a time of day." At Versailles I have heard many shocking stories of her adventures with my mother, and I find her no nicer here than she was in Paris. "For example: *'This afternoon is very lackluster.'* "

"*Ja, ja*, 'this afternoon is very lackluster,'" repeats the queen, beaming. "*Ja, ja*. That is a *goot* word."

Our evenings are generally spent listening to musical concerts or watching plays or gambling. Gambling sounds very exciting, sinful even, but when the queen plays it is decidedly *lackluster*. The younger ladies outdo themselves with excuses to escape the queen's company. But even if they must remain, the queen retires very early and then they are free to fly, like a flock of pretty-colored birds, wherever they wish.

Despite her plainness of manner and looks, the king has eyes only for his wife. The king himself is very handsome—tall and well made and rumored to be very strong. He has a clear complexion and haunting dark eyes, like pools of black velvet. He loves hunting and dogs and has exquisite manners and is unfailingly polite—everyone agrees he is the most mannered man at Versailles. I believe all the ladies of the Court are in love with him. But if anyone compliments another woman in his presence, he is quick to say that the queen is more beautiful. And while that's not really true—the queen is fair but no beauty—no one can contradict him because he is the king.

He visits the queen every day, and though some of her ladies shamelessly seek his eye—Rupelmonde was chastised just last week for the sudden disappearance of her new and fashionable fichu when the king arrived—he only chats politely with us and reserves his keen attention for his wife. It is all so romantic! When I see them together, I think of my husband, Louis-Alexandre, and I feel sad and empty inside.

Today is the feast of Saint Cecilia and it is raining and cold. We are gathered in the Queen's Apartments to read the Scripture and to reflect on Saint Cecilia and her sacrifice. I confess that books bore me. Even the Bible. My mind wanders, and before I can stop myself I find myself staring at the queen. Imagine living in Poland! And Sweden! It must have been awful. She is getting old now, al-

most thirty, while the king is seven years younger. He is my age—
we were born only two months apart. I have heard courtiers sneer
that the queen is like last week's flowers—fading and dying—and
they say it destroys the prestige of France for her to be their queen.
Many at Versailles are as nasty as their words imply.

"Madame de Mailly, my dear, *vot* are you staring at?"

The queen's voice snaps me out of my reverie.

I blush. It is very rude to stare, especially at the queen. "Oh,
nothing, madame, nothing, I was just thinking of this passage I
have read."

"Very *goot, goot* to be contemplating of what you are reading.
Read it to us all so we may contemplate too." *Contemplate* was
yesterday's word.

Her Majesty is not being subtle or snide; she is too good for
that. My friend Gilette is severely wicked and free and says I must
not emulate the queen or I will never find my way at Versailles. I
bend my head and pick a passage from the open book: "'*He leads
the humble in what is right and teaches the humble his way.*'"

The queen grunts in approval. "Very *goot, goot*."

Gilette quivers and coughs. I can tell she wants to giggle.
Gilette claims that the king's eyes are no longer only for his wife,
but I know she likes to exaggerate and will do anything to stir up
trouble.

"And so true, so true," the queen continues, smiling at me.
"Don't you agree, Madame de Boufflers?"

The Duchesse de Boufflers, a formidable lady of great girth
and age who treats the queen more as a recalcitrant child than a
sovereign, smiles in agreement and offers a homily about youth
and humility. Boufflers is a great friend of Tante Mazarin's and is
almost as nasty as she is; she likes to say that one is never too old
for disapproval.

The rain patters down on the windowpanes and my toes curl
in cold as I try to focus on my book and not disappoint the queen.
But oh! How can words, so innocent in isolation, conspire to be
quite so boring when they come together?

Suddenly there is a commotion in the corridor. We all strain to listen, hoping it is the king—wherever he goes he carries with him a commotion like nature's serenade.

It is.

"Madame," he says, striding in to bow to the queen and kiss her hand. The queen's complexion is sallow and she does not blush, but shifts awkwardly and smiles her delight. We rise and curtsy. The king bows to us in greeting but reserves his conversation for his wife; some say he is a very shy person. He has lived almost his entire life in public—he has been king since he was five years old—and sometimes appears cold with strangers and those he doesn't know well.

With the king is Cardinal Fleury, his prime minister and treasured adviser. Fleury is an ancient man with watery blue eyes and no wig. He is reputed to be brilliant but he makes me uneasy; he is a calculating, canny man. Though the king is past twenty, His Majesty still relies on Fleury for almost everything. Even lends him a helping hand when he is paddling his pickle, I once heard the Comtesse de Rupelmonde whisper, and I was shocked that one would speak of the king that way. I'm sure he is a very good king, but perhaps still learning; it must be very difficult to learn *everything* about reigning.

"Madame d'Antin," Fleury says, leaning low over Gilette's hand while the king chats with the queen.

Gilette throws back her head and laughs. "Perhaps you saw my husband this morning?" she asks.

Fleury smiles at her and makes a remark about "relinquishing her hand, but only for now." I fear I don't understand half of what is said here, even though we all speak the same language. When Fleury comes to me I curtsy low and keep my hands clasped in front of me, as though I am about to burst into song. I have no wish for his weak lips on my hand—like being kissed by death. I shudder.

"You are cold, madame?" asks Fleury.

I shake my head guiltily.

"And how is your husband?"

Gilette titters.

Everyone here is most astonishingly free and very few people remain faithful to or even cordial with their spouses. Most have lovers, sometimes even multiple lovers at once. Some of the ladies of the queen are quite notorious for their laxity, even though the queen is very virtuous herself. I suppose she did not have much choice in the selection of her household.

Gossip is a full-time occupation. When I arrived at Versailles I learned that everyone knew that my mother and the one-eyed Duc de Bourbon had been lovers. The duke often visited our house in Paris—my mother always said he was coming for tea, and I used to think how odd it was that the man should like tea so much, and he not even English. I have also encountered more wicked untruths about my father here than I ever heard from the most slack-mouthed servant at home. And if I want to know where my husband spends his nights, for it is certainly not in my apartment, I need only ask the nearest passerby; they are sure to know. The answer, as I have found out thanks to Gilette and many others, is: at the house of Mademoiselle Baudet in town. Mademoiselle Baudet is the daughter of a sword maker. A *sword maker*. Worse than a bourgeois! Imagine that.

Gilette tells me that my husband wanted to marry his mistress—marry a sword maker's daughter, for goodness' sake— but the king, or Fleury, forbade it. That is the reason our marriage happened so suddenly.

"I do believe my husband is fine," I reply stiffly to Fleury. He reaches for my hand and his fingers are as soft as wormy chestnuts.

"Such an innocent," he says, and though everyone here likes to mask the real meaning of their words beneath several layers of falsity, I sense he is sincere. "Stay that way, my dear, stay that way."

Pauline

CONVENT OF PORT-ROYAL

1732

Our Tante Mazarin does not like me, a fact she makes publicly known. She never fails to remark on my dark complexion or bushy eyebrows, and once even said, in a light voice to make it appear as though she were joking, that Mama must have slept with a Hungarian, so horrible was I to look at.

Although it is not permitted to criticize our elders—out loud—the feeling is mutual. I think she is a spiteful old woman who hides her black heart beneath her robes of piety. One time when she was visiting our mother in Paris, Louise and I were brought down from the schoolroom to greet her and sing a song. While we were singing, Tante examined us as Cook might inspect a chicken. Our hands were clasped in front of us in the correct posture for singing (as our foolish governess, Zélie, had taught us), when I had the irresistible urge to sneeze. I did, and unfortunately it was a messy one. And it happened as Tante was standing right in front of me, examining my left ear.

I have to confess it was a little bit on purpose—I could have turned my head, after all—but it was rather funny. Tante was so disgusted that she has barely looked at me since.

So I was glad to be sent to the convent with Diane and not to her house. I was sad for the loss of my mother, of course, but she was never very maternal and we rarely saw her. I was well pleased not to be shut up in Tante's stuffy house with Hortense and Marie-Anne, and I believed I was *finally* going to get an education.

Zélie, our governess from the Quai des Théatins, was complete nonsense. She was a relation of ours, something-something five times removed. As a rare act of charity my mother took her into our household but I don't believe she had any more education than a field mouse, and I don't think she even attended Saint-Cyr, as she liked to claim. During lessons she would spin the globe and tell us stories about faraway places. I was sure she made everything up, for how would she know anything about Québec or India? When I accused her of lying, Zélie would protest and say that being able to entertain was the most useful accomplishment, even if the substance of what one said was in doubt.

I thought that at the convent I might finally learn something. Well . . . to think I ever fancied getting an education here! I feel I have been tricked. Sometimes my head buzzes with frustration and fury, as though a hundred bees were trapped inside my skull.

Every morning for three hours we must study religious books or memorize the lives of obscure saints. Pointless: Why should I care what a virgin Roman girl with an outlandish name did more than a thousand years ago? Afternoons are spent on mountains of needlework. I generally despised Zélie but at least her lessons were secular, and I don't think she even knew how to sew.

The other students are much younger than Diane and me, for I am already twenty years old and Diane eighteen. The girls are sent here by their families for safekeeping until they are released into marriage; no one expects any quality to their education. Without exception they are silly little girls who jump at rats and whimper at thunder and spend hours crying if they find a new freckle on their nose. I call them drops because they are as boring as drops of water. The little drops only care about their future husbands, and they shriek when they hear I am not even betrothed. If one more little drop says she will pray for a husband for me, I will scream.

The days pass, long and dreary. When I declare I have read every life of a saint there is to read and sewn every cushion cover the chapel will ever need, I am allowed to help Sister Claudine in the convent library. We are working to catalog an estimated two thousand books that clog the towering shelves. You might think this would be interesting work, but without exception, and here I will swear on the Holy Bible, all two thousand books are boring beyond belief. *The Canons of Dort?* A bound collection of *Papal Bulls from the Seventeenth Century? Of Exorcisms and Certain Supplications?* Well, that last one does sound a little bit interesting.

There are other boarders here: widows or women seeking refuge from their husbands, or from the world in general. They are very pleasant, apart from one creaky old lady who refuses to speak to Diane and me because of an ancient but well-remembered grudge against my long-dead grandmother. My grandmother was apparently as notorious a slut as my mother, and was once rumored to have slept with two members of the Swiss Guard. At the same time! The ancient lady with the grudge tells me blood is thicker than water and that the seeds of laxness flow through my veins. I snort and retort that I'd rather have lax-seeded veins than her great knobbly blue ones.

But generally the ladies are kind enough and I prefer to dine with them rather than with the little drops. Sometimes we play cards in the evenings and I also borrow books from them; mostly novels and farces. One woman in particular has become a friend, a Madame de Dray, who is in retirement from the world after the death of her husband. He was only a magistrate, so normally we would not be friends, but I find in her a very forthright and funny soul. She has no artifice and hates piety, especially false piety, almost as much as I do. She is also remarkably open about the facts of married life that I have hitherto been in ignorance of. Fascinating, really, the secrets of men.

The convent is not secluded from the world; in fact its walls are as porous as the grilles that box the confessionals, and the lady boarders are free to receive visitors and gossip from Versailles. My silly sister Louise is now at Court and is one of the queen's ladies. I am jealous. Very jealous. I should be at Versailles too, meeting interesting people and living an exciting life. When I pepper the older ladies with questions about life at Court, they describe the concerts and the plays, the fortunes won and lost at card tables, the intrigues and the gossip, the scandals and the power. It's not fair that pitiful little Louise was able to get married and go to Court, simply because she is two years older than me. I am already twenty and no one is planning *my* wedding.

How I long to be there, at Versailles, and away from this convent crypt of monotony. But to be at Versailles one needs both money and a husband. Everyone knows our father frittered away what little was left of our inheritance and that we have only 7,500 *livres* for our dowries, so we're as poor as . . . well, poor people. Not *really* poor people, of course, but we're poor compared to the other people in our world.

Without money you can still get married, but then it helps to be beautiful. Ugly is a strong word, and a damning one for a woman, but I do not believe I am ugly. It is true I am very tall and my skin is dark, certainly, not pale like Louise's, but that is what powder is for. I have nice green eyes—like emeralds—and I like my large eyebrows. I think they make me look distinguished.

My hopes for my future now rest with Louise. She should help Diane and me to get married and get out of this convent. No one else will. I detest letter writing, but I have started to write to Louise frequently. I profess my love and devotion and tell her how much I miss her, which she is probably naive enough to believe. I tell her that I pray that we will one day be reunited (at Versailles) and that she should lead the way to find good husbands for Diane and me.

I am very direct and keep to the point—what does she care if we had eels for dinner yesterday, or how Madame de Felingonge's back pains are progressing? I ask her to invite me to Court or find me a husband. Then I write again and ask her to invite me to Court or find me a husband. Or secure me a place at Court, even if it's in the service of some dreary old duchess. I don't care. I just want to get out of here. But all I receive from Louise are infuriatingly sweet letters ignoring my requests and telling me to trust in God, because only He knows where my future husband is.

And now my giggly sister Diane doesn't laugh as much as she used to. She has taken to praying for five hours a day and even gets up for matins. She declares she is *madly* in love with Jesus, Mother Superior, and with one of the nuns called Sister Domingue.

"Diane, I think you should focus on Sister Domingue; beneath her wimple she is certainly prettier than Mother Superior. Despite her pox scars. And she is probably prettier than Jesus," I joke, trying to make her laugh.

"Sister, my love for Jesus, and everyone else, can never be divided," Diane replies, all haughty and hushy. "And I have asked you at least twenty times not to call me Diane—my name is Adelaide now. Diane is a pagan name. It's not suitable for a woman with a strong religious vocation. You know I hate it and I don't know why you always try to annoy me with it."

"Sorry, *Adelaide*."

The older ladies assure me that professing a great vocation is just a phase every girl goes through, like wanting to marry a duke or play with kittens all day. Some of the kinder ladies ask gently if it would be so bad if Diane, poor little jolly (as they call her), were to find a life of happiness inside convent walls? Not here—7,500 *livres* as dowry will not open the doors of Port-Royal—but they might take her elsewhere.

It is certainly a blessing to have relatives in the Church, but we already have aunts in abbeys all over France. I want my fun sister back. I ask God for this, and while I'm asking for favors, I also remind Him that I want a husband and that I want to go to Versailles. I want to start *living*.

From Pauline de Mailly-Nesle
Convent of Port-Royal
March 20, 1732

Louise,

I am sure you are in good health and happiness. Not I. I do not like life at the convent and I want to leave. I want to get married. I hope you can find me a husband, please ask Tante Mazarin and anyone else you can if they can help me.

I also want to come and visit you at Court, I think you should remember your sororal duties and invite me for a visit. Remember wise Zélie, who always said that sororal love was the highest love? Please do not forget me.

I miss you very much, I think about you every day, sometimes I cry because I miss you so much. Diane cries too. I would love to see you again and I suggest you invite me to Versailles.

Thank you for writing with the news of the Duchesse d'Antin's dress. Imagine a pink satin petticoat sewn with white posies—fascinating! How I would like to see that dress myself! If you invite me to Versailles, I could see it and then I would be even more fascinated.

Diane thanks you for the lace ribbons. She sewed them onto the cuffs of her convent dress but the nuns make her take them off on Sundays. She sends her love; she wishes she could have written but a bee stung her finger and now she has some difficulty holding her quill.

With much sororal love,
Pauline

Louise

The fashions here are simply extraordinary. Gowns of silk and satin, velvet and fur, brocades in winter, fine muslins and gauze in the summer. Everywhere there are ruffles and lace and bows and ribbons and flowers. And feathers and jewels and bells and even little stuffed birds, adorning dresses all the pale colors of the sun and the moon. If one wears a dress too often, friends will remind you that you are not in the provinces and they claim that seeing the same garment too often affronts their eyes and may even cause blindness. They complain that dark colors give them headaches: why wear brown when one can wear pink?

The more daring women push out their legs while seated so their gowns and petticoats fall away and reveal their pretty satin shoes, sewn with pearls and decorated with delicate buckles. Some even dare to show their shocking white stockings and I have heard that the Comtesse de Rupelmonde wears a bejeweled garter that cost more than a pair of horses.

I have a fair number of dresses, but most of them are hopelessly plain when compared to what the other ladies wear. Everything must be beautiful, but everything must be paid for. Not immediately—dressmakers are generous with credit—but eventually. I receive a pension as a lady of the queen, but what are 8,000 *livres* a year when some ladies (and gentlemen too, for the men must be as well dressed as the women) spend five thousand *livres* for just one outfit? How I envy my friend Gilette, the Duchesse d'Antin; her husband is one of the richest men at Court and I have never seen her wear the same dress twice. Never; not even one turned inside out!

I have learned that my husband is rather short on money. I do my best with my old wardrobe and have become very adept at arranging ruffles or bows on old gowns to make them look new again. And original, for though everyone here must speak and act the same, everyone wants to be noticed. Recently, Gilette admired my simple green gown, the stomacher sewn with bands of real white carnations. Gilette usually reserves her speech for snide remarks or gossip, but this time she complimented me on my elegance and creativity. And I think she meant it.

Gilette is also constantly urging me to forget Louis-Alexandre. She has a lover, as do so many women here, but I am adamant that I will be faithful to my husband. I must be accountable for my sins before God. And besides, I don't have children yet.

"But you can have fun without being *strictly* unfaithful," says Gilette in her light voice. "There are ways."

"And where would be the fun of that?" Mademoiselle de Charolais laughs. "Don't be foolish, Gilette." Mademoiselle de Charolais is a sister of the queen's *surintendante,* Mademoiselle de Clermont, but unlike her sister she is very beautiful. She is not married but takes lovers as she pleases and routinely disappears for a month or two, complaining of a "bellyache." I suppose when one is the granddaughter of a king, one can do anything.

"I am surprised you would need to be educated about the ways, mademoiselle," banters Gilette.

"Oh, please, you have no need to insult me." Charolais and many of the women here wear their looseness like a necklace they are proud of, for all to see. "Let's just say I moved beyond that phase long, long ago," she continues. "A very long time ago. Now I am not satisfied until . . . shall we say the hand has been fitted into the glove?"

"Tush, we need to start small," says Gilette, laughing and

squeezing my shoulder with her cream-gloved hand. "A mild flirtation for our little Louise would be a very fine first step."

"On a ladder with many rungs," finishes Charolais with a smirk. "And oh! What delights await you at the top."

I try not to blush. A flirtation might be nice and certainly possible in this palace of a thousand gallants, but I am afraid that if I start down that path I might find myself at the end of it like Gilette and Charolais and so many other pincushions. Though it is sometimes hard to find Him amidst the many Greek and Roman gods that line the walls of the palace, I must always remember that God can see us everywhere, even at Versailles.

But when one is surrounded by vice, that which shocks fast becomes normal.

❧

May is simply the most delightful month at Court; the rooms are warm again and the sun shines and in the gardens the cherry and lime trees molt their blossoms over the ground like snow. One fine afternoon the queen calls for easels and paints to be brought outside that we might pass the afternoon painting.

"We must inspiration," announces the queen. *Inspiration* was yesterday's word.

"Madame," says the Princesse de Montauban in a voice thick with honey and thinned with sarcasm, "your memory never ceases to astound me." Mademoiselle de Clermont, formidable in her position and her birth, fixes a sharp eye on Montauban, who smiles back innocently.

We settle on the grass in the North Parterre, encircled by hedges of strictly cut rosebushes. "Get those away from me," hisses Tante Mazarin as a hapless footman approaches her with a palette of paints. "Not while I am wearing my brown satin. Colored mud—that's all paint is. Stay away."

Then she slips easily into a light voice and sidles up to the queen. "Madame, why would I want to paint myself when I can watch the glory of your art? It would be far more prudent of me to admire your work and learn from such talent."

The queen smiles thinly and settles at her easel in front of a small rosebush. I now believe the queen knows false flattery but is too weary to protest the compliments that flow her way. I watch the half smile that stays on her lips. She is in a good humor these days: she just gave birth to another little daughter and is still enjoying the loose robes of pregnancy.

A few of us take easels and canvas. I like painting; it is easier than reading and it is a wonderful thing to preserve the beauty of nature. Real flowers wither and die but a painting lasts forever. My favorite part is mixing the colors; on this fateful day I search for the perfect shade of pink, a soft blush color, to capture the very inside of the little rose I have chosen as my model. If only I could order a dress of the same color! But I have already ordered two new dresses this year, and it is only May. If I am not careful my bull of a husband will come raging at me about money again. I turn my mind away from those unpleasant thoughts and start to paint.

The Princesse de Montauban is as skilled at painting as she is at sarcasm. She makes me a little bit afraid; for months after I arrived she complimented me profusely on the elegant way I took my coffee. Then Gilette took me aside (though only sometime later) and told me I was doing it all wrong: one never, but *never*, must let the third finger touch the cup.

Soon Montauban's delicate depiction of a bright pink rose is receiving compliments all around, though of course everyone must praise the queen's bush more. A group of gentlemen appears round the hedges. I know most of them, but only in the slight way that everyone knows everyone at Versailles. The men admire the queen's work and Montauban's beautiful rose. Then they turn to Gilette's canvas. Gilette has painted her rose in a very odd manner, concentrating only on the opening of the bud and making it more oval than round.

"Well, well, well, what is this unusual flower you are painting, Madame d'Antin? It is exceedingly beautiful. What do you call such a rose?"

"It is a *cocksglove*," one man declares.

"No, I do believe it is that sweetest of all roses, the Latin name being *Cuntus mirabilus*," another replies.

I giggle despite myself. Such lewd talk!

"I've heard the petals are good enough to eat, though sometimes a little pungent and fishlike," the first man says.

"Such *children*," hisses the Duchesse de Boufflers, steering her great bulk away. She and Tante Mazarin create a protective wall of chatter around the queen. One of the men detaches himself from the group and comes over to my easel. He is very handsome and is wearing an exquisite cream coat sewn with violets. I know his wife quite well, a pleasant woman who always wears a ribbon around her neck—it is whispered that men have been known to faint at the sight of the wine mark she hides beneath her choker.

"It's beautiful," he says softly, looking at me and not at my canvas.

I blush. "Oh, no, sir. I am an amateur."

"The painting, perhaps, though the color is nice. What a perfect shade of pink. But the real work of art, madame, stands before me."

He takes a step closer and I look in his eyes and then a curious thing happens: the world recedes and everything around me—the queen, the courtiers, the bushes and the flowers, Gilette's dirty painting, even the sun and the grass and the heat of the day—they all disappear and then there is only him and I, alone together.

I think: So this is love.

Only the setting sun breaks the spell and returns us to reality. When at last the man draws himself away from me, he bows low and lingers over my hand.

"Would you do me the honor of presenting me with your delightful rose, madame?"

I blush.

He gestures to the half-finished painting.

"Oh. Of course . . . but it's . . . it's not finished."

"It is perfect as it is," he says, with one last long look in my eyes. He leaves with the rest of the gentlemen and I stare after him as they disappear down the path. Gilette skips up and pinches my arm.

"Our little Louise has made a conquest," she says in a too-loud voice.

"Oh, nonsense," I say. "Shhh. He is just a kind man."

"Just a kind man with the most handsome face since Jupiter!" chips in the Princesse de Montauban, poking a brush dripping with cerise paint at me.

"And with that disgusting thing on his wife's neck, he'll be easy pickings, I'm sure," adds Gilette. "Oh, my little Louise, you are starting to climb the ladder. I am so proud of you!"

I giggle despite myself, rather intoxicated by what has just happened. I see Tante Mazarin bustling toward me and I know a lecture is coming.

"Deliver it to my apartment," I call out to a footman, pointing at my canvas, and then Gilette and I sprint up the steps to the terrace, laughing all the way.

⁓

His name is Philogène.

Puysieux is his family name, but I call him by his Christian name, Philogène. What a name! I could say his name for hours. Philogène, Philogène, Philogène. He is so handsome, thirty years old and in the prime of his life. He is perhaps the most handsome man I have ever seen. Dare I say he is more handsome than the king? Would that be treason? But I think it is true. He has big beautiful eyes and an elegant nose and wonderful white teeth and a large mole just below his ear, that I call his beauty patch. He is always dressed elegantly and his favorite color is blue—the same as me! Beside him, my husband looks like quite the country lawyer.

I do believe he is perfect. Philogène, I mean, not Louis-Alexandre.

Philogène, Philogène, Philogène.

In addition to being the most handsome man at Court, he is

also very intelligent and charming. He has the high regard of the king and his ministers, and has traveled abroad many times on Court business. He has even lived in Sweden, a cold country filled with Protestants; he says they are not as awful as one might think.

At first I resist and insist I wish to remain chaste, but my friends are having none of it. They tell me that Philogène is the most handsome man at Court and that he is dying of love for me, and then they remind me again about my husband and that sword maker's daughter.

I feel my will crumbling. I am not a very strong person to begin with and Versailles has definitely changed me. Rather rapidly too. And . . . surely there are greater sins?

The other ladies tease and prod to know how my affair is progressing and ask why it is already July, yet all the world knows I have not given in to Puysieux? I don't ask how all the world knows; scandals here are like spring buds that flower with gossip as their water.

Once a footman, blushing scarlet, carried a ladder into the salon where we sit with Her Majesty.

"The ladder you ordered, Madame de Mailly?" The other ladies peal with laughter, but instead of blushing and losing myself in confusion as I might have done when I first arrived, I say calmly: "No, you may take it away. I don't need it." I wait a beat, then add: "But perhaps in a week or two." Gilette and Montauban cheer and Tante's eyes look to bulge out of their head. The queen beams in confusion, laughing eagerly though she knows not the joke.

Clermont glares at us with icicle eyes then says smoothly to the queen: "Madame de Mailly thought to help you practice *escalate*, madame." *Escalate* was Wednesday's word.

I sink back in my seat, feeling like a true *versailloise*. And I think my friends might be right: Perhaps I could use a different view? My resolve is disappearing like dew on a hot morning.

The next day I kiss Philogène for the first time, then spend the night in the chapel praying away my sin.

Gilette studies me. "Where were you last night? We missed you at the tables."

"Oh, a touch of indigestion." I wave my hands vaguely over my stomach. Gilette peers at me suspiciously.

"Not that kind of bellyache?"

"Oh, goodness, no." I blush. I wish it were. It would be nice to have a child, not with my brute husband . . . but with Philogène? I still see Louis-Alexandre occasionally, so if I were to become pregnant the baby could well be his. Besides, everyone knows the most important thing is to have the child, not who the father is.

Oh, such thoughts, to so quickly undo my night of penance!

Philogène is ardent and seeks every opportunity to be at my side. Soon we are kissing and more in the shadows and spending every free moment in the privacy of the hedge-high gardens and mazes.

It is a beautiful August day of warm wind and sun. We make our way slowly down the vast stone staircase to the Orangery and on every one of the hundred steps, Philogène stops me to declare another reason why he loves me.

"Step thirty-three: your brown eyes with flecks of green— enchanting! Step thirty-four: your little yawns when you are bored. Step thirty-five: that piece of hair that comes loose"—and here, despite my protests, he pulls a strand free from its pins— ". . . and sparkles in the sunlight."

Remaining chaste is becoming harder with every passing day. For the first time, I want a man who is not Louis-Alexandre. I know that with Philogène it would be different. Very different.

"You must think of your sisters," Tante hisses at me. "You must consider Hortense and Marie-Anne." I am becoming adept at avoiding her. Versailles is an easy place to get lost in and I take care to schedule my weeks with the queen for when she is not in attendance. Despite my best efforts, our calendars sometimes collide.

I ignore her and fold a napkin as we prepare the queen's dinner table. The napkins are heavy yellow silk brocaded with red and green vines. What lovely fabric—wasted on table linen. How

I would like to have a gown made of it! How many would I need to make a jacket? Two would suffice for a stomacher, perhaps with my white gown . . .

"Don't ignore me," Tante hisses again.

I pretend I haven't heard her.

"I swore to your dying mother I would protect you from all these evils."

"I thought my mother died suddenly. And you were in Paris when it happened, and she at Versailles. And besides, my mother never cared for such protection for herself." I freeze, avoiding her eyes. Is it love that gives me such courage?

"Insolence," breathes Tante, and I know I have made an enemy. But I don't care.

The next night I invite Philogène to my apartment for the first time.

I dismiss my women and we are alone in the bedchamber. He kisses me slowly and I want to melt into him, to be the wax to his fire. His hands are soft and smooth, both the skin and his movements, so different from the coarse paws of my husband. That night Philogène unfurls pleasures for me that I had heard of but had never experienced, that now come to me like a dream remembered.

Oh.

Why couldn't Philogène have been my husband instead of Louis-Alexandre?

From Pauline de Mailly-Nesle
Convent of Port-Royal
February 20, 1733

Dear Louise,

I have not heard from you for many weeks. Perhaps your letter to me was lost? I hope you are well. The convent is boring. I am almost twenty-one years old and I do not like being surrounded by babies. I wish you would invite me to visit you at Versailles.

Thank you for the news of the queen's artistic talents. How I would love to see her paintings! And yours too! I am sure you paint beautifully; you always had talent though we never had lessons.

Diane no longer wishes to be a nun; instead she also wishes to get married. She is well but she burned her hand with her morning coffee yesterday and so is unable to write. She asks me to send her love. She loves you, but not as much as I love you. Do you remember in the nursery when I used to help you feed all the animals of the Noah's Ark, when you gave a little party for them? I think you know I love you the most.

Thank you and I look forward to your next letter, and most of all, I look forward to an invitation to visit you at Court.

Pauline

From Marie-Anne de Mailly-Nesle
Hôtel de Mazarin, Paris
June 17, 1733

Dear Diane,

Greetings from Tante Mazarin's. Unfortunately Tante Mazarin has forbidden you to come and visit next week; the workmen are starting on the first floor and she said the dust would be bad for your health. I am not sure that is true, but what Tante decides, must be. I know she is not very fond of Pauline and I told her you would visit alone, but she said that it still would not be possible.

I hope you are not too bored at the convent and that Pauline is being nice to you. Do not let her be a tyrant as she was in the nursery. Life is dreadfully dull here. I wish we were back in the Quai des Théatins, we had so much more freedom there. Freedom!

Do you know what happened to our Noah's Ark? I thought Hortense had brought it with her but she can't find it. Of course, we are too old now for such childish things, but I do think it would be nice to have it again. Remember the cats that you loved the best? I liked the tigers.

When you next send a letter, please try to write more clearly. I could not understand your last letter and there was a large smudge over the part about the chicken. Or was it about the kitchen?

Love,
Marie-Anne

From Louise de Mailly
Château de Versailles
July 3, 1733

Dear Pauline and Diane,

Pauline, thank you for your letters, and Diane, thank you for your best wishes. I am well and trust you are well too. I had a slight toothache last month but I am better now.

I am sorry I have not written but life is very busy here. Summer is wonderful! Simply wonderful. I am so happy! I mean because it is summer. I regret I cannot invite you to Court; unfortunately my apartment is too small to host you properly.

A quick note only; I must prepare for the evening—a concert in the Marble Court. Yesterday the Duchesse d'Antin dared to wear her sleeves above her elbows; she claimed the flounces had been burned by a candle. No one complained and we all are very interested to see what she will wear tonight! I will keep you informed.

Love,
Louise

Diane

CONVENT OF PORT-ROYAL, PARIS

1733

I love Louise's letters. How glamorous Versailles sounds! Louise tells me what she wore when, and who was the most fashionably dressed on which day. Pauline says stories like that are a waste of ink; she wishes for news of men and war and intrigues. Not for news about the Duchesse d'Antin's shocking gown*f* of orange roses or the Princesse de Montauban's flowered traveling hat.

Louise writes only occasionally but I wish she would write more. Our governess, Zélie, always said that if one wants to receive, one must give, so I suppose I should write more letters to her too. But I am not very good at spelling—why must letters always sound different in different words? And I hate writing: my fingers get tired so easily and my letters wilt downward, as though they are as sleepy as my poor hand, and the ink always seems to get everywhere. The laundress here at the convent says I am the most careless girl she has ever had the misfortune of dealing with. Luckily our daily wear is brown, so the ink stains don't show much.

I suppose if I were better at writing letters, I would also write to my younger sisters, Hortense and Marie-Anne. I miss them. Though we are not so far away, Tante Mazarin does not like Pauline, and so we are never allowed to visit.

The convent is very dull; lessons are boring and we are rarely allowed to walk out or sing or dance. I like dancing, though we never had proper lessons. A dancing master came a few times to the Quai des Théatins, but then he was caught with one of the serving girls, dancing but in an adult way. After that he never came again. Pauline said dancing was silly and Hortense said it was sinful, but sometimes Louise would strum on an old harp and Marie-Anne and I would dance together. Even when I was younger I was tall (as tall as an Amazon, said Zélie, though I can't remember what Amazons are) and I would twirl Marie-Anne, who was just a tiny little thing, around and around. One time I let her go and she crashed into a chair, which then crashed into a table and the globe fell off and there was the most frightful ruckus. *Ruckus*—I like that word.

I miss our house. And I miss my sisters. I think I even miss my father. And of course our dear dead Mama.

I often wonder what my sister Louise is doing at Versailles. I know she is a lady-in-waiting to the queen, so must attend Her Majesty, but sometimes I find myself wondering, usually during chapel or lessons, what she is doing at that *exact* moment.

If it's morning, perhaps she is praying in the same chapel as the king and queen? They say our queen is very pious. I am of course very pious too, though perhaps not as much as before. I hope God is not angry with me for no longer wanting to become a nun, but I think He has enough nuns already—there are thirty-eight just in this convent alone! I am sure the chapel at Versailles is very grand. If there are candles and mirrors everywhere at the palace, does that mean there are mirrors in the chapel as well? And then here I am, praying in the chapel at Port-Royal with only white-washed walls and dreary religious paintings, so dark and old they look like pieces of weathered leather.

In the afternoon, perhaps Louise is eating at a grand dinner or having a picnic outside. They say the gardens of Versailles are the most magnificent in the world. And I'm sure the food at Versailles is splendid. I wonder if she can choose what she wants to eat? The food at the convent isn't very good and the refectory here is so cold we shiver even in summer. The best days are Sundays, when we are served roast chicken, and the worst are Fridays because I don't like fish or eels very much. Unless they are baked in a pie.

In the afternoon, when we are supposed to be reading our catechism, perhaps Louise is chatting with the queen or helping her dress for an important occasion. The queen's gowns must be magnificent! Much finer than my brown dress, even with Louise's lace sewn on. Though I have heard the queen does not overly care for fashion. But still, she is the queen, so I am sure she dresses very well.

And in the evenings, when we are playing cards with the women boarders or preparing for bed, I imagine Louise dancing away at a grand ball in the grandest room imaginable, far, far larger than any room at the convent, larger even than the refectory.

How different our lives are.

Louise

After more than three years at Versailles I no longer think twice before I sink in respect before Cardinal Fleury. For many months after I first arrived, I worried: Would I fall over? Would my leg collapse over my heel, for the shoes are always too small and tight fitting and the dresses so heavy? But these days I sink as gracefully as Mademoiselle de Charolais, whom everyone considers the most elegant woman at Court.

Cardinal Fleury looks surprisingly healthy for such an old man. He still makes me nervous, with his darting eyes and slippery smile. I trust him even less than I trust most courtiers, though he holds the king's confidence tight and dear.

"Madame, you are looking lovely as usual," he replies to my greeting. Fleury is seated, and Mademoiselle de Charolais is beside him. I wonder why they have asked me here to her apartments. I assume they wish me to spy on the queen, as they have requested before.

"You will be wondering why we have asked you here."

I nod. I do not sit, for I am only a countess and Mademoiselle de Charolais is a princess of the blood and one cannot sit before one's betters unless invited. But graciously Charolais motions me down and I curtsy again to show my thanks, then settle onto a green velvet sofa with shells scalloping the gilt edges. The color of apples, I think, distracted. Rather perfect. I have never been in Charolais's private apartments before and it is opulence in seven shades of green. I'm surprised the furniture is not lavender; she adores that color and wears it constantly. But I do count twelve vases filled with lilacs grouped around us; their scent is cloying and close. Charolais only ever wears a special violet scent, made just for her, and she refuses to speak to ladies who dare to wear the same flower.

"We have a delicate matter to propose to you." Fleury coughs and I see in astonishment that this great man, the king's most trusted adviser, is nervous.

Charolais smiles her too-wide smile and leans in. "My darling Louise." She has a lisping, insinuating voice. "Louise, you are so adorable. So pretty and so refined. Elegant."

I smile and thank her, confused. No one is as pretty as Charolais, even though she is getting older. She sees the doubt on my face and assures me they have nothing immoral to ask of me. Fleury laughs and shakes his head. "Not at all, not at all. Your service to the queen has been well received and well remarked upon."

"My loyalty to the queen is absolute and . . ."

Charolais holds up a delicate ringed hand and the feathers trimming her sleeves flutter. "With the queen's best interests at heart, and with the king's as well, we have thought long and hard about how to accommodate the rupture between Our Majesties."

The rupture? What rupture? The king is not as devoted to the queen as he was before, and the queen will not see him in her bed on an ever-expanding list of saint's days, but a rupture? "I—"

Again the fluttering of feathers and that wide, false smile: "Please, Louise, darling, let me continue."

Generally I like Charolais for her wit and sense of fun, but today she is making me uneasy. She continues: "If I may speak frankly?"

Fleury nods as though giving a cue.

"The king no longer feels everything he used to feel for the queen. It is only natural, you understand? She is so much older than him, and remarkably plain, and with no disrespect intended, she is not the brightest diamond in the necklace."

"Not the sharpest knife on the table," adds Fleury with a smirk.

"Not, of course, that one has to be intelligent to be a good companion," Charolais says swiftly, shooting a worried look at the cardinal.

He takes over: "It is only a matter of time before the king strays from the—ah—marriage bed. And it is important that when he strays, he does not go too far."

Fleury talks of the king as though he were a child, I think, as I watch the two play their game in front of me. After three years here, I am better at reading what is left unsaid or what stays beneath the surface. It is a useful skill but not one that comes naturally; I prefer honest words to artifice. Even so, I have no idea what they want of me. For they surely want something.

"What we are saying, Louise, is that the king is certain to take a mistress."

"A mistress? Oh, no, the king is far too devoted—" I let my words fall off. It is true that everyone is betting on when the king will take a mistress, and who she will be. Gilette has quizzed me about her own chances, and wonders if the king will fall in love with her long dark hair, since the queen is fair-headed. She plots to leave her hair as loose as she dares and unpowdered one night, and claim that her hairdresser was sick.

"No, Louise," says Charolais with just a hint of impatience. "His days of devotion are fast fading. And he is a young man, only twenty-three, just like you. He cannot live the life of a monk forever."

"The king will take a mistress," repeats Fleury. "But who that mistress will be, well . . . That is a matter of *supreme* importance. Even national importance."

They both smile at me intently. Last year the Marquis de Beaulieu came back from India, alive, and kept the Court entertained with stories of snake charmers. It is as though they are trying to hypnotize me with words as their music.

"It is so important, dearest Louise, that the king's mistress be someone we know. And trust. Someone from a good family, of course, an ancient one, and someone who will have only the king's interests at heart. Someone who has no greed or ambition, and who will bring no complications."

The music stops, and suddenly the meaning of this meeting becomes clear. "You wish my help in finding the king a mistress?" I say, looking between the two charmers.

Fleury looks at Charolais, who makes a small grimace, as if to say, *I told you so.* She turns back to me with a dazzling smile. "You are very perceptive, dear Louise. As always. It is true in a way that we wish your help, and who better to help us than the one we wish would help us the most?"

I am not sure I understand. At Versailles in such situations, it is always best to remain silent.

Fleury steps in: "I think we need to talk plainly, and simply. Clearly. Louise, we think you should be the king's mistress. For the king, and for France."

"Imagine, Louise, the chance to be a royal mistress." Charolais almost licks her lips but curls her tongue in at the last minute. Her lips are dyed carmine and rather cracked. "You could be the new Agnès Sorel or Diane de Poitiers."

I look blankly and Fleury raises his eyebrows. "I see your education is as lacking as they say. Try this, my dear: you could be the new Madame de Montespan, or Madame de Maintenon."

He speaks of the last king's most famous mistresses. Of course those ladies I do know—Athénaïs de Montespan, the beautiful love of the king's youth, supplanted in his affections by the devout Marquise de Maintenon, the companion (and secret wife!) of the king's later years. I know well of their fame and their beauty, and of the power they had over that most powerful of men. I don't think I am one such as they, but Charolais and Fleury, two of the most influential people at Court, seem to think I am. It is flattering, of course, but still . . . the queen. And Philogène.

"Puysieux." The cardinal flicks at his sleeves as though to flick the idea of my lover from my mind. "The Marquis de Puysieux, the man you call Philogène, is a nobody. We are offering you the king."

"Think on it, dearest Louise. Think on it in your dreams." Charolais pats me and a feather wisps against my wrist, a little tendril of temptation.

But of course that night I can't sleep.

&

The next day they find me in my apartments. Fleury is brusque and invokes my family name and the chance to do a great service for France. "Your forefathers served their kings on the battlefield," he says, "and now we wish you to serve your king in the royal bed."

"Why me?" I have the courage to ask. "There are prettier and . . . ah, more *experienced* ladies than I at this Court."

Charolais rattles off the reasons: "Louise, you are pretty and pure and virtuous, at least for Versailles. You have no ambitions to meddle in politics, I can see that, and all your friends know you only suffer gossip because you can't get away from it. It is your very virtue, in fact, that has made us decide that you are the perfect woman for our king to love."

They have put a lot of thought into this. "You talk of my virtue, but what you propose is immoral—"

"Puysieux? Was that—is that—not *immoral* as well? You mounted that ladder *very well.*"

Suddenly I feel like crying. "Well . . . I may have already sinned, but the king has not. I would be an adulteress, encouraging him to stray from his wife. And the queen would be devastated."

"No, Louise," says Charolais firmly, rising and coming toward me. She puts her hands over mine. I stare at her gray gloves, delicately embroidered down the back with a row of little purple flowers. I should get some like that, I think. I wish I wasn't having this conversation. I wish I were somewhere else. I really do.

"You must not think like that. You *cannot* think like that. Because if you do not rise to this challenge, someone else will; someone who might harm the queen. Whereas you, you would do all in your power to make the inevitable *situation* as comfortable and pleasant for the queen as you can. We all know your devotion to her."

Fleury nods. "Exactly! Very solid thinking, mademoiselle." He then proceeds to lecture me on how becoming the king's mistress will be the best thing for the queen.

I am never defiant. I always do what is asked of me. I was obedient to my parents and I am obedient to my husband even though I have no respect or love for him. And now I know I cannot withstand this request from these great personages. I feel the walls closing around me; my dress tightens and I sweat even though the palace is cool this September day. I am very confused. The idea is certainly intriguing and what an honor to be loved by the king! But . . . I lay down my last objection and the one that is closest to my heart.

"The Marquis de Puysieux," I say. He is away in Sweden again with the Protestants. "We are in love and what . . . what will happen to him?" Perhaps were he by my side my resolve would not falter, but he is away and I am here, snared and charmed.

Fleury snorts and rises and says he has wasted enough time on this matter already and that he has a country to run. But he senses victory; they can both see I am wavering like a jelly.

"As the cardinal said yesterday, forget Puysieux. Imagine instead the king falling in love with you, and you with him. Imagine that." Charolais's hand tightens on my arm and this time she actually does lick her lips.

Trying hard not to, I do find myself wondering what it would be like to be in the arms of the king, to be kissed by him, to make love with him. To make the King of France happy. Oh, Philogène, Philogène, Philogène. What should I do? The next day I don't stare at the queen, or even look at her, and when the king comes in to pay his daily respects, I slip outside and hide in a corner.

Without waiting for my approval, they set their plan in motion the following week. In Charolais's apartment her hairdresser, a snooty man who wields his hair tongs as though he were conducting an orchestra, arranges my hair and fixes my cheeks with rouge and places two beauty spots beneath my eyes, exactly like tears. I am wearing my white silk gown, now adorned with garlands of glossy, peach-colored rosettes.

I am very nervous but also strangely excited. This is the *king* and it would be false to say I was not attracted to him: every woman at Court is half in love with him. Or wholly in love. He is so handsome and regal. Many say Louis XIV was France's most magnificent king, but I think our Louis is equally magnificent, if not more—I am sure one day he will be known as France's best king.

Charolais pulls a few rosettes from my dress—the king likes simple things and these detract from your charms, she says—and arranges me on a sofa next to a small fire.

"Have some champagne." She pours me a large cup and I take it eagerly.

Fleury and the king's valet, Bachelier, a tall, lanky man with a reserved demeanor, arrive and they nod their approval. So Bachelier is in on this "plot," though I should not be surprised—he controls everything around the king and is, in his own silent way, rather terrifying.

They retire, but not before Fleury has placed his wormy, decrepit hands on me and wished me luck. Then I am alone with the fire, the champagne, and my shaking nerves. Goodness, what am I doing?

The door opens softly and it is the king. It is the first time I am alone in a room with him, but I must remember, as Charolais keeps telling me, that tonight he is not the king, just a man.

"Madame."

He bows formally and we look at each other.

Should I rise? But this is an informal meeting . . . a *very* informal one.

The king stays frozen by the door and I stay frozen on the sofa, my chin starting to shake with threatened tears. What am I doing?

This is mortifying. The king stretches out his hand and starts to study one of his fingernails intently. My champagne cup trembles and I spill some on my skirt. I dart another look at him and see he is as mortified as I am. I burst into tears—why had I ever agreed to this mad plan?—and the king jumps as though stung, then bows quickly and retreats from the room.

Oh, mortification! I will leave Versailles; I will go back to that hated country house of my husband's, anything but stay here. Run away to Sweden and fling myself in Philogène's arms. Philogène . . . I drink the rest of my champagne and give myself over to my tears. I am so humiliated. It was all so . . . so . . . I can't bear to think how awful it was.

Charolais rushes back in. "Don't worry, don't worry," she says briskly, filling my glass with more champagne. "Oh, you spilled some! And stop crying or your rouge will run, and look! One of your patches has slipped." She picks it off and flicks it into the fire. "One is fine. Bachelier is with His Majesty right now. He will persuade him to come back. And I thought I could count on you to cry—the king would never leave a woman in distress."

I don't have any words. I wish the floor would open and I could fall through, away from this room, down into the ground beneath. I wish I were *dead*.

"Stop crying, Louise!" Charolais looks at me critically. "Let's try this. Lounge back, as though reading a book of poems."

I obey, sniffling, and feel myself gradually beginning to float away with the champagne as my guide. Charolais pulls up my skirt to reveal my green stockings and a blue garter.

"You're not powdered, are you? Down there?"

For an awful moment I think she is going to dive in and check. "No, no, of course not." I blush.

"Good, the king hates powder. Anywhere. Good." Charolais takes another rosette off my bodice and slips it under my garter. "This will surely attract his attention."

I blush some more and look up at the ceiling. What am I doing? I mean, really, what am I doing?

"Best legs at Versailles, you know that is what they say about you."

I didn't, but I stop crying. Charolais pats delicately at my cheeks with a handkerchief and declares my flushed face "charming" and my expression deserving of my innocence.

"Don't move. He'll be back."

I am left in my awkward pose, staring up at the ceiling.

The king reenters the little salon and this time he comes directly to stand by the sofa. He takes my hand. I have never been this close to him before. Or this alone. I breathe in and my other hand curls around the arm of the sofa. Our eyes don't meet. My leg feels naked and cold and I am sure he is eyeing my garter.

"Madame, you are lovely," he says in his wonderful, deep voice, and before I can say anything, he has buried himself in my lap, his heavily ringed hands running up and down my leg. Suddenly the world fades away and all that is left is the fire, the king and I and our beating hearts, and his face in my lap.

Tentatively at first, then stronger, I run my hands through his thick hair, intoxicated by the smell of bergamot and fine leather. I'm touching the king, I think in wonder as his hands climb higher to pull at my garter and bare my legs. Then he pushes a finger inside me, a ring grazing the delicate skin. I gasp and he rises to kiss me. I sink into his soft lips and close my eyes and forget about everything—and everyone—outside of this room.

"Madame, you are beautiful."

From Pauline de Mailly-Nesle
Convent of Port-Royal
January 20, 1734

Louise,

I hope you are well. We have not had any news from you for quite a time and I hope you have not forgotten me. I long for your fascinating news—did the Marquise de Villar's new gloves of sable and pink leather keep her warm this winter? How are your gloves?

I suggest you invite me to Versailles. The convent is boring and the younger students are constantly crying for me because I am almost twenty-two and not yet married or even betrothed. But then little Gabrielle de Moudancourt, only thirteen, left to be married and was dead in childbirth within the year, so for a while their pity stopped. But I know it will start again.

Father tried to visit last month but he was turned away at the gate for being too drunk. Apparently he was accompanied by an actress! Unfortunately I did not get to see her.

Remember, Diane and I have no other relations to take care of us and now we have the news that Marie-Anne, only sixteen, is engaged! It is an absolute scandal for a younger sister to marry before her elder sisters. She is to be married because Tante Mazarin has her interests at heart. You know that Tante hates me and will not do the same for me.

Diane is well and she sends you her love. She pricked her hand sewing last week and is unable to write but she does love you, but not as much as I love you. I think you know I love you the most.

Sororal love,
Pauline

Marie-Anne

PARIS AND BURGUNDY

1734

So, I am married.

As of yesterday, in fact. The Marquis de la Tournelle was a frequent visitor to Tante's; she is—was—great friends with his mother. Jean-Baptiste, or JB, as I call him, was quite taken with me and Tante encouraged his attentions. Actually, he was more taken with Hortense, who has become an extraordinary beauty, but Tante suggested I would make the better bride. I think Tante is holding on to Hortense for a better match than Tournelle.

Ours is what they call a "love match," though I don't love JB. But at least I know him and he is a fine enough boy. He's actually my age—sixteen is rather young for a man of no dynastic importance to get married—but he had to grow up quickly because his father died when he was only three. His mother is atrocious; the worst kind of arrogance. She was against our match from the beginning, contending we were both far too young and that my dowry wouldn't feed a bird for a month. She and Tante had quite the fight over it and they are now no longer the great friends they once were.

JB does not have to listen to his mother, and so he decided we should be married. He's not the most intelligent person but he is very much devoted to me, and I must make him believe his admiration is returned, for what choice do I have? One has to marry—it's either that or the convent. So I have married Jean-

Baptiste-Louis de la Tournelle, the Marquis de la Tournelle and the owner of a host of unimportant places, mostly in Burgundy.

It was all neatly arranged and now Tante never ceases reminding me what a wonderful match it is. Surprisingly, she is tickled by the idea of a (suitable) love match. She told me the tale of her disastrous first marriage: she was only eleven when her parents betrothed her to the late king's councillor Phelypeaux. He was not of the old nobility, but of the new and despised administrative nobility: his father was only ennobled in 1678! I know this, having read it in the *Genealogical History of the Royal Family and Peers.*

What I didn't know was that my aunt cried and cried at having to marry such a man. My image of stuffy old Tante as a stuffy little girl is a charming one. When she was twelve she obeyed her parents and married him, but she told her family she would never be happy again and that she would never forgive them. She was correct on both accounts. Luckily, Phelypeaux died and then she married the Duc de Mazarin, fulfilling her dream of becoming a duchess.

So I am now the Marquise de la Tournelle. An acceptable title, not as old or as prestigious as my father's, but still, nothing to turn up one's nose at. As well as becoming a marquise, today I also became a woman, at four a.m. to be precise; the wedding feast at his Paris home was long and protracted and that was the earliest we "smitten lovebirds" (actually one smitten lovebird, and one rather indifferent but a little bit excited and a little bit drunk lovebird) could escape. Within five minutes (and lots of fumbling and one torn chemise), it was over. I am not sure what all the fuss is about, but perhaps time will tell.

Now it is odd to think that there is someone who has more of a claim on me than Tante, or even Zélie, ever had. Someone who can interfere with my private thoughts—or even with my body— at any moment of the day.

JB has the house in Paris but he is frequently away with his regiment and does not have a place at Court yet. Unfortunately his mother also lives in the Paris house and I certainly don't want to live with her. Then it was proposed that I continue living with Tante while my husband is away. Oh, horror.

"I wish to live in the country, at his place in Burgundy," I announce. I keep my expression neutral: I'd rather go to Vienna, or Rome, or a hundred other places, but since those aren't options, I will settle for Burgundy. Anywhere but here.

"Who *willingly* goes to the country? And leaves Paris? And goes as far away from Versailles as it is possible to get?" responds Tante, her voice filled with alarm.

Burgundy is quite close to Paris, but for Tante, anything beyond two hours' drive could as well be in Hungary as far as she is concerned. She considers my request at once shocking and eccentric.

"Eccentricity is all well and fine in a man, especially a rich one," Tante reminds me. "But certainly not in a woman! And definitely not in a new bride."

I stand my ground and JB agrees to my plan. Then I have the supreme triumph of defying Tante and making my first independent decision as a grown, married woman. With the permission of my husband, of course.

I believe I am settling quite well into my new life. On the surface, it appears that I only desire to please. I play the part very well and it is interesting to see JB grow daily more infatuated with me. I have a rather cherubic face that is definitely at odds with my inner being: rosy, dimpled cheeks and a mouth that can be compared to a rosebud have never served a woman wrong. JB says it is my eyes that are fascinating; the rest of my face is like a child's, but my eyes are those of an older, knowing woman. I am much smarter than he is, but I know that I must never contradict a man, or concern him in any way with my wit. Zélie was fairly useless but that lesson stays with me.

My new home has some nice surprises: it lies beside a river of considerable strength and the days are filled with the soothing sounds of flowing water. But the saving grace of the house, and of my life, is the library. There, I am like a man dying of thirst who has just been released into a lake.

"Darling." JB calls me to the bed. I'm on a sofa, crouched next to the fire, reading. The château is icy and everything feels colder here than it does in Paris: I have decided that country cold is different from city cold.

"Yes, JB?"

"You're awake?"

"Yes, you can see I am sitting up."

"What are you doing?"

Does he not see I have a book? "I am reading."

"What are you reading? Come here and show me."

He motions me to the bed and I show him the book. *"Pascal: Lettres Provinciales."* He spells out the title rather laboriously. "Never heard of him."

What can I say to that?

I don't think JB has ever been inside his own library, but it is rather fine, three well-stocked rooms with books towering to the ceiling, extensive collections of literature and philosophy and geography and so much more; his grandfather Nicolas-François was a great reader and intellectual.

"Well," says JB, taking the book from my hands and throwing it on the floor—!—"You don't have to read any more of these dull books."

"Is that a promise?" Or a threat? I hadn't thought to ask his permission to take books from the library.

"Mmm . . . definitely a promise. Move over a little . . . there . . . mmm . . ."

Will I ever get used to cold hands on my private places? His tiresome pawing feels so uncomfortable and so *wrong,* I don't care if we are husband and wife. Though sometimes . . . if he moves in the right way, I catch glimpses and hints of things I cannot quite place, like trying to catch a cloud or a shadow in the night. Something I want to grab and pull back to me, though I don't know what it is yet. I think I'll find it eventually.

Other than studying JB and my books, there is not much else to do at the end of the world in deepest Burgundy. I miss my sisters, except of course Pauline.

I write to Diane at the convent and occasionally she writes back, but I can never decipher her letters; her spelling is atrocious. Hortense writes sheaves of pages and tells me that thanks to my romantic story she now prays for a marriage as filled with love and passion as mine. I don't disabuse her of her fairy-tale follies.

I occasionally write to Louise; even though she is rather dull, she has the most exciting life of all of us. She hinted in her last letter that she has a lover, but I suspect this is just another of her girlish fantasies. I remember her mooning, for years, over that sketch of her dreadful husband. Still, the idea is intriguing. I wonder if we will ever go to Versailles—JB assures me that in the future we will establish ourselves there. Louise could help, of course, but she was always so timid I can't imagine her influencing anyone on our behalf.

Will I be forgotten here, outside the world? Will Louise have all the glory and the love, while all I get is JB? I console myself with a newly found book of *Aesop's Fables*. It is strange to think that we can learn from insects and animals, but we can: he makes good use of humble lessons to teach great truths. Right now I feel a little like the tortoise—my life is starting slowly. Very slowly. Perhaps one day I'll be the hare?

From Louise de Mailly
Château de Versailles
August 4, 1734

Dearest Marie-Anne,

Congratulations, my dearest sister, on your wedding! I am thrilled that you are now a woman and introduced to the joys of marriage. I heard it was a love match, though a suitable one of course, and I am delighted for you. And how marvelous it is that your husband is the same age as you! That is absolutely perfect!

Love is the most wonderful thing in this world. I am talking about true love, of course, not puppy love, or infatuation, or things that we think are love, but about *real love*, the kind that only comes when one has found one's kindred soul, and when one realizes why the world exists and why *we* exist.

That is the love that I have finally, as a married woman, and I hope that you will also find it in your marriage. This rapture, this giddiness, this happiness—would that everyone could experience it so!

Oh, but I am rambling! It is just that I am so happy. For you, I mean. Though I am happy too. The world is wondrous and I am in love!

You must write and tell me of Burgundy. Burgundy! How far away it sounds. I overheard Tante Mazarin (she no longer speaks to me) saying that she feared she had failed in your upbringing, to have raised a child who would wish to live so far from Paris and the Court.

I am sure you miss Hortense and Paris but you will find a replacement, and more, in the arms of your husband.

A thousand hugs and kisses and congratulations again!
Louise

From Pauline de Mailly-Nesle
Convent of Port-Royal, Paris
August 22, 1734

Marie-Anne,

Congratulations on your wedding and your husband. My friend Madame de Dray says it is highly irregular for a younger sister to be married before an older. You are only sixteen, yet I am twenty-two and still not married. And Diane is twenty. Did Tante not consider the scandal?

Diane says we must write more often, that it is not sororal to dislike one's sisters.

I hope you like Burgundy. I'm sure it can't be worse than Tante Mazarin's house.

Pauline

From Marie-Anne de la Tournelle
Château de la Tournelle, Burgundy
September 1, 1734

Dear Hortense,

Greetings from Burgundy! All is well here, though I have to confess married life is not that different from my life before; in Paris I was confined to Tante's house, and now I am confined to my husband's house. Well, not exactly confined, but as there is nowhere for me to go, it is all rather the same.

My days are not exactly boring; the weather is lovely here and the gardens are extensive and good to ramble through. Everything is very quiet. There is a wonderful library with seeming all the books of creation gathered into three rooms and that is my solace and my passion. I have just read *Manon Lescaut*; have you heard of it? See if you can find a copy—I recommend it highly, but don't let Tante find it.

There is not much else to report. My husband was here until last month but has now left to be with his regiment. He is well, though he had a persistent cough he blamed on the summer wind. He says the Austrians are being very aggressive and he is worried. I'm not; Burgundy is miles away from Austria.

Please let me know how life is with you. How is Victoire? Did she have her puppies? How many? One of the gardeners here found a baby deer and I adopted it; it was quite the most adorable thing. Unfortunately it got rather big and the cook complained it would decimate the onion stores for the winter. I had it killed and it was delicious, though I was a little sad.

I am sending you a crate of dried quinces from the orchard here. The taste is sharp but the scent is simply heavenly.

Love,
Marie-Anne

Louise

VERSAILLES AND RAMBOUILLET

1734

A long, aquiline nose. Divine hooded eyes—can I use the word *divine* if not talking of Him?—pale and brown, Anjou pears at the end of summer. His hair is long and glorious, like a bear's pelt, and wondrously soft.

His skin is very fair, a little pitted but only as would make him masculine. He likes it when I tickle and kiss the back of his neck and when I run my hands lightly and delicately over his chest and back. He calls them my little dove fingers.

At first there were qualms and incertitude. Louis had never been an unfaithful husband and the new role rested uneasily on his shoulders. Many nights he and I stayed awake to discuss his misgivings, which were mine as well.

"I don't want to be as my great-grandfather . . . So many women. The people of France . . . They knew him to be an immoral man, and he was not loved for that."

"But, Louis, my love, you are a man. And you love me. How can this be wrong? And you must not care what the people think. You are the *king*."

He sighs heavily. "There, my love, I must disagree. Fleury always says that the love of the people is one of the most important ingredients in this fateful soup that is kingship. The last king was highly admired in his youth, but by the end of his reign the people were tired of him. He was known as the Sun King, but also the Sin King. I must never be called that, never."

"But the people love you, darling!" It is true the people adore their young king; he is seen as the savior who will lead France to recoup the glory it has lost in recent years through endless wars and famines. I'm not sure how he will do that: Louis is just one man, and perhaps even a little bit lazy, but I am sure Fleury will think of something.

Louis sighs again; he has a somber side and sometimes passes days or even weeks in deep depression. During those times he wishes to be alone, or as alone as a king can be, and I do my best to make him comfortable and coax him back to the world again.

"The queen must never find out," Louis declares, with more passion than he has said, or done, anything all day. "I would die of mortification and shame. Dearest, this sin is not a cloak I wear lightly."

I take his hands in mine and beseech him to come to bed. We are in his private rooms, far above his official bedroom, alone in this warm and cozy cocoon. He refuses my hand and continues to stare moodily into the fire.

"Sin is not like a piece of clothing, Louise," he says finally, speaking to the dark and to the demons that haunt him. "You cannot simply put it on, then take it off and be pure again. Once you have sinned as I have . . . as we have . . . there is no return to the straight life."

I feel myself growing cold at the thought of being taken off and placed on a hook, discarded and never to be worn again.

"But, confession, my love . . ."

He waves away my protests. "Confession. How can I confess when I am living in sin? I shall not be confessing for a long, long time." Fortunately for both of us, Fleury supports our love—he was after all the mastermind that brought us together—and as a man of God, as well as Louis's closest adviser, his influence is unique.

I am silent, unsure of what to say or do. Louis is perplexing; underneath the layers of convention and perfect manners, there is a man much more complex. He is a very private man, perhaps because of his strange life: orphaned suddenly at the age of two when his mother, father, and elder brother all died of measles within months of each other; then king at the tender age of five when his great-grandfather Louis XIV died. His beloved governess, the Duchesse de Ventadour, was as his mother, but at the age of seven he was cruelly taken from her and thrust into the world of men; from that time on, Fleury was his father and none but he had his trust.

And he does not want to disappoint his father.

I think back to my time before Puysieux, to my indecision, to the desire to be faithful and beloved in God's eyes, pure. Now that time seems so long ago, just a little girl's fantasies. I am not saying I no longer regret my sins, and of course I still attend Mass, but . . . life must be lived. I think of my husband, Louis-Alexandre, and shudder. Surely love and happiness cannot be such great sins? Surely God understands? A log falls in the fire and snaps Louis out of his reverie. He sighs deeply. Oh, how it hurts me when he is in distress!

"All I want is for you to be happy."

"I am happy, Louise," he says solemnly. "But is He, up there, happy with me? I do not presume to say. Tomorrow, I want you to pray for me."

"Of course, my love. My darling, come to bed now, for soon it will be dawn and I must go. Come, please, I want to hold you and comfort you."

"A sinner, a sinner," he mutters as he climbs the steps to the bed to lie beside me.

Luckily his black moods never last long and soon his doubts subside, and as the months pass we come to know a pure, true love. I cease to think of him as the king. Now he is just Louis, my lover. The love of my life. Oh, how I adore him! I wish I were a Molière or a Racine in my way with words so that I could express completely how much I love him; all I can say is that everything about him is perfect. Everything. From the tips of his delicate fingers, with his lead-buffed nails, to the top of his head and his ambrosial brown hair, down to his toes and the little hairs that grow only on his big toe but not on the other ones. I adore everything about him.

And he loves me. He calls me his little Bijou. Jewel. Isn't that heavenly? I'd sooner have that endearment than all the real jewels in the world. Which is fortunate as Louis doesn't have much money for jewels. He cannot be generous with me because our love is secret, though occasionally Fleury passes me some money. But I am not Louis's mistress because I want a hundred gowns or dozens of diamonds. I am his mistress because I love him deeply and dearly and I would still love him if he were a lowly kitchen hand and we had to sleep in . . . in the kitchen, or wherever it is that kitchen hands sleep.

But Louis is the king, and that cannot be changed.

Now my world is split in two—divided between the hours I spend with him, and the hours without him. Though fortunately Fleury and his other ministers—Maurepas, d'Angervilliers, Amelot—mostly take care of the business of government, there are still papers to sign, ambassadors to meet with, ceremonies and regimental reviews to undertake, public dinners to attend. On those days when the demands of kingship must keep us apart, I feel empty and hollow inside and my stomach flutters with a thousand sad butterflies. The moment I see him again my mood is calmed. He is a drug for me, like the Indian opium that they say floats you away on a boat of blissful calm.

Only when we are finally alone, after a long day spent on the public stage of life, can he truly be with me. When we are alone, nothing else exists. Even though his life is lived almost entirely in public, Louis is a very private person and I know he relishes our secret as much as I do. At Versailles he sometimes comes to me, or I visit his private apartments under the lid of night, disguised with a mask and wearing my woman Jacobs's plain cloak. When the Court makes the annual visits to the royal castles of Compiègne or Fontainebleau, the rigid rules of Versailles still apply; it is only when he travels unofficially, on matters of the hunt or pleasure, that can we spend the entire night, and sometimes even the day, together.

This week we are at Rambouillet, a small ivy-covered château not far from Versailles, owned by the Comte and Comtesse de Toulouse. Some disparage her and her husband and call them faithful buffoons, but I think their devotion to each other is charming. I like the comtesse; she is a kindhearted woman and knows the king well from when he was a little boy, and the king in turn adores her.

When she learned our secret she hugged me and told me she was delighted, and whispered that she had rarely seen the king so happy and content.

At Rambouillet this week we are an intimate group—Charolais, Gilette, the young and very dear Comtesse d'Estrées, as well as the Prince de Soubise and a few other of Louis's close friends. Still, there are those among us who do not know the truth. Bachelier assigns our rooms and I am given a small chamber above the king's, our rooms linked by a secret staircase carved inside the thick stone walls of an ancient tower. My room is decorated in the Turkish style, the walls hung with generous blue velvet and a thick orange carpet on the floor. There are stars painted on the wooden ceiling, and at night when the king lies beside me I look up and feel as though we are in Heaven.

During the day, while the men hunt, I wander through gardens draped with lush bowers of overgrown roses and the last of the summer marigolds. I trail along the river and lose myself in the tranquil outer gardens, aimless and content. I have no wish to sit with the other ladies and listen to their speculation as to which shade of yellow most becomes a brunette (though I do think it is lemon, not mustard, as Charolais contends), and who the king's lover is.

Very few know—our love is a secret kept as hidden as a garter—but many are beginning to suspect. The king's attendance in the queen's bed is vigilantly tracked and it is well noted that he no longer frequents it as before. Everyone accepts that the queen is old and faded and declines to be disturbed on saint's days, so now the question on everyone's lips is: Where is the king putting his ardor, for surely such a young and virile man must be putting it somewhere?

"It must be Geneviève de Lauraguais—those amethyst eyes! Who could resist them?"

"Her husband, for one. Personally, I think it's just a maid, or a few of them—little grimy girls from the kitchens."

A shriek and some laughter. "Not our sovereign, my dear, not our sovereign. He would never touch anything so dirty."

"What is there that some water and a scrub cannot clean? My husband was once positively addicted to some little maid with a dreadful Gascon accent. We must remember the king is a man, no more, no less."

Another shriek. "Treason! Absolute treason. And you, Louise, who do you wager on?"

"The Duchesse de Lauraguais," I say quickly. "Her eyes are so beautiful."

I give the easy answer, then get up and leave the ladies and their gossip and speculation behind. I lose myself down a path of decaying yellow rosebushes, trailing my hand over the flowers and occasionally snapping off a few. I gather a bouquet and sneak it up to my room, and lay it on the bed. Will they last till the evening?

Now the night draws near and the guests depart for their rooms, full of braised boar and sleepy on champagne. The king retires with no ceremony, just Bachelier and a fresh chemise; nights here are longer and more intimate.

Alone in my room I sprinkle rosewater on my wrists and lap, then I pull back the carpet and lie down carefully on the floor. I turn my ear to the oaken slats; where the old boards warp away from each other the sounds from the room below rise up. I feel close to him even though I cannot see him.

"A good day today," I hear Bachelier say to the sounds of a jacket being beaten for dust.

"Mmm, by goodness, that last one was a great beast. And I want word of Pasha—we cannot have that horse lame."

Silence.

"The blue one, I think." I imagine him donning his chemise and robe.

Silence, the sound of a chest being closed.

"Just one candle."

"Shall I light the way, sire?"

"No need, I shall follow my nose."

The two men chuckle and I flush—is this a good thing or a bad thing? Do I wear too much scent, or not enough?

"Sire, I will be here if you need me."

I hope Bachelier can't hear from below as well as I can from above. I get up and open the little door, hidden behind a tapestry on the wall.

"Bijou," he says, coming in to the room and kissing me softly on the lips. "You smell delicious."

I take the candle from him and place it on the table by the bed.

"Kiss me again," he commands, and pulls me to him. "At last," he murmurs, and my heart beats faster.

"Ah, good, you have not undressed."

"Of course not, darling. I know how much you enjoy it."

He sets to work, untying the bows on my gown, unlacing my corset, detaching my skirts, his brow furrowed in determination and his fingers thick with anticipation. My desire grows, as does his. "Damned bows," he mutters, and I giggle. He likes this—a challenge for a man who has had his life served to him, completely.

"I can't help you, Twinkles, you know you forbade it." "Twinkles" is my pet name for him—because his eyes shine like stars. He declares it adorable.

Finally he yanks the last string and I am naked, my dress and petticoats a heap on the floor.

"Victory," he says softly. "You cannot know how I have been waiting for this." He pushes me down on the bed. "All through the meal I was eyeing that gown and I knew it would give me trouble. But now I have you."

You have me. You have all of me, I think in delight.

A gust of night wind finds the candle on the table and suddenly all is inky darkness. Louis wants me to go into the hall and take a light from a sconce, but I resist, just a bit. It is new for me, this power over a man. This power over a king.

"No. Wait," I say. "Let's enjoy the darkness."

"I submit to your desire."

We lie still, holding each other, surrounded by the black of velvet. Soon the room lightens as moonlight casts a silver glow around the chamber. He traces my face with his hands and I smile up at him.

"I love you," he says, and I know he means it.

"I love you too."

Oh, Heaven. After we make love I lie beside him as he starts to snore, and once he is safely asleep I slip out of the warm bed and offer up my prayers, as I do every night, that we will have a child together. Then my happiness would be complete and the world would be perfect.

Puysieux—remember him?—came to tell me he has been appointed ambassador to Naples. He declared passionately that he would stay and defy orders if I just gave the word. We haven't, of course, been intimate since I became Louis's mistress, but apparently he still hopes we will be reconciled.

Never.

I was rather cold to him and honestly I can't remember why I ever fancied myself in love with him. Certainly he is a fine-looking man, but next to the king he is nothing. Nothing. I just wished him *bon voyage* and left him kneeling on the floor. I am glad he will be in Italy and not moping around Court and making me uncomfortable.

I have never known such depth of love; what I feel for Louis is nothing like what I felt for Puysieux. That was infatuation, that was obligation—if one had to have a lover, as it seems is the custom at Versailles, then he was fine enough. But this? Oh. Who could have imagined such bliss?

Diane

CONVENT OF PORT-ROYAL

1735

Pauline listens everywhere and finds out everything of interest. Our friend Madame de Dray says she is like a pig in the forest, snuffling out truffles of information. One evening Pauline sails in to our room, back from a night of cards with Dray and some of the other women. I see her triumphant look.

"Did you win? Oh, I hope so, you know how I would like another box of those dried apricots." I don't usually play at cards—the games are very confusing and I always lose, though Pauline encourages me to play when I have some spare money.

"No—yes. Yes, I did win, but that is not important now. Can you imagine what I heard?" Pauline's eyes twinkle in the candlelight and I jump up and hug her.

"Something good, something good! Did Louise invite you to Versailles? But I saw her letter to you last week, she didn't—"

"No, it's not that," says Pauline impatiently. "Unhook me, I'm not waiting for Sylvie, that woman is so slow."

"Well, what is it? Is Dray's daughter pregnant again?"

"No, it's so much better than that." I sit down on the bed and Pauline pulls off her gown.

"Tell me."

She giggles. I've rarely seen her in such a good mood; normally, Pauline doesn't like laughing or anything resembling joy.

"Guess!"

"Louise has found you a husband!"

Her giggles stop. "No," she says grimly, unpinning her hair and shaking it out. "Though this news will help with that little project, I am sure. But it is about Louise."

"Louise is pregnant!"

"No, she's not pregnant! Goodness, Dee Dee, is that all you care about? If you want a child so badly, look no further than old Bandeau." The porter at the convent has a beaked nose and roving eyes and likes to grab the little girls and exhort kisses from them. I giggle; I know she's joking.

"Tell, tell, tell!"

"So Louise . . . Louise . . ."

I'm going to pop!

"Louise has a lover!"

Pauline sits down heavily on the bed beside me and I tumble back in astonishment. Louise has a lover?

Imagine that! And apparently Louis-Alexandre, her husband, doesn't even care. I think the news very funny—in the schoolroom Louise was always so good and only ever wanted to be virtuous, almost as much as Hortense. She would be troubled if we played with our toys on Sundays and even wanted the maids to double their petticoats in summer so that when they knelt to light a fire, the outline of their buttocks would be obscured. And now she, sinning along with everyone else at Versailles!

I tell the funny news to everyone I meet, even to the little students and the nuns, until one of them slaps me and says if I don't learn to talk of more appropriate things, she will tell Mother Superior to stuff my mouth with bread so I can't make a sound.

I laugh, because it sounds so funny—imagine me with a mouthful of bread!—but it is true. I do like to talk and the nuns are always scolding me for babbling and for not thinking before I talk. But why should I think before I talk? Why would I want to do things twice: First think something, then say it? Surely it's easier to do just one or the other? Only kind Sister Domingue doesn't laugh; instead she just rubs my head and tells me that one day, I'll learn.

Pauline decides the news is excellent and she has doubled her letter-writing campaign. She is convinced that a Court lover will surely have money and influence and therefore can help Louise fulfill her sororal duties. She considers blackmail, but Madame de Dray only snorts at that idea and says that Pauline has a lot to learn about the ways of the world: Who would care enough to pay money to keep such a thing a secret? Especially when it is clear her degenerate of a husband (her words, not mine) obviously doesn't care?

Hortense sometimes visits now from Tante Mazarin's, even though carriage travel makes her sick and she complains that the stream behind the convent smells of rotting fish. She doesn't tell Tante that she visits. I think that she is lonely, now that Marie-Anne is married and gone to Burgundy.

Hortense tells us that Tante now despises Louise as much as she despises Pauline and has made her, Hortense, swear on the Bible to never talk to Louise again!

"I suppose she hates me too," I say. "I mean not because I am a whore, obviously, not like Louise, I mean she's not a whore, Tante just says that, but because I live with Pauline."

"I don't know," says Hortense earnestly. "It is quite difficult following Tante's feuds; she has so many. But she says they are a necessary feature of polite society, for they remind people of their place in the natural order."

Pauline and I share the gossip we have heard about Louise's rich and powerful lover with Hortense, who only blushes and says she shouldn't be listening to such talk. I know she doesn't mean it. Everyone loves gossip, and those who say they don't are just lying; they probably relish it most of all.

From Pauline de Mailly-Nesle
Convent of Port-Royal
March 30, 1735

Louise,

You may think the convent very secluded but it is not, and we hear a great many things here that might shock and surprise you. We hear all the gossip of Court—all of it. I hope you are enjoying yourself and that your husband, Louis-Alexandre, is pleased with you.

You know you can tell me anything, because I am your sister and love you above all else. If your husband—or someone else—were rich and powerful, perhaps he would help you with our project of bringing me to Versailles?

I beg you to consider this. Please remember, I am almost twenty-three and Diane is already twenty-one.

Here is my news: we had delicious rabbit here last night, and carrots. Well, the rabbit was not delicious, it was mostly very tough. My back is not aching. My teeth are fine. I am sure you do not care about these trifles, but Diane says I should include them. She wanted to write but she spilled her inkwell and Mother Superior says she can't have any more ink until the end of the month. She sends her love.

Diane asks me to thank you for the goose pâté you sent, she ate all of it before I was able to take even a spoonful. She said she did not know it was intended for both of us; she claimed she thought I hated goose.

Do not forget us here. With much sororal love,
Pauline

Louise

VERSAILLES AND HEAVEN

1735

In public we must be circumspect and careful but we develop our own language, the secret code of our love. A play is performed outside in the Marble Court, and though we are seated far apart, at the end the king says loudly, "How fair were the jewels on Mélisande's neck!" Jewels! And me, Bijou!

When he visits the queen and exchanges pleasantries with her ladies, he often asks me (but not too often; the others always have their ears pricked) if I am well rested.

Well rested!

How clever he is. I try to think of similar things to say, but I am not very good with double entendres (or even single entendres). Gilette could help me—she is frightfully sharp and clever—but I can't involve her. And I don't want to ask Charolais, for I do everything possible to keep her far from my intimate life.

Instead I buy a bag of mixed buttons from the merchants down by the Ministers' Wing, and when he can, Bachelier brings me the king's coats. I sew a little button on the silk lining inside, right where it will rest on his heart. When I see him wearing one of my buttoned coats, I thrill to know he has a part of me so close to him.

I make him handkerchiefs covered with little doves, hearts and flowers surrounding them, sewn with love. Once he pulled one out, stroked it, and stared at me. My knees went weak and I thought I would faint.

Gilette noticed and poked me.

"Why was His Majesty looking at you in that rather queer way? It must be true that he suffered from indigestion last night. We all thought that was just an excuse to avoid the queen's bed. But it was a strange look—almost as though he was admiring you! But that cannot be—I am sure it was the oysters."

One night he deliberately loses at cards, that I might pocket the porcelain pieces that he just held. I jingle them in my hand, until the Princesse de Chalais snaps at me to stop. I smile at her and slowly rub the smooth pieces. I feel the king's eyes on me, the heat enough to sear me through.

These little tricks and delicious secrets sustain me through the long, boring hours with the queen, through the endless official functions, through the business of the king's public days and even the informality of his private nights, when he is so close to me, yet so far.

Now Louis says he has a gift for me. I cannot hold my excitement, for it is rare that he gives me anything. It is barely noon when Bachelier sends me a note telling me to don my cape and a veil. He comes for me a little while later and hurries me into a waiting carriage.

Inside sits the king, masked.

"What? Where are we going?" I ask, breathless with excitement. Louis smiles and shakes his head, and even as we leave the palace far behind and the carriage rumbles through a thick wood, he refuses my entreaties.

"Patience, and you will see!" he commands, pulling off my gloves and entwining my fingers in his. I stare out at the trees and thickets, my excitement mounting. No more than an hour passes when we pull up beside a small wooden house, set beside a clearing in the woods.

"Shhh," he says, motioning to the driver as Bachelier brings a hamper down and sets it beside us.

"By sundown, sire," he says and climbs back in the coach. Then they are gone and we are alone. I feel as if I have entered a dreamworld.

"And did I say privacy was the one thing I could not command? Well, I shall admit I was wrong. I have arranged it so that Maurepas and the Marine Council think I am meeting with the Turks, and the Turks think I must closet myself with the council. There will be something to pay tomorrow, but for now, Bijou"—and here he bows and laughs—"this August afternoon—I give to you."

I shriek with joy and leap into his arms. He twirls me around until I am dizzy with delight.

We spend the afternoon exploring the woods. I find a bed of daisies and make him wait still while I twine him a crown of flowers. He picks a giant wild rose for me, and bows low as he presents it: "For my Lady of the Roses, the Lady of My Heart."

We pass an old peasant bent double under the weight of his years and the giant bundle of firewood he carries. He calls out a respectful greeting, and when he has passed we both giggle in delight: that man knew not that it was his sovereign he had just addressed.

The meadow next to the little house is enameled with clumps of wild marigolds in decadent bloom. From the food hamper we take cold eggs, a chicken, a bottle of Gamay. We spread a blanket and I drape my head with gauze against the sun and freckles. We sit side by side in the middle of the marigolds, eating and listening to the sounds of the countryside around us: crickets, birds, the chatter of squirrels, the occasional deep hum of a bee. The fairest symphony in the world, played for us in our field of gold.

Louis takes the gauze away and unpins my hair and breathes me in. He spreads his fingers like a star through my hair, drawing me closer, and I hold him faster and tighter than I have ever held anyone in my life. They say food tastes better when eaten outside, and it is true: his lips are the most delicious honey and sugar. We lie in the brilliance of the sunshine, bathed in the warmth of the August afternoon, caressed by the balmy wind and lulled by the sun. Though I lie on the ground I feel as though I am soaring like the hawks that circle above. This is the closest to Heaven that I'll ever be, I think, for Heaven for me is this closeness of Louis in our perfect, sunlit privacy.

"I could stay here forever," he murmurs to me, "until the sky falls down."

I can't say anything, so complete is my happiness. I start crying and he licks away my tears, softly and expertly.

"I wish you were not the King of France."

"But I am, Bijou, I am."

"You are everything to me."

"And you are everything to me," he replies, and something lights inside of me, something that can never be extinguished, and I know I will carry his words, and the memory of this day, through all the years of my life.

Small shadows fall across us and the wind grows chill. No! Don't let the sun go down—would that the world could end, just so this day did not have to. With reluctance we rise and make our way back to the little house.

"We will come again," he says as we await the carriage. In the distance we can hear a wolf howling and the woods draw closer as the sun goes down. "To this, our place. The whole of France is mine, but this wood is my most treasured domain."

We climb into the carriage and head back to Versailles and to our painted, false lives. But he promised we would come again, I think happily as I lean against him in the carriage, and that is all that matters.

Back in the real world, Pauline continues to bother me with mountains of letters that arrive with constancy every week. She wants me to find her a husband and bring her to Versailles. Or just bring her to Versailles. But that, as I have explained to her often, is much more difficult without a husband. And poor dear Pauline, she was never pretty and I've heard she has not improved with age. Though that is very unkind of me to say, it is the unfortunate truth.

I do not know who will take charge of her marriage. Papa is in Paris but unwell and unable to help his family; he seeks a cure with an actress, who has experience playing the role of a kind nurse in one of Molière's plays. And while Tante Mazarin got Marie-Anne married, I cannot ask for her help as we are no longer speaking; our relationship has gone from cordial to chilly to cold. She knows I have another lover and is constantly dropping her pincushion in front of me when we are sewing with the queen.

Of course, I could ask Louis . . . but I would rather not. Here is a little secret: though I am the mistress of the king, and should perhaps be very rich and powerful, I am not. Louis hates, but just hates, when people pester him for favors or seek advantage from him. This is understandable; people ask him for everything every day, at all moments. Just yesterday, the Marquis de Créquy was included in the hunt as a special favor over the death of his mother—a great friend of Louis's old governess, Madame de Ventadour. He made Louis's afternoon very difficult by continually talking about a court case involving a dead horse that he wanted settled. Louis was indulgent because the man was in mourning, and has two excellent staghounds, but then he made the mistake of not letting the matter drop.

"Yes, I could have easily granted his request, Bijou," he complains later, stopping by on a visit. He won't stay, but when he is irritable or worried he likes to wander the halls at night, disguised as a doctor with a silly old wig and accompanied by one of his valets. He has a secretive side to him; I know he likes to roam unknown, pretending he is a servant or a simple nobody.

I anxiously serve him a cup of hot coffee, glad that I bought that stove last week from the Duchesse de Rohan-Rohan. It is made of Meissen porcelain and was frightfully expensive, but it is useful that I might serve Louis something hot and quick on his nighttime promenades.

I bring him a plate of pastries from the afternoon. "Have an apple butter tartine, dearest. I know you love apples."

He waves them away. "No, no. But I would have some duck. Oh, how I long for some duck!" He hasn't taken off his cloak and sits in dejection at the table. I hate to see him like this, peevish and irritable. I feel I should say something, urge him to stay and seduce him, but I am not very good at things like that. Instead I rub his back and murmur in his ear, until he shifts in annoyance. He sips his coffee then complains it is too hot.

"I should have him sent away. Créquy. Harsh, but it would send a message. A message, Bijou! My time at the hunt, it is sacred. When I am in the forest I am not the king, I am just a man on a horse. No one knows the burden it is to be a king."

"I do, Twinkles, I understand."

"Perhaps."

"What a burden!"

"A burden. To be pestered thus, at all hours of the day and night."

"Stay . . . please. I will . . . make you feel better. I could . . . ah . . . could . . ."

"No, no, enough. I would be alone. I shall walk the palace awhile, perhaps go up to the roofs. And it is so noisy here. Those dogs! You should really speak to Matignon." He gets up. "Tomorrow . . ." He sighs. "Tomorrow the Hungarians again. Will I ever know peace?"

He leaves and I sit alone in the room and drink the rest of the coffee. The dogs in the apartment above mine continue barking; a pack of rangy wolfhounds as tall as my shoulders. I should ask the Comte de Matignon to take them away and board them at the kennels, but I don't have the courage. I could ask Louis, of course, and in one lift of his finger he would take care of it. Could a *lettre de cachet* be used for a dog? But I cannot ask that favor of him. I vowed long ago never to ask him for anything, for why would I want to distress the man I love?

Marie-Anne

BURGUNDY

1736

I must confess that I am becoming intrigued by the physical side of our relationship. It is very amusing to see a man become a pleading mess if denied the touch of a certain part of one's body or if one's finger presses ever so slightly on another part. My goal these days, in addition to finishing all five volumes of Piganiol's *New Descriptions of History and Geography of France*, is to see how far and how fast I can reduce JB to quivering quince jelly, and for what length of time. The advantage is that now he will do anything for me, so instead of having a husband whom I must obey, I now have a husband who will obey me.

I find myself waiting eagerly for his trips home. Before, JB never visited Burgundy more than once a year, preferring to spend his free time at his Paris house with his atrocious mother—who, I am pleased to report, is now ill and bedridden—but these days he makes every effort to come to Burgundy and see me. I await him with anticipation, for as the months pass, I am beginning to understand what all the fuss is about. Between the sheets. I have caught the shadows, so to speak, or JB has caught them for me.

Now I spend the time between our reunions scouring the library for inspiration and education. Unfortunately the books there tend to much drier matters, but I did find one very interesting little tome, from India I think. I could not understand the writing, but oh, the pictures! Very informative. So much to do! Even with only two bodies the number of possibilities is quite extraordinary.

Soon we are well practiced and are spending rather too much time in the bedchamber. I have moved our bedroom into a tower room—for the views, I say, but also for the privacy; at the best of times the château still teems with far too many people and the doors are old and ill-fitting.

I open the door a crack to the impatient knocking.

"He's still indisposed," I say serenely to JB's steward. JB is only home for a week this time and I have no intention of allowing him to be dragged into boring estate discussions with servants. I close the door firmly; I will not relinquish JB a moment before I need to.

I go back to the bed and JB pulls me to him.

"Only old Viard."

JB sighs. He has a very skinny neck and a prominent Adam's apple and his ears stick out far from his head like two small pies. He might be a good-looking man when he is older, but for the moment he is rather gangly and unformed. But strong and eager.

"I suppose I must go to the docks. He has been writing me constantly—too many regulations." JB's land includes some fine timber and the logs are cut here and float all the way up the river to Paris.

"Friday, darling, Friday. Visit with him on Friday. And take care of the village priest while you're out—tell him he'll have his roof next year—he's been bothering me far too much. And be sure to pick up some eels when you are at the river; they are supposed to be superb. Now, let's focus on your eel."

JB laughs and lies back. "Sometimes you talk like a camp follower. Not only the words, but the mind as well."

I encircle him gently and gaze into his eyes. I hold the gaze as I feel him growing between my fingers. He gulps and I breathe deeply.

"Do you . . ." I know what I want to ask, but do I want to hear the answer? "Do you—have a camp follower?" I tighten, ever so slightly.

He shakes his head and I believe him.

"Why should I make do with a camp follower when I have

you? You, madame my wife, are far more glorious than any camp follower. Besides, they're usually fat, and rather dirty. And they don't have your breasts . . ." He reaches out for mine and I let him caress them for a while. Oh. I feel my breath quickening.

"Wait."

I push him back on the bed and straddle him. He starts to shake his head.

"No, I cannot, it's too soon." The sun hasn't reached the height of the sky but we have been at it all night. *It*—what pleasure.

"Shhh . . . You have more in you than you can consider. I know your bone like the back of my hand. And I want to give you a gift. Better than pickled cherries."

He shakes his head again. I lean in to kiss him then I slide my tongue down his chest and want to go farther south still.

"No, cherish, not that. We have already discussed this. I am sure, quite sure, the priest would not approve."

I chafe at the hands that hold my hair: if I can't explore the world, at least let me explore the body of my husband. I continue my journey, pulling against his hands. Besides, I know he never resists for long.

"No, no, it is not clean. The priest . . ."

A little nibble as I reach my target. A sharp intake of breath from JB. He tries to pull my head away but at the last minute pushes me in. I close around him and I know all the thoughts of the priest are gone.

"Oh," sighs JB. "Oh, Heaven."

❧

Then he leaves and I feel empty inside. I'm not in love with JB—I fear I am a cold person and will never truly be in love—but I certainly like him, and he is a welcome and pleasurable distraction from the monotony of country life. I have ceased to be interested in visits and suppers with the provincial *comtes* and *marquis* that JB knows from childhood. In fact, I rarely leave the château these days, and I especially avoid the village priest when he comes knocking with his endless petitions about the deplorable state of the stone church in town. I have a few small domestic concerns to occupy me; JB made me promise to make sure that Cook would pickle enough cherries to last through the winter. I did that.

The library continues as solace—and my current passion is for books of exploration and far lands. After I finish Piganiol, I read Las Casas and learn about the savages in New Spain, and then I devour Matteo Ricci's *Christian Expeditions to China*. Fascinating. That people and places could be so different. There is a globe in the library, similar to one we had in the nursery in Paris. Sometimes I spin it and trace my fingers until it stops, and declare that that place shall be my destination. If I were a man I would join the navy and sail around the Cape of Good Hope and on to India, and then I would go to America and grow indigo in Saint-Domingue, and then I would . . . Everything. I would see the world.

Instead, I am in Burgundy, dying ever so slowly of boredom. I do, however, have a new hobby. Our cook interested me in a scheme to grow herbs and spices in a disused set of stables close to the main château. Garnier is a very enterprising young man, and, frustrated by the high prices of the spices demanded by the dishes he wished to prepare, he decided to try growing them himself. Though the cultivation of spices is but an extension of farming and peasant work, I am discovering that there is a limit to the life of the mind. Too much reading has left me hankering for something a little more *real*. If that is the right word.

The roof of the stable had fallen in, so we replaced it with a series of windows to let in the sun. We insulated the rooms and heat them with a collection of braziers. We have a row of ginger root, some precious vanilla orchids as well as many herbs, including mint and marjoram. I am not sure if the whole undertaking is actually economical; the cost of the coal for the braziers must be taken into account . . . but nonetheless I take a strange delight in tending to the plants as they emerge from the ground and begin their struggle for existence, some of them so far from their native lands.

Often I spend solitary afternoons in our little hothouse, surrounded by the spicy pungence of the plants and herbs. I like to imagine I have traveled a long way, to the hot islands where they belong and which I shall probably never see.

Sometimes when we work in the greenhouse together I can feel Garnier's eyes on me. He is a young man, not much older than me, and he speaks with a husky voice that is both rough and tender. Something inside me wants to turn and meet his gaze, to uncover and to learn: Would it be the same as with JB? But too much holds me back. He's a cook, of course, and smells, though not unpleasantly, of sweat mixed with spices and fruit. But what if we were discovered and JB decided to keep me here, forever, as punishment? No, the risk is too great.

I think.

From Louise de Mailly
Château de Versailles
November 16, 1736

Dearest Pauline,

Thank you so very much for all your letters! The nuns must be very generous with their paper, but please do not waste ink and quills on my account.

I am glad you are enjoying life in the convent and that both you and Diane continue in good health. I too am fine; I had a slight toothache last week but nothing that clever Monsieur Pelager, a very renowned dentist, was not able to cure. He prescribed a powder of lead and mint, and it was just the thing. Please let me know if you would like me to send you some, and how your teeth are doing.

Please do not worry about getting married; there will be a husband for you when God wills it to be so. The Comtesse de Rupelmonde told me that her youngest sister married, for the first time, at twenty-six! And the girl had only four fingers (a great family scandal, please do not repeat). So you see it is not too late, especially as you are not even deformed.

You know that I would love you to visit me at Versailles, but that would be very difficult and of course one needs money to live here. My dear husband continues with his numerous charitable causes and money is very tight. Please tell Diane, for I know she is interested in such things, that blue squirrel fur is all the rage this winter at Court; the Princesse de Soubise wore a skirt trimmed with six layers of it and no one could decide whether it was delightful or simply too much!

I tried to find some for you but it is very costly now as all search for it high and low. I send instead these green ribbons for you and Diane; my dressmaker brought them last week and I instantly thought of you and your green eyes. They are a very unusual shade. Madame Rousset (my dressmaker) said the color is called "envy green." They will look fabulous on you and will certainly complement your brown convent dress!

Please stay well and all my love,
Louise

Louise

VERSAILLES

1737

Though many suspect that the king has a mistress, none can guess her name. The king goes less and less to the queen's bed, and perhaps in consequence her list of important feast days grows longer and longer.

"Saint Paphnutius," grumbles Louis one night in September. Outside, the black air is thick and still and Matignon's dogs are mercifully quiet. We are in my apartments, the window open and a single candle the only light. Just the two of us. My favorite part of the day. He indicates his shoes and I kneel down to take them off.

"Saint Paphnutius. I am sure he was an honorable monk and a noble saint, but I for one have never heard of him. And she uses that as an excuse! Not that, of course, my dear, I would rather be there than here with you." He caresses my hair. I have been careful to shake the powder out, for Louis hates old powder with a passion, and often leaves his own hair without it. "But one must do one's duty, and I thought tonight I had the heart for it, and the bone. But no—I found my way blocked by Saint Paphnutius."

I unroll his stockings. Now the king and queen have eight little children but only one son; the poor little Duc d'Anjou, and a sister, died a few years ago. The *dauphin* continues in good health and the king dotes on his little princesses, but still. With only one son it is hard for him to consider his duty over and so he must persist in visiting the queen.

I kiss his naked legs, covered with soft black hairs. "My day can now begin," I murmur, and he laughs and pulls me up by my hair, gently but firmly, and onto the bed beside him.

"And mine as well," he declares gallantly as he takes off his chemise, by himself.

∽

We keep our secret well; not an easy thing in this palace of a million intrigues. We keep it fast and no one beyond our little group—Fleury, Charolais, the Comtesse de Toulouse, the king's valet, Bachelier, and my faithful woman, Jacobs—knows the truth.

No one knows but everyone likes to guess; suspicions and rumors pile like leaves in autumn. Louis prefers intimate suppers, often taken in the apartments of the Comtesse de Toulouse. Tonight we are a small group, just a dozen or so, and he is in a rare good humor—the boar were most obliging on the hunt this afternoon. After the fish stuffed with fennel and the goose brains in gravy, he stands and raises his glass. Chatter stops instantly.

"A toast," he declares, looking up at the ceiling. "To her."

The guests buzz in confusion as we raise our glasses. To her, up there? A toast to the Virgin Mary in Heaven, or to the queen, whose apartments are on the floor above? Or to one of the painted nymphs on the ceiling panorama?

"A toast to my mistress," clarifies Louis, looking around at his guests. "To her." He smiles rakishly and I almost choke with happiness on my champagne.

"But who is 'her,' sire?" demands the Marquis de Meuse, a mincing man who is known for the cleanliness of both his and the king's boots. "You know *everyone* has the utmost curiosity and there is much in wagers riding on this. Why, I stand to be out a four pair of horses if I am not correct with my pick. Do help us win our bets and reveal who the lucky lady is. I beg of you."

"No, I shall not help you with your bets, but I should like to know what the wagers are." There are twelve of us and each throws out their opinion, accompanied by laughter and a running commentary on the king's face when each lady's name is mentioned.

At the end, the ladies leading in the group's estimation are the German Duchesse de Bourbon and an Orléans *princesse*. They are both very young and very attractive, so I find myself in good company. Others vote for young Mathilde de Canisy, newly arrived at Court and so beautiful she was immediately nicknamed the Marvelous Mathilde.

I am the last and throw my bet on Madame la Duchesse, who seems the least likely; she's German, after all. I feel a little cold, though the room is awfully hot, when I think about the Marvelous Mathilde. I hope Louis doesn't get any ideas. That would be awful.

"Well, you are all wrong," announces Louis with a very satisfied smile; he loves secrets. "The lady keeps her honor for another day, and I have the sublime pleasure of keeping my secret, from those who presume to think they know everything about me." He drains his glass and the courtiers do likewise, looking amongst themselves for confirmation.

I hug my secret to myself. I can't smile at Louis so instead I smile down at the table and find my happiness reflected back at me from the glassy eyes of the fish on my plate.

‹›

Gilette presses me: "Your woman told mine you bathe every night in water tipped with olive oil. And you sleep with your hair still coiffed . . . Only a woman who has a lover would take that care . . . do you finally have a new lover?"

People know Puysieux and I are no longer together, though they don't know why.

"Goodness, it's not that husband of yours, is it?"

There I don't have to lie. "Certainly not! Olive oil is good for the skin and I have always bathed in that manner."

Gilette appraises me with her cool gray eyes. We have grown apart under the burden of my secret, but I don't really miss her. She presses on: "You'd tell me if you had? Taken another lover?"

"Of course, dearest, of course." I can now lie like a true *versailloise*—perhaps not a talent I should be proud of. I change the subject. "But what a lovely necklace—are those all rubies?"

There is a part of me, a small part, that wants people to know that I love Louis and that Louis loves me. And then we could be affectionate in public, sit beside each other at the entertainments, talk without fear. Charolais insists I keep our affair a secret for as long as I can.

"Nothing intrigues a man more than intrigue, Louise."

"Yes?" I agree tentatively.

We are sitting in her salon and Charolais is showing me her new cosmetics. Even though she is past her fortieth birthday, she still has the skin of a woman half her age. She knows all the potions and remedies; only she dares to dabble in light magic like her famous grandmother did during the notorious Affair of the Poisons. Thinking on it makes me shudder: babies sacrificed, so many people poisoned, so many Court ladies arrested . . . I hope her lotions are not scented with even a whiff of magic. Though she does have the most remarkable skin.

She pats a rose-scented cream onto my cheek. It stings slightly.

"Once everyone knows about you and the king, he will quickly become bored."

As I smooth the lotion onto my cheeks I search her words for hidden meaning, but this time I think she has said exactly what she meant. The idea that the king is only with me because he likes intrigue is very insulting. Nonsense. Louis is with me because he loves me. I think Charolais might be jealous; Gilette told me she wanted to be the king's lover, many years ago, but that he had no interest.

Fleury has the opposite view and has recently been urging Louis to be open about our affair. Fleury has come to despise the queen and he thinks it is high time that Louis declares himself a man who chooses his own mistresses. I really don't know what to think. I smooth out the rose cream but it feels like my face is on fire. I ask Charolais if I can have more of the patchouli oil she gave me last week—Louis declared the smell transported him into raptures. My cheeks turn even rosier at the memory and Charolais looks at me as though she knows exactly what I remember.

I leave in a bad mood ("Once everyone knows about you and the king, he will quickly become bored"—nonsense!) clutching a vial of patchouli and the pot of rose lotion that smells lovely but feels as though it is rubbing my face raw. The misery of the day is compounded when my husband, at the palace for a regiment display and dinner, stops by my apartment before he returns to his house in town.

Jacobs hands me a note from the king's valet, Bachelier; he will come for me before midnight. I take the note and my heart sings. I was not summoned yesterday but tonight I shall see him! I throw the note in the fire, hoping my husband doesn't notice, and I disappear into the chamber to have Jacobs prepare me.

To my horror my husband comes into the room where I am washing and looks at me curiously, drinking a large cup of wine. Jacobs shoos him out and he leaves, trailing a smell like Brie gone bad behind him.

When I come out he is settling down to eat a savory pie he ordered. He roots around in it and emerges triumphant with a chicken head, which he proceeds to noisily suck on.

"Delicious," he announces. "The regiment dinner was a paltry affair, only twelve dishes and two of them carrots, for goodness' sakes. And no asparagus, though it is in season—disgraceful." He drains his glass of wine and pours himself another.

He looks at me with curiosity. "Is this on my account? The hair and the robe?"

"No." I sit down on the sofa. I can't leave with him here, for he will want to know where I am going.

"This wine is awful—why do you drink it? And this place is so dusty. Makes my eyes swell." His eyes are red and puffy, but I think it's the drink more than anything. He finishes his pie and wipes his hand on the tablecloth.

"So, where are you going, almost midnight and dressed up like a strumpet? Tell me."

I want nothing more than him gone from this room. I want to say he should go back to his sword maker's daughter, but I don't have the courage. And perhaps he has someone new.

He looks at me curiously while picking idly at the little daisies I have arranged in a vase on the table. He snaps the head off one.

I flinch.

He throws it on the floor.

"Don't do that," I whisper.

"What?" He turns to me with a hard look and I realize he is quite drunk. I don't know why he hates me so; I tried to be a good wife to him and he never uttered one word of kindness to me. Not one. I shudder, remembering his hands on me. Thankfully it has been a long time and I push the memories of those nights down into a place far, far away, where I need never encounter them again.

I get up from the sofa and move away from the light into the protection of a dark corner and look out the window. All is quiet above and below. The Comte de Matignon has gone to the country for the hunting, and taken his dratted dogs with him.

"Come here."

I go and stand in front of him, looking as miserable as I feel. I mustn't cry or my rouge will run and I will have to redo it and I hate to keep Louis waiting. Why won't he *go*?

"What are you hiding?"

"What do you mean? Nothing." I look down at my hands. Outside I hear the clocks chime and a thin peal of laughter comes from the courtyard. Midnight is coming.

"You smell like a Turkish whore."

"How would you know?" I snap back, my impatience making me imprudent.

He raises one eyebrow in shock. For a moment I think he is going to strike me, then he chuckles and picks something out of his teeth and flicks it in the fire.

"You've changed," he says, and I can do nothing but stare at him—he never noticed me before, never even looked at me, and now here he is examining me as he would his favorite horse. When did he become so observant? Curses! Why won't he just go?

"So who is waiting for you, little one?" he says, mocking me. He pushes me back down on the sofa and bats my head lightly from side to side. "You want me to leave. I can tell it, I can sense it. I know women." He leers at me. "You're like a hare in heat." I flush and my chin trembles. I mustn't cry.

"Ha! But it's not Puysieux, the whole world knows that."

"I had no idea you followed my movements with such interest," I say bitterly. Why won't he go? Oh, how I hate this man who is my husband.

"You're my wife, fool," he growls, and impatience wells up in me.

"Oh, let me go, let me go," I cry, and to my horror I realize I have spoken out loud.

"No."

I start crying in frustration, and then I say what I know I shouldn't, but at that moment I have to:

"You can't keep me from the king," I sob. "He'll have you sent away. You'll be sent to . . . to . . . ." I can't think of anywhere that is far enough for this man to go. ". . . Louisiana."

"The king?" snarls Louis-Alexandre. "What does he have to do with you?"

But I have already said it, and why not? "It's true," I sob. "It's the king. There, that's who I am going to. He . . . he loves me . . . loves patchouli."

There is a short silence then Louis-Alexandre throws back his head and roars with laughter. He slaps his knee and continues guffawing in glee.

"Our king! That namby milksop . . . Now," he says sharply, "don't go telling him I just said that. But it makes sense, he hardly takes a whiz without Fleury telling him to, and I was always curious as to why that virgin monk was so interested in you."

"Fleury has nothing to do with this," I say stiffly. I had not thought my husband so shrewd, but tonight he is a fox. A hateful, cunning fox.

I keep my head bowed, following his movements around the room from beneath my lashes. He rubs his breeches then laughs. "Eat from the same plate as the king—now that would be a tale for my regiment, I tell you. But no. I have no desire. No desire at all, madame." I don't know why those words cut me, but they do. I continue crying.

"I wonder if all this was behind my promotion last year," he muses on. "And when His Majesty spoke to me in June, he complimented me on my horse: 'A fine horse,' he said, 'a fine horse with strong legs.' Hmm."

My husband pulls me up from the sofa. "But don't let me keep you, madame, don't let me keep you from your duty. Why, I am as loyal a subject as any, and I only aim to please. Hie, hie to the king with your patchouli stink and your red-rosed cheeks. This is wonderful news, wonderful. Gontaut has a set of four white horses I have had my eye on for a long time now . . . I wager he will sell them to me for cheap once he knows."

"Don't tell anyone!" I whisper in horror.

He shrugs. "Perhaps not. You must tell me what makes the most sense, little one. You have the power now." He laughs hoarsely and pours the last of the wine into his glass. "Those horses are such handsome beasts—the purest white! Great good fortune. I knew I would be the one to restore the family fortunes. I am a man of destiny, Louise," he slurs, and sits down heavily. I see a small, ugly man before me, insignificant. I pull my cloak around me and slip out into the corridor where Bachelier waits.

"I'm sorry I'm late," I whisper as I trail along behind him.

Behind me I hear Louis-Alexandre calling out in the corridor for someone to bring him the finest bottle of gin this side of Jamaica.

⁂

The rumors continue, isolated notes of a music that soon blend into a song. Too many people are coming at me with sly looks, hoping that I might confirm what it is they think they know.

"Are you not missing Puysieux? So long since he has been gone!"

"I see your husband driving a new carriage with four white horses. Such an extravagance—why is that?"

"We so rarely see you at suppers at Madame de Villars' anymore. They say you are always at the little suppers with the king? You are fortunate indeed to always be so included . . ."

"The Bible says the meek shall inherit—what do *you* make of that, Louise?"

Then that fateful night, scarcely a month after my husband found out. That afternoon there was an official dinner for the Spanish ambassador but my duties with the queen did not require me to attend. When Bachelier came later with the summons, I donned the brown hooded cloak and followed him through the back rooms and corridors; late at night the candles are few and the way is dark. As we neared the king's rooms Bachelier suddenly grabbed me by the arm and swung me around, saying I must be careful or people would see me. My hood fell off with the force of his swing and the people lounging outside the doors saw me clearly.

Instead of turning around and pretending we were not there for the king, Bachelier ushered me through the doors, and into infamy. By morning the entire palace knew. The gates of gossip were flung wide open and then they all came to me, to greet me, welcome me, reproach me, beg me, smile at me, and reproach me again.

Everyone, simply everyone, is personally offended that I chose not to share the news of my good fortune with them. Gilette is scarcely speaking to me and the Pious Pack of ladies has completely shunned me. Not that I care overly much about them, but I do not like being called a pincushion or a chipped vase every time I pass one of them in the corridors.

So what I dreamed and dreaded has now come true. Charolais's words haunt me: *Once everyone knows about you and the king, he will quickly become bored.*

Impossible. I think. Louis adores me. Why should it matter if the whole world knows?

Diane

CONVENT OF PORT-ROYAL

1737

Today Pauline found out something extraordinary! The news caused her to scream and run out of the room and down to the ends of the convent garden, past the kitchens and the horses, all the way to a small apple orchard at the edge of the smelly stream. I follow her outside though it's rather cold and muddy and I don't want to get my shoes dirty.

I approach her cautiously; sometimes Pauline is rather terrifying. She stomps on a fallen apple and brown goo splatters up her skirts.

"Bitch! Judas! Cain! Anyone who ever betrayed anyone!"

Pauline is upset because we have just found out that Louise is the mistress of the King of France. Our Louise! Imagine that! She's pretty, certainly prettier than Pauline or I, but it is hard to imagine her so beautiful that a king would fall in love with her. The king can have any woman he wants . . . well, perhaps not a nun or mother superior, but anyone else, so you would think he would choose the most beautiful woman in France.

"Dee Dee, they have been together for *years!*" She stomps on another apple. Another brown stain on her skirt.

"Your skirt, you should be careful—"

"She is the mistress of the most powerful man in France, in the *world*, yet she leaves us languishing here at this convent. Do you know what sort of marriages she should have made for us? Do you have any idea the power she has?"

It's strange to think of Louise as powerful. Pauline could certainly be powerful, but Louise? She was always so meek and mild in the nursery.

"I will never, ever forgive her! Never, never! God DAMN it!"

"Pauline!"

She takes a handful of brown apples and flings them against a tree trunk. I know she wishes the tree were Louise. I've never seen her this angry, her face red and her hair bristling against her cap. Now she is hitting the tree trunk with her hands.

"Pauline! Stop it! You're scaring me!"

"Delilah!" she cries, spent, and crumples on top of a mess of rotten apples. "I'm going to shred all her letters, all her stupid letters with her stupid lies and excuses. I'm going to tear them apart. But I will wish it was her I was tearing apart."

I'm so shocked I can't even remonstrate.

❧

Well, Pauline is very resilient, like a cockroach that you can squash but it still survives. I suppose I shouldn't compare my sister to a cockroach; I should say instead she is very resilient, like . . . a . . . a resilient thing. Quickly she turns the news to her advantage.

"Now that Louise is the royal favorite, she can no longer use the excuses of finance or propriety to keep us here. She can do anything she wishes."

We are sitting in our room at the convent the next morning, drinking coffee and eating our breakfast buns. Madame de Dray joins us and brings a tray of candied pears, a gift from her daughter, to contribute to our meal. Pauline has laid out Louise's letters over the bed; she has not shredded them. Not yet.

"She won't have a choice now—she will have to invite me."

"Why do you say that?" inquires Madame de Dray. She motions for me to take another slice of pear and I do, eagerly.

"Well, her excuses always were no money and that it would be improper. Now I know she must have masses of money, and impropriety should not be her concern."

"An excellent point, my friend," says Madame de Dray.

"So here's what I am thinking. I have a plan."

Both Madame de Dray and I put down our cups and turn our full attention to her. Pauline likes to make plans—she often says she wishes she were a general and not a girl with no money or prospects. Mother Superior says she has a mind as sharp as a goat's.

"I now realize that Louise being the king's mistress is simply perfect news. I shall be invited to Versailles, I am determined. And then, once I am at Court, I shall use Louise's proximity to the king to enchant him and steal him away—it should not be very hard. If boring Louise can capture the king's heart, then so can I."

Pauline often astounds me, but this is the most astounding thing she has ever said. Yet she's not finished.

"Through the king, I will become the most powerful woman in France and I shall rule the Court, and the country. That will be my route to power."

I laugh nervously and almost choke on my pear. I always laugh when I don't know what to say.

Madame de Dray raises her eyebrows. "Big words," she says. "Big words, my dear. You are indeed a force of nature."

"A force of nature?" I ask, quickly taking the last slice of candied pear while Pauline is lost in her dreams. "What's that?"

Madame de Dray considers. She has a narrow face and gray skin that makes her look as though she is on the verge of death. That, and the black wool gown she always wears. "A force of nature is something that cannot be stopped. Like a great wind or a fierce rain that floods the land."

She continues in her careful, modulated voice: "It can be used to describe a person of great determination. Pauline is a very determined woman. And I believe determination to be the greatest gift of all. Greater even than beauty, intelligence, or cunning. Determination matters most."

She repeats Pauline's words slowly, wonderingly: "Go to Versailles, meet the king, take him away from your sister, become his mistress, and rule France through him. Yes, Pauline, I believe you *will* do that."

I am not sure what I think of this plan. "What about Louise?" I ask. Pauline always says Louise is silly and stupid, but surely she must still love her? Her plan sounds rather cruel. It doesn't sound sisterly at all. Not at all *sororal*, as Zélie would say.

Pauline snorts: "Louise loves me, as I love her." Then she smiles and says Louise will *want* family around her now, because everyone knows Versailles is a nest of vipers and royal favorites are never safe. Now that the secret is out, someone might even try to poison our sister.

Poison? Perhaps Pauline going to Court is a good idea; she can protect Louise.

In the weeks that follow we hear more interesting rumors about Louise. We hear that she has two secret children with the king; that she is a Freemason, like her husband, and that the king has also become a Freemason, and that she keeps him interested by . . . well, I shouldn't repeat those types of rumors, but we do hear a lot of them.

Tante writes us a stern warning that we must never speak to Louise again, because she is a harlot and an adulteress. Pauline uses the letter as kindling to melt the wax that seals her latest appeal to Louise.

From Pauline de Mailly-Nesle
Convent of Port-Royal
September 30, 1737

Dearest Sister,

Congratulations on the wonderful news we have received from all quarters. You are very honored to be chosen thus; it is a fine thing to be loved by a king.

You are now a very powerful woman and I know that you will use your power with the same skill that you do everything in life.

I do think, though, that at this time of great public exposure, it would be prudent for you to have family close and near to you. You must take as your model the mistresses of the late king; look at how Madame de Montespan and Madame de Maintenon's families prospered from their connection to the king!

I may be younger than you, but only by two years, and I hope to be the one to offer you the love and succor of a mother, in this exciting time.

I am glad your teeth and back are fine. Diane had a slight bellyache last week but I think it was just too much squirrel pie—onions do not agree with her.

Sororal love,
Pauline

From Hortense de Mailly-Nesle
Hôtel de Mazarin, Paris
October 15, 1737

Darling Marie-Anne,

Forgive me for taking so long to reply to your last letter, all has been in upheaval here. The workmen have started on the second floor and everywhere there is noise and dust, dust and noise. Antoine, Tante's brother-in-law, is visiting from Switzerland. Tante is much occupied at Court, so I have been charged with hosting the guests.

Tante has been in quite a state since we heard the shocking news from Court. There has been speculation for quite some time that the king had taken a mistress and Tante has confirmed that indeed he has, and that his mistress is Louise! Our Louise!

When Tante heard the news she went straight to Louise so that she could deny it, but Louise did not! So it is true, and the most shocking thing of all is that she and the king have been lovers *for years!* You could have knocked me over with a feather. I wish I were beside you to tell you this news, but it could not wait. I want you to hear it from me rather than from someone on the street, for unfortunately that is where our proud name now resides.

Tante says we must not correspond with Louise or we will be corrupted. Tante says it is necessary for our good name and especially for me, as such a blemish to our reputation could prevent a good marriage. I will obey and I hope that out of the love you have for Tante and your respect for our good name, you will do the same.

Thank you for the box of mint—Cook used some in a heavenly pie—please send more when you can. Victoire got kicked by one of the horses and now she limps but is still as affectionate as ever. I think she is pregnant again: Would you like me to send one of her pups down to Burgundy for you?

Pray for Louise and her sinning soul.

Love,
Hortense

Marie-Anne

BURGUNDY

1737

I read Hortense's extraordinary letter, then read it again. I shake my head and my lips curl at some of her foolishness. As if it's Louise dragging our name through the mud—our mother did a good job of that while she was alive, and our father is continuing the grand tradition. And since when did a royal mistress in the family prevent a decent marriage? I wager I'd be a duchess by now if this had been known before I married JB. And I'll double wager that Hortense will make an excellent marriage because of this news, not in spite of it.

Well, well, well. Who would have thought? Mild little Louise?

Good for her. Isn't there something in the Bible about the meek inheriting the earth?

I'm tempted to write to Louise, but I haven't written to her for ages and I am not sure what I would say. Things are happening for her, great things, while I am stuck here in Burgundy where nothing *ever* happens. Rather than write to Louise I write to my husband and share the news with him, and ask him to be sure to greet my sister when is next at Court, to see if there is any advantage to be had for us.

Would I like to be at Versailles, now that Louise is known as the official favorite? I'm not sure—it's just so hard to imagine. Mild, pretty little Louise, who never wanted to fight, who only wanted peace and pleasure. She is seven years older than me. When one is young that is a great age difference, but I never really looked up to her as I might have to an older sister. She was always so . . . bland. Boring. Sometimes it was easy to forget she was even there. I remember her mooning over that drawing of her disgusting husband, sighing with imagined love.

And now she is the mistress of the king of France.

If I went to Versailles I would have to bow to her, and treat her with respect. That would be very strange. It's all very strange. Surely the king has the pick of the women in the land, and to choose her . . . Well, I don't know the full story. I don't know anything about him, except that he is the king. Which says everything, for there is nothing that the king of France cannot do or cannot have.

I wonder how long it will last? I can't imagine any man, especially a man as worldly and sophisticated as the king must be, finding solace for long with sweet, simple Louise.

But then again, I've noticed men generally like fools.

Here life continues on much the same: the rhythm of the countryside ruled by the changes of season; a few visits to acquaintances, interesting interludes with JB when he visits—though he did sprain his arm last time, in an unfortunate bedroom accident—and working in the spice lodge with Garnier. Our first vanilla plants have borne fruit, but the results were not as anticipated: the pods were dry and small.

"More water," Garnier suggests. "And perhaps some milk." Other spices have done well and I delight in eating what we have grown, fish flavored with turmeric or ginger boiled with cream; quite the nicest thing on a cold winter's afternoon.

I still spend much time spent ordering books to build up the library, though I have by no means read everything in there. I am currently reading all twelve volumes of *The Arabian Nights*. I spend my afternoons devouring the splendor and the passion of Persia, entirely lost in the hot sands of Arabia, only to come back to reality at the end of the day, blinking in astonishment tinged with despair that I am in this castle in Burgundy, and not in treasured desert sands. If I were Scheherazade . . . but what tales would I have to fill even one night?

Louise

VERSAILLES

1738

The greatest in the land now want to be seen with me and I am always given the place of honor in a carriage or at a table. The Court is full to the rafters, for now that it is known the king has a mistress, everyone believes great changes are afoot and anticipate sure gains if they befriend me. It is all a little overwhelming: Do I really need the Spanish ambassador at my morning toilette?

Before, people treated me with indifference, but now they are either openly hostile or overly sweet. I want to protest and tell them that I am the same and that nothing has changed! But what would be the point? No one would listen. My days and nights are filled with people wanting favors and more favors. And when I refuse, they turn cold on me and now I can count more enemies than I have fingers, whereas before I never had one.

It has been a distressing year. My husband was discovered to be a Freemason, and was put in the Bastille for a while. I suppose I should have been happy about that, but I hate to cause Louis any more problems than he already has, and he positively loathes such scandal. Worst of all, my father finally overstepped the line: to insult the king's creditors is to insult the king himself, and that cannot be. Louis was forced to banish Papa to Caen, which sounds dreadfully foreign and far away, though he assures me it is still in France. I do hope there are some good actresses there, with experience playing nurses.

And worst of all, the man I love is now questioning God about our union, after five years together. Surely He would have shown His displeasure by now, if He did not approve? There are small quarrels creeping in where before we only knew harmony: little disagreements over food or cards, over the guest list for the next hunt. He always apologizes after, and blames the moon, and says he is grown bored with life.

Bored. How I hate that word. Charolais's words are caught in my head, a melody that won't stop: *Once everyone knows about you and the king, he will quickly become bored.*

After too many rebuffs from the queen, Louis declared that his last daughter was not Madame Septième, but was in fact Madame Dernière. He has not spent a night with the queen since, but even so does not call me as frequently to his bed as he did before. The queen is the same toward me, always smiling sweetly and never complaining, but now I feel awful when I must be in attendance on her. I fear I have disappointed her dreadfully.

Perhaps the only good thing to come of this mess is that many of my creditors have disappeared. Not because I have more money—Louis is as parsimonious as ever—but because they assume I will have more money, one day. And it would be terrible for business if they were to pester the royal favorite.

The royal favorite. It all sounds so grand, doesn't it?

I'm sitting at my dressing table in the corner of the bedroom. It's already midnight and I won't see Louis tonight: there has been no summons. I look at my face in the mirror. It is true olive oil makes the skin soft, but it does not stop the small creep of lines around my eyes and mouth.

"Madame? You should go to bed, madame, it's after midnight. Let me take your glass . . ."

Jacobs is a loyal servant and I love her dearly, but sometimes she can be very irritating. "No, Jacobs. It's just gone midnight. I'm not the boring old queen, you know, I like to stay up late." Oh, unfortunate choice of words. I must be more careful when

I drink, for I often say things I regret. But then again, doesn't everyone? "Pour me another glass."

Jacobs looks like she wants to slap me.

"I'm not a little girl," I say plaintively, then wish I hadn't. Grown ladies—especially ones who are the mistresses of a king—don't need to justify themselves to *anyone*. I am important. Or should be. "The Spanish ambassador was at my toilette this morning, you saw him."

"Madame?"

"Just pour me some more."

"You won't feel well tomorrow. You won't look well either; your stomach will ache and your eyes will be red."

"I'm still pretty, aren't I?" But was I ever really pretty? I'm not sure. My two youngest sisters, Hortense and Marie-Anne, they are the beauties of the family. I wish I were truly beautiful. And I wish Louis were my husband and not that boar Louis-Alexandre. If the queen died, and Louis-Alexandre also, would Louis marry me? The last king married his mistress Madame de Maintenon, and her family certainly wasn't grander than mine.

"Would I make a good queen, Jacobs?" Last year the queen almost died in childbirth.

"That's enough! Imagine if someone heard you. To even think a thing like that!"

"Oh, don't worry, don't worry. No one ever listens to me. Ever." I look dolefully down at my lap, a wine stain spreading over my yellow robe.

Jacobs goes to bed after she pours me the last of the bottle. I sit and think and drink, then all too soon it is dawn and the sky is pale gray with orange streaks—the exact colors of a dress the Duchesse de Ruffec wore last week.

The king is having affairs. I am sure of it. Not with me, with other women. Some of them bourgeois, some of them worse. Not affairs, just fucking. Just *fornicating*. I know it's not serious, and not very often, but still, it hurts.

The next day my head throbs rather awfully and my skin is

gray and overcast. Jacobs was right, as always. Tonight I dine with Louis and a small group in the Comtesse de Toulouse's apartment; luckily there are few mirrors in her salon, for mirrors cast a harsh light, whereas candles only soften. We wait for the king to join us and the air is redolent with the smell of a turtle soup bubbling on a silver brazier, the room cozy and close. I love these evenings, when it is just Louis and I and a select few of his friends. Those who are not included complain; they say a king should show himself more to his subjects and not closet himself away like a cripple.

Charolais corners me while we wait for the men. She twirls around to show me her new gown, a gorgeous creation of lavender sewn with butterfly rosettes and mountains of heavenly cream lace from her elbows to her wrists. A great gust of violet puffs off her as she turns.

"Have you given any thought to our little matter?" she demands, as superior as ever.

I flush. Charolais believes I should try some tricks with Louis—in bed. She has a woman she wants me to meet, a Persian who has some type of house in Paris. Charolais says this woman can tutor me and show me . . . objects to use. How disgusting. When she was younger Charolais was the lover of the Duc de Richelieu, one of the most notorious rakes of France. I haven't met him yet, as he is currently serving as our ambassador in Vienna. There is a rumor that when they were lovers, Richelieu had her carry around a carrot inside her all day (and once, when she was feeling very adventurous, a parsnip). At the end of the day he would remove the carrot, cook it up with some cream and cumin, and declare it the most delicious dish he had ever eaten.

Since I heard that horrible story I have not been able to eat carrots, or parsnips.

But I don't even want to think about such things. The king is a very conservative man and I do not want to shock him; we have a familiar routine that works perfectly well for us.

"Well?" Charolais picks at a row of butterflies she has pinned down the front of her stomacher. I don't want to look too closely, but I think they are real.

I avoid her eyes. "I do not think it is appropriate." I wish I were more commanding, and then I would just tell her to stop pestering me with such vulgar matters.

She strokes the row of butterflies and pinches one. "And how appropriate do you think it will be when some other woman nets him?"

"The king loves me." I am the tiniest bit curious, but what if I were to use a . . . these toys she talks of . . . and he is scandalized by my lewdness?

"Have you considered welcoming the king through the back door?"

What is she talking about? "There is no longer any need for secrecy," I say stiffly.

Charolais rolls her eyes. "Sometimes I think you don't understand anything," she says. "Not a *thing*. Try this—the king is a man. Do you understand that?"

I refuse to answer her and turn away to study the fire. Eventually she purses her lips, hisses in disapproval, and flounces off. I move away from the hearth; the small room is getting hotter and I do not want to perspire through my peach satin. Things are suddenly so complicated. Daggers and looks and intrigue. Louis cold, then melancholy, then loving but always with his doubts, worried about what the people think. Now it is not only God and Fleury who know of our indiscretion, but the whole of France, as well as his children: I know he is dreadfully embarrassed by that.

And that hateful woman's words that I can't brush off: *Once everyone knows about you and the king, he will quickly become bored.*

It is all very confusing. I need a confidante. Charolais says I should trust her, but then she also tells me to trust no one. But family can always be trusted. Perhaps Pauline should come and visit? It's just . . . well, Pauline is rumored to be very tall and overly . . . hairy. And sharp and caustic. Louis abhors masculine women. Just last week he made a cutting remark to the Marquise de Renel when he saw her wearing a tricorn hunting hat of her husband's; the poor lady had thought to start a new fashion but instead she was humiliated. And she, despite the hat, the most feminine of women!

It would be good to have a confidante; someone of my own flesh and blood whom I could trust completely. A sister. And Pauline might help amuse the king; in the nursery she always liked jokes and stirring fun. Louis is melancholy these days, as he often is as winter approaches, and a new face might be just the refreshing tonic we need.

Should I invite her? I'm just not sure. I must consider this some more, but the more I think about the idea, the more I like it. What could be the harm?

From Louise de Mailly
Château de Versailles
August 2, 1738

Dear Pauline,

How are you, dear sister? I trust you and Diane are well. Thank you for your news of the convent. I understand you have heard of my good fortune, and though I hesitate to write of the king, he is well and enjoying good health, and yes, it is true we are good friends.

I long to share the news with my family; sisters are truly a wonderful thing. I should like to invite you to visit me at Versailles. Would you like that? A short visit, and of course, you cannot be presented. It might also be an opportunity for us to consider a marriage for you, if you are so inclined.

Have you grown much since we last saw each other? I remember you quite so tall, and we so young still. I am sure the nuns are teaching you comportment and manners? The Duchesse de Tallard has a daughter, who had unfortunate hair on her face but she employed a Persian—they are very good with hair, of all types—and now the daughter has no mustache at all! There are many Persian women here at Court; the Comtesse d'Aubigny has a very skillful one (she needs one, though I will not tell you why).

If you are in agreement, I shall write to the mother superior and make the arrangements. Perhaps we shall see each other soon.

Love,
Louise

Part II

One Takes Over

Pauline

If I have one gift, it's that I know people. Reading people's characters is as easy for me as reading a child's book. I understand things that others don't; I like to think I am one of the few people that recognizes the truth in the world. And I can see this: Louise was the perfect mistress when all was secret. But now that everyone knows, everyone will want something from her and there will be intrigues swirling all around her like wind in winter. She will be helpless and confused. She will need me to guide her.

At least that's what I told her in my letters. And it appears she believed me, for then it came: the invitation. The day I received Louise's letter inviting me to Versailles, a calmness came over me. The buzzing bees that normally inhabit my head fell silent. Completely silent. An enormous hope rose in my heart and for one glorious moment the world stood still, and all for me. The road stretched before me, clear and straight. I will leave the convent and I will go to Versailles. And I will enchant the king.

Diane washed my hair yesterday and today it is still damp—not good for traveling—but I dress it in a cap and put on a hat of Diane's that she has decorated with feathers. She fusses over me; I know she is upset at being left behind, but I promise I will not forget her. Together we pick out my best dresses, and some of hers, to pack into my chest: two gowns, one pale blue but a little plain, with nary a bow or a ruffle, and a rather fine one of green silk. She has spent the last week unstitching a long row of bows from her peach dress and stitching them onto my blue dress.

"I am sure two dresses will not suffice at Court. People will notice and it will be remarked upon," she says with a worried frown.

"The whole world already knows that we are poor," I scoff. "I'm not going to pretend I am rich, when everyone knows we are not."

Diane sighs, a worried look on her face. "I just wish you weren't so tall. I think my yellow chintz would look wonderful on you. But the pale blue looks good too. And please, please, please, remember to use my sleeves."

She has also sacrificed a white summer dress, taking off the sleeves and sewing them with lace to create a cloud of fine ruffles. She counsels me to attach them to my green gown, and then it will be as if I have a whole new dress and people will think I have three.

"I will not win the king's heart with the bows on my bodice or the ruffles on my sleeves."

"But you will be at *Versailles*. With the king and queen! Everyone cares what you wear. It is the center of all that is fashionable and the other ladies will not speak to you if you are not dressed as befits your rank and station."

"I'm still a Mailly-Nesle, whether I wear sackcloth or go nude," I say crisply. "And I don't care about the other ladies."

"But you will embarrass Louise!"

"Perhaps; if so, she can order me some new dresses."

Diane presses her brocaded green shawl on me. "If you throw it over a simple dress it will look rather grand. They say Versailles is dreadful cold and drafty, colder than the refectory here. Even in summer. And you must write every day. I don't want to miss anything!"

"I will."

"No, you won't. You hate writing letters. Well, except for the ones to Louise. But that was because you wanted something. But try. Please. I want to know everything. And keep this hat on your head. Or at least make sure you are wearing it when the carriage arrives—it looks very nice on you."

"I will."

"And be sure to attach the white sleeves to your green gown, after you have worn it once."

I don't answer.

"And you've got all your stockings and chemises and lace caps?"

"Yes, Dee Dee."

"You're not going to write and you're going to simply disappear at Versailles, you'll fall into a giant mirror and be gone." Diane starts to cry. "You mustn't forget our promise. I don't want to be here forever, alone."

I hug her, unexpectedly hard and fierce. "I won't forget you, Dee Dee. I love you and you know that. You will come to Court too: I'll find you a duke for a husband."

Diane rummages through my pouch to make sure I have everything I will need for the journey and my new life: pocket coins, her Bible, extra handkerchiefs, an apple, and a small chestnut cake in case I get hungry on the road.

Mother Superior comes out into the courtyard to bid me farewell. She holds me at arm's length and studies me intently. I avoid her eyes. I don't think she was ever pleased with me. Not once.

"Such an extraordinary young woman," she says, and my ears prick: Mother is usually a woman of few words. "Normally I would be apprehensive of such a journey, and of such a destination, and with such an immoral hostess."

Diane and I exchange a quick look.

"I am sorry if I sound harsh, Diane-Adelaide and Pauline-Félicité, but it is the truth. Your sister Louise-Julie has sadly strayed from the path God would wish for her. Yet oddly, I am not afraid for you, not at all. I believe you can take care of yourself. You have such confidence. Not our doing, not at all; you were fully formed when you arrived. How old were you?"

"Seventeen." It seems so long ago—nine years in fact.

"Seventeen." She shakes her head. "Even at that age, such assurance and confidence. Though I can't imagine where it comes from, for you are not blessed either financially or physically."

"She is morally good." Diane chips in to champion me. I don't say anything; I think having confidence is a good thing, but the abbess speaks of it as if it's something found in a chamber pot.

"Oh, you are a fine Christian woman," continues Mother Superior in a dry voice. "And long may that last in that wicked cesspool you go to. If only your strength of character were to be employed to remain virtuous and true. But that, I am afraid, is rather improbable."

"Pauline is a force of nature," Diane says proudly. "Unstoppable, like a blizzard or a flood."

The Mother Superior raises her eyebrows. Her face is poached white from decades inside the cloister walls. "Yes, that does quite describe our Pauline," she says drily.

The carriage arrives and my sister and I hug one last time. Now Diane is truly wailing, but my eyes are dry. I get in the carriage, my heart singing. It begins.

☙

"Sister!"

We embrace and I am shocked. It has been so many years since we last saw each other and Louise is far prettier than I remember. She is positively radiant; the slightly scared, slightly ovine expression on her face has been replaced by a serene, poised mask. Her dress is most elegant: luxurious green with flounced yellow lace at the neck and elbows. She looks sophisticated. For the second time in my life, my confidence feels burned; apparently it takes a sister to do this.

"You look lovely," I say, and I mean it. I wish I didn't.

"Thank you, dearest!"

She smiles and I notice she has two symmetrical orbs of rouge on her pale cheeks, a beauty spot centered in one.

"And you too my dear, you look . . . well. So well! And what a nice hat! Pretty feathers. The journey was not too tiresome?"

I look around her apartment, keeping my mouth shut so it doesn't gape like shutters in the wind. The room is not large but it is beautifully decorated, the panels painted with sprays of flowers in every color. Gilded cherubs keep watch over the doors and windows. The plain white walls of the convent suddenly seem very far away.

"But this is beautiful!" I exclaim despite myself. In one corner there is a pink sofa with a curved scalloped back, flanked by three pink chairs; on another wall a bronze statue stands guard between two narrow windows.

"Come and see my bedroom."

Louise walks me up a few stairs to a smaller chamber where an enormous blue-canopied bed takes up almost the entire room. Two women sit sewing on a bench and they stand to bob when we enter. And this, I think, looking at the vast bed that rises like a ship from the parquet, is where Louise and the king make love. We return to the main room and some of my old confidence returns. Only two rooms! For the royal favorite!

"Two rooms. He must love you very much."

Sudden fear floods her face. She is like a damaged vase; from afar everything appears smooth, but up close you can see the hairline cracks.

"These were Mother's rooms. Versailles is so terribly overcrowded, you wouldn't believe where some people live. Even the Duc de Villeroy! He has only two rooms, and by the east privies, and even my friend Gilette's apartment has a chimney that constantly smokes. Here at least I have a nice view."

"At least," I murmur, looking out onto a narrow sunless courtyard. Strange to think this was where my mother slept. Perhaps with her lover, the Duc de Bourbon. And perhaps even with my father.

"I have a surprise for you." Louise comes close and squeezes my hand. Her brown eyes lighten and I smell jasmine and something deeper and more expensive.

"Tonight . . ."

"Yes?" I am holding my breath, and the bees have returned and are buzzing quite madly.

She claps her hands together. "The king will dine with us here tonight and has graciously allowed you to be present."

I too clap my hands, and the bees are silenced.

❧

I wear my pale blue dress with Diane's peach bows and Louise lends me a fan and some of her scent. As we are having our hair done we sip champagne and Louise fusses over my dress. She declares it impossibly plain and only reluctantly concedes it will do. Why do women think clothes are so important? Only women care how they are dressed; my friends in the convent told me that all men want to see is some bosom and a pretty face. My breasts are rather nice, and my wit will be my pretty face. I am like a pineapple, I decide, hiding my luscious interior beneath a rather scaly exterior.

I could get used to this, I think, sipping champagne and luxuriating in the softness of the sofa. Lamb's wool! From Turkey! I take mental notes from Louise on the king's best points—his charm and his manners. She lists his likes—pretty women and fashion—and tells me of his dislikes—being pestered; smelly cheeses; thunderstorms. And masculine women.

Everything in Louise's apartment is tenfold more luxurious than the convent, but as we sit I spy the little economies and signs of hardship: paint is peeling on the wall by a window, and one of Louise's petticoats is ragged with age. A single dying daisy in a glass vase graces the side table. Her woman, Jacobs, is running around borrowing candles from her neighbors, coming and going with bundles, followed one time by two footmen bringing in a pair of enormous candelabras. They are placed carefully to flank the table where we will dine.

"Isn't the room well lit enough already?" I ask. I've counted six sconces as well as a twenty-candle chandelier.

"Oh, no! Everything, everything must be brilliant for the king. He rarely dines here, and I want everything to be perfect," says Louise. She chews her lip. "It can be hard, keeping up with the king's demands. Candles are expensive. Especially the musk-scented white wax ones that he prefers."

Why is she mewling about expensive candles when she is the mistress of the most important man in the world? Well, most important after the pope, but the pope can't have a mistress. At least not these days. Louise, I realize, deludes herself into thinking that the king will love her more for her reticence and lack of greed.

Finally our hair is done, the champagne bottle is empty, and the servants bring in heaping dishes to lay on the table, among them a stuffed goose, an elegant porcelain stove piled with eggs for an omelet, and an enormous raspberry jelly that quivers with anticipation. Diane would love it here, I think, and then there is a commotion outside and the door opens without even a scratch. He is here, in all his glory. King Louis XV of France.

"I call him 'Twinkles,'" Louise whispers in my ear, sharing her pet name for him with all the solemnity of a state secret. "Only in private, of course. Because his eyes twinkle so."

Louise introduces us and I fall in a quick curtsy, then pull myself up to my full height. I lean in close and make my eyes forceful and brilliant. The king smiles but takes a step back and I can see I have unsettled him. Just a little bit. That is good. He should know from the beginning that I am not my sister.

Other guests arrive and introductions are made and people generally ignore me. They do not think I am important, even though I am Louise's sister. Or perhaps because I am Louise's sister? If so, then that is the opposite of the way things should be.

The meal begins. The men talk of the stag they failed to catch at the hunt. The king describes the rack of antlers on the beast. The prolonged efforts to corner the elusive animal caused him to miss a visit with his children. Everyone listens, rapt, their attention as overdone as the goose.

The talk turns to politics and I perk up, but I can't follow the details as everyone debates the Austrians and the upcoming Treaty of Vienna. I don't know much about politics, but I suppose I will have to learn. I notice Louise doesn't participate either, but just nods and follows every movement of the king.

Then the woman next to me, Mademoiselle de Charolais, fearfully pretty and fearfully important, entertains the table with a description of a troop of traveling monkeys she saw in Paris.

"The monkeys were trained to do tricks, and one even played the harpsichord. But it only knew Prussian music!"

The guests lap it up. Louise is the very picture of perfect attention, giggling and cooing and sighing at all the right moments and never taking her eyes off the king. At one point he tells her to move her chair away, saying the room is too hot and she is suffocating him. At this she doesn't even blush but just shifts over, her eyes still smiling.

I study what the women are wearing—Charolais has eight layers of lavender ruffles on her sleeves—and memorize the food so I can describe it all to Diane. I feel a pang; I miss her and part of me wishes I could sleep tonight in our bed at the convent and not with Louise in this strange and magnificent place. What weak thoughts!

I mentally push myself back to the table and compliment Mademoiselle de Charolais on her sleeves. Her list of conquests would put my own mother's to shame, and her face is as creamy and beautiful as her grandmother Madame de Montespan, King Louis XIV's most famous mistress. It is a delicious thrill to be sitting next to the woman known at the convent as Worse Than the Whore of Babylon.

"You should see my silver satin." She twirls her wrists and little silver bells, hidden in the lacy folds, chime softly. "Sixteen layers of lace at the sleeves." She looks me over to see how she may return the compliment but comes up short. Instead she motions down the table to Louise. "We call her Poor Goose," she whispers to me, then elegantly spears a mouthful of the roasted one. Charolais knows full well I am Louise's sister, yet she bothers not to hide her disdain. She then turns her daggers on me: "What an interesting perfume you are wearing. I smelled something like it in Paris last week . . . by the dancing monkey's cage."

Near the end of the meal, the Marquis de Meuse absentmind-edly plays with his spoon in a dish of pears with cream. The king shakes his head in annoyance and remarks that the marquis must have had neither manners nor music lessons when he was young, for the sound of the spoon on the porcelain is neither polite nor melodious. Meuse blushes beneath his powder and looks cra-venly down at his pears, laying his spoon on the table as quietly as he can.

Quickly I tap my champagne glass with a fork and sing a little scale to accompany the beat. "Come," I say, "his music was not so bad. With the right accompaniment, we could have an orches-tra and it could be quite melodic. We could call it Pear Poetry."

There is a dark silence. I feel Charolais shrink away from me and Meuse looks as though he wishes oubliettes were still in use that I might fall into one and disappear.

The room holds its collective breath.

Then the king laughs. Quickly, everyone laughs as well.

"Mademoiselle." He addresses me, and I see a flash of under-standing in his eyes. "You have a fine ear for music. What would you call this?" The king taps the rim of the omelet plate lightly in a three-beat with his knife.

"An Omelet Opera, of course," I say quickly.

We all laugh again and then there is instant cacophony as the others fall over themselves, clamoring like monkeys in a cage, to make "Soup Sonatas" and "Raspberry Rhapsodies."

The king's eyes are still on me and he is still smiling.

Triumph.

⁂

After the guests leave Louise fusses around with her servants, su-pervising the dismantling of the table and food. I sink into her luxurious pink sofa and nibble on the remains of a goose wing. Louise has a fuzzy little frown on her face and I know she wants to say something.

She sighs, starts to speak, stops. She turns away, a perfect pic-ture of indecision, and orders Jacobs to wrap the rest of the goose and save it for tomorrow. "But you can take away the jelly . . . how I hate things that *quiver*."

I suppose I should make this easier for her. "There is something you wish to say to me?"

Louise looks at me cautiously. She was never good at confrontation—in the nursery the little ninny couldn't say no to a kitten; even the maids would boss her around.

She takes a deep breath:

"You do not know—you could not know—everything on your first night here. But to do as you did . . . it was very . . ." She searches for the perfect word, so as not to offend. "Very . . . naive? You did not know. How could you? You have been cloistered in the convent for so many years, and our manners here at Court must seem very strange to you."

"What did I do wrong?" I ask, trying to hide my amusement. I think of the king's eyes on me, the little sparks of connection. I finish the goose wing and hop up to the table to see if there is anything else worth eating. I pour myself another glass of champagne and spoon the last of the cream and pears before Jacobs can spirit them away. Mmm, this is the life. I think back to the Mother Superior's horrid words to me: *Not blessed either financially or physically.* Well, I am blessed in other ways.

"You should not have spoken to the king without being addressed first. And you contradicted him! You almost insulted him! He does not like to be treated in a familiar manner by those he is not familiar with. He is very shy, you know."

"Oh, he didn't mind."

"Oh, but he did mind! He minded terribly. He would not show it because his manners are perfect. He will forgive—he is a very forgiving man, and I know he will be indulgent with you, to please me—but he was insulted. Believe me. I know him well, better than you."

For now. I finish my champagne and change the subject.

"That dreadful woman—Mademoiselle de Charolais?"

"Oh, yes!" says Louise, sitting down in relief, the difficult part over. "She's ghastly, simply ghastly. But she's ever so influential and Twink—the king, I mean—is ever so fond of her. But that lilac powder in her hair!"

"And oh, how she reeked of violets! And nastiness. And what is wrong with her voice—she sounds like she is six!"

"It's true! Some say she sounds like her eldest sister, who is shut up in an abbey and rumored to be ill in the head. And another sister, Mademoiselle de Clermont, the *surintendante* of the queen's household, is as false as a—oh, I know I shouldn't spread gossip, but that is just the way it is here at Versailles."

Louise hugs me, happy now that she thinks she has an ally. We get undressed and I can't help but stare at myself in the mirror, the candles flickering, my face enriched by the gilded surroundings, glowing from champagne and the memory of the dinner. I see myself as the king must have seen me, and shiver inside. I climb into bed with Louise and she hugs me.

"Oh, Pauline, I am so glad you are here. This is just like old times! Do you remember when there was a fire in the nursery, and Diane's bedcovers were ruined, so she slept in Hortense's bed, and then we all piled in, coughing dreadfully?"

"No, I stayed in my own bed." Away from Marie-Anne.

"Oh. I don't remember that. I thought we were all in bed together."

Eventually Louise falls asleep. I lie awake, listening to the strange sounds of the Versailles night, so different from the convent—dogs barking and whimpering, the sound of marching guards in the courtyard outside, carriages coming and going, giggles and whispers floating in from the rooms around us as people flit and fly through the night, the magnificent palace giving up its secrets and its whores.

This is going to be fun.

From Hortense de Mailly-Nesle
Hôtel de Mazarin, Paris
November 10, 1738

Diane!

Tante is at Versailles for two weeks, so if you want to come and visit, please do. You must be lonely at the convent without Pauline. Tante has not expressly forbidden you to step foot in her house (as she did with Pauline), so please come if you can on Thursday or Friday.

I trust Pauline is having a good visit with Louise at Court. Tante has not seen her and she says that that is just as well. She heard that Pauline has dreadful manners and that she insulted the king! Well, not to worry, it's only a short visit.

If you come next week you can see Victoire's new puppies. One is very, very small and has the strangest red fur. I also received a letter from Marie-Anne; I will share her news with you.

Please, when you reply, just write yes or no so I can understand if you are coming or not.

Hortense

Pauline

VERSAILLES

Early Winter 1739

Versailles is an enormous place but everything that is important is small. Hidden amongst the peacocking of the courtiers, beneath the winking lights of a thousand candles reflected in a hundred mirrors, the devil, as they say, is in the details.

Little scratches at the door, smaller for some, louder for others. A greeting that is a second too long, or a second too short—what does it imply? A look given or withheld. A coat worn one too many times; lace used inventively but too often on the same bodice; the crackle of a fresh satin gown, where before there was only wool. Where one sits at Mass, where one sits to dine, in which carriage you ride—second behind the king, or third? The room assigned to you when the Court is at Compiègne or Fontainebleau: larger than last year, or smaller? Minuscule details yet so infinitely, infinitesimally important.

What a strange life! What a strange existence! The day after my dinner with the king, this country (as the courtiers like to call Versailles) was all abuzz and I saw how here, gossip travels faster than a carrier pigeon. Louise's rooms were crowded with people eager for a glimpse of me. I heard whispers, caught stares, and felt enormously content.

"They are in vogue, these strange creatures, like those monkeys at the exhibition in Paris."

"Novelty and newness; I suppose that has to count for something."

"I shouldn't be so direct, my dear, it's not proper, but: I just don't understand. I. Just. Don't. Understand. Where is the attraction?"

The snipes don't bother me at all; I very quickly see that it is just the language of Versailles, one that I don't think I'll bother to learn.

The king likes a small group around him at all times; Louise tells me he feels alone if he is with fewer than four companions. All vie, often in vain, to be one of the chosen few. There are hundreds, if not thousands of people who would give their teeth, real or not, to be included on the magic lists of invites, be it for the hunt, a supper, a night of games. And when one is on the list? What power!

There are endless petty struggles over precedence, mounted with the precision of military campaigns. The battlegrounds are the pews in the chapel, the sacred stools, the queen's table, the king's antechamber. Such things as who may be carried through which rooms, or who should have the honor of taking off the king's boots, are matters of central importance. And any contact or access to the king, no matter how humble, is considered worth more than a dozen diamonds.

Frankly, I am feeling very rich right now. I am part of the chosen few, along with all who are fashionable at Court: Charolais and her sister, Clermont, equally evil; the Duchesse d'Antin, whom Louise claims is a good friend, and the Comtesse d'Estrées, both harmless ninnies whose only virtues are their pretty faces and bland, easy conversation.

Oh, and there is Louise, of course.

☙

The footmen fluff the white cloth and it descends like snow over the vast gaming table. Outside, real snow blankets the world: we are in the middle of the harshest winter in living memory. As cold as a dead man's cock, as Charolais so charmingly puts it.

Outside, there are reports of starvation and even death, but inside, in the king's private salon, the world is toasty with a fire blazing and the heat of too much hope steaming up the windows. On top of the table the footmen place an enormous *cavagnole* board surrounded by candelabras covered in golden and green acanthus leaves. The guests gather around the table.

There are those privileged with entrées to the King's Apartments, and then there are those that the king has decided may join us for this night of gambling in his private rooms. Many are scandalized that I am here tonight, for I have not been officially presented and am therefore nothing in their eyes. Most refuse to address me, or even look at me. Fools.

I decide I prefer to watch, since I don't have money to gamble, and besides, I don't like games of chance. Silly games like *cavagnole*, solely dependent on luck and cheating, bore me rather completely.

"It is perfectly all right if you don't want to play, sister. You can sit by the fire and enjoy the warmth." Louise is dressed in a heavy cream gown sewn with blue fur, which she insists is fox but that looks rather like squirrel to me. Charolais sneered at it earlier and told me it was dreadfully passé.

"No, Bijou, what are you thinking? Mademoiselle de Nesle is our guest here, and she must partake of all the pleasures that we offer."

Well, if the king insists.

I sidle into place between him and Louise, poking her with my closed fan to push her over enough.

"But, Pauline, you have no money to bet with," says Louise, slipping around to the other side of the king and displacing the old Princesse de Chalais, who snorts in disapproval and moves down the table, taking a plate of cheese tarts with her.

"Perhaps you could bet 7,500 *livres*?" offers Charolais sweetly from across the table.

"No. I'll play with this," I reply as I unhook one of my pearl earrings.

"Oh, no, Pauline, don't do that! Those are from Mama."

"Ha! We are intrigued, mademoiselle, intrigued." The king looks at me with admiration. "You are very brave. If you win, I shall arrange for the banker to give you sixty-four additional pearls, enough for a fine choker. Nothing would please me more than to give you a pearl necklace." I know from the way the king watches me that he wants to be close to me, to touch me. It is the first time I have tasted this particularly feminine form of power, and it gives me a rare giddy feeling.

"Bijou, you will hold the bag tonight, we all know you are dependable and honest, and you have not the money to be playing again. Besides, I dislike the bad humor you have when you lose." Louise curtsies and takes the velvet bag, soft and minky like a little animal, and shines with misplaced pride. She told me she lost thirty thousand *livres* at cards last month, an enormous sum, and a debt that the king keeps promising to pay for her, but hasn't yet done.

The king turns back to me: "So, what number shall be your lucky number tonight, mademoiselle?"

"Well . . ." I search his face for inspiration. We are very close, no more than the length of a candle apart and I can feel the lust rising off him.

"Fifteen," I decide, and go to place my pearl earring on the board.

"Wait. Let me bless it with good luck, for this pearl has the number of my history on it." He takes the earring from my fingers and touches it to his lips, all the while looking at me. I open my mouth ever so slightly. He hasn't kissed me yet, but I know he wants to. And I want him to.

"Ah, Majesty, but that was my pick. I also thought to honor you in that way," announces Meuse from the end of the table in his high-pitched, annoying voice. "Instead let me honor you by choosing the number of the boar Your Majesty killed this week." He places his stack of counters on the number forty-eight.

"Indeed." The king turns back to me and grins. I have noticed the king can be cold, even aloof, with those he doesn't know, but once one is inside the charmed, magic circle he relaxes and becomes a very friendly, witty man. Louise keeps insisting he's shy, but I don't think he is, really.

"Now, mademoiselle, would you do me the honor of choosing my number?"

I raise my fan to shield us from the others, that none may hear my words and improper address. I lower my voice to draw him in even closer and whisper: "King, you will be twenty-nine soon."

"Yes," he whispers back. "And you, mademoiselle, you are twenty-six?"

"I am."

"I believe fifty-five will be my luck tonight," replies the king, catching my meaning quicker than a wink. "I like the way you think, mademoiselle. Together, we make the perfect number."

Louise shakes his arm, intruding on our little world. "Fifty-five? Oh no, dearest, you must play your special number seven."

"But all last month that number did nothing for me, nothing. I will change. Sometimes, change is just the tonic that is needed."

The other courtiers decide their bets, the Marquis de Mezières ostentatiously placing a high tower of coins on three and thirty-six, announcing to no one in particular that he was blessed with a dream last night in which those numbers appeared. The Princesse de Chalais stops nibbling on a cheese tart long enough to place a bet on number twenty.

"Twenty—is that for the number of tarts you have already eaten, or for those you plan to eat?" inquires Charolais in a voice as smooth as an egg. The princess observes her with a cold, un-blinking eye, then, without losing her grip on the gaze, slowly reaches for another tart. Madame d'Estrées and the Chevalier de Cocq banter obliquely about the number of times they "visited the Fountain of Venus" last month, and decide it was sixteen, though she claims she visited twice without his knowing. Soon, the board of seventy numbers is an uneven landscape of towered coins and porcelain tokens, low and high.

"The time has come!" announces the banker grandly, tapping lingering hands with a gold-tipped cane and collecting the list of bets. He gestures to Louise and she spins the bag delicately. All eyes are on her as she pulls a bead from the black velvet.

"Forty-eight!"

The young Princesse de Guémené squeals like a pink piglet and jumps so hard that a pearled begonia falls from her hair. "Now I shall have that ruby ring! It has been denied me too long—I *knew* I would be lucky tonight."

The Marquis de Mezières bows solemnly and declares some forgotten obligation, and departs the room with an unsteady gait. The Princesse de Chalais throws a half-eaten cheese tart on the floor in disgust.

"Ah, I am sorry, mademoiselle, the numbers were not in our favor."

I shrug. "Nothing ventured, nothing gained. Besides, it's just a game of chance and luck. They bore me."

"So you do not believe in chance and luck?" The king raises one eyebrow in amusement.

"Oh, but I do. How else does one explain the success of people that have no merit?" I look down the table at Meuse, picking his nose while mindlessly rooting through a bowl of dried figs.

The king chuckles. "Ha! You are so unkind, mademoiselle, so very unkind. Now, if these games bore you—what do you suggest?"

"Chess," I say promptly. Madame de Dray was a keen strategist and we spent many long evenings playing together at the convent.

"But that is not a game for a friendly evening!" declares Madame d'Estrées, contorting her lips into a ducklike pout as she attempts a flirt.

"Ah, chess—the game of kings. Fleury taught me, many years ago, but I must confess I have lost the knack in recent years. No willing partner, perhaps?"

"There is a set in the Wig Chamber, sire," offers Meuse, hastily swallowing a fig. "The gift from the Spanish?"

"You are right as always, Meuse. Goodness, it has been a long while. But I must agree with Madame d'Estrées; chess is not the game for the group we have here tonight."

I don't murmur that I agree, but continue to smile at him. He hesitates a flinch, then makes up his mind: "But perhaps tomorrow evening—that concert in the Queen's Apartments does not interest me. We shall play chess, then, yes, with Mademoiselle de Nesle!"

"Wonderful. I shall polish my plays and I have no doubt you will be in checkmate by the end of the evening."

The king licks his lips and stares at me, then shakes his head as though he had forgotten there were others around us.

"That chessboard is ever so pretty. Such dainty little carvings, made of ivory, I think," chips in Louise in a rather worried voice.

The king turns to look at her and for one brief moment it is as though he is looking at a stranger. Then he claps his hands: "But for now, another round of *cavagnole*."

I take the other pearl from my ear, and place it on the one. Why not? Louise jingles the bag again and the air is thick with anticipation and greed as those with the most of everything pray for only more.

"One!"

Ha! I clap and spontaneously reach over to grab Louis's arm and he hugs me back. It is the first time I have ever embraced a man; I don't think my father ever hugged me, and certainly not a strange man.

Oh.

"Sixty-four pearls, for a pearl herself. Mademoiselle, I will see the banker and have your winnings made into a necklace. And I shall add sixty-four more, for your presence here gives me much pleasure."

At the end of the evening I walk back with Louise to her rooms. I'm in delirium—perhaps skill and strategy are overrated? Perhaps all you need is luck? And tomorrow we will play chess—alone.

"You are very lucky, Pauline. The king was in a good mood tonight," says Louise as we wend our way back through the candlelit corridors to her room, the giant mirrors throwing ghostly reflections back at us, her voice soft because who knows who lurks in the shadows? "It is rare to see him in so fine a mood; usually he is quite melancholy in wintertime. And he was very friendly with you—so friendly. I wonder if it was the arrival of the young Prince of Lichtenstein, yesterday, that put him in such a good humor?"

Her voice is slightly worried, but hopeful, as if by airing her thoughts she can rid them of unwanted suspicions.

From Pauline de Mailly-Nesle
Château de Versailles
April 3, 1739

D—

You know how much I hate writing letters, but I am going to write you a nice long one to apologize for my tardiness. I want to share with you everything that has happened here. It has all been quite exciting. I have met many powerful people. Cardinal Fleury, the king's adviser, is the oldest man I have ever seen and frightfully powerful even though his father was just a country lawyer or some such thing.

Mademoiselle de Charolais, the late king's granddaughter and a complete whore, has pronounced herself my very best friend and showers me with gifts and advice. Mademoiselle de Charolais is dreadfully false—everyone here is, apart from our good Louise—and loves intrigue. I always do the opposite of what she counsels. I even sleep in her apartments sometimes, though I am averse to the lavender she stocks everywhere. Still, it's preferable to sleeping with Louise; her room can be very noisy at times.

But I should let you know that my plan is coming along marvelously. The king thinks me the most fascinating woman! I know this, for he said it himself. He marvels again and again that one such as I should emerge from a convent: I tell him it's because I never listened to a single word the nuns said.

The king is wonderful. And very handsome and kind. We have become satisfyingly close and I now consider him more of a friend—a good one—than my sovereign. I hope spies or Mother Superior don't open this letter; it feels strange to be writing thus about His Majesty, almost like using His name in vain!

I believe he is positively infatuated with me. He says he loves my intellect and my fierce green eyes and the unexpected and sometimes inappropriate comments that come from my mouth (but always, he declares gallantly, always forgiven; for him I can do no wrong). He says I am the most exciting woman he has ever met. Most—all—of the courtiers here are as boring as sheep, so I have no doubt that what he says is true.

If I can say this—goodness, I hope the spies are not reading this—I am his mistress in all but name and, well . . . I will share more details when I next write.

The indigo ribbons I'm sending are from Charolais—I don't have any use for them but I know you will like them. I hope they will make up for the sleeves you sacrificed. She also had a beautiful ivory and strawberry silk fan, and when I suggested to her that you might like it, she gave it to me! So here it is, enjoy it and keep it out of sight of the nuns—I am sure they would consider it far too luxurious and sinful for Port-Royal.

Show this letter to Madame de Dray—it's for both of you. I simply don't have time to write twice. And perhaps Madame de Dray could write back on your behalf? I didn't understand much of your last letter, and I should like to hear your news.

Louise is very happy—she sends her love.
Pauline

Pauline

The king could not hide his fascination and desire for me, and did not. From the beginning there was no scuttle-bugging down darkened corridors as he had done with Louise; ours was not to be an alcove affair. Openly he sought my company and never even apologized to Louise for his marked change of affection. I didn't apologize either; it's not my fault if the king is bored with her and wants to be with me.

Of course, she is still his mistress and he still often passes the night with her. She is familiar: I now know that the king is a man who clings to routine and stability. At Versailles there is a routine to the routine; the music all sounds the same and the plays are all funny in the same way, or identically tragic. At gambling it is always *cavagnole*. Louis used to prefer quadrille, but this year it is *cavagnole* and only *cavagnole*. I do not see why this should be so, but this is how he likes it.

How he *thinks* he likes it.

Once I am married and my position is assured, I will banish Louise. For now, I cannot deny she serves a useful purpose. Six years is six years and she knows the king intimately, both in body and mind, and I can quiz her endlessly about his likes and dislikes. Though I am sure the last thing she wants to do is sit and expose the soul of her beloved to me, Louise is unable to say no to anyone. This is a deadly flaw at Versailles. Here, soliciting for advantage is a full-time occupation and Louise spends far too much time fulfilling others' wishes, always with her little fuzzy frown. It's irritating. People asking her for things, I mean, though I suppose her face is also irritating. Sometimes I step in and put an end to the carping; they do say that blood is thicker than water, and when people disrespect Louise (which is fairly often) it is as though they disrespect me. Which will not do.

Just yesterday Gilette, the Duchesse d'Antin (whom Louise claims is a friend but who looks more like a fiend to me) darted into our rooms and demanded to borrow Louise's porcelain stove, claiming hers had been knocked over and shattered by one of her husband's dogs. Louise, who needs it for heating our chocolate and coffee, was about to say yes when I stepped in and told the woman that we need to drink just as much as she does, and that she could not have it.

But I'm glad Louise can't say no to me. I ask her freely about the king, and meekly she replies. She tells me he likes the smell of carnations above all other flowers; that he is only truly happy during the hunt—the morning he killed twenty deer is one of his most cherished memories; how he dislikes Hungarians more than all the others of Europe; how he admires his great-grandfather, yet does not want to be like him, for he vows never to legitimize any of his bastards (though to Louise's knowledge he has as yet none and certainly none by her). She tells me how he dislikes smelly cheeses, more specifically smelly cheeses from Normandy; how he hates hair powder that gets on his clothes, and how he dislikes, above all else, situations that make him uncomfortable.

And she tells me about his dark times and depressions and his fear of death and Hell and of his unformed memories of those months when he was but a babe and lost all his family, memories that haunt his soul still. He was only two when his father, mother, and elder brother all died within weeks from measles, and it was only the intervention of his governess that saved him. Madame de Ventadour still lives, and the king is very devoted to her.

"He visits her every day," Louise informs me solemnly, "even when there is the hunt."

"Ah yes, I've seen the black-shrouded woman."

"And the Comtesse de Toulouse is equally dear to him; he considers her the mother he never had."

"Mmm." Louise always gushes about the *comtesse*'s kindness and says she is just the nicest soul, but I disliked her from the start. The king often has his informal suppers in her apartments, and I always catch her eyes on me, full with the wary watchfulness of a mother bear.

"And you must never, never ask him for anything," Louise warns me, glancing at my cup of coffee.

We are sitting together in her salon; the king is occupied with visiting Turks. I like to make outrageous demands on Louise, just for fun. Today I told her I craved orange-flavored coffee and would she find some for me? It is a new craze here but the stuff is deadly expensive and very hard to procure. I sip the sweet treat and ask her to give me the rest of the box so I can send it to Diane, who will be delighted.

"Are you sure? The whole box? It's a rather large box, and it was so very expensive."

"Diane loves coffee, you know that. And oranges."

"But so do—oh, all right. Poor Diane, stuck away at the convent while we are at Versailles! I will send it tomorrow. But as I was saying, you must never ask the king for favors. He very much dislikes being pestered."

I snort. Of course the king wants to be asked for things: How else can he show his love? "So is it true what they say? That the king makes love like a porter and tips like one too?" Charolais has been sharing with me many stories about the king's parsimonious nature and his miserliness toward Louise. I already have a list of trifles the king has given me, including a pair of Chantilly vases and a choker of flawless white pearls—but all he's ever given Louise is a little engraved box from China. And something about a meadow—a watercolor perhaps?

Louise's lips start to quiver and red creeps up her face.

"Sister, you are not married! How can you talk about such things? How can you even *know* of such things?"

"I'll be married soon enough," I say confidently. To a duke, I hope. The king has been discussing possibilities for some time. There was talk of a match with the Comte d'Eu, who is a prince of the royal blood; that would have been *very* suitable. Fleury was opposed to the match. Not to worry; it's been noted. Whenever I see the old crapchard I think: your treachery will come back to bite you, just like the fleas that are rumored to live in your robes.

"But still, this is not proper. You are an unmarried maiden and you should not ask such things. You should not even *know* of such things." I don't even bother snorting. Besides, I doubt Louise has much to teach me in that area; I imagine her lovemaking to be as dull as her conversation. I'll rely on what my friend Madame de Dray told me back at the convent, little tricks mostly centered around their penis thing.

Charolais has been pushing me to give in to the king and sleep with him. She thinks I am a fool but I am not. I can't sleep with him until I am married; adultery after marriage is acceptable but fornication before marriage is simply unthinkable. Look at what happened to Mademoiselle de Moras—such scandal! It didn't happen at the convent of Port-Royal, worse luck (we never had the exciting scandals), but of course we heard about it: she ran away with an entirely unsuitable suitor, and then she was entirely ruined, and he sentenced to death!

Of course, Charolais is not married and she certainly fornicates, but as the granddaughter of Louis XIV, her birth puts her beyond even convention. She can do anything, and she does. Last year it was whispered she slept with ten men, including one of her own footmen, and one from the household of the Comtesse de Toulouse. Imagine that! No, I will not sleep with the king until I am married. Besides, Louis is a hunter and everyone knows the deer most chased is the deer most cherished.

I make it my policy to be well informed about government and current events, but surprisingly, Louis is not all that interested. He largely leaves the business of government alone, content to sign what his ministers require, content to go where Fleury leads. I think he should be more involved; if he doesn't know any-thing about France or governing, how will he ever get out from under the gnarled thumb of Fleury?

When he is with me I make sure that he is constantly chal-lenged, spurred, thinking. We talk about politics, about war, about the situation in Europe. At first he was reluctant, saying that women should not meddle in such matters. I replied that it was not to meddle that I wished to involve myself, but rather to support and understand my king.

I too have a lot to learn but I am a quick study. And so I learn of the poor wheat harvest and all the consequences—who knew a lack of rain could be so disastrous? I learn how unrest between the Russians and the Ottomans influences the price of treasured Turkish carpets—strange that something that happens so far away should have such a direct impact on us here in France. I regret the time wasted at the convent; I should have been seek-ing out newspapers and learned books rather than reading silly novels or pawing through religious books, looking for scraps of interest.

I learn about the Polish war and the Treaty of Vienna. And about our enemies, the Austrians and the British. Especially the Austrians; Hapsburgs are known to have extra fingers and many have enormous lower jaws with protruding lips, evidence of their ungodly ways. Many say we are heading for war with them, a path that Fleury violently opposes; he is, as they say, a dove.

೧೦

We are at Rambouillet, only an hour from the palace. A small group of us have come on ahead and now it is evening and the king arrives. He joins us in the wood-paneled library, peevish and peckish.

"What a day, what a day. How nice it is to be gone from that tiresome place. Man, bring me a cup of something hot. Bouillon."

"Darling, what is it?" Louise reaches up for a kiss. Since her position became known last year, Louise does not hesitate to make public her affections. Charolais tells me that everyone finds it insufferable and all preferred her when she had to keep her love secret.

I watch them, curious. Louise clings to the king as a barnacle to a ship. Even when it is plain the king only wants to be with me, she refuses to leave, no matter how surplus we may make her feel. All the while Louis and I are growing more intimate and there are many evenings after supper when we retire, just the two of us, to one of his even more private rooms, where we are free to talk alone and kiss as we will. Louise never asks about these evenings; I think she prefers to pretend they never happen.

The king sighs again. "All Fleury can talk about are the peasants and the lack of flour at the markets. It appears serious."

"The flower market?" asks Louise in a worried voice.

"That is right, my dear, no flour at the market. A cause for grave concern."

"But why do the peasants need flowers? I don't understand. Can't they just gather them in the woods if they need them so badly?"

Meuse sidles up to join the conversation. "It is dreadful, sire, dreadful. Ruffec returned from the country with news that the situation is dire—hard to even have a peaceful dinner without the peasants gathering in the courtyard and crying their misery. Even worse, the only bread available was an inferior gray stuff—eating it caused his wife to chip a tooth."

"And I've heard the peasants are eating grass, like animals," adds Madame d'Estrées. "Shocking, simply shocking—have they no manners?"

"Ah, we must not believe these reports. We all know it is the peasants exaggerating and making drama as usual. Surely these are only fanciful tales, grown with the telling?" The Duc de Duras is another of the king's intimates, a genial man with a tiny, prim mouth.

The king shakes his head. "But still, it worries me, worries me to no end. Of course, it is not my fault—nature I cannot control! We must have more public prayers, perhaps a whole week this time."

"There is another solution, sire," I say loudly, and the room falls silent.

"Now, what would your pretty little head know about such matters?" queries the king, coming over to where I am seated by the hearth.

"Anything of interest to my sovereign is of interest to me."

"Oh, Pauline, you mustn't bother His Majesty with work, not here at Rambouillet. We must talk of lighter things." Louise scuttles over and possessively puts her hand on the king's arm. He casually detaches it, then removes his gloves to fret his hands over the fire.

"And so, Mademoiselle de Nesle, what would you propose?"

"The government should buy grain and store it, then resell it when it is scarce. If you don't do that, grain speculators will, and they will keep the prices too high," I reply promptly. I have become an avid reader of the *Gazette de France* and often pigeon-hole Orry, the king's controller general, to test my theories. I think the man replies to my questions more out of shock than anything else.

"An interesting proposition, mademoiselle; I have heard Orry talk of the same. You must tell me more, later. But for now I would change and ready myself for the evening's entertainment." He takes a glass of warm bouillon from a footman and signals to Bachelier. "I hope there will be duck on the menu tonight? And something tart for dessert, gooseberries perhaps?" I hear him say as they leave the room.

By the fire Louise stares at me with rather an empty look. One of the king's greyhounds wanders over and nuzzles at her skirt. She tries to push it away, her eyes still on me.

"He really doesn't like to talk about work once he leaves Versailles, Pauline," she finally whispers. "Oh, get off me, dog. Why won't it leave me alone?"

"You mustn't confuse what you like, dear sister, with what the king likes. You're not the only one who knows him well." It is a deliberate arrow, but it is also the truth; we are daily becoming closer, and try hard as Louise might, she is a fool if she doesn't see it. Soon . . .

Charolais swoops in. She was in the carriage with the king; I had forgotten she was coming.

"So you presume to know what the king likes now, do you, dearest Mademoiselle de Nesle?" She is wearing an enormous cream cloak, patterned with purple and blue flowers, and she brings with her the cold and a strong scent of violets.

"I do know what he likes. He has become a good friend," I say more smugly than I should. Sometimes triumph feels good, and anything that trumps Charolais makes me feel simply *superb*.

෴

When we talk of the future—our future—Louis is most concerned about Fleury and what the "people of France" will say if he takes a new mistress.

"The people of France?" I quiz him. "What do you mean by that?"

"The common, ordinary folk. A lawyer or a shopkeeper or something. A peasant, even. They are a highly moral people, and I do not wish them to see or think of their king as a . . . libertine." Louis has a deep, sonorous voice, water flowing smoothly over well-rounded rocks.

I don't snort as I might for I see he is deadly serious. He really cares what a lawyer or a peasant might think of him! How strange. Certainly it would be nice to have the love of his subjects, but his right to rule comes from God, so at the end of it all, why should he care what "the people" think? This is not England: it is not as though they can chop off the head of their king if they are unhappy.

"Dearest, you are the *king*. You are above the opinion of the people—they have no right to cast judgment on you."

There is silence. We are in the room assigned to me at Rambouillet, a cozy room, decorated in the Turkish style; the ceiling is painted a deep midnight blue dotted with a hundred silver stars and the thick stone walls are hung with luxurious tapestries.

Louis lies on the sofa looking up, lost in the heavens above. I am sprawled by his feet on the plush orange carpet with my hair unpinned. Charolais has shown me how to wash it with Moroccan oil to soften it, and make it less bristly.

The king runs his hands through my hair in a distracted circular motion. I appear relaxed but in fact I am ever alert. Though Louis likes to be pushed, even the most pliant branch must eventually break.

"But what judgment . . . what judgment it would be. Incest . . ."

"Louis, you mustn't read those pamphlets!"

"It is rare I agree with them, but you know the injunction against sleeping with one's wife's sister. A law embedded in morality since the beginning of time."

"But you aren't *married* to Louise."

"I know, I know. I am not sure if that makes it better, or worse. Still, the priest . . . He did mention incest."

This is serious.

"Louis, you are not *married* to Louise," I repeat. "If I were the queen's sister, then perhaps there might be some concern—"

The king shudders and holds up a hand to make me stop. "Were that you were just Louise's cousin, or unrelated. Then there would not be this added . . . complication."

"But then you might never have met me. Nor I you," I say lightly. I don't like where this conversation is heading. If only I knew who was starting and spreading the stories around Paris. I tried to talk to Marville, the lieutenant general of police and a man fast becoming a friend, but he said that trying to stop the pamphlets and songs would be like trying to stop the wind: an impossible feat. Charolais claims they come from Maurepas, one of the king's ministers and the son-in-law of Tante; needless to say, I don't think we will be friends.

"I see, darling, that nothing bothers you, but I . . . I cannot say the same. My soul . . ." Louis is pensive and I see his mind is far beyond the room, far beyond the scattered stars and deep blue depths of the painted sky above. "Sometimes I fear for my soul. It is not so much the judgment of the French people I fear, but the judgment of One much higher." He sighs, the deep melancholy gloom of a much older man. "Sometimes I think I would give all the rest of my days if I could just turn back the clock to the time when I was a faithful husband to the queen, when I was a man who could stand straight before God. But then there was Louise . . ."

Louis was recently forbidden Communion by his confessor, a rat-faced old Jesuit called Father Lignières. Without confession he can no longer touch and cure the leprous. A small thing, I would think, and something he should be glad of—disgusting lepers!—but it weighs heavily on him. I smell Fleury behind this; everyone knows Father Lignières lives under Fleury's scarlet robes.

This is dangerous and rather unexpected territory. I run my hands softly up and down his legs; we are not fully intimate, yet we are close in many ways. Louis knows the rules as well as I do and assures me he will find me a husband soon. This melancholic, spiritual man is a new Louis, and a rather worrying one. Louise had warned me of his black moods but I had assumed they were just a reaction to her company.

"But dearest, God understands. You cannot, you must not be chained to the queen, a woman who rejects you from her bed. God understands." I make a mental note: Lignières must leave.

Louis continues to talk up to the ceiling. "When I was first with Louise, we would spend hours together, asking for forgiveness for our acts of sin. Hours we prayed, even as we sinned before and sometimes after. But gradually . . . I believe I have lost the way of the righteous, and that the only path ahead of me is the one that leads straight to Hell."

But Louis's moods are like spring winds that blow inconstant. He soon abandons his religious qualms, and his insistence on finding me a husband increases. I cannot agree more: What is taking him so long?

From Marie-Anne de la Tournelle
Château de la Tournelle, Burgundy
May 2, 1739

Dear Louise,

Greetings from Burgundy! I trust you and your husband are well and thank you for your news of Court. My news is not very exciting: my husband was home over the winter, but he has since gone again and will not be back for some time. We are deep in rains this spring: last week the river beside the château rose and flooded the kitchen cellars; our stores of apples and vegetables were completely ruined. Soon we may even be as hungry as the peasants! That is only a joke, of course.

How are you and, if I may be so bold, how is the king? I do apologize, but news of your relationship is quite open knowledge, so I do not think I am being impolite. We are sisters, after all. Hortense writes that Pauline is now at Court—how curious! She had heard some strange rumors—*very* strange rumors—but I am sure they are not true.

Is Pauline as ugly and foul as ever? Well, I suppose I should not write such things—imagine what Zélie would say!—but you all know that Pauline and I are not as close as perhaps sisters should be.

Thank you for the book you sent at New Year's—how nice that you remembered I like La Fontaine's poems!

Please accept this box of cardamom seeds that I send to you, grown by my own hand. Well, not my own hand, but Cook's, though I did supervise everything and am very pleased at what we have been able to accomplish in our humble greenhouse. At the end of the summer I will send you some more of our quinces; the orchard here grows the most abundant and delicious fruit.

Please send me news of Court and Pauline.

Love,
Marie-Anne

From Louise de Mailly
Château de Versailles
June 15, 1739

Dear Marie-Anne,

What a nice surprise to get a letter from you! Every time I receive one I do think we should write more frequently. Ah, dear Zélie, yes, she always said the truth: we must be more sororal.

Life at Versailles is wonderful. I and my husband are well; he sends his regards. Thank you for asking after His Majesty, and of course I do not begrudge you the question. It is no secret that I am in love with him, and he with me. He is well, troubled by a slight nose infection at the end of May, but nothing to be concerned about.

It is true that Pauline is at Court with me now. Still. She has been here quite a while now; I thought she was coming for just a quick visit but she proved to be surprisingly popular. Many at Court begged me to allow her to stay longer, and so I consented. I suppose it is more interesting for her here than at the convent, and she can be very charming and witty when she is in good humor.

I am of course very happy for her but I do worry about Diane all alone at Port-Royal. I should like to urge Pauline to consider returning there, for her position here is awkward as she is not married, and she does not know well the manners and customs of Versailles. It would be kind of her to return to Diane at the convent, but you know how Pauline is—she is often too busy to truly think of others.

Thank you so much for the cardamom. It was very popular and I am sad to report that I have none left, so eager were others for a pinch. I am glad, dear Marie-Anne, that you are happy in Burgundy. I hope you have a wonderful summer.

With love,
Louise

Louise

For all that Pauline used to complain about our governess, Zélie, and what a simpleton she was, I still mind many things she taught us. One lesson in particular I treasure: Zélie taught us that to show our emotions was to be naked.

"Your emotions are like your buttocks or your shoulders," I remember her saying, and we were so young then that we would blush and titter at this image. "Emotions, just like your buttocks or shoulders, or legs, must be covered in decent society. If anyone sees your emotions, consider yourself naked."

If we cried, or looked angry or resentful, Zélie would make us stand on a chair and lift our skirts to show our legs. I remember those lessons well and now I cover my emotions completely, so none may see how I die inside.

It is a Wednesday afternoon and the queen's daughters are giving a small concert. We ladies must applaud and flatter and praise the young princesses as though they were the Muses themselves. Madame Elisabeth, the eldest, has a particularly flat ear and gauche fingers. Madame Henriette, her twin, and Madame Adelaide are passable but hardly the musical paragons their mother so proudly proclaims them.

First the Princess Elisabeth woos us on the harpsichord, playing a zarzuela piece she has learned in honor of her upcoming marriage to the infante of Spain, her thin body rigid with self-importance as she pecks the keys. She will be twelve next month and the wedding is fixed for shortly after her birthday. Louis is distraught at the prospect; last year he lost his four youngest daughters to the abbey at Fontevraud (Fleury insisted, claiming the expense was too much to keep them all at Versailles) and now he will lose his eldest daughter to Spain. In exchange, the *dauphin*, Louis's eldest and only son, will marry a Spanish infanta. The *dauphin* is just ten years old, so that wedding won't be for another four or five years.

We clap with polite enthusiasm when Elisabeth finishes. *"Gracias,"* she says as she rises and bows; she has been having Spanish lessons.

"Magnificent, magnificent, madame, you must be so proud," says Mademoiselle de Clermont to the queen in her hearty voice.

The queen beams and I note tears in her eyes; it is not only the king who will miss his daughter. She is very sad these days, for while the king still sees her almost every day, his visits are just routine and quick formality; they live almost completely separate lives. Though her children give her consolation, she must know that one day she will lose all her daughters to marriages far away.

Madame Henriette, taller and softer than her twin, takes up the strings of a viola and strangles a piece of Lully. We listen with polite, mustered attention. Their music master, a thin young man, oddly bearded, strums in nervous proxy by her side, as if to will the notes out through the sheer force of his bulging eyes.

While I am stuck here they—the king and Pauline—are away together at Choisy, a new palace he has recently acquired. Pauline has no formal engagements at Court, so she is free whenever the king is. I think she urges him to travel during the weeks when she knows I must be with the queen.

"Vanderful, vanderful," says the queen in delight as Madame Henriette finishes her piece. The queen smacks her knees to applaud, a vulgar fashion of the Poles. She has been in France long enough; surely she should know our manners by now? These days I find myself irritated with everyone, even with the poor queen. I believe she now pities me as I used to pity her; I have learned that to be pitied is a dreadful thing.

Madame Henriette gives an awkward curtsy.

"Again, magnificent, madame, magnificent: how proud you must be."

"We will practice a group symphony, yes, and playing for all. All of us together, before Elisabeth leaving."

"But nothing could be more horrifying!" says the Princesse de Montauban sweetly as Clermont snaps her head around in censure. "If we were to miss this wonderful opportunity."

A flustered footman struggles to wheel in an enormous harp, one of its wheels broken, his face popping peach with exertion. Little Princess Adelaide, all nine solemn years, then settles in front of it and twitches her tiny sausage fingers at the strings. The afternoon is hot and interminable—how I wish I were at Choisy with Louis! How I wish I were *alone* with Louis at Choisy.

What hurts the most is how quickly it all happened. The day after that awful dinner all Louis could talk about was Pauline, Pauline, Pauline. At first I thought he was just being courteous, to give me pleasure. But then he sought every opportunity to dine with her and spend time with her, and then, so very, very quickly, they were inseparable.

I told myself it was just a passing phase. But before I understood what was happening, I was on the outside looking in, watching the man I love fall in love with my sister. What despair, what torture. My world is broken and seemingly nothing can make it right.

I know she wants me gone, and truth be told sometimes I think a convent would be preferable to this version of Hell that Versailles has become for me. But a convent would mean never seeing Louis again, and there is nothing, not all the humiliation in the world, not all the grief in the world, that could be worse than that.

And so I stay.

Now we are oftentimes all together, like some awful three-headed monster from a Greek myth.

When I am alone with him, I cry. I don't want to but I can't help myself. When I see the distance in his eyes and his aura of guarded familiarity, the tears flow so fast they run away with my rouge. I know he hates crying women but I cannot stop. And then he slips further and further away until he is like a star at night that I can only see from afar and can never hope to draw nearer.

In front of everyone, I never cry. Instead I smile and take his arm and take Pauline's arm and exclaim in delight when she suggests one of her outlandish games, or listen with interest when she talks of politics or finance that she has no business even thinking about.

I am never naked before the world, but once alone in my apartments I can only cry and cry and cry. My woman, Jacobs, says I must have a river in my head, for she has never seen anyone produce so many tears. She never asks me why I cry because it is obvious—who would not in this dreadful situation?

What have I done to deserve such a fate? Is this God punishing me for being unfaithful to my husband? But I love Louis, I truly love him. How can that be wrong?

Oh, despair.

I love him in a way that I know Pauline cannot. I believe she is incapable of true love, for it is clear to me and to everyone around us that she is ambitious and loves power, and power only. For her, Louis is but a hill she climbs on her hungry quest, but for me he is my world, my life, my everything.

Most people do not like Pauline, no matter how they may flatter her. But there is something in her they admire. They even admire her ugliness. They say she is ugly but in a unique way that has its own charm: *jolie laide*.

I have come to hate this place and I hate Pauline and I hate the shifty-eyed courtiers who whisper, not even behind my back:

"My darling, how do you bear it?"

"Dearest, your eyes are so red! Red! Have you been crying? Understandable, of course. Why, if I were in your place, I would cry my eyes away. But then again, I would never be in your place . . ."

"Let me be a shoulder to cry on in this time of need. You must be so sad, so humiliated, you must feel *so pathetic*."

"Straight to the convent. Straight there. I wouldn't hesitate for a minute. Isn't your great-aunt the abbess at Poissy?"

Charolais hugs me tightly, suffocating me in a field of her loathsome lavender, and whispers: "We always suspected the king did not have the most discriminating taste, but this is beyond anything we might have imagined."

Still I smile and curtsy with grace. For what else can I do?

❧

It is a hot summer morning in July. I have no duties with the queen and I am in a tired, sour mood. Last night I drank too much wine, waiting for the summons from the king that never came, then was unable to sleep for Matignon's dogs that barked the entire night long. I must confess sometimes I find it hard to get out of my robe on the days I am not in service with the queen. Today it's too hot to dress and I can't be bothered to do my hair.

I sit by the window, working on a doormat for my room, a piece of stiff tapestry that I am embroidering with the word *welcome*. I concentrate on the *W*, the difficult curve of the letter as it turns at the top.

"I don't know why you insist on doing that yourself! Why don't you get one of your women to do it, if you really think you need another doormat?" Pauline is sitting at the table, munching on a carrot and leafing through a stack of old *Gazette de France* magazines she has procured from somewhere. "Did you know *too much* rain can be as bad for crops as too little? That doesn't even make sense, does it?"

She's not dressed either; it is too hot to even contemplate putting on a formal gown. Later, in the evening, it will be cooler and we will get dressed. There is a display of fireworks planned this evening for the Spanish delegation's arrival, down by the Grand Canal.

"You know I like needlework; it calms me. Besides, I don't have a doormat. That is why I am making one."

The door flies open without a scratch and it is the king. Oh! How unfortunate, I had thought he was busy all morning with the Spaniards. I quickly stuff a few hairs into my cap and catch a glimpse of myself in the mirror, then wish I hadn't. And the room is a mess, old pastries from yesterday scattered and crumbing all over the side table—Pauline picked out the fruit from all the tarts and left the shells.

"My dear—" The king stops rather awkwardly when he sees me. "You are not with the queen, dearest," he says. "I had not thought to find you here."

"No, I changed my day with Madame de Villars," I say, keeping my voice steady as I realize that he came to see Pauline, not me.

"Well . . ." The king hesitates a fraction, then plunges on: "This good news concerns your family, and in particular your sister."

"Majesty!" Pauline bounds up to him. They embrace cordially, as if they are old friends from childhood, and Pauline leads the king to the table and offers him a chair.

"Pauline, you're not even wearing your robe! You can't greet His Majesty like that!"

"Oh, he doesn't mind," she says, grinning at him, and a look of such intense admiration passes between them that I almost faint.

"No, no, I will not sit. I cannot tarry. The contracts will not wait, but I wanted to come to you the minute it was confirmed." He looks between us but I know he only means Pauline. Suddenly I know what he is going to say next, and my spirit flakes like yesterday's pastries.

"My dear," he says to Pauline, "all is confirmed, our little project. Your husband has been decided—the Comte de Vintimille."

Pauline claps her hands but doesn't hide her grimace.

"Well, I suppose d'Eu was too much to hope for."

"Indeed, but the *comte* is a . . . a . . . well, he is young and of good family. The Italian blood has surely passed out by now. And healthy in many ways, I believe. His great-uncle the archbishop was gracious enough to consent."

"Mmm. Well done!" says Pauline, and the king glows as though he has been praised by Mother Mary herself. They stare at each other, both grinning madly, and I know they are thinking of what it means once she is married.

The dogs upstairs erupt in a cacophony of barks and the spell is broken. Pauline goes back to flicking through her journals and munching on her carrot.

"Isn't that wonderful, Bijou," the king says, turning to me at last. "A year of great marriages, with little Elisabeth next month and then Pauline." He makes no attempt to hide his joy, even though he must surely know the news is not happy for me.

"Well, I must get back to the council. A long day, a disgracefully long day, the Spaniards making last-minute demands that no Frenchman would consider. Might not even make the hunt this afternoon. And, Louise, you must really talk to Matignon about those dogs—this apartment can be unbearable sometimes."

He leaves and we are left alone. Pauline beams at me and I notice, not for the first time, how radiant she is looking. She was outside playing *boules* last week, without a hat, and her slightly darkened skin makes her eyes shine like little emeralds.

"Isn't this wonderful news!"

"Yes," I say quietly. I look down at the *W* I have sketched on the tapestry. Should I embroider the letters all in pink, or trim them with blue?

"You know what this means?"

I think I am going to faint. Instead I start weeping.

Pauline looks puzzled. "Louise, what is the matter? Are you not feeling well? You certainly don't look very well. But why are you crying?" Once started, the tears pour out like rain onto my doormat.

"Oh! But you are not crying because I am to be married?" She is the most hateful person that ever walked this earth. "But it is no secret the king wants me to get married. We all know the king desires me, loves me, I suppose. It's not my fault that he loves me more than you, surely you know that. Stop crying, it's very irritating."

I try as best I can to stifle my sniffles and change the subject to something more pleasant: "The Duchesse de Ruffec has invited us to dine with her tomorrow. Will you come?"

"You should be happy for me, Louise! This is ridiculous. Thank goodness I am going to be married soon and I can leave these rooms. I don't know where Vintimille has his apartment— oh. Perhaps he doesn't have one? But I am sure the king will award him one, as a wedding gift. I shall go and find out right now."

She skips out, humming a little tune to herself. I am left alone with my sorrow and my throbbing head. My only hope is that once he sees her naked he will recognize her for the beast she is, and will return to me.

Oh, despair.

From Pauline de Mailly-Nesle
Château de Versailles
August 10, 1739

D—

A quick note to share my good fortune. I have momentous news: I am to be married! The king has finally found me a husband. His name is Jean something something de Vintimille. He's very young, only nineteen, and has terribly spotty skin. His great-uncle is the Archbishop of Paris—you remember the fat one that married Louise.

The king has arranged it all! He is the most generous of men, and is even helping with the dowry. Oh, D—I wish you could meet him. The king, I mean, not Vintimille.

Once I am married and presented, I shall always be at his side and we will rule France together! I don't think the spies open these letters, but why should it matter if they do—everything I say is true.

Louise is very happy for me—she sends her love. The Court is all abustle with the celebrations for Madame Elisabeth's Spanish marriage. The king is melancholy but it will be good to have one gone at least; they all manage to be frightfully disapproving even though they are hardly more than children.

I enclose a hat of Louise's—you will love the orange feathers. I think she has worn it enough and so I told her it would be best if she gave it to you. Send my love to Madame de Dray. Do you think she would also like a hat? Louise has a rather somber brown one, also with feathers, that I think would suit her well.

After my marriage, I promise I will pester the king for a fine husband for you—no less than a duke!

Love,
P

Pauline

I can't say anything, for the first time in my life. I can't breathe either, though I have no stays holding me in. I am naked and staring at Louis, and he is staring at me.

"You cannot know," he says, leaning in to kiss me, down there, "what a pleasure this is for me." He tugs gently at my hair with his teeth while he presses his hand against himself. I don't know what to do. I shiver and look at the ceiling. This uncertainty is new for me. There *are* things I don't know in this world.

He motions me down to unbutton his breeches and I look at his cock in amazement. All of Madame de Dray's stories could not possibly have prepared me for this moment. Now, in my hand I hold it, the source of all mystery and vitality, stiff and harsh as wood. Impulsively I lean in to kiss it.

Louis gasps in delight then we fall back on the bed and he pushes into me. The pain is nothing, not even to be considered. Once he is inside, my hands instinctively find his back and I feel my hips move to meet his. Yes. Yes. Someone from above, perhaps my mother, I think as I stare up at the ceiling, motions me onward and tells my body exactly what it needs to do. I pull him farther in, because it is France inside me, my future inside me.

When it is over, Louis shakes his head and wipes his brow.

"You, my dear, are like no virgin I have ever had the pleasure of parting. We are not disappointed."

But more importantly, now that I am officially the Comtesse

de Vintimille (after a cordial handshake Louis replaced my husband in the nuptial chambers; how scandalous!), I shall be properly presented at Court. As part of the marriage settlement, Louis gave one hundred thousand *livres* in addition to my paltry dowry, and I am assured of a place in the new *dauphine*'s service. The talk is of a marriage in three or four years; may they take their time. I want to enjoy life and am in no hurry to attend to a Spanish infant.

And I am to have my own apartment. It is the old apartment of the Duc de Bourbon, once a lover of my mother's and the prime minister until he was dismissed by Fleury the year after Louis's marriage. The apartment has four rooms, all large and well appointed, one of them a delightful salon with three windows overlooking the Court of Honor. It will do for now. At the time it was whispered my mother aimed very high, taking as her lover the Duc de Bourbon, then the prime minister of France. But look at me, aiming even higher! I think she would be proud of me.

When I am made duchess I shall need a much larger apartment, no fewer than eight rooms and with my own kitchen and chef. But for now four rooms will do nicely. They are situated in the part of Versailles known as Noailles Alley for the proliferation of Noailles hereabouts; that family breeds like rabbits. The late duke had twenty children. *Twenty.* Who knows, perhaps one day it will be known as the Avenue of the Vintimilles? Though I am not planning on having twenty children; I want at most four of my own. Including at least two sons, who will take after their father.

My young husband is very naive and seems to be the only one who is not aware of how things work in this world. One of my women has just finished cleaning a giant mirror that lies between the windows in the salon, wiping away the dust and grime of the previous occupants. I am admiring myself in it when Vintimille comes and stands awkwardly next to me. We look at each other in the mirror.

"Do not be afraid," he says stiffly, putting a hand on my chest.

He gulps. "I will be gentle." The woman grabs her rags and scuttles into the next room.

"Oh, get off me, you pimply virgin."

"You are my wife," he says, his Adam's apple bobbing in distress. He tightens his grip on my breast. The boy looks like he had the most terrific case of smallpox, but apparently they are just adolescent pimples. Disgusting.

"Don't be a fool." I unclench his hand from my breast and push him away. "Did your uncle not explain anything to you? You know about His Majesty and me, I assume?"

"You are my wife," he repeats nervously, backing away.

I advance forward. "Since you appear to be lacking in any knowledge about the finer points of life, let me explain them to you: Your great-uncle the archbishop continues in favor with the king. You yourself are one hundred thousand *livres* richer and have the right to hunt with the king *whenever you want*, which, by the way, I think is excessive and was not an honor I supported. In return, my little boy, you are to leave me completely alone. Completely. Don't ever presume to touch me. In fact, I would recommend you find yourself alternate accommodation, perhaps in town. These rooms are not big enough for the both of us."

Really, children can be *so* tiresome.

I turn back to the mirror and call my woman back—the bottom is still streaked.

⁀

Louise has been so mopey recently, positively in despair, I would say. I need her red goose eyes and mournful misery gone from this place. She affects my mood, as well as Louis's. He hates unpleasantness, and much as she tries to hide it, she is simply unpleasant. I'm thinking Poissy—our great-aunt is abbess there and the country air and days of devotion will calm Louise's spirits.

But for now, more important concerns: a deep silver dress with panniers two feet wide, pale webbed lemon lace and trim, the skirt pulled back to show a patterned gold petticoat. Soft, scandalous white stockings and a pair of specially made shoes, wide enough for my feet and even, if I may be so bold, quite comfortable. A pair of brilliant emerald earrings—a gift from him, of course—and my hair piled as high as fashion will allow, which unfortunately is not very high. Two beauty spots, both on my left cheek, and a fair amount of white powder and rouge for my face. Liberal amounts of my favorite perfume, a special blend of sweet pea dashed with carnation.

That is what I will wear for my presentation. Though I may have scoffed at them before, now I understand that clothes signal many things, including power.

I must remember to write to Diane with the details.

From Françoise de la Porte-Mazarin
Château de Versailles
September 30, 1739

My Dear Niece Marie-Anne,

I hope you are well in Burgundy. I bring you sad tidings from Court. I cannot entrust Hortense to relay this news, and besides, she knows not all the details. Your sister Pauline was married last week to the Comte de Vintimille—a man with far too much Italian blood and whose great-uncle the archbishop is a well-known lecher. It is not a marriage your sainted mother would have been proud of and it appears now that it was a complete sham—the king replaced the bridegroom in the nuptial chambers on the wedding night!

The scandal here has consumed all of us and burns the paper I write this on. Two sisters. It is bestial and base and beyond belief. They are fortunate the pope does not excommunicate them; the scandal is enough to make your father turn in his grave, were he dead. I can only be thankful that you are far from this soup pot of sin and remain pure and chaste in Burgundy.

Fortunately, Hortense is soon to be married—I trust she has already written you the news—and then I will thank my stars that you will both be safe and secure.

I command you to swear on the Bible, in front of your confessor, that you will never follow in your adulterous sisters' footsteps. I will write to him to that effect, and I insist you comply with my wishes.

In sainted judgment,
Your Tante Mazarin

From Hortense de Mailly-Nesle
Hôtel de Mazarin, Paris
October 23, 1739

Dearest Louise,

Greetings from Paris, my sister. I am in the most delirious of spirits, for Tante Mazarin has arranged a marriage for me! I wanted to write you myself, as I know that sometimes Tante overlooks to share important news with you.

His name is François-Marie de Fouilleuse and he is the Marquis de Flavacourt. The wedding will take place in January of next year! So soon!

I do hope that Marie-Anne will travel from Burgundy for the celebration. You know I would wish for you to be with me on the wonderful day, but Tante is firm that your duties at Court will prevent such a happy occurrence.

So many weddings: Pauline, and now me! Of course, my wedding will not be the scandal that Pauline's was, and I am determined to remain faithful to François.

All my love,
Hortense

From Louise de Mailly
Château de Versailles
November 12, 1739

Dearest Hortense,

My darling sister, how wonderful your news is! The Flavacourts are an old family and your new husband is very well respected for his military devotion. Unfortunately, Tante Mazarin is correct; my duties with the queen will prevent me from attending the wedding, but you will be in my thoughts and prayers.

Life is wonderful here at Court. Pauline is of course now married; her husband is youthful but he will be a good influence on her and his unfortunate skin condition seems to be improving since the wedding. I am sure that they will be very happy together and that Pauline will be a good wife to him. Now that she is married she has been officially presented: the queen was simply enchanted by her.

She charms everyone. I suppose I should not be surprised: Do you remember how spirited she was in the schoolroom, always chasing us in fun and teasing us with those little spiders? Her wit has captivated everyone. Even His Majesty. They are good friends now and it is one of my greatest pleasures to spend an evening with them, just the three of us. How wonderful it is to have family so close!

I enclose a large piece of silver gauze that was part of my wedding dress—perhaps it can be used on your gown? Think—when we next write, we shall write as married women. If Marie-Anne travels from Burgundy for your wedding, please send her my love. We must not forget her, even though she is so far away. It has been too long that we are all apart.

All the best for the New Year. 1740—how modern it sounds! May it be a good year, and a good decade, for all of us.

All my love,
Louise

Marie-Anne

BURGUNDY AND PARIS

January 1740

My hairy sister, Pauline, is married and is now the Comtesse de Vintimille! But even more shockingly, they say the king replaced her husband on the wedding night. My first thought is that the poor adolescent *comte*, her husband, was probably more relieved than anything. But my second thought was: How on earth did Pauline manage to seduce the king?

Now I hear she is presented at Court and never leaves the king's side. They even whisper that the king does not wear a coat without Pauline's permission, or request a meat for the menu unless she approves. It seems she has replaced Louise completely in the king's affections, and that her marriage was just for convention.

I am simply dumbfounded by everything. Pauline? Pauline is just about the ugliest thing possible. Tante used to say that my mother must have mated with an ape instead of our father to produce her. Or a Hungarian, I can't remember which. And Pauline with the king? This is even more of a shock than Louise was. It is most definitely treasonous to even think this, but: Is there something wrong with the king?

Ironically, I had finally started to consider the idea of going to Court. Burgundy is all well and fine, but really, it is time to see new horizons. JB has little interest in foreign affairs and refuses to angle for a position abroad, so Versailles it must be. But now that Pauline is there . . . Well. I think it best I stay out of her way—

the schoolroom or Versailles, it's all the same. I still remember her marshaling the toys and locking them in the cupboard, and her contorted face when I exacted my revenge.

I was a revolutionary when I was young and I was able to defy her, but one can't be a revolutionary at Versailles. Pauline always had the makings of a tyrant and now she is one of the most powerful women in France, while I am stuck in this backwater surrounded by pigeons and pigs, where nothing changes from year to year. This is unfair and unexpected.

Most unfair.

&

In the heart of the January cold I travel to Paris for Hortense's marriage. I move back into my old room at Tante Mazarin's and in some awful way feel as though I have never left.

I don't know much about Hortense's husband, the Marquis de Flavacourt. Hortense is moony-eyed in love and describes him as a paragon of kindness, humility, and courage. From others, I have heard that he is a rough military man and has forbidden Hortense from going to Court. He tells all and sundry that she is the most beautiful woman in France, and given the king's predilection for Nesle blood, he avows he has much to fear. He declares he will kill her, and the king, if he so much as touches her. A stupid thing to say, and more than a little treasonous. If those words are any indication of his character, then I am afraid he is a blustering blowhard.

The day before the wedding, as Tante and the Flavacourts, along with their lawyers and the archbishop, are finalizing the marriage details, my sister Diane comes to visit. Diane left the convent a few months ago and is now living with the Dowager Duchesse de Lesdiguières, an elderly aunt and distant relation.

We leave the elders to their negotiations in the grand salon and drift upstairs to a smaller, cozier room that Hortense has claimed as her own. It is the first time in many years that we are three sisters together, and we hug and exclaim at how little we have changed. It is true; Hortense is as beautiful as ever, her porcelain skin delicately flushed with the excitement of the occasion. Diane is still the same, though perhaps a little fatter than I remember. The food is probably better at Madame de Lesdiguières than at the convent, I remark, and she nods vigorously and launches into a long description of the pies the cook bakes, especially for her.

Well. We look at each other eagerly and expectantly, not sure where to start. There is only one thing I want to talk about, but it must wait. Hortense pours us all a cup of chocolate and passes around a plate of buns with blueberry cream filling.

"Sisters, this is the first time we three have been together since our days in the nursery!" says Hortense softly, and she looks as though she is about to cry. She is very weepy and emotional these days; she says it is her impending marriage.

"Do you remember," says Diane, "how we used to sit around the table like this and feed our Noah's Ark? Remember the fruit-cake that Cook would make, if we pleaded well with her?"

"And we would pick out the currants to feed the animals!"

"They liked the orange peel the best," says Hortense in delight, remembering our childish folly. "I used to worry about feeding them the raisins, do you remember how they made Pauline's throat tickle and what if they did the same to the lions?"

"And the cats!" exclaims Diane. "The real ones, not the wooden ones—do you remember Loulou and Poupou? How we used to swaddle their kittens?"

"Oh, and, Marie-Anne, remember how you used to rescue the mice and keep them in a little box, warm and cozy by the fire, away from the cats?"

I make a noncommittal gesture—they have obviously forgotten my little experiments.

"Marie-Anne," says Hortense kindly, motioning to the maid to take the pot of chocolate and warm it, "you are not sharing in our reminiscing."

I shrug. "I was so young, only twelve when we left."

"Old enough for memories, sister! Do you remember when we all slept together in the same bed, the night of the nursery fire?"

Instead I say: "I think we should talk about them."

There is a little silence and Diane giggles nervously. From downstairs we can hear Tante haranguing someone, a lawyer perhaps, and it makes me smile to remember her dealings with JB's mother before my marriage. She is like a wolf protecting her cubs; I suppose we are lucky to have her. But I'm surprised there is any bone of contention with so little at stake—you could sneeze away Hortense's dowry of 7,500 *livres* on two horses and a banquet for twenty.

"Them?" inquires Hortense politely, pursing her lips and examining her bun.

"Pauline and Louise," I say baldly. "You know, our elder sisters. And the king's mistresses." Hortense looks distressed. Diane giggles again.

"Oops, I shouldn't giggle. It's all so scandalous. The priest says it is . . . *incest*. Oh, that is a horrid word. Like pest or insect." Diane lowers her voice, in case Tante is around. I shiver. It seems wrong to even say that word here, in the sacred house of Mazarin.

Then Diane giggles again, thinking of something else. "You know they are saying our family motto is very apt."

"'*Frappe qui voudra*'—'Knock who will'?"

"They say the king is definitely knocking at the Nesle door."

I laugh with delight; there is a depth to the gossip here that is impossible to obtain in Burgundy. I am enjoying this. Hortense buries her head in her hands and wails. "Oh, I am lucky my husband loves me or else he would never have consented to marry me."

"How do they explain the attraction of the king for Pauline?" I ask Diane, but she only looks puzzled. I remember that Diane always worshipped Pauline, who could do no wrong in her eyes. Instead I scold her: "Really, Diane, your penmanship must improve! I would love to hear more news from you. This gossip is simply delicious and the whole situation . . . incest or not . . . it's certainly interesting."

"Tush," says Hortense. "If Tante were to hear you . . ."

"And then what?" I demand. "You'll understand soon enough—

by tomorrow you will be a married woman, not a young maiden under her care." This is not entirely true: Hortense will continue to live here, as Flavacourt has no suitable house in town and she prefers to stay in Paris over his estate in Picardy.

"You must come and visit me in Burgundy," I say, but Hortense only grimaces.

"Three days in a carriage, or more because of these dreadful winters? Thank you but no—I would have vomited half my body weight by the time I got there. Oh, I'm sorry, that was rather a crude thing to say. Please forgive me. Jeanne, bring the pot, I would have another cup."

"Do you hear from her?" I ask Diane. "Does Pauline ever write?"

Diane licks out an enormous amount of blue cream and starts to speak with her mouth full. "I have letters occasionally from Pauline, but I am sure she is very busy, and you know Pauline hates writing, I mean, except when she wants something, she sent soooo many letters to Louise begging to be invited to Court . . ." She trails off and looks a bit awkward.

"Louise sometimes writes to me," says Hortense rather wistfully. "She appears cheerful but she must be very sad."

"Oh, no," says Diane, "Pauline writes that Louise is very happy these days."

Hortense and I look at each other and I know we are both thinking that it's not only Diane's body that is as thick as a tree. I see a surprising amount of compassion in Hortense's eyes.

Diane brightens up. "I have letters from Louise occasionally. She tells me all about the fashions at Court." She gets up to twirl around and show us the gown she will wear for the wedding tomorrow. "Apparently stripes are all the rage now—do you like my underskirt?" Diane has sewn three rather crooked strips of pink silk across her white petticoat. "And isn't the color divine—like a juicy ham."

"Oh, yes," says Hortense dutifully. Diane twirls once more in satisfaction and her skirt clips a spindly-legged table. Hortense's cup falls off and shatters on the floor. "Oops. Whoops. Madame Lesdig always says I am as clumsy as an ox."

When the mess has been cleared away and she has sat down again, I pursue the issue: "Do they ever . . . does Louise ever write about Pauline?"

Diane considers. "Not really. She just said that the king adores her, but then again who wouldn't adore Pauline? She is so funny and so nice"—sometimes I think we are talking of different people—"well, I know, Marie-Anne, you never got on well with her, but she *is* very nice. I think if you met as adults you would really like her. I really loved her, I mean I do love her, and so does Louise, so I am sure that she is happy that Pauline is much in the king's favor."

"Is it true what they say, that the king won't piss without Pauline's permission?"

Hortense tuts in disapproval.

"Oh, that I wouldn't know. But I am sure the king does listen to her, she is so very smart. If I were the king I would listen to her, you know . . ."

Diane drones on. I half listen, thinking of the strange situation we five sisters find ourselves in. Three here in Paris, two at Versailles. And those two! It would have been interesting if they could have come to Paris for the wedding, but neither is making the journey. A real reunion . . . it is hard to picture, though it would certainly be amusing. I perk up when Diane says something interesting:

"Pauline says she is going to find a duke for me to marry."

"Oh, sister, but that is wonderful news!" exclaims Hortense. "Then we will all be married! How proud our mother would be."

I smile as well, but inside vinegar curls my stomach and pickles my heart. Diane, a duchess? Here are Hortense and I, with our middling provincial marquis, and, on the other side of the chasm of luck and fortune, sit Louise and Pauline, intimate with the King of France and powerful (well, Pauline at least). And now Diane to marry a duke.

This will not sound very sororal, but Zélie is a million miles away—dead in fact—and I believe it to be the truth: if faces are fortunes, as they usually are, then my elder sisters would not have been pinned for success. By all natural rights, Hortense and I should be the ones enjoying the glory, for we are the most beautiful, far more so than plain Louise, ugly Pauline, or fat Diane. Instead . . . well, it is as if the world is upside down.

I'm not sure even Aesop could explain this strange situation.

From Hortense de Fouilleuse, Marquise de Flavacourt
Hôtel de Mazarin, Paris
February 1, 1740

Darling Marie-Anne,

I write to you from Paris and a place of happiness. Isn't married life wonderful? God could not have sent me a better husband than Flavacourt. My only sorrow is that after the wedding he was too soon recalled to his regiment, and I have only seen him for a scattering of days since.

But oh! What days. What bliss. What . . . Oh, Marie-Anne, I wish you were here and we could talk, face-to-face. There is a limit to what I can write, and though I hold you no grudge for not informing me before of the joys of married life—I understand that such topics are not appropriate when one is a maiden—how I would like to talk about them with you now! About men and the joy of marriage duties. But alas, such talk must wait until we meet again.

I trust Jean-Baptiste is well and that you will see more of him this year than last. What tribulations we women suffer when our men are not at home!

I send you this fan from Madame de Germond's shop—I remember you admiring mine at the wedding and I thought you might like one for yourself. See the rural landscape—perhaps Burgundy is like that, with cows and such? It is rather elegant, perhaps too elegant for Burgundy, but I know you will look lovely with it.

With much love,
Hortense

From Marie-Anne de la Tournelle
Château de la Tournelle, Burgundy
February 26, 1740

Dear Hortense,

Greetings from Burgundy. I am very pleased that you are enjoying married life.

Unfortunately I have no plans to travel to Paris again so soon, so we will not be able to enjoy the conversation you so desire. Please forgive me if I have interpreted your letter wrongly, but if you are curious, I am sending you a book you might enjoy. I found it in the library here—for some reason it was classed amongst the botany books, but it has nothing to do with plants. It is written in a strange text, from India I believe, but the pictures are really all that is important—they are quite instructive.

I have bound it with a velvet cloth; please keep it covered unless you are alone. I think Tante would be highly shocked if such a book were found under her roof. Also, I suggest you do not share it with Flavacourt—even though he may enjoy the fruits of your reading, many men are prudish when it comes to their wives and he might not like to think of you learning such things.

Take good care of the book. If you do not wish to read it, please put it in the chest under the bed in my old chamber and I will retrieve it when I am next in Paris.

Life continues on here as usual; coming back from Paris was quite an adjustment! But spring is just around the corner and the hothouse did not suffer in my absence. My Garnier is a very talented man, in many ways. I enclose a box of vanilla beans—your cook will know what to do with them.

Love,
Marie-Anne

Diane

After Pauline left for Versailles, I received several invitations from relatives offering me their home and hospitality. It's a pity that they couldn't have invited us before: Pauline hated the convent so! I didn't mind the convent, but without Pauline I was quite lonely and so I gladly accepted the Dowager Duchesse de Lesdiguières' invitation to come and live with her.

Madame Lesdig (as I call her) is frightfully old, almost sixty, an aunt of dear Mama's, and a great friend of Tante's. She has a large mole on her chin that looks like a beauty spot, except beauty spots don't have hair.

Madame Lesdig lives in the grand old-fashioned style and constantly compares her current house unfavorably to the palace she lived in when her husband was alive. He died thirty-seven years ago; I hope she hasn't been complaining for thirty-seven years. There are always two footmen walking behind her now, but she told me that when her husband was alive he never left the house without at least sixty of them. Sixty footmen! Imagine that. How did they all fit on the carriage?

The house she lives in now is old and dark, on a road not far from our childhood home on the Quai des Théatins. Madame Lesdig swears that ghosts haunt the stairs and she has two women who sit with her through the night, never sleeping, but keeping an eye out for apparitions. I don't believe in ghosts, I don't think, but to be safe I unpacked a crucifix from the convent and sleep with it in my bed at night. I try to make my woman, Touffe, whom Madame Lesdig has assigned to me, stay awake all night but she refuses. She says if she doesn't sleep during the night then she won't be able to work during the day.

Because of the duchess's grand past, the house is positively stuffed with furniture and vases and candelabras and chairs and statues—some of them naked—and many other strange objects, all of them far too big for the cramped rooms. I avoid the room with the fierce tiger-headed rug, but every time I turn around it seems I knock over a vase from China or a statue from Siam or a giant crystal candelabra balancing precariously on the hand of a bronze nymph. Madame Lesdig sighs and says I must aspire to move elegantly at all times, to be more like a swan than a bullock.

"If I were younger," she says, "I would mind terribly all this clumsy destruction of my pieces of art." She calls them art but truly they are just vases and candlesticks. "But I am old enough to know that things that don't live are usually replaceable."

Madame Lesdig no longer travels much, but there are many visitors to the house and I am often invited to sit with her when she greets her guests. I may also come and go as I please, as long as I am with Touffe or a footman. The house is just over the river from the gardens at the Tuileries and some days I walk there. My childhood home is also very close, just by the river, and once I walked there. It looked the same; I don't know who lives there now.

Sometimes I visit the convent, and Madame de Dray and the other ladies keep me updated on the gossip while I share with them all I learn at Madame Lesdig's. The drops—oh, I shouldn't say that, that's what Pauline always used to call them—greet me and shriek when they learn I did not leave to be married. And me already twenty-six!

At first the food at Madame Lesdig's was not very good; the duchess has lost most of her teeth and prefers soups and mashed chestnuts for her dinner. She says I should follow her diet, for I am, as she terms it, "grossly fat." "Strive to be more like an eel and less like a whale," she says. After I dine with the duchess I go down to the kitchens for my second dinner. The cook is very kind and makes a delicious pigeon pie with sorrel, and if I ask nicely he will even bake me a sugar tart sprinkled with ginger, my favorite, and just for me.

The best thing about Madame Lesdig's house is the cats; there are dozens of them and there are always adorable kittens of every size to be cuddled and played with. The cats roam the house with impunity and trip up the footmen in the darkly lit rooms. I am certain the footmen break more vases and mirrors than I do.

"You see," Madame Lesdig instructs me wearily, "how elegant and spry they are? You must strive to be more like a cat, Diane-Adelaide, and less like an ox." She sighs. "That was from India."

"Yes, Aunt," I say, and she motions to one of the footmen to pick up the pieces. It was once a delicate ostrich egg, carved to allow a candle to sit inside. Now it's just a pile of shell.

From Pauline de Vintimille
Château de Versailles
March 20, 1740

D—

I know it has been a long time, but I have been frightfully busy. Today the king is engaged with an enormous delegation of vintners and economists—this wicked, never-ending winter has killed all the vines and wine may be in short supply this summer—so I have some time free. I shall write you a lovely long letter.

I am glad you like living at Madame de Lesdiguières, though I am sure you will miss Madame de Dray and some of the other ladies at the convent. Did Mother Superior say anything cruel to you on your last day, as she did to me? Probably not; she always liked you.

I am sorry that Madame de Lesdig—as you call her—has hurt her . . . herself. I am not sure from your penmanship whether it was her foot or her tooth that was hurt. Either way, I hope it is better.

Did you attend Hortense's wedding? I heard Flavacourt is a blustering fool who has been saying treasonous things. He shouldn't worry; the king is not interested in Hortense because he is only interested in me! Now that I am married, the king and I have become closer. Much closer. Ask Madame de Dray what I mean. It is wonderful and very exciting—men are such strange creatures. You will understand when you are married. I think he loves me, a thought that fills me with a strange elation I can't well describe. I like him too, well enough. Goodness, I hope the spies don't open these letters.

My husband was quite annoying at first, I think he actually expected me to act as a wife to him. What a pimply-faced fool! But he cannot complain; now he is allowed to ride in the same carriage as the king when they depart on the hunt.

So, I promised I would share with you the details of my presentation dress—I am sorry it has taken me so long to respond. The king and I have been busy at Choisy—he tells me he is renovating the palace just for me! Imagine that—a palace as a gift! It—and I—will be famous throughout Europe. I will insist that one of the bedrooms be decorated in yellow, your favorite color, and it will be where you will stay when you come to visit.

So, my presentation. My dress was of silver satin with pale lemon lace everywhere, six layers at the sleeves! The panniers were dreadfully wide but necessary, the dressmaker told me, to make the right impression. It was very hard to get through the doors of the smaller rooms—I had to walk sideways like a crab. Very annoying. I insisted the hairdresser—Charolais lent me hers—dress my hair high. He refused, saying he was only able to work with modern styles, but I insisted and so he piled my hair a few inches high, and dressed it with ribbons of the same lemon lace. So then I was both tall and wide! And long—my train went on forever. I felt very triumphant and it was wonderful.

The queen was not very happy to meet me, though she was not rude of course. She's rather inconsequential, I think; my presentation was the first time she spoke to me and it may be the last, though I don't care. Thank goodness I am not in her service, as Louise is! Hmm, I don't think the spies read these letters. But I am not saying anything that everyone doesn't already know.

I had my dressmaker remove the yellow lace from my dress and I enclose it for you; I know you will like it. I am also thinking of saving my presentation dress for you—for your wedding. Now that mine is over, it's time to start planning yours.

I promise.

Our sister Louise is well, as always, and is delighted with my marriage and my prospects. For a while she was thinking of retiring to the convent at Poissy but it now seems she has changed her mind and prefers to stay at Court.

Love,

P

Louise

VERSAILLES
April 1740

Zélie used to say the only thing more tiresome than a woman with a tongue is a woman with a tongue who repeats herself. Or something like that. Though it has been more than a year since Pauline came to Court and everything went wrong, the hurt and the despair do not subside. I try to be pleasant and accepting with Pauline. I keep my same smile and light conversation and the care of my toilette as I always did, but inside, my heart is simply breaking. And I do not think there is anything in this world that can piece it back together again.

At the end of the New Year's festivities, especially lavish this year to usher in the new decade, Louis gave a small dinner in his most private chambers and after much teasing presented Pauline with a beautiful gilded oil box. My own gift to him—a pair of candlesticks of the finest Saxony porcelain, decorated with his favorite scenes of the hunt—received only a perfunctory nod. He didn't give the queen a New Year's gift, nor any of his children. And certainly not me. I know Fleury has been urging economies on him recently—and with the continuing famine there is a need to cut expenses—but surely he didn't mean to include New Year's gifts?

Pauline is the only one who received anything. I know I must begrudge him nothing, but the look of pride in his eyes as Pauline accepted her present . . . Something inside me died. I must give up my fantasies of his return to me and accept that as long as Pauline lives, there can be no true reconciliation.

I can only seek what comfort I can in his presence: his occasional tendernesses; the time when he was ill with a fever and declared that only I should nurse him. For three blissful days I tended him and fixed a special broth of turnips recommended by the doctor. He drank it gratefully and declared it prepared by the hands of love. He wanted none but me by his bedside; he understood that Pauline would be useless.

But what can I do—wish continued sickness upon my beloved so that I may be his nurse? No, I cannot do that.

Recently Pauline has been less cold to me, less demanding. I believe she likes me at her side, as a confidante and foil. As I once wanted her to be mine! Oh, how very ironic, how very *unfair*. How I wish I had never invited her. What did I do to deserve a sister like Pauline?

The king is often at his new palace of Choisy with her. There is much work to be done there—improving and redecorating—and he is enthusiastically overseeing all of it. *They* are enthusiastically overseeing it; Louis declares it will be his gift to Pauline and that when they are finished it will be the most beautiful palace in Europe.

He never gave me a palace.

I have been to Choisy a few times and Louis is very energetic there, like a young boy with a newfound passion. He spends hours with the architects and works with the carpenters on their drawings, making changes here, suggesting other designs. The Court buzzes with the news that he has even taken up cooking. Apparently last week he made a delicious soup from the mushrooms he and the courtiers had spent an afternoon gathering from the forest. Gathering mushrooms! Like peasants! Tales of these scenes of easy domesticity burn my ears and deepen my despair—how was I to know that Louis wanted to be like a peasant?

Oh, despair.

I cannot endure this life, I simply cannot.

From Louise de Mailly
Château de Versailles
A dark day, 1740

Dearest Mother,

How are you, dear Mama? Are you happy where you are? I miss
you so much, Mama, I remember when we would come down from the
nursery to your wonderful golden chamber, and you would lie with us
on the bed and hold us and feed us candies. How I long to feel your
arms around me again!

I am so alone, I turned to Pauline when I needed guidance, I had
hoped she would help me but she did not. She did not. She is . . . well, I
cannot write what I think of her, for though she has done me a hateful
service, she is still your daughter. And my sister.

Oh, Mama, how I wish you were here to guide me. Do you
remember how you hugged me the day of my wedding? You said you
would always be there for me, but then you died.

Though it is wicked to think such thoughts, and even more wicked
to write them, sometimes I envy you, for you are in a far better place
and all the grief and the sorrow of this cruel world are behind you. You
are at peace, a state so rare here on earth.

I know it is foolish of me to write this letter but I am so alone. I
have no one to turn to and sometimes my despair threatens me with
such dark thoughts. I do not wish to have them, but I cannot stop
them no matter how I pray. Perhaps we shall meet sooner than later in
the greatest of God's gardens?

I will burn this letter now.

I will love you forever.

Your faithful daughter,
Louise

Pauline

I am beginning to understand that Louis is a weak man. On his seventeenth birthday, the last king, Louis XIV, stood calmly before his ministers and told them that the time of his youth and tutelage had passed, and that now he was in charge. There is little likelihood of my Louis doing that, and besides, the moment has passed: what would have been exemplary in a seventeen-year-old would only be embarrassing in one already thirty.

His ministers still treat him as a child, and Cardinal Fleury, whose influence is continuing and absolute, has, I believe, squashed any independent spirit Louis might have grown. I cannot bear to see the king clinging to his leading strings. If Louis is ever to become a king in more than name, he needs to be out from under the cardinal's domineering thumb.

I decide that the king's new palace at Choisy is the perfect place for him to grow into his own man, one who will listen to me and not to that ancient piece of decrepitude.

The château is partially in ruins, for the old Princesse de Conti did not take care of the place as she should have. Regardless, the location, overlooking the banks of the Seine, is divine, and in spring and summer a brisk breeze comes up from the river and rolls through the rooms. Together we plan the additions and the interior decorations, and for the first time Louis supervises the work directly. At Choisy, Louis can be a man and not a king.

Here, when we are in bed together he is more ardent, as though he left some restraint in his nature behind at Versailles. At Choisy he can go twice a night; on one occasion it was thrice.

Choisy is no more than a few hours from Versailles, but when we are here we shed our skins and bar the door against Madame Etiquette and live simply as though the fate of France were not on our shoulders. Here we are more relaxed than even at Rambouillet. We are not alone, of course; Louis hates solitude, and so there must always be a group of courtiers buzzing around us, like flies on meat.

Even Louise comes with us sometimes.

We women leave off our panniers and float through the halls with drooping, flowing skirts. The men hunt all day and in the evening we have suppers with the food from the hunt and the garden, and even do some of the cooking! At midnight we glide on the river in gondolas bedecked with lanterns, sliding through the water as though we are in another world. The old stuffies back at Versailles tut and hiss and say Choisy undermines the majesty of His Majesty, for who wants a king who acts like a peasant and disregards the sacred etiquette? But it is a testament to my growing influence that Louis ignores all they say.

Louis loves landscaping and gardening even above building. He is planning an elaborate maze and has rediscovered a long-lost passion for growing vegetables: when he was a child Fleury gave him a small garden where he grew lettuces. Now with an exacting eye he oversees the gardens, not just the ornamental ones but the kitchen gardens as well. He ensures the rows are well weeded, the vegetables perfectly planted and tended with water, but also with milk and chicken blood.

Louis still prefers lettuces over all other vegetables. I notice that he likes vegetables that have many layers to peel: sprouts, cabbages, and onions. It is a curious turn of his personality and perhaps harkens to his secretive nature. I couldn't be less interested in gardening myself, but I feign an interest and even get my gloves dirty. Once a *worm* fell on my hand. I crushed it before

Louis could save it—he is remarkably sentimental when it comes to garden bugs.

Every day after Mass but before he leaves for the hunt, we stroll to the gardens and follow the progress of his beloved lettuces as though we were following the growth of the *dauphin* himself (the boy turns eleven this year and, as the only surviving son in a field of daughters, he is even more precious than a lettuce). When the lettuces are ready to harvest, they are carefully picked by Louis and served at dinner with great pomp and ceremony. The guests strive to outdo themselves in praising the freshness, the crispness, the élan of the leaves. It all gets a bit ridiculous.

As satire, I compose a verse comparing His Majesty's lettuce to the sun:

> *Golden orb of green*
> *Covered with layers of Light*
> *Such succulence grown*
> *By the hand of Might*

In private I coax Louis to laugh and see the absurdity of my words; no small feat for a man who has been flattered from birth and who thinks sycophancy is simply normal speech. We agree that when the next "golden orb" is harvested, we will goad our guests to laud the lettuce in verse, and give a prize to the one who composes the most outlandish praise. Seeing the courtiers become ridiculous without realizing they are ridiculous, now that is a delicious thing.

The prize is won by the Duc de Richelieu, a companion of the king's youth and recently returned from Vienna. He is an astonishingly accomplished man, so it was no surprise that his ode comparing the leaves of the lettuce to the cloak offered to Venus, set with a musical score and accompanied by two violinists, won. I think he's in on the joke but you never can tell with that man. He sees everything, almost as much as I do.

❧

Louis is absolutely and completely infatuated with me and his adoration does not diminish with the passing of time. I must confess his ardor makes me occasionally uncomfortable and he can be irritating—just a touch. When I am not in a good humor, I am not always as pleasant and soft as he would desire.

But perhaps that is part of my success: you can never give a man, even a king, everything he wants. If you do he will only grow complacent and I am determined that Louis *never* grow complacent. I am always on my guard, for love is a tenuous thing and can easily be uprooted, like a turnip too easily pulled from the ground.

Initially I had thought to banish Louise, but now I see my sister is no threat at all. I never cease to find it strange that we should be linked by blood yet so vastly different. She is mostly a ghost in our lives but having her around does have advantages. She serves a purpose when Saint Maurice, as they say, makes his visit. And everyone knows that men like variety in all things. Men will eat *anything* when they are hungry.

Of all that surround me, I believe I trust Louise the most. I am a general and she is my aide-de-camp, if you will. She is a good listener and I can always depend on her to be there with her big sad goose eyes and her hangdog face, looking for a kick or a treat. She's so good that if she tried to stab someone in the back, she'd probably just curtsy and hand them the knife.

And it's nice to have at least one friend. I can't say I've made too many others. And there is no end of those who assume that I am too ugly to last, or that I have not enough charm to last.

People *always* underestimate me.

Charolais, with her lisping baby talk and her powdered lilac hair, is plotting against me at this very moment. She's getting older and starting to look like a lavender-colored clown. The king is old friends with her from childhood but I don't like the closeness between them. I think I shall wean him from her. I'll leave the Comtesse de Toulouse alone; Louis needs some mothering and he certainly won't get it from me.

As time passes Cardinal Fleury makes no effort to hide his disapproval of me, and I return the favor. The cardinal is about two hundred years old, but he still has the mind of a much younger man. Ageless and with many, many decades of experience, he is a cunning and formidable opponent. He likes control in all things and it was he who chose Louise to be the king's mistress. I must concede his strategy was perfectly correct: Louise was a very malleable mistress who never meddled in politics.

With me, Fleury very quickly realized that though Louise and I are sisters, we are in fact as different as peas and pears. He had no hand in the king's choice of me; right there, we started off on the wrong foot. I do believe he would have wished me to seek his benediction before I even spoke to the king! The idea is preposterous.

So we are enemies, but I have youth, and time, and charms that he has not when it comes to influencing the king. And surely the old man must die soon?

I am not the only one waiting on his death. His grip on power has been absolute since the king was twelve, far too long for one man, and an especially long time for a man who never played the patronage game. There is a whole generation of capable men and ministers waiting impatiently in the wings, eager for more power and riches.

Despite Fleury's continued presence, my influence with Louis is growing and recently he even made a few decisions without the benediction of the cardinal. Last month I was able to secure the appointment of a friend, Monsieur de Breteuil, to the Ministry of War. Directly in the face of Fleury's wishes.

Others are starting to notice my waxing and Fleury's waning moon. Surprisingly, Maurepas, Tante's son-in-law and a very powerful minister, has openly declared his support for me. He shares Tante's dislike of Louise and, combined with his animus for Fleury, it seems he can forget that I sneezed on his mother-in-law.

But still—things would progress much faster if Fleury were removed. Until he leaves, Louis will never be free to be the king I know he can be.

Richelieu is not an ally—what need do I have of allies?—but I know he understands my concerns. I happen upon him one morning in the Hall of Mirrors, surrounded by a clutch of lesser courtiers. The Marquis de Meuse detaches himself from the group to bow before me and compliment me profusely on my dress.

"Such a dazzling pattern, madame, rarely have I seen a finer material and such exquisite workmanship. Such detail on the wings! Such life in the eyes of the little birds!"

I incline my head and wait in silence until he backs away. Finally, the group leaves and Richelieu turns to me.

"You seem particularly grim this morning, Madame de Vintimille. Not upset by your husband's poor performance at the hunt yesterday?"

I ignore his remarks; why does he waste time on such silly sallies when he knows I am indifferent to them? Together we leave the group behind and I start.

"Fleury—we should work together to have him banished."

"No," says Richelieu baldly. I wait for him to continue but he doesn't. We leave the Hall of Mirrors and the crush of courtiers behind. The Court is full to the rafters with a visiting retinue of Turks, the gossips running out of breath over the story of the ambassador crapping his breeches while waiting to see the king. Nerves or too much liver pie—the verdict is still out. We descend a staircase and walk out onto the terrace overlooking the Grand Canal. It is a fine day, full of the summer that has finally finished the endless winter.

"Continue," I say. Richelieu doesn't like me, but he's far too smart to make an overt enemy of me. We tolerate each other and I know Louis looks up to him; though over a decade older, Richelieu was a constant companion of his youth. From the family of the great Cardinal Richelieu, Louis XIII's most influential minister, he occupies a hallowed place at Versailles. The duke is also known as one of the most debauched men in Europe—rumor has it he even propositioned the fat Empress of Austria during his time in Vienna, and when he was younger he was sent to the Bastille three times: once for a duel, once for trying to make love to the king's mother, and once for conspiracy against the crown. *My* mother even fought a duel with her cousin over him, an episode that is still talked of today as an example of the debauchery of Court life.

He is that sort of man, and in turn, I think he is somewhat wary of Nesle women. Except Louise, of course.

"Madame de Vintimille, the king adores Fleury. The man is like a father to him, the only one he ever had. You don't banish your father."

"But enough of this father talk! The king has turned thirty: What use does he have for a father now? If we work together we could accomplish this coup, and the king need never know who was behind it."

"Let me tell you, Madame de Vintimille, a truth about our mutual friend." Richelieu pats his white wig as he struts, smoothing the little curls over his ears. "One thing our young king does know is the ways of intrigue and ambition. Think of it—he has been surrounded by nothing but machinations from the time he was in skirts. Any plot to banish Fleury would soon be uncovered; it is a fool's errand and one he would not forgive."

We walk down the steps to the next terrace and I open my fan to shield my eyes from the sun.

"I would recommend coexistence. It seems to be working well with your sister."

"Oh, that is totally different," I say in irritation. I know scandals grow like mold on a wet wall here at Versailles, but I hate to be reminded of them, especially by those who matter. "You are too cautious in your approach, I believe."

"I prefer to call myself astute. And I would advise you, Madame de Vintimille, to be astute as well. I knew your mother—she was a fool. As is your sister Louise. But, surprisingly, given your putative parents, you're not." We look at each other. Perhaps an alliance wouldn't be such a bad idea?

A crowd gathers in front of us. A man I don't know, in a too-large red coat, is haranguing a sedan-chair bearer.

"No more than a hundred feet. A hundred feet! And you demand five *livres*? This is outrageous! Outrageous, I say." He glances around the small crowd for confirmation, but everyone just looks on idly and no one murmurs their approval.

We move away from the melee.

"My advice, madame: I recommend we bide our time. The cardinal can't live forever: after a dish of green beans he vomited twice on Tuesday. And my sources tell me his bowel movements had a greenish tinge to them last week. Surely that can't be healthy in one so old?"

I disagree. "Who ever won anything by being patient? The man needs to go! Soon, before it is too late."

"As you wish, madame." Richelieu bows ironically and I decide I don't like him very much after all. An alliance is out of the question and I should take pains to curb his influence with the king. Though I have to admit, his words do have some sense.

We are at the terrace leading down to the Parterre du Midi. Richelieu bows again to take his leave. "I must ask my man in Italy for some cream for your husband's skin—the Venetians are very careful of their complexions and have some excellent potions."

"Do as you wish, monsieur; it is not my concern where you wish to put your time and money," I say coldly as I turn back to the palace.

༄

As we travel down to Choisy in the king's carriage, some awfully ragged-looking people shout and follow us, crying "bread" and "hunger" until the coachmen chase them away with sticks.

Louis is shocked. "But this is the first time I have not heard '*Vive le Roi*' when out in the carriage! Why do they call such things at me?"

"Ignore them. Why, do they think crying at you is going to produce bread? They should better put their energies into working their fields," I say, the jolting of the carriage making me irritable.

"But it is not my fault," he continues to insist. "I did not cause the winter weather—that was God's will. And we are working hard to supply them with grain. Can they not understand that if we lower the price, it will only encourage hoarders?"

"You see where Fleury's advice gets you?" I snap. While the king did follow my advice and bought up the grain, Fleury insisted on keeping the price high, and therefore out of the hands of those who needed it the most.

The king doesn't reply; he is in no mood to be lectured and we pass the rest of the ride in silence, with only Louise's brittle prattle to fill the sour air of the carriage.

The rest of the week passes in rain and more rain and the roads become impassable and we are trapped at Choisy. I regret coming here—the old palace is colder than Versailles and our small group of guests is more boring than usual. When it rains the hunt must be canceled; the king takes to tapestry work and seems content to sit for hours stitching. I know I should feign an interest in all his pursuits, but I draw the line at needlework. I didn't escape the convent to pass my days stitching flowers onto chair covers. I'll leave that to Louise; a common interest she can still share with him.

It has been raining for three days now and all are restless; some hide it better than others. The king and Louise are sitting together on a sofa by the fire, she stitching a cushion cover, he working on a tapestry of a pastoral scene. I am supervising and reading, or trying to, a letter from Diane. What do you think an *Otrish* is? An Austrian? Doesn't she know they are our enemies?

Small clusters of courtiers lounge in the rest of the cavernous salon, chatting, playing cards, sleeping.

"My fingers, how they hurt!" complains the king, throwing his tapestry hoop on the floor. "All morning signing papers, papers, endless papers. They hound me so, even here at Choisy." Messengers on horses can still ride the roads, and the dispatches come daily.

Well, I think in irritation but smile at him in sympathy, you are still the king, even when you are not at Versailles. Louis relishes the perks of kingship, but not the obligations.

Louise murmurs something soft in sympathy. "Shall I massage your fingers, sire?"

The king ignores her and rises. Everyone, except the old Duc de Nangis, who snores in the corner, tenses but Louis waves lazily to let them know they may remain as they are. He comes over to the little table where I am seated and I smell leather and orange blossoms. I inhale; last night was very enjoyable.

"What are you reading, honeybee?"

I can see Louise flinch; she hates it when the king calls me thus. I'm not overly fond of the name myself.

"A letter from my sister Diane."

"I would see it."

"You can but try," I say, passing it to him. He peruses awhile, frowns, and hands it back.

"I could not make head or tail of it. Her hand is like that of a chicken. What is her news?"

I make something up: "The Duchesse de Lesdiguières' rheum is better."

"I should like to meet her," says the king lazily, pulling lightly at a ribbon in my hair. "Your sister, I mean, not the duchess. Though I know the duchess well, from my youth. She is great friends with my dear Ventadour."

A distant clap of thunder rolls through the room; outside, all is gray and the rain beats down on the windowpanes. Any more and the river will overrun. No hunting today, or yesterday. Later we will play cards and drink till we are silly, but before the evening we are fastened here in our boredom.

"You would love Diane," I say, detaching his hand from my head. I am not a cat. "She is very funny, and very jolly."

"What are her physical attractions?" inquires the king, his voice husky in a way I know too well.

Louise fills the ensuing silence. "She has lovely long black hair and . . . soft skin! Though a little dark."

"Yes, indeed," muses the king, picking at my hair again. "I should like to meet her."

"Why not, sire? If she came to Choisy . . . ?" I like the idea; it's been rather too long since I've seen Diane. And I really can't decipher her news very well, though I am sure she has nothing interesting to say. I've heard Madame de Lesdiguières is a rigid old crow.

Louise nods vigorously in agreement. "That would be wonderful! I have not seen Diane for many years!"

"And your other sisters?" inquires the king, his voice silky and careful, and a small frisson of fear climbs up my spine. "The young marquises—Flavacourt and Tournelle. We call them Hortense and Marie-Anne, no?"

"Oh, yes, sire, you should meet them too. They are so charming, and so beautiful," says Louise fervently.

I want to reach across to Louise, take the needle out of her hand, and pop it in her eye.

"So I have heard," muses the king, finally leaving my hair alone to go and stand by the window. He follows a drop of rain running like a tear down the pane, then looks pensively over the flat gardens, shrouded in misty sleet. "I have heard that the Marquise de Flavacourt is one of the great beauties of this generation. Present company excluded," he adds, but rather as a matter of course.

"Oh, yes, Hortense is lovely, simply lovely, we call her Hen, which is funny because she hates eggs, but she is so nice and devout, and Marie-Anne—"

I cut Louise off before she can do more damage. "Well, Hortense may be passably pretty but her husband is very jealous."

The king shakes his head, still staring out the window. "Hot-headed husbands are no concern of mine. The real obstacles are the walls that piety builds—those are inaccessible to even the staunchest of men. I have heard she is very pure."

Before I can jump in, he continues: "And what of the youngest? Not as virtuous, I hope?"

"Marie-Anne is a lovely girl, sire," says Louise, and this time I want to take her cushion cover and wrap it around her head.

"She may be fair looking," I add quickly, "but she is duplicitous and mean."

"Such strange words to describe a young girl!" exclaims the king, and to my horror I realize I have intrigued him.

"Pauline! What a thing to say. When was our Marie-Anne ever duplicitous? She was so sweet, why, I remember in the nursery she used to rescue—"

"She once burned down a cupboard, and blamed it on a lame maid."

"Nonsense!" says Louise softly, her mind turning, as it always does, away from the distasteful; she is like a sunflower that seeks only the sun. "Everyone knows it was Claude's fault. Look at this new dove I have stitched—is it not desirable? I think I will add another, here."

"But we all have our faults." The king's voice comes from far away; I know he is ruminating on a family reunion. That will never be. No more Nesle sisters, perhaps with the exception of Diane, at Court.

"We should have a reunion," he says with more excitement than he has said anything all day. He claps his hands and the lounging courtiers instantly straighten as though he has stroked their spines. Nangis snorts awake with a phlegmy wheeze.

"Here, at Choisy, all five sisters and—" At that moment there is an enormous clap of thunder and the Duchesse d'Antin shrieks and drops her cup over her new magenta-rose dress. All eyes and attention turn to her and my sisters are forgotten in a spill of hot coffee and nervous laughter.

Thank You, God, I say silently to the ceilings. Thank You for the thunder. There are few things in life that I fear, and while I don't exactly fear my sisters, I can't say that Hortense and Marie-Anne would be as . . . meaningless . . . as Louise.

Outside, the rain continues.

Marie-Anne

My husband is dead. I never imagined this would happen. He was so young; only twenty-two.

And now he is dead.

It was a damp November day when JB fell ill. He had been gone most of the year with his regiment, and had only visited Burgundy twice. Then he came home and suffered for five days in a heavy fever that deepened until the sheets were wet and his eyes looked to disappear inside his head. As the fever rose he rambled and called my name but not as much as I would have expected. He often cried out to Fleurette. As far as I know, none of his female relatives come by that name—they are mostly Charlottes and Louises. Either, I decided, a cherished nurse from childhood, or his current camp follower from Languedoc.

If indeed the latter, then how sad that Fleurette will be when he does not return and she learns from his comrades that he is dead. I picture a small heavy-breasted woman with long yellow hair, smelling of wildflowers. I wonder about their nights together when he uses her, as I have taught him to use a woman.

There is a local saying that if you suffer for more than five days in a fever, the end is near. On the seventh day we called the priests and in a few lucid moments JB received extreme unction, and that duty done, he quietly expired. I sat with him in death; he was cold and pale from the sweated fever and looked so young and defenseless. I wished I had been a better wife to him, more loving and less scornful. I wished I had written him more letters.

His uncle's widow descended upon the château with indecent haste. I calculate she started the journey before he even died, for she lives at least a week's ride north in Brittany. Her husband, JB's uncle, died two years ago and now she is the mother of the heir, a little boy of only seven. She arrived with a brother, flushed and nervous looking.

They embraced me and consoled me, but the woman could not keep her eyes off my stomach: a young widow can throw a wrench in the most cherished of plans. Just to spite them, I make sure to wear a gown sewn in the new sackcloth style that falls loosely in the back as well as the front. I wear that gown and wrap myself in furs for the best part of a week and raise my eyes to Heaven when I think they are too near to asking me that most private of questions.

"You are taking this so well," says the woman.

Before she married JB's uncle she was a de Blampignon; everyone knows the de Blampignons are as poor as their name is ridiculous. She has rabbit looks and brown teeth; her brother is pompous and bourgeois. I call them Brown Teeth and Mr. Sweat, for the man drips with perspiration despite the cold of November. Disgusting.

Finally the village priest, tired of my evasions, confronts me in front of them and I tear up and clasp my stomach and say I will know with more certainty in another ten days. In fact, I already know I am not pregnant—my visitor Saint Maurice has shown me the irrefutable evidence that I am not—but something in me delights in creating anxiety for the relatives and the base hopes which ooze from their oiled pores.

When their lawyer arrives, I greet him serenely and announce I will not be sure for at least another week.

Mostly I spend the days alone, reading in my chamber and thinking of the future and tending to the herbs in the hunting lodge. I like the lodge, a cozy womb of calm and serenity. No one knows where I disappear to; they probably think I am praying for Jean-Baptiste's soul in the chapel.

I do not have enough money, or courage, to set out to see the world as I have often dreamed. If I did, I would go to England to see London, and then to the wild coast of Ireland; then I would travel to Canada and see spaces vaster than anything here, and red savages and strange animals. Then I would go to Greece to worship at the site of Aristotle's birthplace. And then I would go to Java and explore the world of spices, and then . . . so many places to go.

Widowhood is the one time in a woman's life when she has some small freedom, but for me there is only one future: I must return to Paris and to Tante Mazarin's house. If I had a son, the castle and the position would remain mine and I would be in that most envied of positions, a young widow with independent means. JB was not wealthy but there would have been enough here to give me some small independence.

But there is no child and so there is no place for me at Tournelle. I will have to leave; leave Garnier and the spice garden and my beloved library. I write to Tante, and to Hortense, and to my father's lawyer in Paris. He promptly comes down and, once it is clear that there is no little JB growing inside me, starts negotiations with the Blampignon pig for the return of my dowry. My pathetic little dowry, all that I have in this world.

As I expect, Hortense comes as well. I am grateful to her because I know she does not like to travel. She arrives in the carriage that will take me back to Paris.

"Sister."

It's been almost a year since her wedding and she is lovelier than ever, cheeks rosy and eyes sparkling. "You are looking very well," I say.

She smiles and shows her dimples to advantage. "Thank you, sister. And you too, you also look well." She frowns. "Are you not grieved at the death of Jean-Baptiste?"

In my letters to her I have only ever played the content young wife, but now I can't be bothered to keep up any pretense. The last few weeks have drained me of any artifice. JB is dead and nothing will bring him back. I will miss him . . . but not that much. I fear I am as cold as I have ever been. I shrug my shoulders. "I saw him but rarely."

"I only see François at most a few times a year," protests Hortense. "That does not stop me from loving and missing him . . ." Her eyes well up.

"Not everyone has a love story such as yours, Hortense," I snap impatiently. I may sound envious but I'm not; I've met Flavacourt.

"Is there no . . . ?" Hortense looks in expectation at my stomach. We are alone, she is my sister, we are two married women (well, one married and one a widow), and yet she cannot bring herself to ask me the indelicate question: Are you pregnant?

"I'm not pregnant," I say baldly, and Hortense flinches a little, just a little.

"Oh, sister, I am so sorry."

"I have accepted the situation."

"Well, that changes nothing. I came, of course, to bring you home."

"Home? I hardly think of Tante's as home."

Hortense is puzzled. "But it is our only home. Where else would you go?"

"There is nowhere else for me to go," I say, and where I see only a bottomless void, Hortense sees acceptance and duty.

What shall I bring from Tournelle; what shall I bring to remind myself of the six years I spent here? My memories of JB; some sweet memories of our time together, certainly.

Alongside my clothes and memories I pack a set of Molière's plays, all of *Artamène* and a few scientific books from the library; neither Mrs. Brown Teeth nor Mr. Sweat look like avid readers. Brown Teeth tries my patience sorely, coming into my chambers on the least pretext and making a show of helping me arrange my affairs, while I know she is only interested in my jewelry. She is trying to determine what belongs to the château and what is mine from the house of Mailly-Nesle. She has a list from the archives that her lawyer, or perhaps mine, has provided but she can't match the descriptions to the pieces in my boxes.

I don't know whether I should keep the jewels that JB gave me, but I won't offer them back unless directed to do so by her stringy lawyer. In the end I pack them all and leave her only a string of black pearls that I never liked. I know there won't be a big fuss; what are a few middling pieces of jewelry when the real prize, the château and the title, are now within their grasp?

A few days before we are to leave, I fall into a deep depression. I am listless, tired, everything is pointless: What does it all mean and what does it all matter? We're all going to die anyway.

JB is buried in the small church not far from the château. I sit for hours beside him in the freezing Tournelle crypt, wishing he wasn't so cold. I read the names of his relatives already dead. Elisabeth-Charlotte, dead at twenty-two. Madeleine-Angélique, dead at seventeen. And my Jean-Baptiste, dead at twenty-two. All of them so young. One day I'll be dead too, and then what will it matter what I did while I was alive?

Everyone leaves me alone, assuming I am feeling some well-deserved, if tardy, grief for my dead husband. I lie in bed for two days and cry because I am not pregnant and wish I were, then cry because I am so confused—I never hankered for a child before. But suddenly the idea of a little JB is very appealing. Or it could have been a little girl, though a female child would not have stopped my eviction. But still. I would have named her Armande, after my mother. Now JB is dead without posterity and who will remember that he ever lived? Soon all that remains of him will be his name engraved in marble, and he will lie with his ancestors in the crypt, alone and forgotten.

On my last day in my dead husband's house, Hortense drags me out of bed and puts me into the carriage. Maybe, I think, burrowing down into the mound of blankets and cushions, for the roads are cold and bumpy from here to Paris, maybe I can be like this forever, doing nothing, saying nothing, no one expecting anything.

I will just exist.

From Louise de Mailly
Château de Versailles
December 10, 1740

Darling Marie-Anne,

I heard the terrible news about Jean-Baptiste and I write to offer you my deepest condolences. What a tragedy! You must be sorely grieved. I too am in the depths of despair. At your news.

I know the heartbreak you are going through, that grief that comes when you lose everything. No one understands this better than I. I know how strong your anguish is—to lose all that you loved in the world, to be turned away from all that is familiar and safe, and only because of one dark dash of fortune. That is loss. That is death. And what is loss but a form of death?

I grieve for you, sister, and I pray that in time you will come to accept your burden. Acceptance is the most important thing, for there is much in this life that we cannot change. In this time of sadness and affliction, I am sure Hortense and Tante Mazarin will take care of you in Paris. You must let me know what I can do to help.

Here, the king is well, a touch melancholy, as he often is when winter arrives. Pauline is also well; she is very happy with her husband, the Comte de Vintimille. He is a fine young man, despite an unsightly skin condition. Pauline sends her love and her condolences. How I wish you two could be friends again! When we were last at Choisy the king talked of a reunion of all of us sisters. I thought it a wonderful idea! Imagine the five of us, together again? Perhaps once your mourning is over?

I send you this handkerchief, embroidered with black doves, that they may comfort you in your sadness.

In loving sorrow,
Louise

Pauline

It has been a year of change and growth, of triumphs and battles, both large and small, most of which I have invariably
won. Louis and I have grown closer and he is still very much
devoted to me. He has a lot to thank me for; I have helped him
make his own decisions and stand up to his carping ministers.
Gratitude is a strong foundation for love.

The fight with the Austrians now brews into war. Charles of
Austria, France's cursed enemy, died in October and left only a
daughter to succeed him, opening the way for France's interests
in Austria to be asserted. Fleury wants to avoid war at all costs:
have us roll over like a lapdog and accept the outrage of a female
Empress of Austria. Not all agree with him, and I certainly don't.

There is a general called Belle-Isle who has spent much time
cultivating my friendship, for he is a smart man and knows where
the true power lies. The gossips say he provides two hundred men
with stipends, to spread good rumors in his favor. It is a strategy
that works. I like subterfuge; I am thinking of employing a verse
writer to write *positive* songs about me for a change, to coun-
terbalance the scandalous drivel. Something comparing me to
Athena, perhaps? It's not that I mind them overly much, the verses
I mean, but the king is still awfully sensitive to them.

Belle-Isle and I both agree a glorious war would be the making
of Louis; the king could emerge like a phoenix from the shadow
of his great-grandfather (Belle-Isle's words, not mine; the man

is quite the poet) and establish himself as a noble warrior king. Louis would no longer be known as a king who only fights stags and boars.

"This is a once-in-a-generation opportunity," repeats Belle-Isle, a hard edge to his voice. The men have been arguing for hours; what started as a simple review of regiment expenditures has degenerated into a polite but tense battle. "We must join with the Prussians and assert our interests while Austria is weakened."

"War is the undoing of countries!" Cardinal Fleury repeats in a wearisome voice. "You do not know anything, none of you bull-headed young bucks . . . you have never lived through war and you know not the devastation it causes."

You've lived through everything, I think sourly. And continue to live; he must be three hundred years old by now. We are in a cozy inner library, hiding from the cold of the council rooms. I leave my perch by the fire to stand beside Louis's chair. "I agree with Belle-Isle: Maria Theresa's right to rule is highly questionable, and this could be the perfect opportunity for French expansion in the region."

"What is she doing here?" Fleury asks in astonishment.

"The Comtesse de Vintimille is always with me," replies Louis, taking my hand and stroking it.

"They say France is being ruled by a woman, sire. It is well known that a monstrous regime of the hymen is the undoing of countries. And is that not why we are proposing war with Austria?"

What a fool—does he really think he can win? While I have now accepted, grudgingly, that Louis will never banish the man, it still irks me that the cardinal does nothing to seek my favor.

"Pauline has more sense in her pretty head than twenty of our best generals, Cardinal, and I would have you remember that," says the king mildly. "We are not in a formal council, and I would have her here." Ha! I have the urge to stick out my tongue at Fleury; if there were not others around the table, I would do it.

"I agree with Madame de Vintimille," says Richelieu, coming over from the window seat where he was having his boots cleaned.

"What the devil—who else is hiding in the shadows?" exclaims Fleury in peevish annoyance. "Who else would join this conversation uninvited? You, over there by the door! Come here."

A frightened footman is propelled forward.

"And do you have an opinion about whether we should go to war or not?" Fleury asks, his voice dripping with sarcasm that the footman misinterprets as interest.

"Well, sirs, Majesty, my grandmother was of Austrian blood, from Linz in fact . . ."

"Oh, shut up!" cries the cardinal. I have rarely seen him so irritated. His eyes bulge and one large vein rises from the web on his forehead to throb vibrantly. All around the table stop as we collectively wait for the attack of apoplexy that will finally, once and for all, scuttle this wretched man.

"Enough!" says Louis. "Cardinal, my friend, calm yourself, there is no need to get so riled. The right decision will be made . . . in time. These matters cannot be decided right now. We must think, plan, ponder."

And procrastinate, I add in my head. Louis seeks harmony and consensus around him and still fears to make his own decisions. He has been long trained to believe that others know better, and it is a hard habit to shake: he is a weather vane that swings with the wind of others' opinions.

"But this is our chance," urges Belle-Isle. "Austria cannot be ruled by a woman! We must—"

"Enough, did you not hear the king?" exclaims Fleury, his vein still throbbing. "You have made your opinions known, but in the end it is my—our king who decides."

Richelieu and I exchange a look, and I know we are, for once, in complete agreement. This war will happen, it must happen, and when it does, Louis will ride onward in glory.

※

Thanks to my influence, Charolais is now only rarely invited to Court. Louis is conflicted, for she was a part of his youth. "That is the exact reason," I tell him, "that you must stop childish friendships and seek new companions." Like the General Belle-Isle.

Even in her absence, all around me there are snipers and marksmen, buzzing with the same hopeful question: When will he be tired of her? It's almost like the bees that used to plague me. They have entirely disappeared from *inside* my head but now manifest *outside* in the form of leering, tiresome courtiers:

"That Marvelous Mathilde is simply exquisite! And so petite and so young, why, she is just a child, not a woman so mature and . . . large . . . such as yourself . . . You are already twenty-eight, no? Positively middle-aged!"

"Is it true, Pauline, that you have not seen the king for two days? I heard he spent all last week with your sister? Old habits die hard, they say. You must be quite worried."

"You are not looking very well these days, not at all. Are you sick? Are you perhaps sick with worry? Is it because of the Marvelous Mathilde? I would be sick too, I swear, simply sick."

Don't they ever get tired? They are all looking for the slightest crack to rend apart into an unbreachable chasm, but when are they going to realize that I am the new Madame de Maintenon? If he were free, I am sure the king would marry me too. But he's not—the queen continues apace, each year older, each year more irrelevant as she is no longer churning out children. Strange, childbirth is such a treacherous time for women, yet she emerged from eleven pregnancies completely alive and unscathed. A bit unfair, really.

Diane thinks I have forgotten her but I have not: I am actively seeking her a husband. Louis is hesitant—Vintimille cost him quite dear—and balks when I insist that Diane's husband be a duke and a peer.

"But, dearest," he says softly, "there are only forty or so ducal peerages in the kingdom. And most of them are married."

"But you can always create more, Louis." He also needs to

raise my husband's lands to a dukedom, but I've decided I'll bide my time on that one. It is more important to get Diane well married and to Court, and two dukedoms in one year for one family, well . . . even I concede that's a bit much.

Louis bristles and pulls away. "One cannot manufacture dukes, like one can manufacture"—he looks around the room for inspiration—"Saxony candlesticks!" He waves to a hideous pair on the mantel, sculptured boars climbing up the sides. "There are only a certain number and that number must be kept limited."

I'm not worried, not like in the early days; we have plenty of disagreements and arguments and even the occasional raised voices, but they do not dull his love for me. In fact I think they make it grow stronger. He constantly tells me that he finds me so *exciting*.

"If I create too many dukes, then the worth of a duke is debased," he continues. "People are beginning to talk. I heard the Marquis de Créquy, of the oldest of our families, declare he would not wish for a dukedom, so meaningless have they become. Surely you, madame, who is so brilliant and so intelligent, can understand that?"

He's beginning to use my sarcasm against me. I stick my tongue out ever so slightly at him and he immediately softens. He says, "I'll ask Richelieu what he thinks, if he can name a suitable duke. He always has good ideas and the man knows everyone."

I have an inspiration. "What about Richelieu himself? Poor Elisabeth being dead and all." His second wife died last year of scurvy.

Louis appears to choke even though he is not eating. "I hope you jest, madame. I believe our dear friend is holding out for a princess of the blood, or at least a grandee of Spain."

I sigh. It's true that Richelieu would probably want a more advantageous match; before Cardinal Richelieu became the greatest of Louis XIII's ministers, the family was scarcely anything and the duke is still assiduously erasing his humble roots.

"Fine, but I agree we should get his opinion."

"Must it be a duke?" asks Louis again. Never one for a long fight, he is, I see, already resigned.

"Yes, it must. A wonderful duke for my wonderful sister. You will love her, dearest." I pull him to me on the bed. "With your predilection for Nesle blood . . . who knows?"

The look in Louis's eyes tells me it's not a subject he is uncomfortable with. He has been dropping hints recently about both Louise and me, together. I absolutely draw the line there. I have no desire to see Louise naked. Absolutely none.

But there's no need to prick Louis's fantasy about Diane just yet. And at least he hasn't mentioned that family reunion again.

From Hortense de Flavacourt
Hôtel de Mazarin, Paris
February 20, 1741

Dear Louise,

I am sure you have already heard, but I wanted to write and tell you the wonderful news myself. I am now the proud mother of a baby boy, Auguste-Frédéric de Fouilleuse. What joy! What wonder and what a gift for my husband. I can now call myself Mother, and you can call yourself Aunt. Eldest Aunt. Or Elder Aunt. Exciting, isn't it?

The birth went well, and after seven days the doctors declared me free of danger. Tante has insisted I remain in bed for two more weeks, and I am only allowed to eat rice pudding and drink heated milk. I cannot complain; she knows best.

I am so proud to be the first of my sisters to have a child. Strange, isn't it, that we are four married, yet I am the only one with a child! I pray that you will as well be blessed, and I pray even harder that you are not using means to avoid pregnancy?

Amidst our happiness, there is still sorrow: Marie-Anne is as sad as ever. She has been in great grief since her return from Burgundy a few months ago. She is as distraught as I am: I cannot imagine how awful it would be if I were to lose Flavacourt. Or my precious little baby.

I suggested to Marie-Anne that to take her mind off her earthly sorrow, she spend more time in the chapel praying for her husband's soul. She just snapped at me, and it seems that she prefers to lie in bed, eating spiced nuts and reading her outlandish books. Grief takes many forms.

Now my little Freddie is crying—I must call the nurse!

Please share my news with Pauline; it is impossible to get a letter out of her, but I do wish her to share in my joy.

Adieu,
Mother Hortense

From Louise de Mailly
Château de Versailles
February 26, 1741

Dear Hortense,

Congratulations. You are indeed lucky.

God has not seen fit to bless me with a child, but I hope that with enough prayers, my wish may yet be granted. I know I am past thirty, and though the doctors counsel against such imprudence, the queen had her last daughter at thirty-four, and would surely have had many more had the king not decided that he would spare her further confinements. And the Duchesse de Noailles had her last child when she was past forty!

Congratulations again on your great good fortune. I send you this handkerchief embroidered with doves, sewn for the baby.

Your sister,
Louise

Diane

Wonderful news! Hortense has had a baby! I am now officially an aunt, though I don't feel any different than usual. His name is Auguste-Frédéric—all Flavacourt names—and I saw him last week. He is rather small and red and puckered; perhaps he takes after his father.

And even more wonderful news—Pauline says she is hard at work preparing a marriage for me, and has suggested I visit her at Versailles!

Madame Lesdig, like Tante Mazarin, is in open contempt of both Louise and Pauline and their immorality. But on the other hand, being a practical woman, she has decided that she may officially despise Pauline while accepting any marriage she may arrange for me, as long as it is suitably grand. I am now twenty-seven and it is high time I am married.

"Diane-Adelaide." Madame Lesdig always calls me by my full name; she is a very formal woman. "When I was your age I had already been married for six years. I had been pregnant five times, though unfortunately God willed that none of my babies should live. I also had my own house and my own carriage."

She says this with a touch of accusation. I shrug my shoulders, for it is not as though I can arrange my own marriage.

"Don't shrug! Diane-Adelaide, be more ladylike. You must strive to be like a swan, elegant and serene, and not like a monkey. I hate to say this, and may God strike me down . . ." She looks up and crosses herself; she is fond of invoking God and talks to Him many times a day. "But you are lucky in some small way that your sister is Pauline."

The way she spits out "Pauline" it sounds worse than *putain*.

"But you must remember that if you accept her help, you are in *no ways* indebted to her. To arrange a good match to clean the Mailly-Nesle name is the least she can do. But once you are married, you must distance yourself from Pauline and that unfortunate Louise. Reputation is as an egg: once cracked, it can never be made whole again. You must never forget that you are a Mailly-Nesle, even if that name has been dragged through the mud."

I laugh at the expression.

"And another thing, Diane-Adelaide," says Madame Lesdig. "You must refrain from laughing so much. If you visit Versailles, you must be as a sweet songbird and not a cackling crow."

I hug the happy news to myself. I shall visit Versailles and soon I shall be married! If my husband is a duke, as Pauline hints, then he should be very wealthy. I shall be a duchess and I shall eat whatever I want, sugar pie every day, and wear wonderful dresses, and life will be heavenly. Perhaps I will even employ a writer to write letters for me? Madame Lesdig has a reader for days when the light is bad and her eyes are pained, so why not a writer for those days when one's hand hurts? That would be very pleasing.

Madame Lesdig suggests I plan my visit for the summer. She says the best time to be at Versailles is most decidedly June, when it is neither too hot nor too cold and when the gardens are starting to bloom. In her youth, when the old king was still on the throne, she lived there with her husband and she never stops despairing at the sprouting of immorality there in recent years. She says in his last years, King Louis XIV was a paragon of a man and a wonderful moral example to his subjects, living in calm domesticity with his wife, Madame de Maintenon.

What will I wear? Madame Lesdig thinks I have gowns enough and grumbles that before she was married she only had two and that was considered quite sufficient. And here I am, unmarried and already with four! I tell her that I sacrificed my best dresses for Pauline when she went to Versailles. She tuts with reproof but eventually promises to have new dresses made for me. She dislikes the new chintzes and bright colors: she calls them "flimsies for floozies." She says that as one gets older, one realizes that fripperies are just a distraction and simplicity is the best design.

"Diane-Adelaide, you must strive to be as a mouse, content in one color, and not a gaudy peacock drowning in useless brilliance." Which probably means the dresses will be plain. Unfortunately. And she is firm that any money from my father's estate—my father is not dead but he is in such a bad situation no one talks of him or even calls him by name but only refers to his "estate"—must be kept for my marriage. I wish I could order my own dresses, of my own design, but elder duchesses and aunts cannot be contradicted.

Never mind, I am going to Versailles!

From Marie Philippine de Braille
House of the Dowager Duchesse de Lesdiguières, Paris
April 20, 1741

Madame de Vintimille,

Honored greetings to you, my lady. Please excuse the impropriety of receiving a letter from one unknown to your most esteemed person; allow me to introduce myself. I am Mademoiselle de Braille and I am employed as a reader for the most honorable Duchesse de Lesdiguières, but today I write to you on behalf of Mademoiselle Diane de Mailly-Nesle, who has engaged me as her writer.

I write on her behalf to inform you that she is delighted with your invitation and looks forward to visiting Versailles and Choisy this coming summer.

She wishes me to inform you that she has had two new dresses made for this momentous occasion, and begs you to consider if she may take back the peach bows from your blue dress, as she is sure you have many, many dresses now that you are the Comtesse de Vintimille. She believes the peach bows are necessary to adorn her new brown silk. She also begs me to inform you that she has a new gray dress and has used the lemon lace from your presentation gown to enliven it. She also wishes to humbly remind you of the green brocade shawl she presented you as a gift several years ago, and wonders if you would be so kind as to return that favor when she is at Versailles, as she has no other shawl that is in any ways as fine as that one.

Awaiting your esteemed response, I remain your humble servant,
Philippine de Braille

Louise

I am embroidering a set of curtains for Pauline's bedroom at Choisy, to match the newly painted walls. The fabric is blue and gold and I sew small white doves trailing up the stripes and stitch a border around them, sewn of our initials stitched closely together. Mine and Louis's, not Pauline and Louis's. *LdF-LdMLdFLdM*. Only if you knew to look would you notice the letters. It is my secret and private revenge on Pauline, but I know she will never notice.

In this new year, I want to love Pauline again, because it is always better to love one's sister than not. I find I can even forgive Louis, and when we spend time together I no longer reproach him. He is the king and a man and can do what he wants, and my duty is to accept and support him. Acceptance is surely better than grief and despair? I want colors back in my dreams and joy back in my life and I was determined that this spring would finally bring me some small piece of contentment. May is a beautiful month, the hardness of winter gone and memories of warmth returning.

But such happiness is not to be. For now comes the news . . . Oh.

The Comtesse de Toulouse, always kind and always a friend, seeks me out before the others could. I am on duty this week at Versailles but have brought the Choisy curtains back with me. She finds me early one morning, stitching my doves.

"Darling." She holds me at arm's length and searches my face. "Have you heard?"

"No? What? Good—bad? Tell me." My thoughts fly to the worst. The king? A convent?

"Sit down, dear." Her voice is calm and motherly, though I can't remember my mother ever using that tone.

"Please, Sophie, tell me quickly, what is it?"

"Your sister Pauline . . ."

"Does she wish me to leave?" My voice is calm, but inside I am being strangled alive.

"No, no. Your sister would never do that! But Richelieu told me last night . . . she is expecting."

"Expecting what?" I blank, sighing with relief that I am not to be banished. Even though we have a good relationship, and have been in harmony this past winter, the fear of being banished always remains, creeping around the corners of my conscience like a cat in shadows.

"Expecting a child, dear Louise."

Oh.

I stare at the *comtesse*. Is this a prank, a joke, a lie? But I know from her face, innocent of powder but painted with kindness, that she would never do such a thing.

"Thank you for telling me," I say softly. "Thank you, really."

She nods. "This world can be too cruel sometimes."

I laugh shortly. "Indeed." The *comtesse* married her last husband for love; they enjoyed fourteen happy years together before he died.

"I wanted to tell you before someone else broke the news, in a rather less kind fashion. Here, you are alone and you can compose yourself before you venture out."

When she leaves I close the door and lean against the wood, fighting the floor that threatens to pull me down to its hard embrace. I send Jacobs out with a quick note of excuse for the queen and crawl back into my bed. My cocoon. My dress lies abandoned on the floor, the symbol of a day aborted.

They will have a child together.

Just when I thought my heart was truly broken, it finds a new way to break and grief runs fresh. They will have a child together. He will never leave her now. And oh! How I wish I had a child of my own, a little daughter to cuddle on my chest and to feel her tiny arms around me; to have the joy of knowing that one person, just one person in this world, loves me wholly and forever. Yet I fear my hopes are for nothing: my husband refuses to see me and now I only have Louis to my bed occasionally.

There is no guidance in the Bible for the situation I find myself in but I need to talk to someone. In my dreams I ask the queen for advice. She is always courteous, though you can still tell she was raised in the Polish equivalent of a hunting lodge.

"I am sorely troubled and I thought perhaps you might help me."

The queen smiles faintly but her eyes stay cold. Though a kindly woman, she is still the queen and must harden her heart as much as she can against the endless requests that surround her like snow in winter.

"No, I want nothing from you, Your Majesty," I clarify. "I only seek your advice."

"*Vor* you, my *dareeling* daughter, I will gladly help you." Once, she might have called me her "darling daughter," but now her pride prevents her from extending such closeness. But this is only an imaginary conversation, so in my mind she calls me her darling daughter and her hand, soft with hard peaks from too many hours of sewing, covers mine gently.

"Madame, I ask your advice: How do you bear it? When you want to be with him, but he does not, and you must wait and wait, and hope and hope. And then when he does come, how do you stop reproaching him and declaring your love and imploring him to stay with you forever?"

The queen points to a tapestry on the far wall, woven with scenes of early Christian martyrdom. "Our beloved saints. They will help you. Fructuosus. Cephas. Phlegon. Onesimus. They are all here to help you. Identify the right one, and all will be well."

I curtsy and lean to kiss her hand but inside I am disappointed. How can obscure saints help me? And who is the patron saint of sinners who wish ill on their sisters?

Even my confessor starts to remind me that repetitiveness is a sin. He has already absolved me of the sin of jealousy and of adultery, and says there is no need to ask forgiveness again and again.

"God loves not those that toil in the wheel and return to where they started. You could try reading the story of Sarah and Hagar—a splendid example of a woman who humbled herself and accepted the trials God sent. And don't forget, there is always the convent for those who feel the secular life too trying to bear. Is not your dear aunt the abbess at Poissy? Perhaps I should write to her?"

Even God is tired of me.

Pauline strumps around like a queen, constantly caressing her stomach—which remains flat—and being more thoughtless and rude than usual. The king is all nervous fluster and clucks over her with distressing frequency. The courtiers are becoming more aware of Pauline's power—even those that have openly professed their disdain—and now invitations to Choisy are like white foxes: rarely sighted and very valuable. Pauline leaves it up to me to decide whom to invite; she really doesn't care for such trifles.

"You see, Lou"—she has started to call me that, though I detest the name; I am not a cat—"they finally understand that I am not a flash of lightning, or a cheap tallow candle that burns too quickly. I will bear the king's son, and we will start a new dynasty, one to rival the descendants of Madame de Montespan. The silly sheep must realize that I am here forever. Forever. I wonder, when they write the story of my life, will they compare me to Madame de Montespan, the great love of Louis XIV's youth, or to Madame de Maintenon, his mistress and wife of his later years? Perhaps both?"

What am I supposed to say to that? I have come to realize that

Pauline is completely unfeeling. Well, perhaps not unfeeling, but she simply doesn't consider other people. Ever. She's even rude to Louis, and astonishingly, he never seems to mind.

"Everyone loves you, Pauline," I murmur. What else can I say? We are standing on the wide stone terrace in front of the palace at Choisy, debating whether to take the carriage out to meet the king in the forest. An overwrought footman has come back with the news that two stags, antlers entangled, have been spotted and that it will be a momentous kill.

"I think it is going to rain," I say. "We can see it—them—when they bring it—them—back to the palace." I am tired and would rather lie in my bed, and cry, than ride out with Pauline and watch her caress her stomach and see the king squeeze her shoulder and beam at her.

"No, I think we should go. The rain will hold off. Just get your shawl. And bring me my green brocade one. Beauchamps, get the carriage, we ride out to His Majesty. We must be there to share this wonderful happening. And we go alone—I can't have the Duchesse d'Antin ruining this occasion with her silly laugh." From the salon on the second floor the Duchesse d'Antin and the Comtesse d'Estrées glare at us through the glass. Pauline ignores their icicle eyes.

I turn slowly back into the palace. I feel like I am bearing an enormous load. One small little addition, one tiny piece of straw more, and I will break.

Simply break.

Pauline

This summer is hotter than any before; I cannot breathe. I have a small black page—a gift from the Duchesse de Rohan-Rohan—who fans me without stop, but even the light breeze scorches. It is as though we are in Hell: flowers droop and at dinner jellies melt into great puddles of bloody liquid. I am pregnant and very uncomfortable, and I want to scream. My ankles are swollen and my fingers too puffy to wear the rings that Louis gives me. I dream of the winter and of the ice that forms on the inside of windows and of frozen beds that take forever to warm up and of how, if you are seated too close to the fire, you can simply move away and be cold again.

I remain at Choisy, for the heat here is slightly more bearable than at Versailles. I have the idea to make the wine cellars into a retreat. Perhaps we could bring down some chairs and drape the walls with velvet and dine down there? Perhaps even sleep down there? Unfortunately the cellars are rife with rats and the palace rat-catcher cannot guarantee our safety. Seeking comfort, I wear a loose muslin robe I designed myself, with no front or back or even waist. The others whisper that it's scandalous, that it looks like a chemise, only suited for the bedroom. And I sometimes go barefoot. I don't care what anyone says.

I find I am not as interested as I used to be in war and politics. I don't really care about Austria and all that is happening in the Elbe Valley. I am not even interested when the king wants to talk about the unrest in Saint-Domingue or about the peasants that continue to starve all over the country. I really only care about the child growing in my belly. Unexpected, really, that something so small could occupy me so completely.

It will be a boy even though no one else believes that. Including Louis. It is a joke of long standing that both of our families are very proficient at producing girls—my mother had six daughters, if one includes the little bastard she had with the Duc de Bourbon. And out of all her pregnancies, the queen only succeeded in giving birth to three boys, one stillborn, alongside eight girls.

But I know our child will be a boy.

Louis has always declared—though not directly to me—that he will never act as his great-grandfather did and legitimize his bastards. Courtiers, including the many who are descended from those royal bastards, don't hesitate to remind me of his pledge. I'm not worried. My son will be acknowledged by the king, and he will marry a Condé or a Conti. Or Richelieu's little daughter.

Here is the truth: I am smarter than Louis. It is rather annoying to constantly make sure he does not perceive this. Even though flattering and puffing up men has been the task of women from time immemorial, it sometimes feels as though I am taking care of two children: the one who grows in my belly and the one who hangs around me like a little yapping dog. Pregnancy—and this heat—make me irritable and I can no longer hide my annoyance as well as before.

Louis feels impotent that he cannot change the weather and he is bored, for the hunt has also suffered. The dogs and horses are too hot to move and only want to sleep all day. I think Louis should stay at Versailles—he has a kingdom to run and I can send him my instructions and thoughts perfectly well by courier, several times a day. Then I could just pass the next two months lying in the shade by the river with little Neptune and his fan, and rest in peace until this ordeal is over.

But instead Louis travels regularly from Versailles, accompanied by a clutch of courtiers with their noises and their smugness.

He pesters and pesters and pesters me with his attentions and his crawling hands and his constant solicitations, a hopeful look in his eyes that I will grant him a smile or a caress. I could scream! He reminds me of Louise! At first he didn't let me sleep alone and was constantly pawing me. The sexuality of the king is the virility of the nation—France is in good hands there—but sometimes it all gets rather too much. Now he is banished to Louise's bed. My idea. No matter how annoyed I am, I can never forget the danger that lies when there is a king and an empty bed.

In private I speak to him as I would to any man, but in public he is still the king and I must mind my words. Even at Choisy.

"Imagine, they come from Nantes and Bordeaux, and before that even farther afield. The south of Spain . . . Sometimes I wonder what it would be like to travel to those places."

We are seated in a small pavilion, seeking relief from the heat by the river. A boat is docked and we watch as sheep, and crates of wine and sherry, are unloaded and carried up to the palace. I think of my sister Marie-Anne as a child, dreaming of far-off lands, and my fingers curl with impatience. Why travel to outlandish places when the world is right here?

"You're France, Louis," I say without sympathy. "You can't leave. That would be like . . . Oh, I don't what it would be like. All I know is I am too hot." The terrified bleating of the sheep leaves my nerves taut and I would rather be lying down on my bed than be here near this smelly wharf full of flies and commotion. No matter how sweet the river breeze may be.

"We are all hot, madame," Louis says a little stiffly. "And I do not believe it is a fault to have dreams and desires, no matter how impractical."

One of the men carrying a crate of bottles slips and falls into the water, and for a moment I envy him. How wonderful to be a fish, surrounded by cool rushing waters all the long day. Another man jumps in to catch the floating bottles while the terrified man is pulled to safety with a rope.

Why are we here? I would lie down on the floor of the

pagoda—inviting, cold stone—but there are too many around us and I couldn't support their hushed shock right now. "I want to go back to the palace," I say, flicking my fan at Louis.

"We will wait until the last of the crates are off. I would see the boat depart." While Louis is generally solicitous, sometimes he is so used to coming first that I honestly don't think he understands that other people have feelings too. Especially hot, pregnant women.

"Why? Have you never seen a boat depart before? You're like a child sometimes, Louis."

I know I have insulted him but oh, how I want to get out of here!

He draws himself up stiffly and I see in his eyes that I have gone too far.

"Madame, you are being very disagreeable these days. I believe the only cure would be to cut off your head and replace your blood with that of a lamb. You are simply too disagreeable."

He stalks off up the hill toward the palace, surrounded by a clutch of courtiers bleating their displeasure at my coarse words. I know what they are thinking: Is this it? Has she done it? Is it over? Should they arrange for the Marvelous Mathilde to come for an unexpected visit? I sit in the pagoda watching them, my eyes hooded with heat.

Of course it's not over.

But as for this interminable pregnancy . . . well, that's never ending. I have taken to sitting in the dairy, enjoying the coolness of the tiles and trailing my hands in the tubs of cold water from the underground springs. It's all so awfully inefficient. Pregnancy, I mean, not the dairy—that is quite the modern wonder. I watch the cows with their baleful eyes. The dairy master tells me that a cow stands, in no apparent discomfort, for all of her gestation and then on the day of the birth: a few moos and it is over. But for us women? Nine months of torture and then the agony of the birth. I tell myself to be patient, that soon it will be over and I will have a son, and my body will be my own again.

I startle, unfamiliar with the sensation. What . . . ? Then I realize what has just happened: my baby kicked me! And, judging by the strength of those little feet, my baby will be a strong boy. I laugh in delight; Madame d'Estrées startles at the strange noise but I avoid her questions and go up to my bedroom. I dash off a quick note to Louis, telling him that he must come immediately. Through the afternoon and into the evening I hug my secret to me and enjoy the sensation. To think there is a little baby inside me, that will soon come out and be my child . . . It is all rather miraculous, isn't it?

The heat does not let up even at midnight and I am lying naked on my bed when the king arrives. He rushes in, all concern and apprehension.

"No, darling, it's good news, good news." We embrace awkwardly, my stomach a barrel between us.

He stops and shakes his head. "I was so worried, trumpet. So worried. I thought the worst. All through the ride I was beside myself, wondering what could have happened . . ." He takes off his hat and rubs his eyes. "You appear well."

"I'm sorry." And I am. "I'm really sorry," I repeat, and stroke his back and tickle him with my fingers. "I should have said it in the note, but I wanted it to be a surprise."

"And so—what is the surprise, dearest?" He sits down heavily on the bed.

"I want you to feel something." But the baby, riotous all day, is now frustratingly silent. Louis caresses my belly and I slap it lightly, but nothing happens.

"He kicked for the first time this morning! I thought it was indigestion and I was not looking forward to Estrées crowing—she told me not to eat those frogs last night—but then I realized it was the baby!"

Louis laughs with delight and kisses me. "It will be a fine, strong boy."

"No one told me this might happen." I jump up and down,

giggling, trying to get the baby to kick again. "Silly baby. Why isn't he kicking? Is he shy like his father?"

"Private, not shy," says Louis, sticking his finger in my belly button and wiggling. Still nothing. "Adelaide kicked something tremendous, I remember the queen complaining about it. And she was an exceptionally healthy little baby."

"Shall we sing to him? Perhaps that will wake him?"

"Wait, I have an idea." The king disappears and comes back a while later with a small violin. I chuckle.

"Where did you get that?"

"Let's see if this works."

He strums a few strings and we wait, laughing.

"Should we call the musicians?" he says, only half joking. "We could set up a whole symphony. He may not respond to my poor tunes but better music might rouse him to express himself again."

I laugh. "No! It's too hot to get dressed again. Perhaps he's just being as stubborn as his mother."

"Dearest." Louis abandons the violin and pulls me down on the bed. He plays with my breasts and I stroke his head, and apologize again for the note that caused him such worry. I'm so glad he came and suddenly feel very tender toward him. He is a fine man. I nuzzle at his neck.

Then I feel it. A kick.

"Oh! There, there, put your hand there!"

The baby kicks again and Louis feels it too. And then again!

Suddenly I feel wonderfully, deliriously happy. We fall asleep in each other's arms, the baby still kicking occasionally.

From Pauline de Vintimille
Château de Choisy
The hottest day of the year, 1741

D—

I am sorry you can't come. I just simply can't do anything in this heat, and cannot have any more distractions or guests. The heat is unbearable. We are being cooked alive. How I wish I was a fish and could spend all day in the river!

You must come after the birth: the doctors say it is due in the middle of September. I have already told K that you will come in October or November, and stay for a month. I am to have new apartments when I have my child, and so there will be plenty of room for you.

I will also have a new chef, only for me, and I can imagine how much you will love that! He will make you anything you desire, even mugar pie? What is that? Sorry I did not understand when you wrote of your favorite food. I enjoyed and understood the letter written by Philippine the Writer—perhaps you can employ her again?

Enclosed please find the peach bows, Rose picked them off, there are twelve in all. They will look nice on your new dress.

Excuse me but I am going to lie down. It's too hot for the wax to seal properly, so do not worry if the letter arrives half-open.

P

From Hortense de Flavacourt
Hôtel de Mazarin, Paris
August 1, 1741

Dearest Louise,

I am glad to hear that you are enjoying the summer at Choisy. And what wonderful news about Pauline's condition—the Comte de Vintimille must be very proud. Now you will be an Elder Aunt twice over!

Thank you for inquiring after my husband. I have not seen him for two months, with all the trouble with the Austrians. He writes me from Silesia—I dread to think where on earth that place could be, with such an outlandish name! I pray every night for France's enemies to be afflicted by an act of God. An earthquake would be very suitable, or a fire to consume the whole city of Vienna. I am sure God will hear my prayers.

Poor Marie-Anne has still not passed from the grief over her husband. She snaps at me—you remember she was never very patient— and claims she is not missing her husband, only dying of boredom. I know that is the grief speaking. I sometimes think I pray more for her husband's soul than she does, but you know Marie-Anne, she is very private. I am sure she spends much time on her knees when she is alone.

We see Diane now occasionally. Tante is never very keen—she says Diane is as badly brought up as Pauline—but she is allowed to dine with us once a month. Though she does eat an awful amount, her manners are fair, much improved since she has been living with the Duchesse de Lesdiguières.

Thank you for the lovely handkerchief with the doves for the baby. They looked black but I am sure they were not; perhaps just a very dark blue? Freddie took it with him to Picardy, where he will be cared for by his wet nurse. I miss him terribly.

I enclose a crate of lemons; freshly squeezed they make a very refreshing drink, perfect for this heat. Cook recommends adding honey and a touch of salt.

Love,
Hortense

Marie-Anne

August 1741

Widowhood is supposed to be the one time in a woman's life when she is accorded some degree of freedom. For those who escape unscathed from childbirth and the caprices of a husband, widowhood is a season cherished by many women.

It seems that Tante is determined to ruin even this for me.

Life back at Tante's house is almost as unbearable as it was before I went away. While I have changed, Tante has not. She is as dour and disapproving as ever, though the scandal and antics of my two sisters at Court enlivens her slightly; it seems her hate has given her new reason to live. She forbids Hortense and me from visiting or corresponding with our sisters. Like convent girls we must obey, for we are in her house.

Hortense is only too happy living here, content with visits to friends in our neighborhood, writing to her husband, her endless needlework projects. She will hardly even accompany me to the opera or the theater—the last time I dragged her she complained bitterly of the immorality so celebrated in *Tartuffe*, and I realized I had chosen the wrong play.

I miss JB, and it was terrible that he had to die so young, but his memory recedes rather quickly. Now it seems that the mourning dresses that I must wear are the only memory I have that I was ever married. I am sad, of course, but I am not drowning in my grief as Hortense likes to think; rather it is boredom that plagues me and makes me snappish and irritable.

Sometimes I find myself longing for Burgundy, though it felt like a prison while I was there. I suppose, I think in moments of sad clarity, or when I have drunk too much wine and wake later to stare at the walls of my bedchamber, for a moment forgetting where I am, perhaps I am the sort of person who will never be happy, anywhere. I am like those sheep, I think bitterly, that only and forever seek greener pastures. Was that Aesop?

༺༻

"As large as a swollen sow, though with a touch of fever these last weeks. They've been bleeding her constantly. Next week she returns to Versailles and will be installed in the apartments of the Duc de Rohan. Five rooms." The Duc de Richelieu raises his eyebrows at the guests assembled around the dinner table; I think he knows quite well my sisters are the great unmentionables in this house, but his broad smile to Tante implies no artifice. *Do continue and tell us more*, I want to say, but of course I can't.

From Vienna, Richelieu procured for Tante a small piece of a finger bone, rumored to be part of the hand of Saint Septimus, that she desires to present to the queen as a New Year's gift. To thank him Tante invited him to dine when he was next in Paris. With us are Tante's silent, dwarflike daughter, Marie Jeanne, and her husband, the Comte de Maurepas. We are seated in the freshly renovated dining room, a room dedicated to the art of eating, a riotous procession of newly painted nymphs on the walls, others hiding in the clouds on the ceiling. Tante's decorating style shows no restraint. The windows are open to the gardens at the back of the house, the summer evening wind affording some relief from the relentless heat.

"I must update you on the latest decisions," says Maurepas in his reedy voice, turning the conversation, to my dismay, away from Pauline and her pregnancy. Maurepas launches into a pompous screed; he is the minister of marine and on the state council and likes to boast that the king depends on him more than on

Fleury. I doubt that, but then again I have also doubted, in the deep dark recesses of my mind, the king's judgment.

"And so, we must consider, and His Majesty commends me for my prudence, whether increasing the number of ships . . ." Maurepas drones on as the main dishes are served—a rather dry roast beef, two great sides of sauceless pig, a few vegetable dishes. I take some green beans and a slice of pork. Maurepas is rumored to be the author of many of the dirty ditties and songs that make their way from the street, pass through the kitchens, and eventually—thankfully—reach us in our rooms on the upper floors. It's hard to believe he has the imagination to write them: he probably employs a playwright.

I wish one of our guests would tell me what is really going on at Court, with the king and Pauline and Louise. But Maurepas—never. I've only met him and his bat-faced wife a few times and I am not impressed with the man, with his ill-fitting mustard breeches and affected voice. Instinctively I dislike him—there is a shadow about him, and I would not trust a word from his mouth. His wife sits beside him, small as a midget and morosely silent. I don't know what she is thinking, but then decide I don't care.

One of Hortense's women is the sister of Maurepas's valet; apparently Maurepas is as impotent as a frog. Hortense didn't say impotent, of course, only whispered that his member finds it impossible to rise to sin; sometimes Hortense has a hard time reconciling her love of gossip with her full-time piety.

But Richelieu—now, that is an interesting man. As Maurepas drones on about the expansion of the navy, I study the duke. He is a relative, distantly, through my mother. Shorter than expected; a handsome face with a high-beaked nose and large eyes; ruby buttons down the front of his elegant coat, and a wig that shines like silk in the candlelight—white horsehair, I think; no need for powder. He is a man well into his forties but still good-looking, and one who . . . Holding a forkful of beef in midflight, he turns toward me and smiles, a thin, supercilious smile. He knows he has been under scrutiny. Without seeming to, he interrupts Maurepas and steers the conversation away from ships.

"Soubise could be an interesting appointment, but he once told me he gets seasick," he says. "And speaking of Soubise, I heard he was courting our lovely young widow? I've noticed he has a dance in his step these days, and it's not those heels he wears."

I smile and cast my eyes down to the pork on my plate, playing the demure widow. His first wife dead in childbirth, it's true that the Prince de Soubise had been courting me, though rather halfheartedly. He declared me lovely, but he was more intrigued by the dowry of our neighbor Anne-Thérèse de Carignan. She can have him; I'll marry again, someday, but this time it will be my choice. And it will be someone I love. Truly love. That will be my freedom.

"I do not believe he is serious," I murmur.

"Poor man—I will be reproached when he learns that I had the opportunity to dine here and feast on his lovely lady." Richelieu's voice is languid and drawn out, and I have a sudden, shocking image of him eating me. "Feast my eyes, if I am to clarify."

"Not too disappointed," I say, willing myself not to blush. "He ate here last month. But now it seems his . . . affections . . . are better placed with Mademoiselle de Carignan." Though he is young and good-looking, I found Soubise rather boring and boastful. An intimate of the king's—a fact he alludes to constantly—and as arrogant as the rest of his family: the Rohans are said to be even more pompous than the Noailles.

"He should have come and talked to me," says Maurepas in disapproval, not bothering to look at me. "Far too early for Madame de la Tournelle to be thinking of remarriage." I roll my eyes, ever so slightly, and Richelieu catches my look and grins. There is cordial dislike running between the two men.

"Ah, carrots in cream! Delightful!" exclaims Richelieu as the footman sets a large tureen on the table. "My favourite dish. The fame of your table reaches far and wide," he says to Tante, who inclines her head and absorbs the false compliment.

"Needs more seasoning," says Maurepas in his high, reedy voice. "I find them a little bland."

"Well, perhaps my niece has some suggestions," sniffs Tante in her vinegar voice. "Apparently Marie-Anne was quite the little gardener down in Burgundy."

"I grew some spices," I concede.

"I still remember those vanilla pods you sent," says Hortense dreamily. "Cook made such a heavenly pudding with them. I think he even called it Heavenly Pudding. Or was it Pudding of Heaven?"

"Ah," says Richelieu, looking at me with some interest. "A fellow horticulturalist. And what spices would you recommend to enliven this delicious dish, madame?"

"Cumin," I say promptly. "The earthy tones would complement the cream very well, and enhance the flavor of the carrots."

Richelieu's eyes almost bulge out of his face. They quickly recede but his expression remains greedy and alive. It is a look I can't place, but suddenly he is very interested in me. Very interested. What have I said?

"Carrots cooked in cream and cumin? Madame, an *excellent* choice. Nothing, *nothing*," he emphasizes—why is he looking at me like that?—"could be more delightful." He takes an enormous forkful to his mouth and deliberately allows a slim stream of cream to dribble down his chin. He dabs at it with his handkerchief, his eyes still on me—still feasting on me.

I wonder how he would be as a lover. I remember JB's gangly body, his strong arms and large hands; while the duke is smaller and more compact, I sense energy, muscles and more beneath the silken finery of his elaborate Turkish coat. He is said to be the most accomplished man in France, both in the bedchamber and out.

"What's cumin?" asks Hortense. "It sounds *horrible*. Definitely not something found in biblical lands, I'm sure."

"I just think a little more salt would do it. Nothing wrong with good old salt," says Maurepas rather pompously. "All these newfangled spices from the Orient and other places, I just can't—"

"Yet you command the ships that bring those spices in; is the trade not good for France?" I ask, boldly interrupting.

Maurepas keeps eating as though I had not spoken.

"Carrots cooked in cumin. An excellent choice, madame," Richelieu repeats, bringing the conversation back, his eyes still on me.

"Cumin has many uses," I reply. I feel as if I am flirting with him, but about what I am not sure. Carrots? It's flattering, though, and I'm enjoying it. "Good for the complexion, when used in a face cream, or so my Gar—my cook in Burgundy used to say."

"It can be an excellent face cream," says Richelieu, staring straight at me. "Massaged well into the face—yes, it has its uses." It is as though we are having two conversations, one spoken and the other not, but I don't know which one we say aloud. Extraordinary.

After dinner Richelieu apologizes and takes an early leave, saying he will be late for the showing of *Tartuffe*. We all know that the play is no longer in the theater and that he is off to see his mistress, or mistresses: it is common knowledge that he has a soft spot—or is it a hard spot?—for the wives of the Parisian bourgeoisie.

Maurepas watches him leave with a look of frank envy. We settle down in the salon with Tante and a book she will read aloud to us: *A Treatise on the Persecution of the Freemasons*. I keep my emotions better hidden and primed, but I am envious too.

"Thank goodness that man is gone," whispers Hortense to me as we take our chairs. "Though he said nothing untoward, he fair reeks of sin."

The next week a book arrives for me, courtesy of the Duc de Richelieu.

"Illuminations on the Virtue of Goodness," I read in puzzlement—now, why would he think I would be interested in that? Hortense and Tante both receive copies of the same title as well, and I am piqued to be burnished with the same brush of goodness as them. But then I open mine and find the book has been re-covered; it is actually an illustrated copy of *The Academy of Ladies*, a book the priests call Sodom and Gomorrah, combined.

Oh.

I remember the knowing way Richelieu looked at me, the way his eyes casually discarded the stuff of my gown to bare my breasts, and worse. And that strange conversation about carrots and cumin. It was almost as though he knew me, though we had just met that night. But perhaps he does know me, I think, flicking open the book to a rather disturbing picture of a woman, her skirts up, bent over an altar—I snap it shut, then reconsider. He does know me, and why should I hide it?

I wonder again what it would be like to have him as a lover.

I write him back and thank him for the book, and tell him I have passed many pleasant evenings with only it for company. But—rather disappointing—I don't hear anything more from him.

Pauline

His name will be Charles-Emmanuel-Marie-Magdelon de Vintimille. In truth, my baby should be named Louis, for he is the spitting image of his father. But that buffoon boy Vintimille carries on as though the child were his own, ignoring the sneers and loud whispers proclaiming him both a blind man, and a stupid one.

The birth only took an hour, two at most—very efficient. After the birth both fathers collided in my chamber, both exclaiming over the perfection of the baby. It was quite funny really, and I even felt a rush of tenderness for Vintimille—after all, it's thanks to him that I am married and with the king. I suppose I should allow him his small moment of triumph. Perhaps he can move back into his apartment when I move into my new one?

Vintimille assumed naming rights, and so Charles it is. But I call my precious babe Demi-Louis. And how delighted the king is with his son! Just hours after he was born Louis was at my side, kissing me and stroking my arms. He held up the baby and examined every perfect inch of him. He laid him out in the crimson cradle and crowed over him as though he were a new *dauphin*. For all his children with the queen, Louis has only one son living. I feel such triumph that I could give him this ultimate gift.

He was there beside me almost every hour before the birth and now he showers me with letters and tender visits. He promises my new apartments will be ready by the end of the month, and I have already met the man Degas who will be my personal chef— he prepared me a white cake with coconut, prescribed by doctors for building strength after a baby. Though plain, it was quite delicious, but I only managed a few bites.

I am resolved to be a better consort to him in the coming years. He is truly a magnificent man. The king, I mean, not the chef. He truly loves me. And I . . . I might even be falling in love with him. He is so patient with me, so enamored of me—how can I resist? We are a true partnership, lovers yet also friends, and now we share this miraculous little baby.

The wet nurse comes to feed Demi-Louis several times a day. I watch him as he suckles and then I take him in the bed and spend hours marveling at his flawless little fingers and tiny, tiny toes and his soft white skin. My passion for this child is stronger than anything I had imagined; had you told me I would be among the most maternal of women, I would have knocked you over with my laughter. But that was before Demi-Louis was born.

I was delighted when I became pregnant, of course, but mostly for the additional power a son for the king would bring me. But now . . . can love be stronger than even power itself?

Did my mother feel like this at my birth? Daughters are not sons, but still. Did she marvel at our perfection? Did she fall in love with each of us in turn and forget for a time the world outside the doors of her bedchamber? Perhaps. Perhaps not. But oh, what a wonderful feeling. For the first time I feel as though I understand the purpose of my life: to provide this precious little son of mine with all that the world can offer.

Now Demi-Louis is starting to fuss. I hand him to the nurse then ask the attendant for a cup of weak wine. I eat one last mouthful of the white cake, spitting out the little shards of coconut that I care not for. My head is beginning to ache and I feel uncomfortably hot. I will see Louis in the morning and I am determined to be up and at his side within the week, even though my insides still hurt and my ankles are swollen like a pig's.

But now my head is aching terribly and I feel so very tired. I seem to hurt everywhere. The nurse closes the curtains and leaves me in darkness. I hear Demi-Louis's whimper as he is taken from the room. And that is the last sound that brushes my ears before I fall into sleep, and darkness.

Diane

auline gave birth to a son! The doctors declared her free of all danger and the baby fine and healthy. Now she is a mother and I am an aunt of the king's son! How grand it all sounds. Madame Lesdig says I must not get too excited, for these days are not like the old days when the royal bastards all became royal princes. This king, she says, will not acknowledge the child, and I must always refer to him as a Vintimille. Not to worry; I am sure Pauline will change the king's mind.

I am impatient to see the child, and of course Pauline. We received the good news five days ago, and now I eagerly wait to hear the name of the new baby. Will she name him Louis? Would the king allow that? The first message said the baby looked very like His Majesty. Madame Lesdig snorted: "Such foolery. The only thing a baby resembles at two days old is a crumpled little crab. More importantly, we must pray it is healthy, and leave such trifles as appearance for later."

Perhaps Pauline's husband will want to name him, in which case it might be a Vintimille family name, perhaps Félix or Gaspard? I hope she doesn't have to call the baby Gaspard—I have never liked that name. I don't know why; perhaps because it sounds like bastard, or custard.

We are sitting in the salon on the first floor of the house, an old-fashioned room with dark red walls hung with gloomy portraits of men on horses. Madame Lesdig is sorting through old letters; when she finds one from a friend who has died, she gives it to me and I roll it up and tie it with a black ribbon and place it in a small enameled chest.

"So much death, so much death," says Madame, shaking her head. "But as I am sixty, I suppose it is only natural that half my friends are gone. So many who died so young."

I roll a long letter from the Comtesse de Marbois.

"A friend of my youth," says Lesdig with a sigh. "From our convent days. She hated birds—was terrified of them really—and then she married a man whose heraldry included a hawk, and her entire home was decorated with them. Quite unfortunate. Poor Clémence."

I tie it with a ribbon and pop it into the coffin box of dead letters.

"Dead in an accident, she was only twenty-two—or was it thirty-two? The wheels rolled over a flock of chickens and the carriage overturned."

I giggle. "Death by chicken!"

Madame de Lesdig tuts. "Don't be disrespectful, Diane-Adelaide. Here is another from Marie-Clémence. Roll them together. Maurice, get down." She takes a large ginger tom off the table and deposits him on the floor, where he slinks off into the shadows. I don't ask what she's going to do with the letters in the box, especially as she's probably going to die soon herself. It's hard to talk to old people about death, though I am sure she must think about it a lot.

Then I hear the clatter of a carriage outside on the cobblestones.

"Oh, it could be news. From Pauline!"

"Diane-Adelaide! You must remember that curiosity is for cats, not ladies!"

I leap up and skitter outside, ignoring Madame Lesdig's pleas for more decorum. It is a footman in the Noailles colors; his face is solemn. Messengers are trained so their demeanor matches their news, and I stop short, something cold suddenly creeping over my heart.

"Gaspard?" I squeak, before I can stop myself. Is that the bad news?

The man bows and hands me a letter. I see the black feather, sealed under the black wax. Oh no. The baby . . . Oh no, Pauline will be devastated. The baby . . .

The floors are no longer as level as they were before, and I walk carefully back to Madame Lesdig. Wordlessly I proffer the sealed note, though I would prefer to burn it and pretend it never came. Madame Lesdig slices it open with one gnarled nail and reads. She closes her eyes, her face marble white.

"The baby? Is it the baby? Is he dead?"

"No, dear heart, it's not the baby."

She hugs me and I am enveloped in rosewater and love. Suddenly I wish it was the baby, because I know what she is going to say next. "No, dear heart, no. It's not the baby. It's your sister."

"But the doctors said she and the baby were fine . . ." I whisper, beginning to cry.

"She is dead. Pauline is dead. It must have been poison," Madame Lesdig says. "They do that," she declares, shaking her head and pursing her lips. "Take advantage of this time in a woman's life when she is most vulnerable. And the news after the birth was so positive . . ." Now she is crying too and her tears are as real as mine.

Oh, poor Pauline! Dead. I cannot bear to think of her cold and all alone in the ground. She always hated the cold. And the heat. She hated everything. I cannot believe she let herself die.

Poison? No, surely not.

∞

Pauline is dead. My sister Pauline is dead. How can this be? She was invincible, she was supreme, she was Pauline. She was my sister. A force of nature.

Later we hear more details of her death. She died so suddenly that there was no time for the sacraments. Her body was quickly taken from Versailles, for no one but royalty may lie dead under the palace roof. She was taken to the sacristy in a church in town and left unattended; a mob found her and desecrated her corpse.

They desecrated her body. Her poor, cold body. Why? Why did they hate her?

I cry and cry and I think I may never laugh again.

When she hears what happened, Madame Lesdig is so overcome she retires to her room and stays within for days, anguished at the idea of Pauline dying without last rites. I think, but surely God will understand? If there is no time, there is no time; you can't stop the night from falling or the sun from rising the next day. But the mobs . . . they tore . . .

The images I conjure in my mind don't leave me alone, not for a second.

To distract myself I mix up my dresses, cutting the bodice of one and attaching it to the skirt of another. I drink too much brandy until I fall asleep, but even in my dreams I cannot get the images from my mind. They tore her body apart. They tore it *apart*. And cut off all her hair.

They stuck firecrackers in her body and lit them and then laughed. Why? She made the king happy. She never hurt anyone . . . well, perhaps Louise a little bit, but never anyone else. Certainly some at Court didn't like her and not everyone at Port-Royal did either, in fact many did not like her. But that was only because they were jealous of her intelligence and her wit, which was quick but sometimes too sharp. She never really wished anyone ill, they were words only, and in her actions and deeds she never did anyone ill. Except, again, Louise.

It is because she sinned, they say. Her awful death punishment for her many awful sins. But where was the sin? She loved the king and he loved her—how is that a sin? People tell me I don't understand but of course I do.

I want the baby to come and live with us at Madame Lesdig's, but Louise writes and tells me that his father—she means the Comte de Vintimille—will occupy himself with the boy's future.

But when the boy is older I will tell him all about his wonderful mother.

A stray dog wanders from the street into the dining room,

followed by several hissing cats. Before the footman can shoo it away, it comes straight to my side and sits and looks at me expectantly. It is looking at me with the eyes of Pauline, and though of course the dog is not Pauline, I feel in some way it brings a message from her.

"It's because you are eating chicken," says Madame Lesdig harshly, but I do not agree.

I pick up the dog and ignore Madame Lesdig's horrified cries. I leave the room with the dog and my plate of chicken in my arms. I cuddle it as though it were Pauline and we are children again in the nursery on the fourth floor.

That night, the cook makes me pigeon pie and sugar tarts and I eat until I wish I could vomit. My stomach hurts it is so full, but my grief is an empty pillowcase that nothing can fill. What will become of me now? Pauline assured me my future was in good hands, but now she is gone and my life must go on, and I do not want it to go on at Madame Lesdig's forever.

Oh, Pauline. I will pray for you for the rest of my life.

From Marie-Anne de la Tournelle
Hôtel de Mazarin, Paris
September 20, 1741

Dear Diane,

Hortense insisted I write to you; she said you would be devastated by Pauline's death. As we all are. Hortense says only I truly know what grief is, because of my husband's death. So, I must write to you. Still, you know Pauline and I were not close; nonetheless I would not wish such a terrible end upon even my worst enemy, and certainly not on my sister.

I am truly sorry for your grief; you must come and visit and we will cheer you up. I am very bored back in Paris; Tante's house is the same prison it always was. Does the Duchesse de Lesdiguières have any books she could lend me? Anything is fine—I've quite run out and Tante has nothing more of interest in her library. Please come and visit, and bring the books. We can have Cook prepare something special for you, perhaps plum cake or some almond tarts?

Do not be too sad, everyone has to die someday.

Love,
Marie-Anne

From Hortense de Flavacourt
Hôtel de Mazarin, Paris
October 12, 1741

Dearest Louise,

My greetings to you in this time of sorrow. How terrible that our dear sister should die, and in such a manner. Tante says Pauline died without sacraments. She is very satisfied that God's plan included this vengeance on one so shameless (those are her words, not mine). Tante knows that sinners always pay in the end.

Is it true they talk of poison? Surely not? Who would want to poison her? I am sure she had enemies; well, in truth we heard she had many, but to wish to kill her? Oh, I cannot imagine. I do hope it was just the perils of childbirth. My confessor told me that women who are lax in their prayers or who lead a wicked life are more apt to die at that time than other ladies. I survived my confinement, and so you can see the truth of his words.

You must be very sad. And His Majesty as well.

We saw Diane yesterday. Poor poppet, she was distraught and not even interested in the plum cake that Cook prepared especially for her. Her grief must be deep. Tante told her that her notions of poison were silly, for even though Pauline was a curse on the nation (her words, not mine) she wasn't important enough to poison. I do not think Diane was comforted.

Marie-Anne has not cried but I am sure she has done so, in private or in the chapel.

In loving grief,
Hortense

From Louise de Mailly
Château de Versailles
October 20, 1741

Dearest Hortense,

We are devastated, devastated. The king is in deepest mourning. He takes the death of each of his subjects to heart—he calls them his children. Pauline was a good friend of his, and of course my sister, and he knows how deeply I grieve for her.

The autopsy revealed nothing, and though there are rumors about Fleury, I would not, could not believe them. This is not the last century, for goodness' sake! These are modern times and poison is an ancient trickery art that is out of place in our civilized world.

No, we must just accept that she died from her confinement and the fever that strikes women far too often at that time. I am not sure that prayers influence such matters; I know of many wicked women who have survived their confinements without being struck down.

Excuse the blotches on the paper; I am crying as I write this.

Your sister,
Louise

Louise

CHÂTEAU DE SAINT-LÉGER

December 1741

What a miserable winter it is. Louis is broken, simply broken.

"Why am I being punished?" he asks, then answers himself: "I am being punished for living in sin, such is God's wrath." He turns to me, beseeching that I might contradict him, but all I can do is murmur condolences. For if he sinned with Pauline, then what has he done with me? These days Louis finds some comfort in my arms, though we embrace only as brother and sister; we have not made love since before the birth of Demi-Louis.

He has not returned to the queen's bed or to mine, and loves nothing better than to hear stories of idyllic, platonic love. Libertines now declare it the highest of callings and suddenly celibacy is more fashionable than pink-powdered hair. The staid Duc and Duchesse de Luynes, notoriously dull and faithful, are suddenly in much demand at dinner parties.

At Court, my sister's enemies snigger and roll their eyes and ask, again and again, more openly now that she is gone and the months push her memory further back, how it could be that the king, the most handsome man in France, not to mention the king, could have been so enamored of such a green monkey and be now so devastated by her death?

"She must have had a very fine cunt."

"Blinded him with her ugliness, simply blinded him. I hear there is an insect in Guinea that does such a thing to its mate."

"One shouldn't crow, of course—after all, my mother and two of my sisters died in childbirth, not to mention my wife—but it is all very satisfying."

"An insect's cunt—that's what she had. Now let's just thank the Good Lord she is gone."

They talk thus in front of me and I try to ignore them, as they ignore me. Louis prefers to shut himself up alone with his black moods. We spend weeks closeted away at the small château of Saint-Léger, Fleury and his ministers grumbling that he needs to come back to Versailles, that they need his signature and his interest.

The king allows only a few friends to share his mourning and passes his days in silence and prayer, and even needs to be coaxed to the hunt. In the evening he prefers deep discourses on the meaning of life and death to a game of backgammon or cards. I have never seen his mood so black, not even after the death of his little son Philippe, cruelly taken the same year as one of his little sisters. A wax figure was made of Pauline's head after she died and in the evening Louis has it brought out and placed on the mantel. It watches us with sightless, waxy eyes. I hate it. I want to remember Pauline, but not like this.

On particularly mournful nights Louis will read Pauline's letters to him, over and over. There appear to be thousands—I am reminded of my own mountain of begging letters when she wished to first come to Versailles—and they give him consolation through the long winter evenings. We sit in silence, all heavy hearts and melancholy.

"Ah, Bijou, Bijou," he says to me, thumbing slowly through the papers, "you are such a comfort to me. Such solace. What would I do without you?"

My heart warms when he calls me by my old pet name. Is it possible that happiness can come from despair? Can one be on top of the mountain at the same time as one drowns in the sea? I am genuinely grieved by Pauline's awful death, but I luxuriate in my new closeness with the king and receive much consolation from his need of me at this dark hour. Perhaps I might even venture to call him Twinkles again? It has been so long since that was possible.

"Should I burn them, Bijou?" he asks, staring at the fire.

"No, sire, you must not. They are our most precious of mementos."

"But she is dead and gone. She is not coming back, and soon I—all of us—we—shall all be dead, and so what is the point of keeping them?" Louis is lost in the flames and in his unshaven sadness. "To read them makes me sad, yet at the same time gives me comfort. How can that be?"

"Please do not burn them, sire. Please. If it grieves you so, give them to me and I will keep them until you wish to see them again. Unless you command, I need never show them to you again."

Louis shakes his head; he is far, far away from the room. "She was a good woman. A kind woman. She was kind to me. That must mean she was kind, not callous, as others say. Don't you agree, Bijou?"

"I do, my dearest." He puts the letters carefully back in their box. He locks it and then throws the key into the fire. I gasp.

He turns to gaze at the wax head of Pauline. "When I wish to read them again, I shall have Bachelier take the box to the locksmiths. Everything can be fixed. Everything except death. That is final."

Often his sorrow gives way to anger—sometimes in the course of one evening. He claims her poisoned, for all the doctors—and there were many—declared the delivery a success and the mother out of danger. Only Richelieu dares speak when he is in these moods.

"It happens, sire. My dear cousin Anne-Marie of Soubise, newly married to the prince, was brought to bed of a healthy boy, and seeming in impeccable health, yet eight days after the birth, she died."

"Eight days? Pauline was six. Did we suspect foul play with Anne-Marie?"

"No, sire, she had not an enemy in the world."

"And what, Pauline—she had enemies? What are you suggesting?"

"Pauline had no enemies," says Richelieu smoothly. He lies very easily. He is a very handsome man, and when he is with the king it is like seeing twins, so close is their resemblance both in body and habits, though the king is a trifle taller. "There were some not as fond of her as you were, sire, but she had no enemies. An *enemy* is a very strong word."

"As *hate* is a strong word, sire," I add, remembering Zélie's words: one may dislike, but one may never hate. "No one hated her, though some might have been jealous."

"Who was jealous?" demands Louis.

Richelieu gives me one of his inscrutable looks and I feel like I might faint. Then he says: "Some of the ladies, perhaps, sire, for your charms are abundant, yet you had eyes for only one. Someone like . . . Mademoiselle de Charolais, for example."

That's going a little far, even for Richelieu. Charolais is out of favor with the king—Pauline saw to that—but she would never poison anyone. And her cold sister, Clermont, died just before Pauline did. No; Fleury and his cabal would be the most likely culprits.

"Impossible!" roars the king. "But if it were poison, I should consider it high treason, for it is as though they poisoned me."

We mutter dutifully. But there is no real fear in the room; the king has been talking of poison for months but the autopsy revealed nothing. We all understand that the king needs to blame. In his grief he needs to make someone accountable for a life that suddenly went terribly, hideously wrong.

☙

Charolais worms her way back to Versailles for the New Year entertainments. There is a masked ball in the little princesses' apartments, but it is a subdued and melancholy affair, with none of the gaiety that anonymity usually brings. Only beyond the sight of the king are there are spurts of laughter and gaiety. Charolais sidles up and pulls me aside. "The king is getting bored with all this mourning," she says, and raises one of her delicate little mouse-hair eyebrows, tinted the perfect shade of lavender to match the bows in her hair.

Life was quite pleasant when she was banished. I recall Pauline once referring to her as a lavender-colored clown, and smile. "The king will never forget Pauline."

"Maybe not, but it's all so dull here." Charolais shrugs. "And don't think for one minute that you're the only one concerned about who will warm the king's bed. You know how easily he gets bored." She looks at me pointedly and I know it is a remark at my expense. I remember her words to me from long ago and how awfully they came true: *Once everyone knows about you and the king, he will quickly become bored.*

I look at Charolais and I realize I hate her. I wish I could have her banished like Pauline did, but I don't have the power.

I look her up and down. "Poor dear. Bows on the side of your head . . . why, that hasn't been seen since '39. They fell right out of favor. As if they were *banished.*" Rather an evil thing to say, but it did feel good. Very good.

Charolais's berry-stained mouth opens in surprise. "I see the ghost of Pauline is alive and well," she says tartly, and turns on her heels, all indignation and ruffled lavender. As she goes she lobs one last parting shot: "But ghosts can easily be swept away, along with other *cobwebs.*"

Suddenly I miss Pauline. It sounds strange to say, but the relationship we had suited us, in some odd and definitely sinful way. I crave the comfort of family. Perhaps Diane should come and visit? She must be missing Pauline dreadfully, and Pauline often talked of inviting her to Versailles.

My woman, Jacobs, thinks Diane will do as Pauline did, though I tell her over and again that Diane is nothing but sweetness and folly. I have a strong need right now for sororal comfort—is that so wrong?

Jacobs looks at me with determination, a wolf defending her cub.

"My lady, sometimes I feel as if I am your only protector."

"I don't need your protection, Jacobs," I say, as sternly as I can.

Jacobs does not reply but continues to look at me with her steely eyes. I know what she's thinking but I also know she's wrong.

Yes, I think I shall invite Diane.

From Louise de Mailly
Château de Versailles
January 3, 1742

Dearest Diane,

New Year's greetings to you! Thank you (and Philippine) for your latest letter. Life here continues in sorrow, the king is crushed and so too must the whole world be. We are partners in our pain and we are grown very close again, like brother and sister. His need for me touches me deeply, though we do not touch, I mean.

I know that Pauline wished you to come and visit her at Versailles, and I think to honor her memory by inviting you to stay. It is lonely here—for so many years I was blessed with Pauline's company, and now I find myself longing for sororal comfort. It would greatly please me if you would come and visit. Of course, you cannot be presented but perhaps you might travel with us to Saint-Léger, or Rambouillet, where the rules are less strict? You might even meet His Majesty!

Do not worry about what you will wear; I have saved many of Pauline's dresses for you and we can have the women tailor them when you arrive. I also kept aside Pauline's favorite green brocade shawl; she said it was yours. It is very handsome and will be most appropriate to wear as the days continue cold in this most dreadful of winters.

In loving sorrow,
Louise

From Marie Philippine de Braille
House of Madame the Dowager Duchesse de Lesdiguières, Paris
January 8, 1742

Madame de Mailly,

Honored greetings to you, my lady.

I write to inform you that Mademoiselle Diane received your letter and invitation and has made arrangements to visit in the middle of the next month. She is most excited.

She is delighted that you remembered about the green shawl, and though her sorrow over her sister knows no bounds, she will be pleased to inherit her dresses.

Respectfully,
Philippine de Braille

Part III

One in Triumph

Marie-Anne

Suddenly life is interesting again. Very interesting.

In the New Year, Emmanuel-Armand de Vignerot du Plessis, the Duc d'Agénois (whom I last met at my wedding, six years ago) arrives at the house and he is far more handsome than I remember, wearing a coat the color of blueberries, cut in the modern style and with his hair pulled back in a neat tail. He is tall with strong blue eyes, one of the pupils shaped like a star. After making small talk with Hortense and myself over wine and almond cakes, full of commiserations about Pauline and JB, but also with some ribald memories of their military time together, he boldly asks if he may speak a moment with me alone. I am startled but assume he has something private to tell me, perhaps something about that mysterious Fleurette that my husband called to when in delirium? I look at Hortense and she looks at me as though the man has requested permission, right there and then, to rape me.

I decide that as a widow, I shall take care of my own reputation, and I tell her I will be fine. Tante is at Versailles this week and we are alone in the house. Of course there are twelve footmen and twenty other servants milling around the house and gardens, and workmen hammering away in the chapel, but we are without chaperone. Hortense leaves, reluctance dragging her feet, and Agénois leaps from his chair to sit beside me on the sofa. He takes my hands, and before I can remind him that there are two footmen just outside the door, he launches into an astounding question.

"Do you believe in love at first sight? The *coup de foudre*, the heart falling into the stomach, the moment when Cupid's arrow breaches the iron armor of even the hardest of hearts?"

My goodness, he is quite the poet. How precious.

"No, sir, I don't think so . . ."

"Nor myself. Until I saw you at your wedding. You were wearing a pink dress and a silver cape. A vision of beauty, Venus incarnate, and then the *coup de foudre*! Why? It was everything, the whole of it. Not just the dress—everything about you touched my heart."

It is over a year since I was widowed; he said he would have come at one year and one day, but he was away in Silesia with his regiment and only arrived back last week. Today, he decided to seize the opportunity and make his affections known. I gaze at him, my eyes as large as life. I don't think I have ever had quite such an astounding conversation. Ever.

Agénois gets up to stride around the room. His confession leaves me shaken but I am also secretly rather pleased. He is a remarkably handsome man. Very strong and well built, and those eyes! Quite the opposite of JB, whose image grows skinnier and skinnier with each passing month.

I hardly know anything about him, except that he is a nephew of the Duc de Richelieu, and therefore remotely related to me—but then again who isn't? I wonder briefly if his uncle talked about me. I have heard nothing from the great duke since the gift of that book last summer.

As I gaze at Agénois I can sense he is not a weak man, nor an insignificant one. His declaration is flattering and something stirs inside me . . . Cupid's arrow grazing my heart?

Agénois sits back down and grasps my hands again with assurance—has he done this many times, is this just the ruse of a master seducer?—and announces that he must leave, but begs my permission to visit again the next day.

A footman shows him out and I sit bemused in the gloomy salon, the sun and the day blocked out by heavy velvet curtains and a row of dense yews. Tante has been renovating the house for several years now but has only succeeded in updating the rooms on the first floor. Up here, the house remains stuck in the last century. Or the one previous to that.

I mull over Agénois's words. Such a handsome man—what eyes!—and he said he loves me. Has always loved me. I search for ulterior motives but find none. He has no reputation that I know of; these days a man's reputation travels farther and faster than a woman's, and everyone knows the libertines. He is not one, I am sure, and I do recall that JB once described him as a serious young man. Something tells me that he is sincere. I see again his large blue eyes and the high cheekbones, how his hand, rough and coarse, felt as it held mine, and the way his eyebrows shot up with every word he emphasized. And he said he loves me.

His carriage rumbles out of the courtyard and Hortense rushes in.

"Well?"

I want to be alone with my memory of what has just happened, to unpack it and savor it, then wrap it up again to hold for later. I shake my hand, as though to wave away Agénois and our little conversation. "Just some private memories of JB," I say.

Hortense narrows her eyes. She has become a little Tante Mazarin, both of them provincials though they live in Paris. They are entombed in this house, alike in their habits and their routines, and it is assumed that I too will become as them.

That is not what I want.

Agénois returns the next day, and the next, and all through the week until Monday when Tante returns from her duties at Court. We spend hours in the salon talking, sometimes with his chapped hands clasped around mine. I find myself missing him even before he leaves and looking forward to the next day. I never thought I could be or would be in love, but I truly think I am. And all in the space of a week. Isn't life extraordinary? I think back to the despair I felt upon leaving Tournelle and it is as though I think of a stranger's life.

He introduces me to the poetry of Louise Labé, and quotes to me at length:

> *"Your cold, appraising eyes entice me still,*
> *And cause a hundred thousand sighs.*
> *Again, and yet again, I wait and wait in vain.*
> *The night is dark, the way is all uphill."*

For the first time in a long time, I am no longer interested in my books. The set of ten *Artamène* novels from the library at Tournelle gather dust in my room. I'd rather lie daydreaming on my bed, reading and rereading his letters to me, filled with romantic sonnets:

> *If only I could master that rare art*
> *Of loving you in subtle ways that please,*
> *By putting wayward passions in deep freeze!*
> *I feel too much the ardor of my heart.*

Sometimes I slip out to wander along the Seine with only my thoughts for company, wearing a cloak and mask for protection against the sun and strangers, daydreaming about my new suitor. And unfortunately a suitor he must stay; he's already married.

By his fourth visit Hortense knows something is afoot and sulks behind her disapproval.

"What are you going to tell Tante?"

We are eating in the dining room, watched by a footman and, from the wall panels, five nymphs feasting on grapes.

"That I have an admirer," I say, concentrating on my pea soup. I don't like peas, but when they are crushed beyond all recognition and spiced with mustard and black pepper, I like them well enough. I feel a pang of guilt for not writing to Garnier as I promised. "It is not a crime to have an admirer, and I have had them before." Soubise's courtship was very staid and uninspired; he only ever visited when Tante was home and sometimes I forgot I was supposed to be the object of his affections.

"Agénois is a nephew of the Duc de Richelieu," Hortense observes with disapproval. "The most debauched man in France."

"Only that." We are having a rehearsal conversation, a prelude to the one I will surely have with Tante when she learns of the situation. "Richelieu is only a distant uncle, not his twin."

"And you a widow only a year."

"More than a year."

"Marie-Anne, he's *married*. Tante was understanding about Soubise, but that was a genuine courtship. This—what is this?"

I put down my soup spoon. "Would you have me wilt away in this house, pining for my dead husband, like you wilt away, pining for your living husband? Is that what you want?"

Hortense tries to hold her lips firm in disapproval but they quiver gently. "I am only concerned for your reputation."

"No, you're not."

There is silence and I press on: "It is not forbidden to have visitors. And if the visitor happens to be young and handsome and not born in the last century, then so much the better. It is not a crime. If he admires me, I am glad of it. I admire him too. There is nothing more to it."

The footman takes away our soup and lays the main dishes on the table. We serve ourselves some fish and I start to eat with gusto. I am determined to be unperturbed by this conversation. Agénois has appeared in my life like a ray of sunshine, one that has managed to pierce through the yews and the thick curtains of Tante's house to find me.

"I find his company entertaining," I say into the silence.

Hortense stares down at her plate, not eating. Why is she so upset? I only spoke the truth; she does pine for her husband, who is constantly away with his regiment.

"I'm sorry," I say softly. "There is no harm or shame in missing your husband. It is admirable that you do."

A tear falls silently onto Hortense's plate and mixes with the sauce. I try a joke: "I think the fish is salty enough already." No response. But I do have one thing to say that will make her feel better. "Besides, he won't be bothering Tante, or myself, or yourself, for a while."

Hortense looks up at me. Even when she is crying her skin doesn't redden. Her tears magnify her eyes, glassy like a fish's, and they shine in her sorrow.

"He leaves next month for Languedoc."

I fear it will be a long, dry summer.

Surprisingly, Tante is not as censorious as expected. She knows Agénois personally—his wife is one of her granddaughters—and not just by association with his notorious uncle. She is on good terms with him; it appears that everyone is on good terms with him. He is, improbably, the perfect man, and Tante declares him welcome if he desires to visit. It is understood that nothing beyond "visiting" will happen. To my relief she doesn't demand to follow our correspondence.

"Though I often say the contrary, family is not everything. If it were, you would be as sullied as your sisters and father. Instead, you are known as a young and virtuous marquise, devoted in mourning." She looks pointedly at me. "Make sure your reputation stays that way, at least until you remarry and are out of my care."

"Yes, Tante," I say in a sweet voice, sugared with the practice of many years. I burn inside. I am not a child, yet here I am, trapped.

જી

"Only a quick visit, mind you," says Richelieu; he strides into the reception room and casually flings his cloak over a statue of Hestia, blinding her. "I have some building works to attend to." I hide a smile. Paris is abuzz with his latest scandal: he bought the house adjoining the one belonging to his mistress's husband, then had a secret entryway constructed through the chimney hearths.

"My dear Madame de la Tournelle. So nice to see you again. I hope you enjoyed the book I sent."

To my credit I don't blush but regard him rather coolly.

"Well," he says eventually, "I just had to visit the woman who has so captured my nephew. Pining, positively pining, my men tell me. He is even resisting his deployment to Languedoc."

I smile inwardly. I'm resisting it too. To Richelieu I say: "The Duc d'Agénois was a good friend of my husband's. And he is married to kin."

"Mmmm." Richelieu contemplates me rather lazily and does nothing to advance the conversation. I am not one of those that feel the need to fill empty air with nervous chatter; I hold my silence and gaze back. I know he's here for a reason, but I don't know what it is yet.

"I'm surprised, frankly. Just a little. Yes, he's a fine-looking man, but I would have thought you would have wanted someone more—substantial." I admire how the elegance of his delivery masks the impudent meaning beneath his words. "Agénois is a married man, my dear madame," he continues. I don't dignify his statement with an answer—we both know the situation.

"Have you considered . . ." he pauses, and by doing so lets me know that something important is to follow . . . "coming to Court? Keeping your dear sister Louise in comfort in this time of her grief? Helping her, with . . . matters?"

"No, I have not," I say truthfully, though Pauline's death had definitely removed a barrier. I have decided that if I am to get married again, I shall seek a husband with a position at Court. Where Agénois will be. No more provincial marriages for me.

Richelieu regards me with a gaze as long as a sermon. There is a queer energy pulsing off him and suddenly I realize what he is implying. The world can talk of little else: Who will be the next mistress of the king? Now that Pauline is gone, no one seems to think he will be content with just Louise.

"Well, regardless, we must see more of you at Court," Richelieu says finally, assured that his question has been understood.

"Attend the pre-Lenten festivities. I think I can persuade your Tante—she's been rather in my thrall since I gave her that bone," he whispers conspiratorially, and I can't help but giggle. Though wary of him, I sense a keen kindred spirit beneath his elegant exterior; he is a sharp man with a sharp view of the world. He picks up his cloak from Hestia's head and takes his leave.

I ponder his words. I do not think I misunderstood, but—three? Three sisters? With that, the gossips would not sleep until the next century. The idea is intriguing, and I am certainly flattered he is thinking of me—I am sure he has many other tongs in the fire, as they say—but I am not interested. I love Agénois.

Diane

VERSAILLES

January 1742

Louise embraces me. She looks just as pretty as ever but also quite worried. I promise her I will not do to her what Pauline did: the words burst out before I can stop them. A world of hurt opens up in Louise's eyes and she turns away to gather composure.

"I am sorry, Louise! I should be more like a fish!"

Louise looks back at me, confused.

"Fish don't make any sound at all—they are the most silent of God's creatures. Except of course when they splash, but that is not speaking, just making noise. Like I do! Oh, I am so sorry. Pauline was my favorite person in the world, but I would never do what she did."

"Of course you wouldn't," Louise finally says, very softly.

"Never. And I am so sorry I said it, I didn't mean to say it at all. I just meant that I will always love you. Not that Pauline didn't love you, I am sure she did, in her own way, I mean I *know* she did . . ." I hear Madame Lesdig's warnings all the time but they do no good—I cannot seem to think before I speak. To stop myself talking, I hug Louise as tightly as I can.

☙

Now I understand why Pauline always said her life could not begin until she made it to Versailles. How wonderful it is here! I have laughed more in the last few weeks than I did in a lifetime at the convent or at Madame Lesdig's. I cannot help but giggle, even though everyone here is so serious and they pray before Madame Etiquette as though she were Mother Mary herself.

The courtiers are overdressed dolls with exquisite outfits and accessories. I'm still in mourning for Pauline, but I study the fashions that surround me for the day when I have money and can dress as they do: diaphanous silks and gauzes as light as angel's wings; petticoats embroidered with flowers or heraldic crests; modern gowns printed *à la indienne* with willow trees and scenes from China, and the passion this year is for roses, roses, roses everywhere. Louise points out the Duchesse d'Antin, famous for the luxury of her dress, and Madame de Montbazon, who once wore a jacket made entirely of snakeskins! I meet my half sister Henriette, the daughter of my mother and the Duc de Bourbon. She is now the Marquise de la Guiche and has a small dog with a squashed face that apparently only understands Chinese; she carries it everywhere in a basket painted to match her gown.

I am introduced to many important courtiers who look straight through me in dismissal. Louise says I mustn't mind, that people at Versailles don't know how to be kind—something happens to them when they pass through the golden gates and enter the mirrored halls.

Everyone's manners are impeccable but no one talks straight: their words are sinewy and slippy like eels. The courtiers play word games with double and sometimes triple entendres; compliments are not compliments yet they are; meaning depends not on the words but on who is speaking, and about what, and everyone . . . and everyone is extremely assiduous in telling others unpleasant truths. My head whirls. They compare me to Pauline and their words are silken though the meaning is far from soft.

"Your hair is so crinkly, just like your sister's."

"Your sister enjoyed eating as much as you do; perhaps you enjoy it even more."

"Your voice brays just like Pauline's; how charming to be reminded of her in such a loud way."

All is uttered with the utmost elegance, every word stitched perfectly into place as though by the finest of tailors. When they whisper, it makes me want to talk even louder, though I am not sure why.

The food here is simply fantastic. Whether she is there or not, every afternoon pastries, compliments of the Comtesse de Toulouse, are delivered to Louise's room. Every day! Usually there is a cake and tartines, occasionally meringues such as I have never tasted, flavored with cherries and apricots and even once coffee! The queen is also a fine gourmand and sometimes Louise contrives to bring me tasters from her dinners, little squares of duck fat seasoned with sherry, an elegant artichoke, slivers of lamb crusted with rosemary.

I have not met the king yet; sometimes I attend the crowds when he dines in public, alone or with the queen. Once I saw him with the *dauphin*, a serious young boy of twelve with a rather fat face, and with his eldest daughter, Madame Henriette, who looked too young to have such highly rouged cheeks. I gawk at the king along with the rest of the rabble from behind the velvet ropes, watched by the steely eyes of his guards. Six violinists play lightly in the background and I jostle against the crowds for a better view. One day I am fortunate to see the king top an egg; the elegance of his movement is legendary throughout France. When he slices the top expertly, a bareheaded man with a rented sword offers up a cheer that sweeps through the crowd with much laughter.

"Riffraff," scoffs Jacobs, who has been assigned as my chaperone. She pulls me away. "Nothing but unmannered Parisian day-trippers. You spend far too much time here."

Whenever Louise is on duty with the queen, Jacobs takes me out of the apartment and parades me up and down the great state rooms. She tells me I am too fat and need to walk more. Louise agrees and says I should obey Jacobs, for she is very wise and kind and reminds her of our dear governess, Zélie. So walking we go, up and down the endless halls with their slippy parquet floors, around statues and plants and courtiers planted like obstacles at every corner.

If it is not too cold we walk outside through the magnificent gardens, all the way to the Menagerie, where there are zebras and monkeys and a miniature doe with beautiful velvet eyes, from Africa and not more than a foot high, as well as a great number of small catlike creatures. There is also an aviary with hundreds of birds in every shade of paradise. All are gifts from foreign lands; it is like our Noah's Ark from childhood come to life.

Jacobs was raised in the country and finds nothing interesting in large cats with huge ears or striped horses. She says she doesn't like animals—when she was younger a goat bit her on her leg and now she needs a special shoe just to be able to walk.

The animals huddle miserably in the cold and the tiny doe with its soft eyes looks sadly at me. I know it would rather be far, far away, anywhere but here in a smelly cage in the middle of this gray winter. They say in Africa it never snows; never even gets cold.

Then I am invited to spend a few days at Saint-Léger. Louise tells me it is a great honor to be so included, and though I am excited to meet the king, at Saint-Léger the mood is melancholy and dull. I think I like Versailles better. In the dining room there is a fearfully creepy wax head of Pauline, sitting on the mantel above the fire. It looks nothing like her at all and every time I see it I want to cry.

Despite the cold, the men hunt all day and the ladies gossip and spend hours on their toilette. Mademoiselle de Charolais's master cosmetics man comes from Paris to grace us with his presence, bringing dozens of small pots of powders, creams, and rouges, which he displays as though he were showing us all the wonders of the world. We are allowed to try what we will, and I find a particularly orange shade of rouge that I think is pretty, though Charolais lets me know it makes me look like a carrot. I don't think I like her very much.

Monsieur Buisson spends time with each lady, rubbing her

face raw of makeup and reapplying it in his own style. He paints the Duchesse d'Antin's lips with a shocking carmine, followed by a thin smear of beeswax to prevent cracking. He recommends the palest blush powder for Louise's face, which is looking rather gray these days.

"For you, mademoiselle . . ." He holds my face in his hands and turns me toward the light from the window. "For you . . . well . . . well. Certainly not that orange on your cheeks, that must come off."

"Just give her anything," drawls Charolais. "It's not going to make any difference, is it?"

Buisson drapes a cloth around my neck and smooths on a thick white powder that smells faintly of potatoes. I'm hungry; I miss the afternoon bakery delights of Versailles, and here the kitchens are not welcoming. If I want a morsel between meals, I must wait until supper. But when it does come the food is very good: yesterday we had a delicious roast swan stuffed with onions and apples, and tiny turtles, baked in their shells and covered with cheese sauce.

"This will have to do," says Buisson sadly, swatting me with a brush of the softest bristles, softer than kitten fur. I look at myself in the mirror and a painted white fool looks back. I giggle.

"Don't laugh at art, little Philistine," snaps Charolais with disdain. I giggle again.

Tonight at supper the king looks tired, but then he was hunting all day. I like being this close to him; I can study him when he is not looking. He is very handsome, with silky brown curls and a kind face. When he addresses you he never meets your eye; perhaps he doesn't like to look at people when too many people look at him.

The dinner is over; we had a minced lamb pie with chicory and great mounds of eels slipping in cream, and all manner of vegetables draped in butter. The king is very elegantly dressed in a pale blue coat with silver beading and large pearl buttons; he looks finer even than Richelieu, who wears a cherry coat he claims is from Venice and spun partly of spider silk. The king fiddles with one of his buttons, staring at the wax head of Pauline. One of the buttons falls off his coat and quick as lightning a footman is beside him bearing another coat. The ladies turn away as the king changes; the old coat is whisked from the room as though it had shamed itself. I wonder where it will go to be punished?

The king sighs and examines the buttons on his new coat—gold squares this time—and pulls at them with a distracted air. Richelieu fiddles with his buttons in sympathy and everyone watches the king anxiously. This king too is like the sun: When he shines, everyone shines. When clouds cover him, we are all dark and somber.

"Why don't we play cards?" I ask to the silence. "Or charades?"

"Oh, no, we are used to quiet times at Saint-Léger," Louise quickly demurs. She motions to Pauline's wax head on the sideboard.

How I hate that horrible thing! It's not how I want to remember her. It's not how anyone should remember her. "But Pauline loved games. She would not be happy to see us sitting around like buns in an oven, waiting to be cooked!" I laugh, imagining how quickly the wax head would melt in an oven.

There is a shocked silence and Louise puts a protective arm around the king, as though to shield him from the impropriety of my words.

"Pauline would want it," I say, looking around the room at the impassive faces of the other guests. Everyone keeps their faces blank until they know what expression they should wear. They are cats waiting to be fed, expectant and alert.

"Pauline would want it," repeats the king thoughtfully, then slowly claps his hands in delight. "But it is true, it is true! Come, let us play something, for by doing so we will honor the memory of our most beloved sister."

The others applaud as well and declare themselves most eager to serve the memory of their dear Pauline in this manner. Richelieu motions a footman to get the dice and a table is set for hazard. I am given a bowl of dried cherries to bet with, and we play for hours into the night, joking and drinking champagne. By the end of the evening my stomach is full to bursting and the king has won more than anyone else.

"You see!" I say triumphantly, and I address him not as a king but as a man whose spirits need cheering. I hate to see anyone sad. "Pauline has blessed you with luck! It is meant to be."

The king is pleased, though also a little drunk. He drains the last of his champagne and throws the glass into the fire, where it shatters and crackles. He comes toward me and hugs me closely, and calls me his sister. It is the closest I have ever been to a man. I smell musk oil and face powder and feel his arms on my back.

He pulls away. "Pauline is blessing us," he says. "A fine thought indeed . . . You remind me of her. Just a bit." He smiles at me sadly and I feel something queer inside. Louise comes quickly to his side and detaches him from me. The spell is broken; the king turns away and claps: "And so, to bed."

He raises his hand for Richelieu and his valet. After they leave the room Charolais comes to stand in front of me. "You have done the king some good," she says, and pats me on my arm as though I were a pet dog.

"I like to be tickled behind the ears too." I giggle, the champagne and the king's touch making me giddy. Charolais snatches her hand away as though burned; the others snicker and someone barks lightly.

Before we sleep, Louise hugs me and I know she is happy. "Thank you, sister, thank you. You did him a great wonder tonight."

From Louise de Mailly
Château de Versailles
January 30, 1742

Darling Hortense,

Greetings to you! The weather here is wonderful and all are in good spirits with this delightful and sudden thaw. Of course, we are still stricken, and though he tries, the king refuses to come out of his melancholy. In this time of his need he is like a child and I his mother. I delight in this role (you will understand). I know I shouldn't be so happy but his need of me, the need of a son for his mother, is truly wonderful and has put me in great spirits. I am so happy and have new hope for the future!

As you know, Diane was here last week for a visit, just a short one. She was good tonic, though I was afraid she caused some hurt to the king by her physical resemblance to our dear departed sister. He did remark on the resemblance, but you know Diane, she was oblivious and thought it a compliment! But she was very jolly and on occasion even made the king laugh.

I do hope you are well and I look forward to seeing you soon. Perhaps at Court? Diane's visit was delightful and I wish to extend the same invitation to you, should your husband permit. And Marie-Anne, of course, we must not forget her in her grief. There will be a ball next week to begin Lent; perhaps you might attend?

I enclose a passel of hyacinths from the hothouse. They do so remind me of the coming spring! What a wonderful time of year!

All my love,
Louise

Marie-Anne

Before Lent begins, there is a tradition for a masked ball to be held at Court. Agénois insists that we attend—he is leaving soon with his regiment—and he is even able to persuade Tante to come along. (Agénois has told me some shocking things about Tante: apparently she is not the prude she wishes to be known as. I now look at the ancient Marquis du Mesnil, a frequent visitor to our house, with more interest.)

So we are all going to the ball: Tante; Hortense and her husband, Flavacourt; myself. I am going as Spices of the World and Hortense dresses as Saint Agnes in a long white robe draped around her body to resemble a Roman toga. Tante will not dress up; she declares she will be "dressed as a chaperone." I want to ask what the Marquis of Mesnil will dress as—Male Virtue?—but I refrain.

Agénois does not have to think about his costume; he is going as part of the king's entourage and this year they are all dressed as bats. He is very pleased; he says all the ladies will want to dance with him, on the chance that their bat is actually the king. Especially this year, as the bat is perceived to have a great hunger. For fruit and other delights. Agénois says the ladies will positively flock to the bats; it is rumored that many will be dressed as the peaches they are known to love. Then he bows and says he is sorry, my sister being so recently dead.

"Not at all," I say. "You know how I felt about her. Or didn't feel about her."

"But she was your sister."

Poor Pauline. Still, I am glad she is not around; I don't think I would even contemplate going if she were there.

Agénois has high hopes for the ball. He leaves for Languedoc soon and has been courting me ardently. Though my feelings for him grow stronger, we have not progressed further than many long hours of kissing in the library. I don't want a quick roll in the hay, as they say in the country. How would it be done? Bent over one of the sofas or up against a bookcase in the library, watched by the statues that stand guard at the door? I shudder. No. But Agénois has been alluding to his very private quarters at Versailles and the back corridors we can take so no one will see us leave.

"Even the most private of exits will not fill my bed," I counter. "Tante will do a head count."

"We don't have to wait until the end of the ball," he says passionately.

I look in his dark blue eyes and think how nice it would be to spend the night with him. Naked. With no one else, not the ghost of JB or the image of Agénois's wife, to impede our pleasure.

ↄ৯

"You smell delicious," declares Hortense. "Like a fantastic cake."

I am dressed in a simple white gown, and green satin pouches, filled with caraway, coriander, mint and more, hang around my waist. My women thread ribbons with cloves and nutmeg nuts and drape the strings around me. Tante's hairdresser is doing our hair and I have a handful of juniper berries and some bay leaves I want him to glue to my curls. The cook is not amused; he wants everything back by tomorrow, untouched by my sweat.

"Excuse me, madame, I meant *perspiration*. Untouched by perspiration."

Hortense twirls around in her toga, enjoying the lightness. No panniers for this Roman! She is in a rare lively mood; she told me this morning she thinks she might be pregnant again.

"I know it's indecent, but I think the Romans were very smart. This would have been quite the thing to wear in hot weather."

"You look naked," I tell her as the hairdresser weaves pods into my hair. "It looks like you are wearing your chemise."

"I don't look naked," says Hortense, a little timidly. "I look like a Roman?"

Tante clucks nervously, for it is true you can see the outline of Hortense's body rather too well. "I am not sure this is appropriate."

"But, Tante," says Hortense, "we will be masked. No one will know who I am."

"You look naked," says Hortense's husband, entering the room. Hortense sways across the room—you can see her hips move!—and gives him a kiss on the cheek. Usually a dour man, tonight Flavacourt is in a surprising good mood and insists only on her donning a big cape, which he forbids her to remove. He is supposed to be dressed as an Arab, but I think he is far better as Glowering Husband; he looks as though he will reach for his curved sword should any man so much as smile at Saint Agnes.

When we finish with our hair we put on our masks—mine decorated with dried vanilla pods painted white—and descend to the carriage. It's a cold winter afternoon: the drive from Paris should only take two hours but today the rutted road is clogged with carriages, all going to the ball. It will likely take four.

☙

Agénois swoops in on me immediately, for he knows my costume. He looks faintly ridiculous, swathed all in black—even his stockings are black. "My dearest," he whispers, and spreads his arms, revealing two stretched wings made from black velvet. "Boning from a pannier," he whispers. I giggle, but I'm not sure I like the idea that I may be making love to a bat tonight; there is something sinister, if not ridiculous, there.

"My dearest," he says, enveloping me with his black wings. "You smell delicious. I could eat you."

The crowd parts around us, and a murmur runs through it—is this bat the king? The sense of possibility and anticipation is high with the freedom that a masked ball brings to those who are always watched. Will tonight be the night? Before Agénois can pull me away to get in line for a *contredanse*, a Roman general takes my arm. "Another Roman!" I exclaim. "There are so many this year."

"It is the year of the Romans," the man declares, and I recognize Richelieu's voice. "Come, there is someone who wants to meet you."

I dip a finger in one of my spice pouches and hold it up for his inspection. "First you must tell me what spice this is."

Richelieu sniffs. "Coriander," he concludes quickly. "Or, as they say in the native language of the Hindoos, *dhania*."

He is a most astonishing man.

He leads me down a small corridor and up two flights of stairs and we turn into a small room, paneled in white with a window overlooking the Marble Court. From this height, the crush is enormous; the giant courtyard a menagerie of people and colors, spilling out from the main rooms. Though the night is chilly, steam rises from all the perspiration and even the lanterns seem to flicker in the heat. Against my will I feel my heart starting to beat faster—I think I know who it is that Richelieu wants me to meet.

"Sire, I come bearing this delectable platter I have been telling you about."

A tall bat, one who has discarded his wings and stands alone in solemn blackness, turns to me and bows deeply. That it is the king there is no doubt; beside him, the rest of the colony shrinks in comparison, and even his mask cannot hide the shine of his velveteen eyes. He bows and brings my hand to his lips. My knees go weak and I think I am going to faint, something I have never done before in my life.

"My condolences on your sister," he says, and I hear compassion in his deep treacle voice.

"*Majesté.*" I sweep into a curtsy.

"Monsieur here is simply a bat, Madame des Épices," says Richelieu reprovingly.

"Monsieur le Bat." The king laughs. "Yes, I like that. To you, dear madame, I am but Monsieur le Bat."

He leads me to a velvet-covered bench, and as we sit he leans in and sniffs appreciatively. "Vanilla. Nutmeg," he says in surprise. "And cinnamon?"

"All the spices of the Far East, *Maj*—Monsieur le Bat."

"Armand, you told me she was beautiful but you never told me she was so intelligent. I can hear it in her voice. It is delightful, low and melodic."

Richelieu is watching us, his eyes darting back and forth, missing nothing. "I have never met a more intelligent woman, sire," he says, then catches my eye and winks.

At some imperceptible signal from the king the other bats and Richelieu fly away, leaving only one—the king—alone with me in the little room. We talk an hour, about my deceased husband, about his children, about his projects at Choisy and the progress of the hunt this winter, then embark on a lively debate about the merits of Voltaire's *Letters on the English*. Though I try to pull away, something pulls me in. Sheer flattery, I think. Knowing that down in the crowd a hundred—nay, two hundred, nay, a thousand—perhaps every woman down there, married, single, widowed, is searching desperately for a certain bat. And yet he has called me here.

"May I ask a favor?" he asks suddenly.

"Of course, Monsieur le Bat." I know what he is going to ask. I can see it in his eyes, childish hope mixed with arrogance. To prevent him from asking or even begging—for that would not a king make—I untie my mask and bare my face.

"By God, you are pretty!" he exclaims in delight.

He returns the favor and up close he is as handsome in person as he is in paint. It is strange to have seen so many portraits of this man and yet now here he is, in the flesh, seated beside me and leaning as close as my skirts allow.

Richelieu comes back and says that duty calls. "There is a little angel related to the spice woman who wishes to see you."

So Louise is an angel. How unoriginal.

"Madame. Enchanted. Absolutely enchanted. I hope to see you at Court soon. Very soon."

I lower my eyes demurely.

The king leaves but I stay; I don't want to go back just yet to the crushed masses below, where sweaty hopes mix with perspiration and too much scent. I look down into the courtyard and spot a dejected bat leaning against a pillar—Agénois—and a small crowd around a rather naked Roman lady who seems to have lost her cape. I wonder what Agénois would say if he knew the king had been wooing me. Would he be as Flavacourt and declare he would run his sword through the king if he so much as looks at me again? I doubt it; where Flavacourt is a rough military man, Agénois is the consummate courtier and would as soon run naked to the queen than insult the king. No, Agénois would step aside quietly, of that I am sure. If . . . if that were required.

I stay by the window for another hour, trembling in the chill air and alone with my potent soup of emotions—flattered, confused, elated; flushed with the tumble of thoughts that the extraordinary encounter has inspired in me. The power that comes from being desired. Below I see a large black chaperone, looking like a bat herself, circling the sides of the courtyard, and I know Tante is looking for me. I'm no simpleton: by tomorrow, news of the king's time with me will be all over the Court. Will he order me to come to Court? Can he do that? What would I do if he did? I try to imagine the king kissing me. What would it be like to be kissed by *France*?

Once I am back in the world, Agénois berates me for avoiding him all night. I can only offer a feeble excuse: the anticipation of our passion frightened me, and so I withdrew. Now the timing is wrong and we have no opportunity to slip away. There is a part of me that regrets not leaving with him by a back door when we had the chance, for he will be gone most of the spring and summer. He declares that the only thing that will sustain him through the lonely months to come is the thought that my sweet nectar will be here, a prize for him, when he returns. Rather silly words—I refused to blush when he declared them—but still, his departure leaves me as empty and hollow as an echo.

A few weeks later I am alone in the house—Hortense is visiting her son in Picardy, and Tante has remained at Versailles—when there is a commotion in the courtyard. I wonder who it could be, for it is past ten and visitors at a late hour only bring bad news. I brace myself as the footman enters and regally announces: "The doctors you sent for, madame."

I haven't sent for any doctors.

"Show them in," I say.

Two men wearing voluminous black wigs, a ridiculous fashion left over from the previous century, enter the library. I recognize Richelieu first and am about to demand what he is doing when I realize who the other "doctor" is. Oh. I immediately curtsy and motion them to chairs. "Some . . . some spiced wine," I tell the footman.

"Spiced wine!" chortles the king. "How I should love to drink that."

That spring I am visited twice more by my "doctors," and with each visit I sense possibility in the king's eyes. I am not sure whether I should run toward that future or flee in the opposite direction. What would Tante say? Hortense? Louise? Do I care? Three sisters—improbable and potently impossible. And Agénois . . . ? Is it possible for a heart to be split in two? Surely I love Agénois, but as for the king . . . well, I have always longed for adventure.

One night as the "doctors" are leaving, Richelieu leans in and whispers that the king is so smitten, he is impervious to the scandal. "A passion quite strong enough to overcome the infamy of fucking three sisters—now what do you think about that?"

"I think your words are as filthy as your mind." I stifle a smile; his boldness is sometimes attractive.

"And show him some encouragement," continues Richelieu. "Will you, on our next visit? He's not used to singing for his supper. Or barking for his bone, for that matter."

Then the visits cease, and though I strain for the clatter of a carriage on the cobblestones, all is silent. Hortense comes back from the country, now visibly pregnant. I don't share my secret with her and take solace, rather guiltily, in my letters from Agénois and in my rather fading memories of our kisses and embraces.

Hortense and I pay Diane a visit at Madame de Lesdiguières. After our greetings Madame de Lesdiguières settles into a chair in the salon with us. There are cats everywhere and Hortense's eyes grow red and weepy. A faint mustiness clings over us in the heat.

"Don't worry," whispers Diane. "She'll fall asleep soon."

We are served chestnut pudding and an enormous gray cat with green eyes leaps onto the table and starts licking the wobbly mess on Diane's plate. "This is Joseph," she informs us, stroking his fur. "Isn't he beautiful? I didn't think cats like chestnuts—I certainly don't—but it seems they do."

Hortense shudders. Soon light snoring comes from the corner and we see the old duchess has fallen asleep, fanned gently by one of her women. Diane burbles about her visit to Versailles, telling us about the fashions and the food and the afternoon pastry delights. Hortense asks after the king and Louise, but Diane only looks uncomfortable. "He is still in mourning," she says. From her manner I guess that he is sleeping with Louise again. Well. And then another thought occurs to me: "Did you sleep with him?" I demand.

"Marie-Anne!" exclaims Hortense.

Diane laughs. "You can ask that question, but the answer is no."

"And Louise?"

Diane laughs again, softly this time and shrugs. "The king is a creature of habit. Oh, I'm sorry, I shouldn't say 'creature' when I talk of the king. He is not an animal. He is a *man* of habit."

"Poor Louise," says Hortense.

I look at her in exasperation.

"No, not because of her sin," she explains, widening her big blue eyes. "But because . . . because she is second for him. She is just there, a habit."

It is strange to hear Hortense speak so perceptively, and so kindly.

"What about you?" asks Diane, looking at me and raising one of her bushy eyebrows. So she has heard something.

"Diane-Adelaide! Why would you ask such a thing?" asks Hortense, her voice filled with withering reproach.

"Sorry, Hen. You know I cannot help myself. I know I always say too much. But the king is apparently smitten with our lovely sister. Our lovely sister Marie-Anne, that is."

Hortense's head bobs frantically as it does when she is angry. "How can you say that? With Marie-Anne at home with me, chaste in our Tante's house?"

"I'm not saying she's not chaste. Just that she is giving the king a bit of a *chase*. I've heard he wishes her to come to Court but she refuses. Everyone says she won't come because she is in love with Agénois. Even though Agénois is away. And married. But when the king gets something in his head, it's hard to make him stop, I mean, he is the king and is very used to getting his own way, why Louise says—"

I hold up my hand. Diane's words are like a river that never stops flowing, not even when it reaches the sea. Hortense turns to me for an explanation, her face white.

"We talked awhile at the Shrove Ball," I explain. I say nothing about the doctors' visits.

"You never told me." Hortense looks as though she might faint.

"He was very taken with her, or so everyone says. But talking is not fucking, sister," adds Diane helpfully.

"Diane, you cannot talk like that! This is not Versailles! What if the duchess wakes?"

"Sorry, Hen. But when are you going to Versailles, Marie-Anne? You would have a lot of fun there and the food is beyond compare! A pity that Pauline is not there to welcome you. But Louise is very nice too." Diane falls silent. I know she misses Pauline greatly; it's nice that someone does.

I make a noncommittal gesture. I'm not going to tell anyone my plans. Because I don't know what they are. I change the subject.

"Diane, what about a husband for you? Does Madame de Lesdiguières have any ideas? Hortense, doesn't Flavacourt have a brother or nephew he could spare? Diane would make a great wife."

Diane manages to laugh and snort at the same time and a great quantity of brown pudding sprays out of her mouth.

Hortense is appalled.

Marie-Anne

Richelieu calls on Tante and says he has a message for me from my mother-in-law, which he must deliver in private. We retire to the library and I upbraid him as he smiles coolly at me, looking impossibly smug in a too-bright orange velvet coat, the color of a lurid sunset.

"Now I will have to make up a letter from her! Tante knows I never write to the woman. What am I going to say?"

Richelieu is not a man to be worried about trifles. I wonder, has anyone ever said no to him in his entire life? I should like to be the one. He gets right to his point: "The king is smitten, Marie-Anne. Opportunities like this do not fall like apples in October."

"I understand."

"Or like chestnuts in autumn or nutmeg trees that—"

"I understand, sir."

"That may be, but I don't understand you. What is keeping you here?"

I don't say anything. Is it because I don't want to follow in anyone's footsteps, and all that that would imply? Or is it Agénois? I look out the window to avoid looking at Richelieu, who is staring at me.

"I wouldn't have taken you for a waverer, Marie-Anne. Not at all."

"Tante and Hortense . . ." I begin. It is true I am usually not so indecisive, so confused. I would be second in his heart, if he still mourns Pauline, even third if you consider Louise. I don't want to be a second plate to anyone, a little *amuse-bouche* between main courses. I can't explain this to Richelieu. Yet I also can't explain the sudden leap in my heart that he is here, talking of this matter: my last doctors' visit was over a month ago.

"You're not a fool, Marie-Anne," Richelieu says, and there is impatience in his voice. "The king will not wait forever. He is the king; you can't treat him like a love-struck footman. Yes, he enjoys the hunt and the chase as much as the next man, but eventually the hunter needs to kill to remind him why he hunts. Besides, daggers and more are drawn at Court. It's been eight months since *la grande pute*—oh, I am sorry, I keep forgetting she was your sister, forgive me . . . it has been eight months since Pauline died, and though it appears Louise is warming his bed again, there is a great vacancy. A *great* vacancy."

"And you want it to be me."

Richelieu inclines his head. "Like I have said before, you are not a fool. Though we have scarcely met a few times, I feel as if I know you—perhaps better than you know yourself. You would make a wonderful mistress for the king. Ask yourself—why did I pick you?"

"I do not wish to imply I am ignorant of the honor you do by your consideration of me," I say, rather coldly. I don't answer his question but ask him one back: "And what is your interest in this matter?"

He snorts. "The same as everyone else. We all know Louise won't last, and the race is on to fill the king's bed. There is the ravishing Mademoiselle de Conti, and I'm sure you've heard of the Marvelous Mathilde? But she's too young and silly; she'll never keep his attention. But you, on the other hand . . . it is my belief you would be perfect. Simply perfect. Beauty and brains—a potent combination. And we would make a great team. I have a hankering for the position of prime minister, once that virgin monk dies. My sources tell me he hasn't shat since last Tuesday. He must be stuffed up like a goose—surely a hundred-year-old bottom can't handle that pressure."

Well. It's true Richelieu would be a very powerful ally, and it's flattering that he thinks I might help him become the next prime minister, if . . .

"I will think about it," I say, still staring out the window. An overwhelming urge to run away comes over me. I could go to Venice, I think. Richelieu has been there and is rumored to have slept with more Venetians than there are fish in the canals. "Did you like Venice?"

Richelieu blinks but to his credit doesn't answer. Then: "You're not pining over Agénois?" he demands, comprehension dawning in his eyes. "Agénois is a boy. I am offering you the king, Marie-Anne, the king! And you would pine over a *boy*?" He pauses, makes a decision. "Perhaps there is something you should see."

He takes a letter from his coat and passes it to me. As I read my heart sinks into my stomach and my hands start to shake. "This is false," I finally say, giving him back the letter. It is from Agénois to a woman he calls his "Precious Gabrielle." I can't bear to finish it. "It's not him. This is—this is a forgery."

"Look at the handwriting, Marie-Anne," says Richelieu patiently. My heart falls from my stomach down to my little toes and stays there. I know Agenois's pen like I know mine, the stiff slope of his letters, the extra little curl on the *g*. And a quote from Labé I know only too well:

> *When Love arrives, I hide myself away,*
> *Though filled by burning torments of desire,*
> *That scorch and sear and scar my breast with fire,*
> *And flames devour my heart both night and day.*

"Where did you get this?"

"Sources," says Richelieu carelessly. "One can always find out what there is to find out. In this case, the pity is that there was something to discover."

"I don't believe you. You . . . you have plotted this. I know it. You sent . . . you sent a woman there . . ."

Richelieu shakes his head sympathetically, but there is the trace of a smirk on his face. "Agénois is a man. You are a woman of many charms, Marie-Anne, but a man far away in Languedoc is a man far away in Languedoc."

I turn away and close my eyes. All of a sudden I feel I have lost something, something enormous. This is not JB and his Fleurette; this is Agénois.

"Get out." I don't care what Zélie used to say; I'm angry and I am not going to hide it.

"Madame. You mustn't be angry with me. I am not the one who—"

"I'm not angry," I shout, and wish I could punch him in the middle of his preposterous orange coat, right in the stomach. "If you think this will change my mind, you are wrong. Wrong. This is a fool plot you have concocted."

A footman comes in at my raised voice and I turn away to hide my tears. A large portion of my heart has just been devoured by those inky black words.

Richelieu takes his leave. "Madame de la Tournelle, her poor dear mother-in-law has great troubles these days," he tells Tante on his way out, putting his hand over his stomach to imply the old lady suffers from an unmentionable illness.

From Louise de Mailly
Château de Versailles
August 22, 1742

Darling Hortense,

Thank you for your last letter and the peaches from Picardy—they were very sweet and refreshing. I am glad you and your husband are well and am delighted with the news of your latest pregnancy. I am well and my husband too, though it has been several months since I saw him. He is frightfully busy.

I do wish Marie-Anne would write! I know she must still be suffering in her grief for poor Jean-Baptiste, though I have heard troubling talk about her and the Duc d'Agénois? I hope these rumors are not true; little Félicité, the Duchesse d'Agénois, is a friend of mine and she is the sweetest girl. I am not one to write gossip, but I do wish for the truth, if only to console my friend.

I have also heard rumors, I mean . . . I am sorry I am not sure how to write this. The king speaks often of Marie-Anne. I know he paid her a courtesy visit at the Shrove Ball—once again, I must lightly recriminate both of you that you did not seek me out while you were here—but from the way His Majesty speaks of our Marie-Anne, it appears he has met her more than once. But that is not possible. Is it? Of course he holds our family in high esteem and it would gladden my heart were he to take an interest in Marie-Anne, especially in this time of her sorrow, but I must separate truth from gossip.

Darling Hortense, please write and calm my heart on both of these troubling matters, for my dear friend Félicité and for myself.

Love,
Louise

From Hortense de Flavacourt
Hôtel de Mazarin, Paris
August 30, 1742

Dear Louise,

Thank you for your news. I am glad that you and your husband are
well.

I shall be truthful: I was shocked by your last letter. I am sorry
to say this but I am disappointed. You are my elder sister, but as a
married woman, I feel I may talk and lecture you as an equal. Marie-
Anne entertains the Duc d'Agénois occasionally, and corresponds with
him, but only to honor the memory of her lost husband (they were
great friends and military comrades).

If Félicité is worried about her husband straying, she must not
impugn our sister's name; instead she should look to her own actions
and appearance. I have heard she is fair enough though several of her
teeth are almost black—perhaps if she had them removed her husband
would be more attentive?

Please do not spread evil rumors about Marie-Anne, there is no
need for you to sully our name further—Tante says you have already
done a good enough job yourself. Those are her words, of course, not
mine. For your sake, I hope it is as the very old and very virtuous
Marquis de Mesnil contends: that the king is once again with his wife
and that fidelity has become the new fashion.

I enclose a small Bible I had covered in leather for you. Tante has
agreed to carry it with her when she leaves on Wednesday; normally
she would not, but since the gift is a Bible she will rise above her
judgment and consent. Proverbs and Romans have some excellent
verses about the abomination of gossip—I recommend you read them.

In sainted judgment,
Hortense

Marie-Anne

PARIS AND VERSAILLES

September 1742

Tante is dead! Poor Tante, that dour, solid, pious woman, is dead: it started with a sore throat and deteriorated from there. It was so fast and so shocking: one minute she was wishing us a good week from her carriage and reminding us to have the winter carpets brought down from the attics, and then a few days later, news of her death from Versailles.

We are phantoms, Hortense and I, floating around the house as though in a dream. I ensure the windows are covered and swathed in black and I put on my heaviest mourning clothes, the same for Pauline so recently put away, and before that for JB. Here I am again, pulling on a heavy black dress and dusting off my black lace caps. Another death. What is wrong with the world? What is wrong with *my* world?

They brought Tante back from Versailles and now she lies in the chapel; the marble walls keep the body well enough. I sit alone there one night, long after the servants and Hortense have gone to bed, alone with my aunt and my memories. Tante was not my favorite person. Though I was careful to hide my dislike, she was no fool and I think she sensed beneath the surface something she didn't want to see. She was always closer with Hortense, like a mother to her, but never to me.

Not two days pass before we receive word from her son-in-law, Maurepas, that he and his wife will be moving into the house and that we are to leave. In sum, we are evicted. In the rudest manner: by a note, instructing us to vacate at the earliest possible time, and before next Tuesday. Coward, that he could not even come and tell us himself.

I remember the instinctive dislike I had for Maurepas; unfortunately it seems my intuition did not do me wrong.

This is our home. We have lived here since our mother died, and where else do we have to go? Our eviction brings home to me with force all that is odious about my life: I am young and without independent means or protector. Hortense lies in bed, as if stuffing her head under the pillows will block out what is happening. She is heavily pregnant and has buried herself quite completely in cushions and tears.

All the responsibility for our futures lies on my shoulders. I have written to her husband, Flavacourt, to ask what we should do, but he is away with the interminable Austrian troubles and we will not receive news back for at least a week.

I may have capable shoulders but I don't want this responsibility. In a moment of weakness I wish Agénois were here beside me, but I have not written him since I saw that dreadful letter to his "Precious Gabrielle." He has sent me many letters imploring to know the reason for my silence, but I am sure Richelieu will let him know eventually.

I spend the night on my knees in the chill chapel next to Tante's body. Outside cold rain falls heavily and muffles the noise of the street, but I can hear the clop of horses' hooves, reminding me of a clock, ticking forward—to what? Hortense is overjoyed by my piety and devotion, and smiles for the first time since we heard the news, but I am not praying.

I am thinking.

It is true that I am not usually indecisive. I enjoyed my burgeoning flirtation with the king, but kept myself and my emotions on a tight leash. My love—or was it love?—for Agénois kept me back, but now that has gone. And Tante has gone. It does seem as though Fate is conspiring to push me in a certain direction. Paths have narrowed, and at the end, a gate is open. And with

no nagging from stern-faced Tante, bless her soul . . . well . . .
the king is an attractive man—a *very* attractive man—and he has
much to offer. And Agénois betrayed me.

And I have nowhere else to go.

I keep my eyes closed though I am not praying. When I open
them, a decision has been made. My own decision—perhaps the
biggest decision I have ever made in my life.

I will do this.

I send for Richelieu—my note is short and curt. He is an un-
trustworthy man, and manipulative—I am more convinced than
ever that he sent a woman to tempt Agénois, to break our love—
but now is no time to be turning against influential friends. We
will make a good team.

Richelieu arrives with indecent haste, bouncing with smugness, and I show him Maurepas's note. He crumples it and goes
to burn it over a candle, then thinks the better of it, saying it
might be useful to keep. "Besides, Maurepas is no friend of
mine. And the proof of his base nature is right here." He waves
the note.

"Not a nice gesture," he says after a little rumination. "And one
he might regret. Turning two vulnerable marquises out onto the
streets. There's the makings of some good theater in there, I would
wager. Two beautiful young marquises pitted against one medio-
cre impotent man and his stringy wife. If I were a betting man—
that is to say, I *am* a betting man—I would bet on my young
marquises. And though I didn't put Maurepas up to this note, he
could not have played it better had he been my marionette."

He leers at me and I smile back.

"You are thinking that the death of Tante is an opportunity
sent from Heaven," I say. "Coupled with our eviction."

He bows ironically. "I feel the nymphs of Luck caressing me
hard these days."

"Shhh, sacrilege," I hiss. "Hortense may be creeping around."

I take a deep breath.

"I have decided," I say, slowly and carefully, "that I shall petition for a position at Court. The place with the queen, vacant after Tante's death."

"Ah, madame! I am so delighted you have decided to play the game," says Richelieu, looking as though he would like to hug me. "A place with the queen—ambitious but excellent thinking. Maurepas will want it for his midget wife, but I doubt she would even be tall enough to hand the queen her shoes. And with the right amount of public opinion working against him, thanks to this letter"—he waves the crumpled note—"he may be persuaded to cede the place."

"I won't rely on Maurepas," I say firmly. I would rather die than ask him for favors. He's as much of a tyrant as Pauline was in the nursery. "I shall not beg anything from that man."

"I like the fire in your eyes, Marie-Anne. Finally."

I rise, decisive. "I will secure a position at Court and then we shall see about that matter with the king. And if all happens as it should, I will destroy Maurepas. And I won't be powerless again. Ever." Oh, dear, this does sound like theater.

Richelieu laughs, delighted. "Dramatic words! I should have guessed you would be motivated by revenge. And there I was thinking I was a good study of character."

"Live and learn," I say sardonically, even insolently. One day even he could be within my power. I say as much and he smiles thinly.

"We will make a good team. And this is indeed a happy day." He embraces me and kisses me twice on the cheek then holds me at arm's length. "You have made the right decision, Marie-Anne. But hurry while the sympathy of Maurepas's enemies—and they are legion—is on your side."

‹›

I choose a becoming mourning dress of black and white wool and braid the last of the carnations from the garden to my bodice. The king told me carnations were his favorite flower; I won't see him today, but in some way the flowers give me strength to do what I must do. I take Tante's carriage to Versailles—we still have two days before the house and everything else reverts to her odious son-in-law. As we trundle along the roads, clayed and swollen from the recent rains, I feel as though I am leaving one life behind and starting another.

I regret my dramatic words to Richelieu. *I will destroy Maurepas. And I won't be powerless again. Ever.* Goodness, what was I thinking? All I need is a position at Court and a place to live. And as for the king . . . we shall see how that matter resolves.

I watch the passing scenery from behind the gauze of my traveling veil, the bare fields newly harvested and waiting for winter, the peasants walking with their burdens. So many worlds, so many people, so many different lives, so many paths to take. Was this the right one? The carriage rides into the town of Versailles and the great palace looms ahead of us, pulling all in to its gilded sphere. This country, the courtiers call Versailles: *ce pays-ci.* Perhaps it will become my country too.

I can do this, I think again.

I go straight to Cardinal Fleury, surprising everyone who knows our situation. Fleury is my sister Louise's ally; he is perhaps her only supporter, but he is not a stupid man. He must know it is only a matter of time before the king leaves the comfort of the familiar. He consents to an audience but I can tell he is shocked to see me. I make my request for Tante's position with the queen.

"I will do my best, madame," he says, scratching a fleabite on the back of his vein-streaked hand. The man is ancient. His gray hair straggles out from under his cap, and his face is a labyrinth of lines and veins. I look at him straight in the eye but he avoids my gaze. He examines my gloves and studies the carnations on my bodice. "But this is very unusual, improper even, to have this conversation yourself . . . There is no man?" Before the words have a chance to air, he has run through my personal situation: my father, my lack of brothers, Flavacourt away with his regiment. He sighs. "The Comtesse de Maurepas, of course, has the greater claim, but . . ."

He lets the words dangle and I nod.

"If not the place of the Duchesse de Mazarin, may God bless her soul, then another position. We will see what can be done. But mind, I make no promises."

I smile with as much gratitude as I can muster. Even if Fleury wants to sit on the fence, the king has the final decision and I know which way he will want this matter to fall.

As I leave I curtsy and greet those I know but don't tarry to talk. Let them guess what the audience was about. I get in the waiting carriage and leave. I don't even visit Louise. I want to send a message, from the beginning: there will be no coexistence.

From Louise de Mailly
Château de Versailles
September 15, 1742

Dearest Hortense,

I do apologize for my last letter, you are indeed right that this is no time to be spreading dreadful rumors. I hope you will accept my sincere apology, and I assure you I have done my penance in the chapel, and will continue to do so. I completely agree with you about the evils of gossip and I thank you for the Bible. I did read the recommended verses.

My condolences on losing Tante Mazarin. You must be suffering greatly. I know Maurepas—this is not gossip but the truth, I heard it directly from Madame de Maurepas's cousin—will take possession of Tante's house and that you will soon be homeless. What will you do? Perhaps Picardy?

Also I know—again, this is not gossip but the truth, for many saw her, though I did not—Marie-Anne came to Versailles. Alone! And spoke with Fleury. I would love to know why and what she talked about with the cardinal. I only ask you directly, dear sister, in order to avoid listening to the scandalmongers.

I was saddened Marie-Anne did not request my help. You must let me know what I can do for you. I do not brag, of course, but my influence with His Majesty remains strong and I do believe I could be of help to you.

Please accept this handkerchief, embroidered with black doves, to comfort you in your time of sorrow.

In loving sorrow,
Louise

Marie-Anne

PARIS AND VERSAILLES

September 1742

The morning after my trip to Versailles, I tell Hortense where I have been and she stares at me with her big eyes, now rimmed and red from crying. She has a letter from her husband—he will be back in Paris within ten days—and the news has cheered her. She is sitting in bed and sniffling over a cup of drinking chocolate.

"We're going to Court," I say, "and I'll secure the position with the queen, and so will you, I'm not sure how but we will find a way. Then we will have our own apartments and we need never speak to Maurepas again."

"Flavacourt will not like it," she says after she hears my plan. "He won't like me being at Court, near the king and Louise . . . In his letter he suggested Picardy . . ."

"Picardy? Flavacourt should not be so unreasonable."

Hortense looks down at her saucer. I pour myself a cup from the pot and sit beside her on the bed.

"Careful, you'll spill."

"No, I won't. Look," I say, as though I am explaining to a child. "Even if Flavacourt could provide you with a house in Paris, you could not live there alone. And Picardy? You hate the country. Remember how appalled you were in Burgundy? The goats and the mud? Versailles is the only option. And I will be there to protect you."

"Where do you get your strength, Marie-Anne?" murmurs Hortense, closing her eyes.

"We must leave in two days. By the time your husband arrives, all will be done and we will be installed at Versailles." Hortense nods cautiously but she doesn't look convinced. She would cry if she knew the rest of my plan.

"Now get out of bed," I plead. "You must get your hair combed or it will be full of rattails and you'll have to chop it off, and then people will think you had lice."

∞

How things change, and how fast! Within a week, less than ten days after the death of Tante, we are triumphant. I am a lady-in-waiting to the queen and I have been awarded the apartment of the Bishop of Rennes, away in Spain as our ambassador. Hortense is installed in rooms next to Louise's. We have a small reunion—Louise, Hortense, and myself—in my apartment and the three of us hug and cry. Or at least they cry and I pretend to. Louise is wearing a drab green gown, the color of cooked spinach. She looks rather old, and I calculate with a certain satisfaction that she is now past thirty.

But she is smiling as always, and declares this to be one of the happiest moments of her life. She says she is thrilled to have the family together again. "I will do all I can for you, I promise," she says earnestly, holding our hands, her eyes bright with joy and emotion. I think: But what could you do for us? And what have you ever done for us?

Even more astonishingly, though I do believe the Court talks of little else, she fails to see the danger that I may pose to her. That I will pose to her.

"We must get Diane here for another visit! She can stay with you, perhaps, Marie-Anne, as you have so many rooms. So many. And so big." She looks around my salon with an empty face. We hug again and they leave, and then I am alone.

Four rooms, lavishly appointed. The salon is painted with willows and pagodas and boasts a plush carpet spun of red and gold.

I take off my shoes and stockings and dig my toes in deep, deep. Kittens, fleece, all that is soft in this world.

I am alone in my own apartments—not shared with Tante and Hortense, not shared with *anyone. Mine.* Wonderful. I sprawl back on the sofa and hear Tante's shocked voice telling me to sit up straight and to stop lounging like a monkey. I push her voice back into the void: we won't be needing you anymore.

My woman, Leone, has come with me from Tante's and she watches me anxiously, afraid I am having convulsions. To scare her some more I roll off the sofa and onto the thick luxurious carpet. I bury my face in the soft pile and smell tobacco, dog, and cloves, but I don't care because there is nothing, nothing in this world as wonderful as this.

"Come and feel this carpet, Leone." I pull her down with me. Leone giggles and lies beside me. The ceiling above is painted with clouds held up by a small army of angels. We're silent as we enjoy the view. I could get used to this, I think happily, and it is as though the future has opened up before me, in a long road that leads directly to the heavens painted above.

Louise

Maurepas is a bad man, as evil as Fleury says. I know Tante detested me, may God have mercy on her soul, and now this proof of his black heart. He put Marie-Anne and Hortense in a dreadful situation. Then Marie-Anne came straight to Court to seek a place with the queen. Such courage! And sure enough, she was able to secure Tante's place for herself, even though a dozen families were vying for it.

Richelieu quickly suggested—he is everywhere these days— that I resign my place with the queen in favor of Hortense. Then he will ensure that I become *surintendante* of the infanta's house-hold when she arrives to marry the *dauphin*, in the next year or so. A wonderful opportunity!

Fleury is angry when he hears what I have agreed to. He looks at me as though he wants to spend a very long time telling me something I don't want to hear, but then his watery blue eyes, now tinged with yellow, smoke over and he turns away, his shoulders slumped in defeat.

When I share the good news with the king, he looks a lit-tle embarrassed but says that it is a fine idea and that there is no prouder love on this earth than sororal love. It's rather an odd thing to say, but I am glad he approves.

❧

"My sisters Marie-Anne and Hortense have arrived at Court," I tell Jacobs as she undresses me for the night.

"Young Marie-Anne," says Jacobs in surprise; she remembers her from Paris, when we gathered at my mother's death.

I look at my reflection in the mirror. I am already thirty-two, almost at the end of a woman's beauty. The candle that flickers beside the mirror flatters, but I know in sunlight I look older. I smile at myself and open my eyes wide so the skin around them pulls taut and smooth.

"Marie-Anne is twenty-five now, not a little girl, and she is to take the place of Tante with the queen. And I have been advised to cede my position with the queen to dear Hortense. When the infanta arrives I shall be the *surintendante* of her household. A great honor, to be sure."

Jacobs says nothing; she rarely does these days, but I see by her face she does not approve.

"You don't understand, Jacobs," I say, feeling the need to convince her. "You don't have sisters. There is no greater bond."

Jacobs's face tightens. Perhaps she does have sisters. Actually, if I remember correctly, she had three, all of them dead. But that is not my point. "I must do all I can for my family," I say gently.

"They say you did enough for Pauline, madame."

They, they, they. The mysterious "they" of Versailles, as though it is the palace itself that talks, as though the statues and mirrors can speak. "I don't want to think about what 'they' say."

"Yes, madame."

I take a deep breath. It was the right thing to do. Certainly. There is nothing more important than family, and Hortense and Marie-Anne are not like Pauline. They are both so very sweet. I remember in the nursery Marie-Anne loved nothing better than to dress and undress her doll Agathe, and Hortense, always so quiet and gentle, playing with the Noah's Ark, her face puckered in concentration as she lined up the animals to be counted. What a pleasure for us all to be together at Court! And we will get Diane married and find her a place—perhaps also in the infanta's new household—and then we will all be here.

Everything will be fine.

I rub some pomade on my face and pull at my cheeks. "Jacobs, why do you think Marie-Anne did not seek my help with the cardinal, to obtain the position with the queen?" Even as I say the words aloud I think: But there is only one answer.

"Surely she did not want to bother you, madame."

"Mmm. The cloth." I wipe the excess oil off. How I wish I was eighteen again and still had my life to live over. How I wish I was twenty-two and the king still loved me as he did back then. "This new pomade is very greasy, I don't like it at all. Tell Bernier to stop ordering it. And it smells. Of wet dog." I throw the pot on the floor and suddenly feel terribly unmoored. I want to cry.

"Don't worry about Marie-Anne," says Jacobs kindly. "You cannot get inside someone else's mind, and you should not try."

The king comes by to say good night. He doesn't stay, just squeezes my shoulder, mutters something about Saint Caprasius, and leaves.

Jacobs combs out my hair and swats the powder out of it. I climb into my chemise and then into bed and Jacobs draws the curtains. I think about my sisters: to my great sadness I do not have children of my own, but it is as though my younger sisters are my children and I their guardian. A nice thought.

But then as I drift off to sleep the demons of the dark come out to hound me. Marie-Anne, speaking directly to Fleury. Demanding an audience. Demanding the position. Pauline was the same—fearless. Today the king attended one of the queen's concerts, which he rarely does; his tastes run more modern and light than the queen, who adores Lully from the last century. But he attended, and sat with the queen, and then spoke with Marie-Anne afterward. I saw them talking together: when she laughed the king stared at her with a look of thirst and hunger.

A small snake wraps itself tight around my insides. I try to shake it free: Marie-Anne is nothing like Pauline. She was such a sweet young child, quiet and good. I remember her rescuing small mice from the cold and the cats, and keeping them alive in a little box, lined with cast-off wool. She was so gentle, so caring. Surely people don't change that much?

From Louise de Mailly
Château de Versailles
October 5, 1742

Dearest Diane,

Thank you for your last letter; I must confess it was rather difficult to read. I do think that you wrote that Philippine died of small ducks, but I am sure you meant smallpox. A dreadful disease, I hope she was sent away as soon as the infection appeared.

What happy times these are, with both Hortense and Marie-Anne together with me at Versailles! Of course, the death of Tante was a sudden and awful thing, but she was quite old and I am sure that God knew what He was doing when He called her home. My sisters are now in the service of the queen. They must be bright and polite in the midst of their grief, but everyone remarks on how well they look, Marie-Anne especially.

The king is in a much better mood these last few weeks, though I do not see much of him. He is very careful to show consideration to Marie-Anne and Hortense, knowing that they are my sisters and are in a time of sorrow. The king honored the first anniversary of Pauline's death by enjoying a special hunt, while wearing a black hat. How thoughtful he is! I believe he still misses her dreadfully.

You must come and visit again. It has been too long. It would be such fun, the four of us together!

I enclose as a gift the silver silk fan you so admired when you were last here; I am sorry I did not think to present it to you before.

Love,
Louise

Diane

We are waiting for the king, just a few of us in one of the private inner rooms. I think the king a wonderful man; he loves animals almost as much as I do. Tonight one of his cats, an adorable bundle of silky white fur, waits with us in the room where we will dine. To amuse us one of the footmen dips Snowball's paws into a cup of champagne and we giggle as she licks them clean. Can cats get drunk?

It is the last night of my visit and my name has been added to the supper group as a special favor. The other guests are all very grand, but not very exciting: Richelieu, the Duc d'Antin, the Marquis de Meuse, Charolais, a few others whose names I don't know, as well as my sisters. We are all four sisters here in the room, together for the first time since the Quai des Théatins and our mother's death. I only wish Pauline were here to share it with us, but she isn't, and luckily neither is her wax head—that's still at Saint-Léger. But above the mantel hangs a beautiful portrait of her, commissioned by the king after her death. I love the painting; it makes me both sad and content. The callous courtiers snort and say it looks nothing like her, and that Nattier the artist should have his fingers chopped off for creating such a work of fantasy.

Charolais sidles up to the table and starts stroking Snowball, who is attacking a piece of celery. "Hello, little pug."

"Don't call me that." I'm not very good at being polite to people who aren't polite to me.

"I was talking to the cat, not you." Charolais is dressed tonight in a particularly lurid lilac color. The yellowish shade makes her complexion sallow and unpleasant.

"Her name is Snowball," I reply stiffly. "And why would you call a cat a 'little pug'?"

She stops stroking the cat and smirks at me. Snowball wobbles off the table and falls onto the floor with a stunned *meep*.

"So, congratulations," purrs Charolais, kicking the cat away. "The Duc de Lauraguais. Not bad, not bad at all. You are indeed fortunate in your influential friends and relations." She glances over at Marie-Anne and Richelieu, laughing together under the portrait of Pauline.

I giggle in nervous surprise. "How do you know?"

"Oh, mademoiselle, I knew before you did. I knew it on Tuesday." It's Saturday today and Richelieu informed me only yesterday. Since then I've been floating on a particularly happy, fluffy cloud. I am to be married!

"I'm not sure how his family convinced him—his first wife, Geneviève, was a great beauty. Her eyes were extraordinary," continues Charolais.

Louise comes to rescue me, bringing Snowball back to the table. "It's wonderful, wonderful news." She beams, and I know she is truly happy for me. "Diane to be married, and to be a duchess! Soon she'll be at Court full-time. Her husband has a very spacious apartment. Very spacious."

"Mmm." Charolais looks disdainfully at Louise then turns back to me. "We thought it would never happen. I don't know *anyone* who married for the first time at the age of twenty-eight. Remarkably old. Let's just hope it hasn't *closed over*," she adds in a low whisper before slinking away.

"Don't mind her, Diane." Louise squeezes my arm again and I smile back. I see Louise is nervous, but I don't know why. She has been looking a little lost and gray this last week; she says it is because she is bored, now that she is no longer in attendance upon the queen. She frets her fan and watches Marie-Anne and Richelieu. She has little black circles under her eyes that she tried to disguise with white powder, but it hasn't worked very well.

Hortense is sitting in comfort with a smile on her face, wearing a loose gray gown that flows over her in a river of chiffon. She is now very pregnant but even more beautiful than before: her face is innocent of rouge but somehow her cheeks glow perfectly. The other ladies, even Marie-Anne, pale in comparison, and I notice that Charolais keeps well clear of her. Hortense is enjoying Court life and declares often that even one as beautiful as she is can be pious here. It's not a very humble thing to say—Madame Lesdig always says that the pride of the peacock is an abomination before God—but I suppose it's true.

Marie-Anne is also very beautiful tonight, though she too takes care to stay away from Hortense. She is very simply dressed in a white silk gown with black bows—I tried to get her to add some flowers or lace, but she says that sometimes simplicity is the greatest grace and that there is a difference between elegance and fussiness. She sounds just like Madame de Lesdig! She's very confident, and seems even prettier here than she did when she was living at Tante's: it is as though the grandeur of Versailles suits her. Marie-Anne tells me it was she and Richelieu who arranged my marriage; I'm not sure how she did that but I am beginning to think that she can do anything.

"But what is going on?" The king strides into the room and extricates Snowball from a bowl of salad on the side table. The cat meows piteously. The king recoils at the smell of alcohol: his senses are as refined as his manners. "Is this cat drunk?"

"Sire." The footman Jonglon bows, laughing and sweating. "Snowball turned out to be a right *bon viveur* and enjoyed his champagne greatly."

The king frowns and the atmosphere shifts and the air fills quickly with opprobrium for the thoughtless Jonglon and his dreadful prank. The cowed footman retrieves the cat from the king's arms and exits, with a promise to sit by the animal's side until she is fully sober.

No! I don't want Snowball to go. "Oh, but, sire, it was so funny, you would have laughed if you had seen it, Snowball tried to shred the celery and . . ."

The king smiles at me lazily. Everyone tells me it is inappropriate for me to talk to him when he hasn't addressed me first, but he never seems to mind. And he's the only one who matters, isn't he? Sometimes I feel him looking at me, and when I catch him he always apologizes, even though he needn't, and says I remind him of Pauline. I am like a sketch, a shadow, he says, for the painting that would become Pauline. I think that is a compliment?

The king sits at the head of the table and with a wave indicates that we should seat ourselves at will. I giggle to watch everyone falling over themselves to appear polite, yet wanting to sit as close to him as they can. Only Louise smiles like a saint and takes a place at the far end of the table. Zélie was right: humility inspires admiration. Hortense is helped to the chair of her choosing by the gallant Duc d'Ayen. I am torn between following Snowball and taking a seat, but I suppose I'd better sit down—Louise was telling me all day what an honor it is for me to be included tonight.

I plop down in the middle next to the Marquis de Meuse, whom the king likes but no one else does. Marie-Anne goes to sit beside Louise at the far end of the table but at the last minute she looks back at the king. He smiles at her and she comes shyly back toward him, as though unable to resist his lure. The king grins heartily and leans forward, and Marie-Anne blushes. I think Marie-Anne is a very good actress, which I suppose is a good thing—didn't Zélie always say we should hide our real emotions? But what is she trying to hide?

"All of us, here together," observes the king as the footmen fill the table with plates from the warming room next door. Oh, good—the centerpiece is a pair of roasted rabbits, smothered in sage and onions. Delicious. "All of my favorite family." He looks around the table: Marie-Anne, Hortense, Louise, me, the portrait of Pauline watching over us. His gaze comes back to linger between Hortense and Marie-Anne. "To the charming Nesle sisters," he says. "Each with their own charms, each unique. I would that I had known your mother well, ladies, that I could have thanked that most honorable woman for her efforts in producing such angels."

"I knew the mother well," remarks Richelieu with a vicious grin. I once overheard Madame de Lesdig talking to one of her old friends about him; she called him a rabbit racing around, mating with everything that moved.

"I'm sure you did, Richelieu," answers the king neutrally. "We would be hard-pressed to find mothers of any of our guests here tonight you *didn't* know."

We all laugh dutifully but the king still seems fixed on us four sisters. I suppose it is rather exciting for him: all of us here together, and he does seem to like our family so. Louise says he holds us in kind regard, for his love of her and the memory of Pauline. But he does seem to be liking Hortense and Marie-Anne quite a bit—last week he chose to ride to the hunt with them in his carriage and left Louise back at the palace. Louise said she was glad, because it meant she could spend more time with me, but I don't think she was very happy.

The king raises his goblet. "To my favorite sisters. All so different, yet all so charming. Would that we could be together like this, every evening." He commends us to drink to the health of the perfect Nesle sisters and to our lost Pauline.

I drink quickly, hoping the dinner will start soon. Rabbit is not nearly as good when it is cold; it gets tough and the sauce will soon start congealing. I see Louise smile, as deeply as she can, and I relax a bit, for she seems genuinely happy at the king's words. Hortense blushes an even more perfect shade of pink and lowers her eyes. Marie-Anne trembles with delight.

"And why can we not, sire, have more evenings like this?" asks Hortense in a shy, silky voice, and the king swallows hard and looks as though he is straining against his breeches. In her hair she has sewn three perfect pink lilies and I think she looks like a living flower. "It is indeed delightful to be so entertained, and I would count myself the happiest woman in the world if it could be thus every night."

Marie-Anne frowns. She and Hortense are not getting on very well these days. I am staying with Marie-Anne in her fine apartment, and Hortense rarely visits. When I ask where she is, Marie-Anne just waves her hand and says she's probably pretending to pray or something. It's surprising, because they were very close before. I hope they don't become enemies, like Pauline and Marie-Anne were. I like both of them and wouldn't want to have to choose.

"But too much of a good thing—what is that quote?" asks Marie-Anne, drawing the king away from the angel in the middle of the table.

" 'Can one desire too much of a good thing?' " supplies Richelieu helpfully.

The king nods. "An excellent question, as posed by Shakespeare, my friend, but I think the answer to be no. In this case I do not think I can desire too much of a good thing, too much of these beautiful sisters."

I want to giggle but I hold my tongue. I must be silent like a fish! I must not even splash. But it's true; the king certainly likes our family. I wonder if Marie-Anne will become his mistress? Or Hortense? And Louise—would she be sad? What if the king wants to sleep with *me*? I'll be married soon, and then I can probably sleep with anyone I want—apparently my future husband has a dozen mistresses—and of course if the king asked, it would be hard to say no. But how strange that would be, if the king slept with *all* of us? Had all of us as lovers?

Marie-Anne laughs lightly. "Oh, Shakespeare was a fine writer, but he is not a god. I think that too much of anything leads to boredom. And, Your Majesty, I would hate to think of you bored. Besides, Diane leaves tomorrow, so we shall lose one of our *members*." There is a little husky trill on her last word and the king puts his glass down sharply and again looks as though his breeches have just popped.

Finally we start to eat—apart from the roasted rabbit there are rashers of juniper-smoked bacon and an excellent venison pie that everyone declares is the finest they have ever eaten, made as it is from the stag the king killed that afternoon.

"Victory mingles perfectly with the tender meat and spices," ventures Meuse in his craven, high-pitched voice.

The conversation turns to the scandal of the day: the death of the old Duc de Nangis, who left twenty thousand *livres* to his chief valet. A debate rages about whether they were lovers or not. I want to inform the other guests that such a thing is not possible, but the shadow of Madame de Lesdig falls over me and keeps me silent. I concentrate on the food and help myself to a sweet lemony sauce, perfect when poured over the rabbit and mixed with the onions.

Later, when the meat is eaten and the champagne is near finished from the bottomless bottles, the room grows warm and close with the fire and the sweat of the restless courtiers. The king stops the talk and raises one finger.

"Do you sing?" he asks Marie-Anne. She opens her rosebud mouth a touch, just a touch, and looks at him with soft, quizzical eyes. I know she has a beautiful singing voice, so I am not sure why she doesn't just say that.

He looks down the table to Louise. "Bijou, I know you can sing, a bit. What about your sisters? I would love nothing better than to have the four of you sing before me. An aria or a country ballad. Anything."

"Oh, sire, a magnificent idea!"

"Splendid thought, *Majesté*!"

The courtiers twitter their approval. Richelieu picks his ear and looks around in amusement. Louise laughs a little nervously. Her voice is fair enough but a little thin, and certainly not as fine as Marie-Anne's. "I'm not sure our education extended that far, sire," she says with pleading in her voice, which the king ignores. Marie-Anne doesn't agree and she leaps up.

"What fun!" she declares, and simpers at the king. "The four of us, singing for our king. It would be our honor. Come, Diane, stand, and Louise, you too." We gather around Hortense's chair.

"Let's sing 'Souvenirs de Pauline'!" I cry, realizing as I speak that I have drunk too much and that my voice is even louder than usual.

"No, no," hisses Marie-Anne, pinching my arm. "Shut up."

Hortense suggests "Le Mari et la Mariée," and all declare that the perfect song.

"Yes, yes," cries the king. "But you must get closer, closer. With your hands around each other's waists. Hold each other, touch each other. Yes, like that, closer."

Like crippled marionettes we bunch together, panniers crushing, laughing and starting to sing. I'm not a good singer but I do like it, and so I sing lustily. Next to me Louise speaks the words softly and I can see the unease running down her cheeks, wet with champagne perspiration. Marie-Anne's fine voice trills above the others, her face turned to the ceiling, while below her Hortense sings with the voice of an angel. The king's eyes dart between the two of them.

Poor Louise, he's not looking at her at all. I grab her tighter and pull her close to me, for I think she needs comforting. Funny, because she is the elder and I so much younger.

From Hortense de Flavacourt
Château de Versailles
October 22, 1742

Darling Husband,

Greetings from Court. I am glad you insist on these daily letters; they are a good time to reflect on my love for you and my desire to be a devoted wife. I swear to you, again, that I am not being changed by this scandalous place and that I remain faithful to you in heart and body.

Unfortunately, I cannot say the same for everyone. I am afraid that Marie-Anne may follow the path of Louise and Pauline (and possibly Diane, though this I cannot ascertain and certainly do not want to spread gossip). The king is a handsome man; not as handsome as you, my dear husband, but a good-looking man nonetheless, and I think Marie-Anne is infatuated with him. I don't think he is that excited by her; he has spoken to me alone several times and declares me the fairest of all my sisters. Please do not be jealous or angry—you must know that I have only you in my heart—but if my sovereign wishes to compliment me, I cannot prevent him.

I pray for Marie-Anne, that she will not follow the path of our harlot sisters, but she seems impervious to my pleas.

I enclose a lock of my hair. I hope I have chosen the right hair; I do believe this is what you requested in your last letter. If I have erred, please forgive me and know that I would not have done such a wicked and dirty thing if I did not think it your wish.

I am waiting anxiously for the end of the year when we will be reunited.

In loving devotion,
Your faithful wife,
Hortense

Marie-Anne

VERSAILLES

October 1742

Versailles has some of the world's finest greenhouses and vegetable and fruit gardens. The king promised me during a doctors' visit in the summer that it would be his pleasure to show them to me. And I must not forget Garnier—the king has said I may take what clippings I want and send them to Burgundy.

The king forgoes the pleasure of the hunt to spend the afternoon in the gardens and greenhouses with me. A small group of courtiers accompanies us as the king shows me the hothouses and the numerous vegetable plots and fruit orchards. Louise is with us, wrapped like ivy around the king's arm. Hortense is feeling very ill with her latest pregnancy—thank goodness—and could not accompany us.

We wind our way through the pea and bean plots to the figgery—figs in October! The king picks one from a tree and expertly splits it open. He sucks on the ripe red inner flesh, his eyes on me. I'm suddenly very hungry.

"The best figs in the world," declares Meuse, pushing his way to the front of the group. "Known the world over for their sweetness and softness, only such as could come from this palace, why La Fontaine once compared them to the thighs of Venus and said—"

"Finish it, my good man," says the king easily, and hands him the remains of the fruit.

One of the gardeners brings us a pail of tiny, perfect strawberries, and another proudly shows us the new arrivals in the herb gardens. After selecting a delicate little fenugreek plant to accompany a fig-tree cutting for Burgundy, we head back toward the palace. The afternoon is brilliant; the crisp autumn air warmed by the sun, the sky clear cerulean. The king dismisses the chairs and insists we walk.

"Oh, Marie-Anne, your Mr. Garnier will be very happy with his plants," says Louise cheerfully.

"Indeed," I murmur. We walk along the vast smoothness of the Lake of the Swiss Guards, reluctant to turn back toward the palace and end the afternoon. The king has a slow, stately strut and we fall easily into the same pace as we drift along.

"One day, I should build a proper botanical garden. Like the Jardin des Plantes in Paris. A wonder of the world, with all the plants, every single one, growing in the hothouses. It is one thing to grow fifteen types of pears and more even of apples, but how much do we know of other fruits? Other flowers? Herbs? What a thing it would be to have every plant, from every far land, here at Versailles."

"A venture I would keenly assist with, sire." The late sun glints off the smooth water of the ornamental lake; everything feels heavy and slow. And special. In the distance something is burning, a sharp peated smell cutting through the crisp warm air.

"And what else, sire, do you enjoy as much as your plants?" I ask.

"Astronomy is another interest of mine."

"Oh, reading the future is so much fun! Though a little sinful."

"Astronomy, not astrology, Bijou," says the king patiently. We are walking slowly, one sister on either side of him. I am on the right side.

"Well, stars are very nice too!" says Louise enthusiastically.

"Astronomy?" I arch my eyebrows and smile at the king. "I would not have thought you a star-seeker."

"There is so much in this world to know. Lacaille—what an

astonishing young man. I do believe he will eventually catalog us all the stars in the heavens." We look up at the vast autumn sky; a hawk floats motionless above us. "I have a telescope, a present from Frederick of Sweden, a man as interested in the natural world as I am. A wonderful instrument. You know what a telescope is?"

"I have heard of them, but have never seen one."

"Then I must show you mine. It is long and powerful, very powerful."

"And what it is made of?" I banter back. "Something hard, I hope?"

"Oh, don't be silly, Marie-Anne," chips in Louise. "A telescope can't be soft." Goodness, but she is annoying.

"Made only of the most rigid and durable of materials, madame. As hard as bone, in fact."

"How I should love to see it." I skip a beat. "When the time is right, of course."

"The time is right whenever you, madame, desire it to be so."

We continue walking, taking the long route back to the palace. We turn down the aptly named Alley of Autumn.

"It is so warm today, how nice it is to be in October yet still like summer," Louise remarks to the indifferent air.

"Yes, we thought summer gone, then it reappears," the king replies.

"Some call it an Indian summer, I believe." I am careful in sharing my knowledge; no one wants a Hypatia, but I find the king has an interesting and curious mind, alive with the quest for knowledge and trivia of all kinds.

"An Indian summer—because in India it is hot the year round, perhaps? Beaulieu said it was so devilishly hot there, there was no need to cook the meat. Or was it the vegetables?"

Our dreamy path through the languor of the afternoon continues. We have been flirting for weeks, but nothing has happened. Not yet, despite the rumors that run rife and rampant and over the walls. I even heard that Maurepas, enraged at the paucity of the intelligence provided by his spies, threw one of them against a bookcase and near broke the man's arm.

I think I'll keep them guessing.

The Duc de Villeroy trots up on his horse, accompanied by three barking bloodhounds. He greets the king then stops to talk with the courtiers trailing us. We three leave the group behind and choose a smaller path through the yews, bordered with rose-bushes and red-berried hawthorns.

"Ah, one that yet lives." The king picks from the bush a small rose, the color of ripe oranges, and recites:

> *"Gather ye rosebuds while ye may,*
> *Old Time is still a-flying,*
> *And this same flower that smiles today*
> *Tomorrow will be dying."*

"Your own, sire?" I ask, even though I know it's not.

"But no!" The king smiles easily; in private he can be humble and quite funny, very different from his public persona of aloofness mixed with majesty. "I would not presume to think myself sufficiently talented to write thus. An English poet, I cannot remember the name. But it was a favorite of mine from childhood, though perhaps a little morbid for a youth. And yourself, madame: Do you write?"

"The same as Your Majesty. Why would I spend my time to produce inferior work when I can enjoy the fruits of others?"

"Bow your head," says the king, stopping suddenly. I do as he commands and he leans over and tucks the rosebud into my hair. "A vision, madame."

The intimacy of the moment leaves me speechless, his hand on my head, the closeness of his body. He didn't even ask; he just did it. I want to lean in and have him take me in his arms, right now, but all I can do is stare.

"You look very nice," says Louise faintly, standing rigid beside us.

Then the world rudely intrudes and breaks our spell; Villeroy canters off in a clatter of gravel and dogs, with the courtiers shouting their adieus. We start walking again, slower this time, losing ourselves in the vastness of the gardens and the promise of the late-afternoon warmth. I hold the bud in my hair, afraid it should fall.

"You enjoy the Pléiade, madame?"

"I do."

"And who else do you favor when the time comes for losing yourself in words?"

"I am partial to anything romantic," I lie. In fact, I am partial to La Fontaine's wit and sharp words, but I can sense the king's romantic heart beating beneath his corded yellow waistcoat. He put a rose in my hair! "My favorite is Louise Labé."

"Ah, but there you disappoint me, madame. We have no time for women poets. Only men, I believe, have the heart and the courage to plumb the depths of emotion required for great poetry. You must surely agree with me."

I tread carefully over a fallen hawthorn branch and the mild dismissal of his comment. I take a deep breath and put my hand on the king's arm to stop him. Louise flinches as though burned, but he stops and turns to me, surprised.

"Permit me one sonnet to change your mind about the poets of our fairer sex. Just one." I come as close as I can without touching and stare directly at him.

His head inclines but his eyes never leave mine. "Convince me, madame."

I take a deep breath: "*I live, I die, I drown, I burn—*'"

"And then she said to the footman, get it out of me!"

"Silence!" The king roars his displeasure at Meuse, loudly gossiping with the group of advancing courtiers. "I would hear this fine poem, in fine company, and in fine silence. Get away! All of you."

The courtiers bow and stumble back, muttering their apologies, Meuse's face as red as the pansies on his coat.

"Bijou, you too." The king's smile is kind but there is frost underneath as he casually dismisses her. I think: This is a man who rarely thinks of others. Very rarely. If it weren't so hot, I would shiver.

"Of course, dearest. I am sure you will enjoy the poem: Marie-Anne has such a lovely reciting voice." Louise's expression is neutral as she turns away and walks slowly down the path toward the palace, a lonely figure in front of the honey-colored bricks lit gold in the late-afternoon sun. We watch her go but there is no limp of defeat in her careful, elegant walk.

Poor Louise.

The king takes me by the arm and leads me around a corner to a copse with a bench and a small, statueless fountain. A brown rabbit startles and hops away, and then we are all alone.

"Privacy in the middle of Versailles? Are you Majesty or magician?" I say lightly.

"For you, dear Marie-Anne, I can be both," he says, using my Christian name for the first time. We sit together on the stone bench, his arm still on mine.

"Let me fix the flower." He leans in and for a moment I think he is going to kiss me, but he tucks the bud in again, smooths my hair, and leans back. I look him in the eye again and wait a beat before I start anew:

> *"I live. I die. I drown. I burn.*
> *I shiver with cold and perish with heat.*
> *I leap from anguish to delight; from sweet to bitter.*
> *No two moments are the same.*
>
> *"I live. I die. I drown. I burn."*

Silence.

"Madame. I am"—a soundless pause—"convinced."

He leans in again, and this time he does kiss me.

♋

Richelieu visits me even more than the king does, and while I am grateful for his help, our strategies differ considerably. Sometimes I feel I have two masters to please and only one, the king, is malleable. Richelieu wants me to give in to the king now, on the grounds that he has been chasing me long enough. But I prefer to wait. To increase the anticipation as well as to make sure my requirements are met before the king samples my "sweet nectar," as Agénois used to say.

I have a very specific list of demands: first, the title of duchess. Diane will be married in January, and then she will be a duchess and well positioned to present me when I receive my own duchy. Of course, I will also need an income befitting a duchess. My fortune must be independent and separate, to protect against future upheavals. I don't want to get chased away at the death of the king and forced to live out the rest of my life in a cold convent somewhere, dependent on charity. It's unromantic to think like this, but it must be done.

Then I'll need my own apartment at Versailles, suitable for the first lady in the land—perhaps not first in precedence, but first in everything else. I want only the finest. I am not going to be like Louise—two rooms for a king's mistress! Madame de Maintenon had magnificent rooms; I should have nothing less. And I want legitimacy for any children of our union. Pauline's son, Demi-Louis, is technically a Vintimille and is treated by the *comte* as his own; our children must not be hindered thus. They must be recognized by the king. Finally, I'd like an independent house, either in Paris or Versailles—perhaps the king can buy me back my childhood home?—and a carriage with a minimum of six horses.

When he reads my list, Richelieu grows purple and screws his mouth into a little ball. "This is preposterous! A few presents or baubles to—seal the deal, as they say—the carriage, for example. Perhaps a necklace—"

"One must start as one plans to finish," I murmur. "The wise man does at once what the fool does finally."

He raises his eyebrows. "Sounds like Machiavelli. Though

where a young lady such as yourself found such reading matter, I dread to think."

He returns to the list. I look serene but inside my nerves are tied in knots. If you don't try, you don't succeed, I tell myself. Who would have thought Aesop and his little rodents and beetles had all the answers?

"You know the king hates demands on him."

I know it, but think it strange—what is the role of the king but to answer demands?

"And that's why you, Richelieu, are going to be the one to ask him."

Richelieu barks once in annoyance and leaves.

My hands are shaking. It's a strange thing to ask for so much, especially when I've never really asked for anything in my life. I hear Hortense saying: *Where do you get your strength, Marie-Anne?* I clasp my trembling hands together and press them tight until they are white and still. I can do this.

And there is one more condition that I didn't mention to Richelieu, but on which I am determined. Louise must leave the Court. Immediately. And she must never return.

Louise

It has been a month of anguish, torture, full of slights and in-sults that only wine can soften, when I am alone in my room and wondering if he is with her.

Marie-Anne is cool with me, and when she looks at me (which is rare) her eyes are icy and distant. And the king: I try to remain light and easy in his company but I cannot get too close, for if I do I know I will break down and make a scene. I remember how much he hated that, when he was with Pau-line. He visits the queen more often these days, but they say it is more for her lovely new lady-in-waiting than for any of his wife's charms.

"Not surprising, really. We all knew he couldn't mourn that hairy beast forever."

"Well, she's certainly prettier than that dog of a sister."

"It's almost as if he seeks out scandal, deliberately. Surely there are other women, other families?"

"Another one! Another one! What is this king's obsession with this family? Oh, hello, Louise, I didn't see you there. Rest assured I'm not talking about *your* family, I was referring to those painters the king likes, what are their names, van some-thing Dutch?"

Some are still friends and they seek me out to comfort me, the kind Comtesse de Toulouse assuring me the king will never forget our bonds, and even Gilette, who is sick these days and herself in need of comfort, hugs me and tells me to be strong. How can I be strong? I am weaker than water.

"I could be your partner, Marie-Anne," I say softly. We are at cards and leisure, a small group. I have tried to get her alone, to talk, to plead, but she avoids me with cool, easy calculation, not hesitating to leave when I enter a room and ignoring my requests to visit or dine with her.

"No, I prefer to play alone," she says coldly, and I hear the room fall silent around us. Even Meuse stops twiddling on about his new black horse; the whole room hangs breathless.

"But quadrille is meant to be played with a partner," I plead.

"I have no desire to play this game." She fiddles with her fan—a well-preserved Watteau original, a gift from the king—and looks bored.

"But . . . but . . ." I do not have the words to persuade her otherwise, and especially not in this room full of smirking courtiers, now watching us with daggered intent. I feel myself start to panic and my breath doesn't come easily. "But we could be good . . . you are my sister . . ."

"No, we would not make a good team. And being a sister has nothing to do with it. Nothing. Oh, but I am tired, this room is stuffy and hot. I would walk awhile in the halls."

"Madame, I shall accompany you. Quadrille is not for a night like this." The king rises and offers her his arm. I watch them leave, followed by a clutch of twittering courtiers.

The kind Duc de Luynes beams broadly at me and says he would be honored to be my partner if my sister does not care to play. A footman helps lower him and his gouty leg into the chair opposite. Numbly, I call for more champagne.

"Ah, you are thirsty, thirsty, my dear madame. But it is true the room is hot. Shall I ask the man to dampen the fire some?" Tears almost come at the old duke's kindness. Is it possible he doesn't know, doesn't see? But I can see—I am a lamb being led to the butcher's block. I know what is coming, and though I may squeal and bleat, all protest is futile.

ᴄⁿ

Bachelier summons me and I follow behind him in a trail of misery. Tumbril, scaffold, stakes, and fire. Before the king can even open his mouth, I know what he is going to say—it is written in the whiteness of his face. In some small, meager way there is perhaps even some relief: the last few weeks have been a dreadful nightmare, and now it is time to wake up.

"My dearest . . ." He turns away from me to look out the window into the frosted evening. "My dearest. You must leave us. Leave Versailles."

"No," I whisper softly. "No, this doesn't have to be. Please. Please."

"I'm sorry," he says, and when he turns to look at me I see he is crying too.

"Please, please, Twinkles, please don't—"

"Oh, Bijou, you must know I suffer too. This is not an easy decision. Not easy at all. I suffer too," he repeats sadly.

Out of habit I try to stifle my tears but they won't stop. And then, through my tears, for the first time I think: And why shouldn't he suffer too? He who makes others so miserable. I wail for my treacherous thoughts and collapse on the floor. I will not leave this room. I will not leave him. I just won't.

Louis blows his nose, silent and uncomfortable. I wail louder: "Please, please, Twink—" I reach out for him but he steps back, and then a familiar look of peevish displeasure slides over his face. In a flash he slips back into majesty, a role he wears easily, the cloak of kingship guarding him against all that is unpleasant in this world. And I have become that which is unpleasant. A bolt of black lightning splits my heart in two. Oh my God, oh my God, where are You now?

"Pray leave us, madame," he says coldly, staring down at me on the carpet as though I am a weeping stain, something to be cleaned up and removed. "We will not forget the fondness we have for your family and the services you have rendered, but for now you must follow my wishes. You must leave."

What will I do? Where will I go? I thought I knew despair, but this . . . oh! This is the darkest day of my life. Oh Lord, help me, help me.

☙

"Madame, madame." Jacobs shakes me awake. I sit up, disoriented. Why am I on the sofa? Why does my head hurt like . . . oh. In one awful instance I remember and fall back with a cry.

"My dear Comtesse de Mailly."

What is Richelieu doing in my apartments? I do not think there is anyone I would less like to see at this time. Except, of course, *her*. "What are you doing in my apartment?"

"Madame, it is no longer your apartment."

I fall back on the sofa and start crying again.

"She's been like this all night, sir," I hear Jacobs whispering to him.

"She must stop. There will be time enough for tears later. Now she must understand she needs to leave, and not make this more of a scandal than it already is."

When Louis and I were first in love, I would cover my face with a hood and slip down the dark corridors in the middle of the night. When I arrived he would slowly, carefully, pull back the hood then hold my face in his hands while he kissed me and then we would—

Richelieu pulls me up off the sofa and slaps my face.

"Ow."

"Don't be a fool, Louise," he hisses, and his face is so close to mine I cannot help but look in his detested eyes. I see an unusual amount of pity there and my tears stop in astonishment.

"Cry as much as you want, but later. Please, madame. Please. For now, you must gather your affairs and leave the palace. Toulouse will welcome you in Paris. You still have friends, but you must accept this."

"My duties with the queen . . ." I start to say, but then I remember I am no longer in her service. I realize in a rush I have been tricked and the ground opens up and swallows me, whole.

"Madame!"

Richelieu drags me up from the floor and pushes me into the arms of Jacobs.

"Please, madame." And now his voice is again the silky, odious one I know and hate so well and his eyes are blank. "Pull yourself together. I will leave you and you must leave as well. But not in this state. No one must see you like this. No one. Do you understand that?"

I stare at him and my eyes well up again. How can I accept this? If I leave then I may never see Louis again. I may never—oh!

"Go to Paris. For now. Wait a few days and then we will see how the world turns."

But how can I trust what Richelieu is saying? He is a snake like Marie-Anne. He is one of *her* snakes. Perhaps if I ran to Louis, if I could urge him to have pity, for surely this is not forever, surely he is just dazed by her? We have been in love for almost a decade; he is my world, my life. Surely it cannot end like this?

As if reading my mind, Richelieu crosses to the door and blocks it. "There is no time now for negotiations. You have the king's wishes. You must obey. You must. Do not make me get a letter. But I should not have to tell you that."

He turns to Jacobs. "Make sure she stays here until she is presentable. The king has generously offered one of his carriages, tell Levesque it is agreed. Just, for God's sake, get her out of here without a scene."

❧

I twist inside the carriage as we pass through the gates and I look back at the receding palace, the numberless windows like a hundred blank eyes watching me and mocking me, shunning my grief. In a rush I remember my first sight of the palace, all those years ago. I was only nineteen and I thought then that my life would begin here, in this most glorious place in the world. What a wretched life, that it should end thus! I sink back into the furred cushions and weep with all my soul.

Eventually the rocking of the carriage dulls my senses and I have no more tears to cry. Pauline scared me, at first, but I realize now she was nothing next to Marie-Anne. Snake. Viper. All that stupid talk of spices and farming, she was probably making spells and learning witchcraft down in Burgundy. And now she has entrapped the king with one of her vile potions. May she be exposed as a witch and burned at the stake.

Oh—what am I become that I think like this?

What has she made me become?

The coach reaches the outskirts of Paris and we head for the Hôtel de Toulouse. The place my exile will begin. All is drab, no green, no joy, and the grim November world mirrors the bleakness of my soul. I feel a sweep of jealousy for the simple folk outside, for they will never experience exile and banishment. Or betrayal by their own flesh and blood. I see a woman walking unsteadily along the side of the road, her arms heavy with firewood. For a moment I wish I could be her, but then I see she has no shoes and her feet are blue and muddy with cold. I shudder and my toes curl around the lamb's wool stuffed in my own shoes. I start to cry again.

"Madame, you must compose yourself. We are almost at the Louvre."

"Oh, what does it matter, Jacobs? I am not going to see anyone. They will understand. I will go straight to bed."

Straight to bed, in a strange bed, away from the man and the place I love.

Oh, despair.

Marie-Anne

As the sun rises I stretch in the bed, the king sleeping silently beside me. I run my fingers lightly through his grease-smoothed hair and contentment fills me through and puffs me up. Oh, what a night. I look around the sun-streaked room. Let me count the ways that my happiness is complete and my triumph assured:

One room, one woman, and one man.

Four enormous windows, thirty-two panes of glass.

Eight curtains embroidered with little doves and bordered by Louise's initials, drawn back to let in the pale winter sun.

One fireplace, embers already cold.

Six mirrors to reflect back my joy.

Two bronze statues, Eros and Pothos, watching closely from the doorway.

Six candles, dribbled down to the wick.

Three cats sleeping in the sunlight.

Two glasses of wine on the table by the bed.

One bottle of fine Shiraz, empty.

Two piles of clothes, strewn over four chairs with scalloped backs.

Two earrings and one fine pearl choker, flung on the floor. Gifts from the king, appraised at 30,000 *livres*. (Unsolicited gifts, I should add. I believe Louis really is a generous man and has simply been waiting for the right woman. I am that woman.)

Four shoes, one broken red heel.

One sword, crossed over the lilies on the carpet.

One magnificent bed, mahogany and marble.

Three shades of pale blue on the velvet hangings.

One set of fine linen sheets, softer than satin.

Two years, to the day, since my husband died.

One king, sleeping beside me.

Three times . . .

Well, I won't say anything else. Except: I doubt the king ever had such a night, with simple Louise or dour Pauline. Oof, let me not even think their names. But a quick memory rises, unbidden: Louise comforting me at the death of our mother, making a black lace veil for my doll. I close my mind and harden it, snap it shut against the memory. This is no time for regrets, and in every war there must be casualties.

I should get this redecorated, I think, looking around the sun-streaked room; it's simply moth-ridden with too many of their memories.

But for now . . . eight months and the long battle is over.

Forward to 1743.

Triumph.

From Louise de Mailly
Hôtel de Toulouse, Paris
December 2, 1742

Dearest Hortense,

Thank you so much for not forgetting me in my time of need! I weep as I write; I cannot even pretend to be happy. I show you my emotions as Zélie forbade us for so long. Away from that place of painted deceit, I can only speak and write candidly. Please forgive the smudges, for my tears are real and the pain is almost unbearable.

I must know. You must tell me everything, do not forget anything, even if you consider it gossip, please know that my heart is breaking and I beg you with all your heart to show me some mercy. You must tell me everything.

I dreamed of him last night, we were in a meadow, he was so young and so was I. It can't be the end, can it? I know you think dreams are nothing but Satan's work, but it was so real. What we had was real, it cannot end like this, can it?

Please speak to her for me, remind her of how I was with Pauline. I should come back, I know him well, I can help her, I can help *him*. She did not need to do what she did. Oh, sister, please help me.

Please accept my apologies for not writing before to congratulate you on the birth of your daughter. I will knit her a winter bonnet—my days are free and empty—let me know if I should send it to Versailles or Picardy.

Please,
Louise

From Hortense de Flavacourt
Château de Versailles
December 20, 1742

Dearest Louise,

I regret my harsh words to you in our earlier correspondence and conversation. What Marie-Anne has done to you is truly shocking and perhaps the biggest scandal that our sainted family has undergone. I had suspected for a long while that Marie-Anne was not what she appears to be; underneath her soft face and pretty smile lie many thorns and much evil.

I regret I cannot speak to her on your behalf, for we are no longer close. In truth, I think you should forget any dreams you have of returning to His Majesty's favor. You will be happier away from Court. Marie-Anne is not Pauline, she is altogether something different, and it would be best for your soul, both now and in the afterlife, if you were to stay far away from her.

She has become a swollen river of pride and greed, a monster. Her only act with the slightest redemption was to arrange that marriage for Diane. She crows about having a duchess in the family, and how soon she will be one too. When Hell freezes over, I hope.

Sister, embrace your new life and keep your trust in God and He will hear your prayers and bring you happiness again.

Thank you for your offer of a winter bonnet for the baby. Please send it to Picardy, the child went there last week. She is well made and healthy, but I was hoping for another son. We have named her Adelaide-Julie, for yourself and our sister Diane.

You are in my heart,
Hortense

From Louise de Mailly
Hôtel de Toulouse, Paris
December 21, 1742

Dear Diane,

Please write to me, please. I know Philippine is dead but your writing is not as bad as you think, I can make out most words, and I must have news. I must know what is going on. You must help me.

Do not trust Marie-Anne, though she may appear sweet and kind at heart, she is an evil woman. Remember I was a friend to Pauline? I helped her and I cannot understand why Marie-Anne does not want my friendship and my companionship. I cannot bear to be apart from him. I dreamed of him last night, I dream of him every night, but in morning's light it is the purest of agonies to wake without him, and without hope of seeing him.

Please, I beg of you, help me. Speak to her, or to the king. He once said you reminded him of Pauline—surely he holds some affection for you?

You will be married soon: congratulations. I know you must be busy with your preparations, but please do not forget me. And once you are a duchess and a woman in your own right, you must distance yourself from Marie-Anne and seek only Hortense's company.

Please, Diane, write, and tell me what you know, and what I must do.

In love and sorrow,
Louise

Diane

When I first meet my future husband, Lauraguais, he is drunk and takes no pains to hide his distaste for me. The feeling is mutual; I find him a grisly boar with no manners, and besides, I have only heard bad things about him. He is the same age as I but recently widowed with two small children, so now I have two small stepchildren. I haven't met them yet—they live in the country outside Paris—but I should like to know them someday.

Lauraguais turns with large pleading eyes to his mother, and starts to whine: "But, Mother, you thaid—"

His mother, the Duchesse de Brancas, cuts him short and pushes him toward me. We are in the salon at Madame Lesdig's house. Lesdig squeezes my hand to reassure me, but I don't care. I am not romantic or starry-eyed like Louise used to be. It doesn't matter that my husband is unattractive and unkind, because I will be a duchess and I will live at Versailles and have my own apartment. Husbands, of course, can make a wife very unhappy—Madame Lesdig has assured me of this—and her advice is to avoid them as much as possible.

Lauraguais makes an exaggerated bow and almost topples over, then steadies himself against a delicate table that wobbles precariously. A sour, drunk smell wafts off him and brings me directly back to the nursery on the fourth floor and to memories of my father. I shudder; I hate the smell of drunken men.

"Oxen oaf!" whispers Madame Lesdig under her breath.

Lauraguais rights himself and waves at me.

Startled, I wave back.

"Hello—no, no. Your hand, give me your hand. Paw. Cats! All around . . . so many."

I reluctantly proffer my hand. I can hear Madame Lesdig breathing heavily beside me, ready to pounce should things go wrong.

"Mademoiselle," and his voice is slurred and his eyes wander wildly. "It is my most great and grandest, most great . . . grandest . . ." He loses concentration, momentarily. "Cats, so many cats. Why?"

"Privilege," hisses his mother.

"The most grantest privilege to be united in matra . . . matra . . ."

"Oh, shut up, Louis. You're embarrassing yourself." His mother, Angélique, smiles at me and reaches over a lemon-gloved hand to tweak my earlobe. She is pleasingly plump and has a kind face. "Out too late with the men. Celebrating. Dearest daughter. He is overcome, simply overcome with his great good fortune. We must get you some earrings for those pretty lobes."

As they leave she presents me with an enormous diamond that she says has been in their family forever, and promises to send over a bolt of the finest white ermine for my wedding cape. Their family will profit too: Marie-Anne, who is adored by the king, arranged for him to pay a handsome dowry for me. Well, actually the Jews of Lorraine paid for it, they were taxed because they are . . . well, because they are Jewish. But it was the king who made the new tax and made sure the Jews paid it, so in a way it is he who paid.

❦

We are married in the cathedral by the fat Archbishop of Paris, who also married Pauline. I wear one of my black mourning dresses, in memory of her. At the wedding feast Lauraguais is very drunk, his eyes red and his breath terrible. "You smell," he declares. "Can't you bathe for your own wedding day?"

"It's not me," I retort. I really hate the smell of drunken men. "It's this dress." Why waste water washing a dreary black dress I will soon discard? Besides, my new white ermine cape doesn't smell; it is quite the finest thing.

The wedding feast is wonderful, with more than twelve varieties of pies—including my favorite pigeon pie and of course sugar pie. The reception is at his mother's house on the rue de Tournon, not far from our childhood home on the Quai des Théatins. It is true what Madame Lesdig has told me: my husband's family is very rich. The house has enormous gardens, now a field of snow, and inside, it is almost as luxurious as Versailles.

Marie-Anne attends, and because she is there, Louise cannot be. That makes me a little sad, and of course Pauline cannot be here either. A few people helpfully point out my husband's "special friend" amongst the guests, a tall woman with unpowdered red hair and slanted cat eyes. I admire her hair color—it seems painted on. Did she dye her hair as they might dye cloth?

When I have finished eating, my new mother-in-law shows me around the house.

"But you must call me Angélique, or Mama, or Mama Angélique," she says, and I think I am going to like her.

Each of the reception rooms is a different color and all the curtains and the chairs and the sofas match the walls. I like the yellow room the best. There are fires blazing everywhere, and even though we are deep in January, the rooms are toasty and warm. In each room footmen stand silently in curved niches, ready to leap out at a moment's notice to fluff a cushion or fetch a cup. They are dressed not in the gold and blue of the Brancas livery, but in a uniform that matches the color of the room. They blend into the walls to great effect.

"Waiting for the bell is so tiresome," Angélique explains, and shows me how it is done. We are in the Pink Salon; she drops a handkerchief and a pink-coated man leaps nimbly from his perch in the wall and restores the cloth to her.

I giggle. "Why not paint their faces the same color?" I ask.

"Unfortunately they sweat too much with the paint. And a sweating footman is simply distasteful."

Touffe, my woman from Madame Lesdig's, shows me to a bath. Down below I overhear my new husband screaming at his mother: "I won't touch her until she bathes! You promised!"

The bath is unlike anything I have ever had, lakes of steaming hot water in a large marble tub. I luxuriate and think: I could get used to this. They do not have such baths at Versailles, and certainly not at Madame Lesdig's. I decide I will come here once a month—no, once a week—and have a bath that lasts at least three hours. But even with the stoves ringed around the tub the water finally starts to cool and I must get out, for my husband is waiting. Below I can hear the sounds of the wedding party continuing in a great carouse of song and music. Somewhere a glass shatters and a woman laughs. I climb out reluctantly, sleepy from the hot water and the champagne and too much sugar pie. But it is time to go: the life of a duchess must be paid for.

As I enter the bedchamber Lauraguais quickly releases a chambermaid. She grows as red as the walls and runs from the room without looking at me. I am relieved she does not scamper into a wall niche, for I do not want eyes on me at this time. Though I have to laugh at the thought.

"You shut up. Always laughing." Lauraguais pushes me down on the bed. It is unpleasant, very unpleasant even, but soon he snores from his drunkenness and I am alone, thinking: Now I am a duchess and soon I will live at Court. I am the last to marry and so the last of my sisters to know the reality of the marriage bed. I wonder what Marie-Anne and the king do together in their private apartments, and I wonder where Pauline is now. Is she watching me, perhaps laughing and raising one of her bushy eyebrows over her little green eye? She would be happy for me, I decide.

I fall sleep and dream of a pigeon pie, an enormous one, larger even than the table. Around it folk discuss and poke it and some attempt to eat it, but then the crust breaks and out of the middle flies a blackbird. It disappears into the black-painted walls and everyone claps.

ↂ

So now I am a duchess; therefore I am the envy of everyone who is not a duke or a duchess, which even at Versailles is still a great many people.

After the wedding I spend a few weeks with Lauraguais in his family's apartment at Versailles. He is not always drunk and I discover he is even rather funny, and quite nice. We compare eyebrows: they are of exactly the same size and that makes us laugh. I am a woman and could replace mine with elegant ones of gray mouse hair, but he is stuck with his.

We are lying on the bed drinking cinnamon-flavored coffee, the latest breakfast drink.

"God, but I love your breasts," he says, smothering himself in them then coming to rest against one. "A woman's breasts—two, or one if big enough—are simply the best pillows. Far superior to anything those Turks can make, finer even than goose down. I must see about having a serving girl just for that purpose. One with large breasts, purely for my relaxation. I will call it"—he takes a puff on his pipe for inspiration—"a chest coddle."

"Your family has strange ideas about servants," I say, watching the smoke from his pipe curl up under the canopy of the bed. The smell is strange, an animal roasted too long on the fire. "The priests say we must remember their humanity."

Lauraguais puffs languidly. "And this, from the woman whose grandfather knocked out the teeth of all his maids, to render them unattractive and remove his temptation."

"But those were different times!"

He takes another deep puff. "Ah . . . I wonder what that would be like?"

"Oh, very painful, I'm sure! Once I had a tooth that ached so I—"

"No," he interrupts me, "not the tooth removal, but a tooth-less suck. Now, that is something I wish to experience. What would that be like?"

"You only ever think of one thing, you're like a squirrel constantly searching for nuts."

"It's true, it's true." He doesn't deny and returns to his favorite subject. "So come on, DouDou," he wheedles.

"DouDou? Who is DouDou? Is that what you call your red-haired slut?"

"Which one?" He grins and shakes his head. "I cannot abide the name Diane. Never could. Had a nurse when I was younger called Diane. Such a stupid name. She was quite the witch."

"Then call me Adelaide. Not *DouDou*."

He pulls himself up on one side, balancing the pipe: "So tell me, DouDou. Is it true what they say, that the king can make love twice, with no rest?"

I laugh. "Who is 'they'?"

"You know, the people that know. I've heard it said that he can do it twice in a row, and even twice in a row with the same woman?" He looks at me expectantly.

"I wouldn't know. I have never slept with him. I have only ever slept with you."

He lies back down on the bed and drops his pipe on the floor. "Is it true?" he asks again, and now there is a strange look in his eyes, glazed as though he has been hit on the head. "That you and your sister have slept with him, together? At the same time?"

I shudder. I could not, would not. "No, no! I told you I have never slept with the king, with or without Marie-Anne."

"And Hortense? They say she is there too, but she does not participate, she just supervises. She's too much of a prude to join in, but she is naked. She puts her hair down and—"

I smother his mouth with my breasts. "Oh, shut up, shut up!"

Lauraguais wriggles free. "But you'd tell me if you did? You'd tell me everything? The details?"

"If I did what?"

"Slept with the king. With your sisters. Especially if it's with Hortense. They say she lets her hair down and she licks—"

"Oh, please, Lauraguais! Stop it! That will never happen."

❧

After the rather pleasant interlude with my husband, I return to Paris to visit Madame Lesdig. She tells me I am a married woman now and must conduct myself like one, and not like the feckless, giggling girl I still appear to be. I know beneath her disapproval she adores me, so to make her happy I promise her I will no longer be like a chattering squirrel, but instead will be as proud and as stately as a lioness.

I then visit Louise. She is now in her own house, a small one the king provided for her on a funny, narrow street near the Louvre; Madame Lesdig's predecessor—another Dowager Duchesse de Lesdiguières—used to live here. The rooms are unfurnished and so bare she could be in a convent. She doesn't even have a carpet on the flagstoned floor, just little cut-up squares in front of the chairs to rest her feet on. One says *Welcome*, stitched in pink and blue, but there is nothing welcoming about this room.

"You look well," says Louise, but she does not look well at all. Her skin is more gray than white and she is already like an old woman, though she is only four years older than I. She always used to take such care of her appearance but now she is dressed entirely in black with no rouge, nor even a beauty patch.

I laugh nervously: "You look like a nun, Louise."

"That is a compliment," she says softly, picking at a simple wood rosary in her lap. "I am thinking of taking orders."

"Oh, don't do that!"

She raises her eyes to the ceilings. "Whether I do, or don't, is immaterial—I have devoted the rest of my life to God. To expiate my sins."

For once, I don't know what to say. There is a deep dark hurt oozing off her, filling up the room. "Would you like news of Court?" I ask brightly before I realize that any news of Court must include news of Marie-Anne. And the king. "Of the queen, then?"

"How is Her Majesty?"

"Oh, very well, Marie-Anne tells me . . . I mean, Marie-Anne is now in her service, well, of course you knew that, you gave her your place, well, not to her but to Hortense . . . Marie-Anne says she is well . . . and . . ."

I trail off helplessly. All roads lead to Marie-Anne. Actually, Marie-Anne has no good words to say of the queen. She is a very good mimic and does a very funny impression of the queen's Polish accent: *Goot, goot, goot.* Marie-Anne says the queen deserves to be mocked for not losing her terrible accent after almost twenty years in France.

Louise's eyes flicker with pain when I say Marie-Anne's name. There is silence and I struggle to think of something else to say.

"Do you like it here? These rooms are very . . . very . . . white. White! White is good, it's so calm and serene. My apartment at Versailles is so cluttered, my husband's family has more money than dukedoms and all they do buy is furniture and I keep knocking things over just like I did when I lived with Madame Lesdig, so I . . . this is nice. Your room. Calm."

Finally she says: "It doesn't matter to me. This, that, all of it."

She makes another noncommittal gesture and looks up at the ceiling. It's as if she's not alive anymore, like her soul has gone from her body and left a shell where before she once lived. It's very painful. When I leave I promise to write to her often but I know I won't. What can I say to her? I have no comfort to offer.

Poor Louise. I don't understand why Marie-Anne had to banish her—why could Louise not have stayed with us? Wouldn't that have been kinder?

"Habits are a hard thing to break," hisses Marie-Anne when I broach the subject. "And Louise was a habit."

"But was she not a harmless habit?" Louise never hurt anyone.

"Nobody ever won by being kind," says Marie-Anne, and I

know by the way she says it that I should not ask anymore. But what is she trying to win? She has already won the king's heart, and I am sure he will make her a duchess very soon, and then she will have all she desires.

I am not happy about what Marie-Anne did to Louise, but I cannot say it out loud. There is something about Marie-Anne. Something . . . cruel. I remember when she was young, how she used to gather mice in a little box then starve them, to see how long they would take to die. I think I am a little afraid of Marie-Anne. Just a little.

Despite my fears, Marie-Anne and I are becoming closer and we spend much time together. I do have an awful lot of fun in her company. She is Marie-Anne—she can do anything. With her, I feel I am at the center of Versailles, which means I am at the center of the world, which is a very satisfying feeling. I like the king too; he has a good sense of humor and likes my jokes. I know Marie-Anne doesn't really like them as much, but she tolerates me; she says I should go and live on the rue des Mauvaises-Paroles in Paris—the Street of the Bad Words. I don't think I should like that; it's rather too near a fish market.

The Marquis de Thibouville, an aspiring playwright and a confirmed dandy, has adapted *Cupid and Psyche* into a short pastoral play, and we are all to star in it. Well, Marie-Anne and the king are to star in it, but there are several other parts for the rest of us. Marie-Anne originally wanted to do something by Molière or Racine, but decided amateurs, even royal amateurs, might lessen the majesty of those fine works. I have been given the role of Marie, a young maid.

"Marie—that doesn't sound very Roman? Are you sure that's a Roman name?"

"We'll rename you Claudia, then," says Marie-Anne in irritation. I throw myself into the role: this is better than our games in the nursery! I leap around and offer my services to anyone that asks, or doesn't. I swat away a mosquito from the Duc d'Ayen's wig; take drinks from the footmen and serve them myself; hold

Meuse's snuffbox; fix Madame de Chevreuse's hair ribbons, and all in all enjoy service immensely. I can't wait for my costume to be ready—I shall have an apron!

It is a Saturday and we are just eight, practicing; we hope to present the play next week, to a small audience of our friends. Outside the doors of the private apartments the grumblings and whining multiply, for eight is a small number and the king has been more absent than usual these last few weeks, locked away with the rehearsals.

The king seems to enjoy being a Roman god and forbids any of the players to address him as king, and no one is to wear powder or swords. It is all very informal and jolly.

I curtsy to the king. "Sire, Maid Diane at your service. May I straighten your cravat?"

"I'm a god now, Diane, not a king. And I'm not even sure the Romans wore neckpieces. But thank you for your offer."

"O god, may I straighten your cravat?"

The king chuckles. "That sounds faintly sacrilegious. But why not, my good maid?"

I'm busy straightening it when out of the corner of my eye I see the Duchesse d'Antin has dropped her fan. I leap off to assist her, then rush to open the door for Meuse as he leaves, pushing one of the real footmen out of the way in my zeal. The king finds it all very amusing but Marie-Anne only tolerates it.

"Diane, if you don't stop being so stupid, next time you're not going to have a part at all. I'll put you in charge of opening the curtain." Marie-Anne looks lovely, dressed in a white shimmery dress that might not be a dress at all, but just several light chemises.

I bow to her in delight. "Like a footman! I shall open that curtain and I shall assist the guests and I shall foot the—"

The king laughs and Marie-Anne offers a fake sigh and sits on his lap, to finish straightening his cravat. There is none among our little group who is stunned by this impropriety; we can pretend for a day that we are not even at Versailles at all, but in some other fine world where everything is allowed and disproval is banned.

❦

For a while I think Lauraguais and I have accomplished something, but then one night I have awful stomach pains. I assume it was the wormy oysters I ate the night before, but that wasn't it. Whatever was responsible, the little girl—for it was a little girl—was not destined to be my daughter and we must accept God's will. I write to Lauraguais to tell him the sad news and then suggest we try some more, because suddenly I do want a child. Awfully.

Lauraguais surprises me by arriving unannounced the next week. He kisses me and holds me close and tells me not to be sad, that we will succeed, for his seed is as strong as mustard and any babe should be happy to grow inside my delicious warm cradle. I giggle and hiccup through my tears and hug him back. He suggests we start right now, and though it is only just gone noon, I shoo the servants out and lock the door.

Marie-Anne

Fleury's death in January—finally!—marked a turning point for Louis. He now has a new motto, taken from his great-grandfather Louis XIV: "Listen to the people, seek advice from your council, but decide alone."

I had hoped that with the flea'd old man gone, Richelieu would be paramount in the king's counsel, but Louis refuses to nominate another prime minister. Richelieu had to be content to be named one of the four gentlemen of the bedchamber; a fine honor, to be sure, but not quite what he was hoping for. Irritatingly, Maurepas's influence grows daily. He is the only blot on my existence, the only flat note to mar the perfect tune of my life.

Everything else is quite splendid. I am the envy of every woman at Versailles. Even the Pious Pack and their ilk must secretly be jealous of me, for how can they not be? And why wouldn't they be?

Think of all that I have:

I have tradesmen and merchants falling over themselves to supply me with the latest in finery and fashion. They don't even demand payment! I have the money to pay them, of course, but there is a delicious sense of power in not doing so, in knowing that the grace of your business is enough for them. My father used to think like that—or still does—but he was only an overblown marquis, whereas no one doubts that I am now the most important woman in the land.

I have ambassadors and ministers and bishops coming to pay me homage and remind me of our family connections. They bow and scrape before me.

I have the literary and artistic world at my fingertips. I have to confess I don't read much anymore, but I do like the idea of extending my patronage into the arts. Not only can I order the latest works of Voltaire, but I can invite Voltaire to the palace to read for me! Actually I can't do that, as he is in Prussia at the moment. However, Rameau has asked permission to dedicate his next opera to me, and I have granted it—I did enjoy his *Dardanus*.

Louis has a fine aesthetic sense, and the arts are an interest we share. He is a very intelligent man, though it took me some time to find this out; his lively mind was well hidden beneath the trappings of kingship and the enforced idleness of his cosseted life. He enjoyed our little play last month—during rehearsals, he was able to shed the final vestiges of royal restraint, and I know that made him very, very happy.

I wonder if I should ask Voltaire or Lesage to write something especially for us, for our next performance? Perhaps it could be an allegory, something with a suitably famous Greek goddess at the centerpiece? The story of Hera, perhaps?

Music, poetry, fine books, stimulating conversation . . . how different my life is from what it was in Burgundy. It is a charming, charmed existence. This, I sometimes think in satisfaction, is the role I was born to play. I am an excellent mistress—Louis tells me I am the perfect woman, and I in turn find him a very satisfactory man: gentle, polite, eager to please in many ways. He is very easy to love, and love him I do. Agénois—I thought I was in love with him but I was merely confusing seduction with love, weighing gallantries against boredom.

The only blot, apart from Maurepas, is that I am not yet a duchess. Before such a momentous happening can occur, there are many legal and administrative steps. But soon . . . everything will be perfect.

∽

It's morning, very early. I wash myself and Leone comes in with my damask wrap. It's May but the chill of the winter still lingers, trapped in the corners of the palace behind the statues and the plants.

I take a deep breath and settle at my dressing table. The private part of my day is over, the public part about to begin. The stage is set: the chairs and settees dusted; the windows cleared; fresh heaps of heliotropes flowering over in their vases; a pot of chocolate warming over the stove; pastries and a splendid fresh-cut pineapple on the sideboard. And I, at the center.

All is quiet in the theater but soon the curtain will rise and I will be onstage. I am not nervous; the days of shaking nerves and clenched white hands are over. Outside, the birds are chirping and in the corridor I can hear the soft murmurings of the courtiers as they wait for my doors to open. Chirping as well.

"A large crowd today," I say to no one in particular. I am well pleased; lately my toilette has become even more crowded than the queen's, a subtle shift in power and one that apparently has upset Her Majesty. The thought makes me smile, both inside and out.

My valet announces the hairdresser and the Spanish ambassador, as well as a host of lesser courtiers who range themselves around the room and around me. I will speak to all of them in turn, dispense a kind word, or a not so kind word, and receive their requests and supplications with grace. Perhaps I will eventually tire of it; I know Louis hates to be asked for anything, but I still enjoy it. Influence, the giddy face of power and patronage.

"Might I present this letter to you, madame, and trust it will find its way to the king?" the Prince of Campo Florida inquires anxiously.

"And today, madame, what will you have?" my hairdresser inquires at the same time.

"Madame?" The Spanish ambassador stands, holding the letter, awaiting my decision.

"Madame?" The hairdresser stands, his tongs poised, awaiting my decision.

The room falls silent. My choice of dress will influence the other ladies; no one wants to compete with me. No one *dares* to compete with me.

"I shall wear the pink and silver gown tonight, for the concert, and the cream bargello for the day. So, Dages, for the hair something simple. With plenty of these . . ." I motion to a box of silk butterflies in varying shades of pink and brown. "Butterflies, for spring."

To the Spanish ambassador I say: "We shall see what can be done." I take the letter then pass it to Leone. In truth, I don't really care about the minutiae of government and things like taxes and trade; that is the ministers' job. I'm not like Pauline, who many say wanted to rule France; no, I will leave that boring job to the men. Why would I want to spend hours meeting with ministers when I could be meeting with a cherished author? Reading briefs when I could be dancing a minuet? Choosing appointments when I could be choosing shoes?

Diane rolls in, looking sleepy and a little untidy despite her sumptuous gown of green patterned roses. She flings herself on the couch. We are informal here in my rooms; normally a lounging duchess would require a discreet rearrangement but no one rises for Diane and she doesn't care.

"Long night?" I inquire. Dages starts to brush out my hair. The smell of cloying violets wafts over me and in the corner I see Charolais has crept in—she is not looking well these days.

"Lauraguais is back in town," Diane says with a grin. She is glowing and has an odd expression on her face.

"You look well." Diane accepts the compliment with a lazy smile. She is really the most unaware person I have ever met, but she does have her charms. She motions for someone to bring her the tray of pineapple. She takes a slice and dips it in her chocolate and sucks greedily.

"Careful, you'll get fatter." I have a sharp eye and have spotted two panels of a slightly darker green where her jacket has been let out.

Diane giggles. "I don't care. My husband likes women with curves."

I curl my lips. "Your husband likes women who *breathe*."

"Even that is in question," she says with a laugh, and is about to burble forth but I hold up my hand to stop the river. Goodness, but I don't want to know. I had hoped those rumors were baseless. He may be a duke but the man is a degenerate and completely disgusting. Unfortunately he must stay; a wife shares the punishment of her husband and I need my Diane here at Court.

The business of the morning continues.

The Marquis de Vaucouleur bows before me and updates me on the new appointments in the Swiss Guard. I listen with feigned interest. I then ask him about the grippe and fever that is spreading in Paris, and he replies with what he knows.

The Comtesse de Châtelet speaks to me of her recently married daughter, and how suitable she would be for the new household of the dauphine. A date has been tentatively set for the wedding and arrival, just under two years hence. The fight for positions in the new dauphine's household has already started, and will only get more vicious with time. I have decided I shall be the *surintendante* of the new household—and Diane shall be the *dame d'atour*. The *comtesse* is Richelieu's sister; he told me to expect her visit. She is comfortably ugly, with a thin mouth and too many freckles—did her parents not mind her when she was young? If her daughter looks anything like her, I would be happy to welcome her to Versailles.

The Duchesse d'Antin swirls in, a vision in mint and pink.

"Just a peck, my dear, just a peck, I promised Rochefoucauld I'd see him before Mass." She kisses me lightly and takes a piece of pineapple. "Heaven!" she exclaims as she twirls out the door.

A tradesman from Paris presents a design for a clock I have ordered for Louis. The king loves clocks, an interest that neatly couples with his morbid side: time always marches on—to death. I like the design, but I don't want to be too generous. "Something more intricate over here." I run my hands across the top of the sketch. "It's too plain. More . . . more of everything."

"Yes, madame."

More of everything.

Diane dangles a pastry before my little greyhound, a gift from the Comte de Matignon. The delicate dog barks in delight.

"She's adorable, Marie-Anne, simply adorable. Even more than a cat! I want one. What do you call her?"

"Marie-Audrée."

Diane giggles nervously. "You didn't name her after the Marquise de Pracomtal, did you?"

"Hush," I reply with an impish smile. Perhaps I did—but then some women need to learn they can't order the same citrine slippers, with the fashionable upturned toe, and expect to be forgiven.

Richelieu sweeps in, resplendent in a snow-white coat brocaded with ruby silk. The Spanish ambassador takes his leave and the two cross paths, bowing profusely. Dages finishes combing out my hair with his hot tongs, to silken the skeins. Now he takes tiny strands and curls them, pinning them to my head and affixing each one with a silk butterfly. I shake my head and the butterflies tremble in an imagined wind. Perfect.

Finally the petitioners and the unimportant file out and I am left alone with Richelieu. He is my most important ally and has all the news: he has spies everywhere. It's been a few days since I've seen him and I am sure he will have plenty to tell.

"What news, my dear friend?"

Richelieu sits and sucks on a piece of pineapple. "Mmm, delicious, delicious. I heard this one came straight from Martinique—exquisite." He wipes his mouth delicately with a red handkerchief that matches the brocade on his coat, and smiles at me. "The Marquis de Thibouville . . . Found last night in a Paris gambling house with a footman of Noailles."

Interesting. I never would have thought . . . The marquis always had some flamboyancy in dress and action, especially when directing our play, but everyone here at Versailles is flamboyant.

The drabness of the previous reign has been permanently erased in a shower of pastel fluffery.

"Where is he now?"

"Being held at his Paris home."

Richelieu looks at me intently. I rack my brains, trying to think of what I know of Thibouville and his family connections. I come up short. I really should have paid more attention to those schoolroom genealogy lessons. Who knew that Tante and Hortense would prove to be right?

"What do you propose we do?" I ask, carefully smoothing white cream over my face. It smells faintly of eggs and apricots.

Richelieu sucks another piece of pineapple. "Nothing, for now. We will keep the knowledge for later, when it may be of use. Of course, if it happens again, the king must be informed and it will be the Bastille for him."

I nod. I have a lot to learn from Richelieu; he has taught me well the importance of information. Nothing, nothing, not even the pearl choker Louis gave me last year, is as valuable as information. Richelieu has not been appointed prime minister: Louis is adamant he will rule alone. Rather surprising, but I suppose it is a good sign and at least Richelieu's position as a first gentlemen of the bedchamber ensures both of Louis's ears are in his hands. Between the two of us, the king is never alone. Never.

"What else?"

Richelieu waves his hands. "More songs, of course."

"Let me hear them."

He takes a crumpled pamphlet from his coat pocket. "This one is making the rounds from the Bastille to Saint-Denis. Marville is having a devil of a time finding the source. But we'll get there." Marville is the lieutenant general of the Paris police. I suspect the verses come from Maurepas, but proof is impossible to come by. He reads:

> *"One is almost forgotten,*
> *Another almost dust,*

The third is on her way,
While the fourth is waiting
To make way for the fifth.
Loving an entire family—is that faithlessness or fidelity?"

I take the pamphlet and study the verse. One is forgotten. Yes—everyone has accepted that Louise is over. Pauline is certainly dust, thank goodness. And Diane, well, she could be said to be on her way, though I am not sure where she is going. But . . . the fourth is waiting to make way for the fifth?

Hortense is the fourth sister, and I am the fifth.

"This makes no sense, none at all." I frown. "This implies that Hortense is waiting to make way for me? But she is not with the king. I am! It makes no sense." My voice pitches a trifle higher and the butterflies in my hair flutter in sympathy.

"I've rarely seen you so disturbed, Marie-Anne. Even that lewd piece from last week didn't raise your ire so."

I try to smile but I can feel myself shaking. I stare at myself in the mirror and will my fingers not to tremble as I circle rouge onto my cheek. Richelieu watches me with amusement. I'm used to his condescension—only he can get away with it.

Hortense is my weakness. I don't care about the little sluts that Louis sometimes feels the need to visit; I don't care about that beautiful child Mathilde de Canisy, now married to the Comte de Forcalquier, with her youth and extraordinary cupid mouth; I don't even care about that bourgeois charmer from Paris that everyone is talking about. Well, I do care about her, but not as much as I care about Hortense.

I follow Hortense's Mass attendance: once, of course, is the minimum and a must—God must be placated—but twice a day or more indicates true piety. Normally Hortense goes twice a day, but lately there have been days when she attends only once. As long as she keeps her piety, I am safe. If not . . . if not . . . I have an inspiration: Hortense needs to get pregnant again. Fast.

"Why don't we recall her husband, Flavacourt, from the front?

Find him a ministry or secretariat or something? Away he is useless to us. Hortense needs him here. As do we."

"That might be difficult. We are almost at war, as you know."

"Mmm." War—games for men and boys. What is it good for? I pat my hair and admire the flesh-colored butterflies. They will go well with my pink gown for the evening. I should have had a few made in silver, I think with light regret.

"Pretty," I say to Dages and dismiss him. He bows and sidles out with his tools.

"And one more, Marie-Anne," says Richelieu, eating the last of the pineapple.

They never stop, this tidal wave of songs and verses and sonnets, watering the buds of every scandal like April showers. Where do they come from? Some say—many say—they start at Court and come from Maurepas, Charolais, Marville, anyone. Anyone could be my enemy. Perhaps everyone is my enemy. Richelieu reads once more:

> *"Madame is exiled, all in tears*
> *Goodness, but sisters are a thing to fear!*
> *Once one was all beloved*
> *But now something new*
> *Looks like a coup*
> *From one so beautiful*
> *Goodness, but sisters are a thing to fear!"*

Goodness, but sisters are a thing to fear. I laugh drily. It's funny, and it's true.

Richelieu bows out and Leone comes in with my cream gown. I read the verse again. *Goodness, but sisters are a thing to fear.* As I dress, a memory comes to me of Louise's wedding day; she was so young then—we all were. The five of us together in the nursery. She in her wedding dress of silver, the rest of us in our matching everyday dresses of yellow muslin. We hugged forever and we swore we would never let each other go. And now look at us.

Pauline dead, Louise banished, Hortense and I barely speaking. At least Diane I can trust.

I think.

Where did it all go wrong? Or is that even the right question? In the weeks after I banished Louise, she would sometimes intrude on my thoughts, unbidden, and leave me with a queer sinking feeling, but then I would see the king, and all my qualms would disappear. It was the right thing to do, and now as the months pass, I think of her less and less. And never with regret.

Once dressed, I sit by the window, cradling Marie-Audrée and losing myself in her soft fur. I need a few moments to prepare for the coming day. Well, I will need more than a few moments: I will need stamina, courage, wit, and duplicity. And many other things.

I stand up reluctantly. It is time. First to Mass, then to greet the king. The butterflies are deliberate. *Butterfly* is his pet word for my pussy and now I wear them in my hair, subtly swinging every time I turn my head, to remind him all the day of what is coming in the night.

Perfect.

Goodness, but *I* am a thing to fear.

Louise

I live in a humble house now, far away from the glitter of Versailles or the proud mansions of the nobility across the river. He provided it for me; I knew he never would forsake me entirely. I live simply and in no real comfort; I keep no carriage and rarely entertain those I used to know in my previous life. Jacobs, my dear, faithful Jacobs, stays with me and I know I am lucky to have such a friend.

For the first time in my life, I know what I am and I know what I am not. I am nothing special. Because I was born to a family of nobility and prestige, I thought—nay, I *knew*—that I was better than other people. How wrong I was!

I never knew how the poor lived. Our servants were invisible. They were not deserving of our pity or our compassion; they worked for us and it was thanks to our grace that they survived. We were taught that anyone who was not noble was not fully human, and that their lot was not our concern. Charities had to be done, of course, but only by rote obligation and we were free as flies to ignore the suffering around us.

Apart from our servants I do not ever think I met a poor person. Even as children, when we ventured out from our nursery to walk along the Seine or enjoy the gardens at the Tuileries, Zélie and our attendants formed a shield around us to protect us from the beggars and the ragged ones. I remember once I saw a small child lying by the side of the road, almost naked. It was cold outside but she had no shoes or cloak. I asked Zélie why the child lay like that and why she did not go warm herself by a fire. Zélie told me that the poor have thicker skins than we do and so do not feel the pain, and that the little girl lay like that because she was lazy.

Lies, all lies. We are all the same, our skin and our feet and our hands. Pain is universal; it does not lower itself for titles or wealth.

I live as plainly as I can. I have a few visitors but truly I am not interested in the news they have to tell. Their lives are so small and so petty. Artificial. Clothes, food, entertainment, who said what to whom, what it meant, who won at cards, who the king smiled at. I think with repulsion now of that life. I feel only disgust when I meet a courtier wearing a coat that could feed a family for a year, or a lady with fresh roses in her hair, a single one of which would buy a meal for ten. How can they be so blind?

How could I have been so blind?

I sinned with Louis, but that sin—adultery—was not the real sin. No, the real sin was the ignorance that I lived in, my oblivion to the suffering of my fellow man. And so I dedicate the rest of my life to the poor, to making their lives on this earth a little better, a little kinder, a little softer. I will not retire to a convent; I believe I can do more good out here than cloistered behind thick walls.

Jacobs comes in with my cape, the same brown one I used to wear when I prepared to sin with the king. Now I wear it not as a nostalgic memento, but as a reminder of my guilty days. I also contemplate wearing a hair shirt, for I have a growing need to remind myself in more physical ways of how wrong my old life was and how great my penance must be.

"Rain this afternoon, madame," she says as she ties the cape around me. "And Marie tells me the butcher brought the kidneys he promised, she'll be sure to make a nice pie with them."

"Did he also send the bones?" I ask anxiously.

"Of course, madame. And he added a few pounds of fat, for he is a good man. Marie will be sending it all to the hospital at Saint-Michel."

"Good, good."

We walk out slowly on the streets, the hint of rain following us as we make our way to the church. I come here to Saint-Eustache every morning, and most nights too. I slip into my favorite pew, the worn wooded oak like a familiar cushion beneath me. I am home, and at peace.

I pray for Louis, even though we are no longer together. I don't pray that he will take me back as his mistress, but I pray that one day he will see the errors of his ways and repent and return to his queen as a good Christian man and live in virtue, not in sin. Though I pray for him, I can also see, finally, truthfully, his faults: he is a weak man, and a selfish one.

And I pray for my sisters. I hear rumors, dreadful rumors. I shudder and am filled with a deep, aching shame that I could once have done as they do now. I could repent a lifetime, but that would not be enough for God.

And I pray especially for Marie-Anne. She will be punished in the afterlife, of that I am certain, but it would also be very gratifying were she to be punished in this life. Very gratifying. I pray that it happens thus, and then pray that I might be forgiven my vengeful thoughts.

As I rise to leave a man in the pew next to mine turns and looks at me. Our eyes meet and I see he knows me, as so many know me. I don't know how: Did they circulate portraits along with those scurrilous songs?

"Whore," he snarls, with true venom in his voice. His words shake me, but then they spread out to balm my soul.

"You say it as you see it, monsieur," I say calmly. "You are an honest man, and I thank you for that." I hold his gaze a few moments longer, and soon he drops his head in shame. "Thank you," I whisper again.

Jacobs and I walk home in silence, and on the way it starts to rain, the drops falling heavy on my thick woolen cloak.

From Louise de Mailly
Rue Saint-Thomas-du-Louvre, Paris
September 30, 1743

Dearest Diane,

I trust you are well and settling into the life of a married woman. Heed your husband, but remain true to yourself. My husband was a dreadful man, and though I pretended otherwise, there is no need to lie: even a lie of politeness is a sin in the eyes of God.

I beg you to distance yourself from Marie-Anne. For your own sake, and here I speak humbly and truly: Marie-Anne is not a nice woman, and she is cold and calculating and she will not hesitate to slay or discard people as it pleases her. She is guided by no higher power and restrained by no moral compass.

Please, Diane, write to me and say that you have renounced Marie-Anne, as I am pleased to say Hortense has done. It is for your protection.

Thank you for the lovely Persian carpet you sent. It is very fine indeed and has made my small house here a little warmer and cozier. But please! Do not spread rumors that I live like this because of penury; it is my choice to live simply and as far removed from my old ways as I can.

I have friends and I am happy. I devote my time to good works and I pray if you would make me further gifts, please instead donate to the poor children at the Hôpital Saint-Michel. They have so little, and we have so much.

Love,
Louise

Marie-Anne

I heard that Louise washed the feet of the poor last week in Paris. A group of ladies went to watch; I should have liked to have seen it for myself but thought it best to remain at Versailles.

"It was disgusting, my dear, simply disgusting. A more scabrous lot of peasants could not be imagined."

"It was as though the Church rounded up the worst of the Paris trash, just for her."

"And she smiled through it all, and even seemed to enjoy herself! Oh, the horror."

"She wears a hair shirt now—and she with her skin so soft from all that olive oil! And no rouge. I repeat—*no rouge.*"

So Louise has become pious. She even writes to Diane and lectures her on our wanton life, but really, who is she to judge? Only our betters may judge us, and Louise is certainly not my better. Especially now, for I, Marie-Anne de Mailly-Nesle, the Dowager Marquise de Tournelle and the official favorite of the king, have become a duchess. Louis has bestowed upon me the duchy and peerage of Châteauroux. The duchy is a very suitable one, with more than eighty thousand *livres* in annual rent. I can safely say I shan't ever be poor or at anyone's mercy. Ever again.

Diane led my presentation, and amongst my entourage were several other duchesses, including little Félicité, Agénois's wife. Strange, don't you think? Hortense was also there, brooding dis-

approval and clucking at me under her breath. I'm not as afraid of
Hortense as before; her attendance at Mass is solidly twice a day
now, and occasionally even three times.

When I was presented to the queen, I spared her a brief smile.
What a time she has had with the Nesle women! I've heard she
has even asked her doctors to investigate our blood and compare
the shape of our heads, that she may understand what it is about
our family that so attracts the king. I have instructed Richelieu to
let me know if there is any result of her inquiry.

The king continues devoted and enthralled. Still, one can
never be complacent and I must always plan ahead. When I am
old and the king no longer loves me—I am brutally honest and
know this will happen—I hope we will remain friends. Sometimes I wish Louis were an older man, that time might have
quelled some of his ardor. They say Louis XIV, after a philan-
dering youth, was faithful in his later years to Madame de Maintenon. And he even married her. My Louis is still so young, in the
prime of his life really, and it is no more than wishful thinking to
imagine he might settle down with me. And of course the queen
lives on, as sturdy as a cow. I read somewhere that Poles have un-
usually long lives, due to the cabbage they constantly eat. The
queen certainly enjoys that dish.

I realize that my sister Louise benefited from Louis's natural
piety. When he was younger, the king had a true fear of God, but
now his faith is fading fast, and he no longer mopes at Easter because he can't take Communion. There were no religious doubts
in his pursuit of me. He wasn't even worried about bedding *another* sister—any fears of incest and eternal damnation have long
since disappeared beneath the waves of his pleasure and desires.

I suspect he has the makings of a true libertine, and I know
that one day a younger, prettier Marie-Anne will come along, and
she will not rest until I am banished from Court. Just as I banished Louise. If—when—that happens I will not go lightly into the
night, donning a hair shirt and praying for forgiveness for my sins.
No, when my day here is good and done, I shall go wherever I will

and do whatever I want. I shall go to Venice and Canada and the hot islands of the Caribbean and see all that the world has to offer. Maybe even China and India. But all that is for the future. Here and now, there are other things to do and other things to worry about.

There is a woman who lives in the forest at Sénart, close to Choisy; of very low birth and with the unfortunate name of Poissons—Fish—though she is now married to a certain Comte d'Étioles. Many call her Madame *d'Étoiles*, because they say she is a star just like her name. I call her the Fish Woman, but I have heard she is not at all like a fish: apparently she is extraordinarily beautiful. When the king hunts in Sénart she rides out, hoping to meet him. She presents a very pretty picture in her little pastel carriage, scarcely bigger than a pumpkin. She drives it herself and matches her clothes to the blue and apricot ribbons wound in her horses' braids.

Now I must ride out with Louis whenever he goes hunting there. I can think of better ways to spend my time, but unfortunately, I must attend. There are too many at Court joking that the little star from the forest will be the next piece of game that the king catches.

We've seen her twice just this summer, always so pretty and charming, and somehow utterly feminine, though she wields the reins of the carriage herself. I would like her banished far from Sénart, but her husband is so insignificant it's difficult to even trump up a scandal around him. Richelieu assures me I am safe; there has never been a bourgeois mistress and there never will be, but he doesn't allay my fears when he waxes long and lyrical about her elegance, her large gray eyes, and her pretty hands.

"You sound like you are half in love with her," I say crossly.

"She is so divine, only the Marquis de Thibouville would not be half in love with her," Richelieu assures me with a wicked smile.

But that is no assurance at all.

I fear these days the king is getting bored. Just a touch, perhaps a slim slackening of interest. A fraction of a second too long to smile and approach when I motion him toward my delights; a kiss that is occasionally more duty than pleasure; the pendulum veering just slightly—oh, ever so slightly—from the passionate to the perfunctory. Nothing overt but my senses are so primed to his that even the smallest change becomes my biggest worry.

Louis is getting bored, and he has an abhorrence of boredom. Naturally: when you have everything, to be bored means you have nothing. We have been together now almost a year, and in that time I am sure I have exposed him to more pleasures of the flesh than he ever experienced with sweet Louise or vulgar Pauline. But still. Every man craves the same thing, but not the same thing.

I can learn from Pauline, but I can also do better than her.

❧

We are at Choisy enjoying the last rays of autumn before winter, a week of fresh blackberries and midnight boat rides on the river fringed with lanterns, bundled snug inside pelts of sable against the fresh wind, surrounded by lanterns that bob like fireflies. It is late and only Diane and I remain with the king in the salon; the rest have long departed but we are here. The king is jolly with drink and Diane more so. Only I am sober, though by my manner you might think me well oiled.

I like Diane, even love her: I could not wish for more in a companion and I am confident of her everlasting loyalty. And she is not very attractive. Alone, the king would never be interested. But I am not proposing she be alone.

I slide over to the sofa where Diane is seated and put my arm around her and kiss her on the cheek. She giggles. I smile at the king. Louis raises his eyebrows, ever so slightly, to imply either a question or disapproval. I in turn raise my eyebrows even more slightly: another question, or perhaps an invitation. I cannot be seen to suggest this, I can only abet once he realizes his desire. I pick out a few pins from Diane's hair and fluff away some powder. She shakes her head and more hair falls down.

"What are you doing, Marie-Anne?" she asks. "Do you want me to look like a horse or a common woman?" She pulls one of her long tendrils and picks a blob of congealed powder out of it, flicks it away, then becomes preoccupied with a wine stain on her skirt.

"The king wants to see your hair." Louis has not asked to see her hair—why would he?—but he doesn't object, and is now starting to watch us with a queer, expectant look in his eye, his mouth frozen in a half smile, like a dog awaiting a bone.

"I'm not sure the king should see me like this," says Diane coquettishly, and giggles at the king.

I giggle too and pretend to take another sip of my champagne. "You've got lovely hair." I bury myself in it and find a month's worth of old powder and smoke assaulting me. Good Lord, is it true what they say, that she bathes only in Paris? Louis is a very fastidious man but a dog can never resist a bone, no matter how smelly or ugly it is.

And two bones? At the same time? Never.

"Lovely hair," agrees Louis as I come up for air. His voice is thick honey and seems to come from a place far, far away.

"She is lovely, just like me. After all, we are sisters." My voice holds an invitation Louis cannot misinterpret. He leans forward slightly as he does when he is aroused, pressing his cock inside his breeches. I lean over and kiss Diane's vast bosom and taste stale sweat behind a veneer of geranium oil. I really must talk to her, I think as she giggles, and the king gets up and comes toward us. She must bathe more. If not for me, then at least for him.

Diane

CHÂTEAU DE CHOISY

October 1743

Oh, Hail Mary, Hail Mary, Hail Mary, I have sinned. I go to early Mass then late Mass but there is no forgiveness there. I pace my bedroom and shout at the maids to leave me alone. I lie on the bed and cry and wait for God to strike me down. Then I realize He cannot strike me down if I am already lying down, so I stand up, but my knees are too weak and I end up on the floor, terrified.

I was a sinner before but only a small one. The wags say that morality is only for the vulgar bourgeoisie, and that what is a sin elsewhere is no more than a peccadillo at Versailles. *Peccadillo*, a funny word. I did not know what it meant until I came to Court. But last night, that was no peccadillo, even if it was with the king. That was a sin, a great God Almighty sin, and surely I will be struck down for it.

Between Masses I blurt out my fears to Marie-Anne.

"The only thing we have to fear is your notorious big mouth," she hisses. "Stop worrying. God cannot see into the King's Apartments, for are they not well guarded and very private?"

I do not think that is correct, but as usual I cannot think of a good reply. If a peccadillo is a small sin, what is a big sin? A grand peccadillo? It sounds like an animal. An awful big, sinning animal.

I lie inert on the floor, waiting for divine punishment, but then the clock strikes two and I remember I am to return to Versailles and dine with Angélique, my mother-in-law, this night. If I do not rise soon, I shall be late.

From Louise de Mailly
Rue Saint-Thomas-du-Louvre, Paris
January 6, 1744

Dear Hortense,

Greetings and New Year's blessings to you. May this year bring continued health and prosperity for you and your husband and two children. Thank you for your New Year's gift of the blue silk chemise, but I must confess I will not wear it. I have grown detached from the cares of my face and dress that occupied me for far too many years; I now no longer wear anything soft next to my skin. If you desire to honor me with a gift, please instead make a donation to a charity; the hospital at Saint-Michel, which cares for many abandoned infants, is a particular favorite of mine.

I pray for you all. I know, Hortense, you are very good already, but I still pray that you may stay on the righteous path you have chosen. I also pray for Marie-Anne and Diane, but I have no hope of their redemption. I still struggle to forgive Marie-Anne, but now I am grateful to her: she helped me distance myself from my old life and see the error of my ways.

I pray for His Majesty's soul, but I do not pray that he will ever see me again. That chapter of my life is closed, a book snapped shut that will never be reopened. No, I pray for him as I might pray for someone I once held dear, and when I think of how I gently prodded him from the pious life he once longed for—oh! Can twenty years of penance ever erase that sin?

Please let me know if your little Freddie or Addie will be coming from Picardy to Paris anytime this year; I should very much like to know them. Occasionally I visit Pauline's son, he is being educated with Noailles's son here, but I must confess it pains me to look upon him, so similar is he to his father. He adores sugar biscuits and I make sure to bring him a box whenever I visit.

My blessings,
Louise

From Hortense de Flavacourt
Château de Versailles
February 11, 1744

Darling Louise,

News of your increased piety has traveled through all circles here and I am overjoyed with the news. I apologize for my inappropriate New Year's gift. I made the donation to Saint-Michel as you recommended, but it was with some reluctance: it is well known that children from such dubious backgrounds only grow up to be lazy beggars and I am not sure they should be encouraged.

I shall not bore you or tire you with news from the Court, though I took the liberty of sharing your latest letter with Her Majesty. We have become fast friends; I know you will be happy, for the affection you had for her was real. The queen dedicated last Thursday, the feast of Saint Veridiana (one of her new favorites), to pray for your soul and your change in life. Unfortunately Marie-Anne was not in attendance that day—she avoids her duties with Her Majesty with a cunning I suppose I should not be surprised at.

She is as evil as ever. The king is bewitched, but I know, as does every God-fearing person of this Court, that even the strongest potion must eventually wear off. I pray the day comes soon, and anticipate with delight the convent she will be banished to. Diane is fatter than ever, and there are some dreadful, simply dreadful rumors and songs circulating about . . . No, I cannot write it, for fear I might faint over the desk.

Your sister in love and God,
Hortense

Marie-Anne

My woman, Leone, tells me of a famous fortune-teller in Paris who is quite astonishingly accurate and is all the rage amongst the fashionable. Apparently she even predicted the sudden death of the Comte de Monville, burned alive when his lace sleeves caught the edge of his bedroom candle; that is quite a recommendation. She is called simply Madame Sybille and has her house on the rue Perdue near Notre-Dame. It is more discreet to visit her than to have her brought to Versailles, so I don a veil and a fur cape against the cold and go forth to Paris to hear what my future holds.

It is the first time I have been to such a woman. They were very much the vogue some decades ago but are now looked upon with suspicion. I must keep the visit a secret; if the Court gossips and the Parisian scandalmongers find out, I am sure I will be accused of witchcraft and necromancy and trying to poison the queen, and a hundred other nefarious deeds.

Leone and I wait for her in the small front salon of her house, a room of plain painted walls and some dreadful old furniture. A dog examines us from the screenless hearth and a three-candle chandelier is the only light.

"Well," I remark to Leone, "she can't be that impressive—she obviously has made no money from her craft. Where would a footman stand in this dreadful room?"

Next to me Leone stiffens, then replies in her careful voice:

"Madame Sybille's husband was a master silversmith. She is by no means poor."

"Mmm." Still, the room is positively frightful. Imagine living like this!

Madame Sybille enters and she is surprisingly young, with an elaborate turban on her head and a loose gown of some cheap gold stuff. Not at all one's image of a wise woman: I had expected someone older and more cronelike. She motions me to sit at what must be their dining table, the grain black with age and one leg broken. She lights several candles that throw lopsided shadows around the darkening winter room, then places a large deck of cards on the table.

I make my selection. She turns over the cards and stares at them for several minutes. I shiver, and not only from the cold of the dreary room. Against my will my breath quickens and my heart starts to beat faster. A strange look comes over the woman's face.

"But what is it?" I demand.

"Nothing, madame," she replies slowly. "I just rarely see such good fortune all in one person." She looks up from the cards and smiles at me, too brightly. Her voice is husky with the strange lilt of the south.

"I see new adventure and action. Influence. I see . . ." She closes her eyes then fingers a card with what appears to be Demeter's grain basket crossed through with a sword. "I see illness vanquished and hopes fulfilled."

A little vague, but generally good. "My . . . lover?"

"A strong year for him. At a distance, calamity and casualty, but nothing will touch him . . . or you."

"And our love?"

"Strong like this tower here." She points to a tower of stone surrounded by high trees and I see her nails are darkened with black paint. "Enduring."

I scan the cards. I want to check there are no fish, or for that matter anything maritime. Or anything with stars. There is one with a shell, cradling what appears to be a baby. "What's this?"

"An oyster, madame. To signify the world is your oyster. You have great power."

Good. I want to ask about the queen, and her health, but one cannot speak such questions aloud. Even in disguise to a fortune-teller. Instead I ask: "And the future? Not just this year, but beyond?"

She waves her hand over the cards. "These tell me your fortune for this year, madame, but beyond that, I cannot see."

I narrow my eyes. "What is one year? I want to know the rest."

Madame Sybille bows her head, presenting her ridiculous turban to me, and refuses to say any more. She also refuses payment to loosen her tongue, and after some haggling I get up to leave in disgust. I find myself shaking—why would this woman not tell me my future? How could a woman foretell so accurately the death of the Comte de Monville, and in such shocking circumstances, yet be unable to see beyond December?

I tell Diane where I have been and she laughs, as I knew she would. She tells me not to worry. She says the witch woman was just being greedy. "She didn't tell you about next year because she wants you to come back again in 1745, and pay her again, and then come back in 1746, and pay her again, and then . . ."

Sometimes, just sometimes, Diane has some good sense.

∽

In the bleakness of April I am laid low for a few days. I coax Diane into the king's bed for a few nights. Alone. I lie in bed sick and the cursed doctor, some provincial recommended by Louis, insists I drink copious quantities of fish soup. It's actually quite good, fish and salt mixed with fennel and another spice I can't identify. I sip it and think of what Diane and the king might be doing, and what we will do together when I am well enough. And then of course I start thinking of that dreadful pretty bourgeois from the forest, the Fish Woman. I get nervous and call Leone to take the soup away.

They now say the Fish Woman received a prophecy when she was younger that a king would love her. I wonder if she heard it from Madame Sybille on the rue Perdue? The Fish Woman is so young, perhaps no more than twenty. And here I am, only a few years from thirty. They say it is a blessing for a beautiful woman to die young, for the pain of fading looks hits a beautiful woman so much harder than a plain one. But I'm not going to die anytime soon; there is too much to do.

We are now officially at war. France has been involved for years, mostly against the British, but now we are formally declared at war against the Austrians, as well as the Sardinians. Louis vacillated and vacillated but finally made the decision, alone. I was proud of him, I must admit; since Fleury's death he has become a king in more than just name, and I water his growing independence as much as I can.

And so—war is upon us. I know this was Pauline's dream; Pauline wished the king to go to war and probably would have liked to have ridden into battle herself! I think of my sister and of the enmity that lay between us, from the time when we were very young. I have definitely won and she has definitely lost, for she lies alone and still in her grave. Without one of her arms. But when I think such thoughts I feel a rare frisson of fear, for such thoughts are evil. No one knows the hour of our death and it was a dreadful thing that she died. Though convenient for me.

But I agree with her that it could be a wonderful opportunity if Louis were to go to the front and command the troops. Far away from the influence of Maurepas. Though he is a trifle weak and indecisive, I truly believe Louis has the makings of a great man. The last king identified with Apollo and was called the Sun King. I cannot quite decide what the right epithet for Louis should be, perhaps the Warrior King? Or Zeus, King of Kings? Zeus, Slayer of Austrians?

I paint Louis a picture of him riding into battle, rousing the troops and honoring them with his presence, erasing the memory of France's bitter defeat at Dettingen last year.

"A very large undertaking," he muses. "The provisions, the furniture and bedding, the utensils that must be transported. Cups. Quantities of powder. For the hair, I mean, not the cannons, though I suppose that must be transported too. If I go, too many will insist on accompanying me, and all must be provided with accommodation befitting their rank. Not an easy thing to manage. And it would be expensive. Very expensive."

"Nothing is impossible, dearest. Make it clear that only a very small group will travel with you. This is not to be a holiday in the country. You must go and live as the generals do. Noailles and such. They manage without large retinues."

He shakes his head and gestures to an embroidered fire screen, a gift from his youngest daughters, away at the abbey where they are being educated. The screen is stitched with four successively smaller brown-skirted stick figures, and it pleases Louis immensely. "Besides, soon I will bring my darlings home and I would be here when they return."

I wish the little princesses would stay at Fontevraud; he still has two daughters and the *dauphin* here at Versailles and spends far too much time with them as it is. And it goes without saying that they do not approve of me: I would prefer not to add another four recriminating little faces to the crowds.

Last month we attended an opera in Paris, and Louis surprised me by suggesting his eldest daughters, the two not yet married and not at the convent, should accompany us. It was a brave and perhaps foolish thing to do, for the whole world could talk of nothing else. I knew his intentions were good: he loves his daughters so very much, almost as much as he loves me, and I know it would please him greatly were we all to get along.

Needless to say weepy Henriette and the cold Adelaide were not friendly with me; Adelaide is only twelve but not too young to ooze disapproval from every pore of her little body. Henriette was at least polite, and after the final act she was as enraptured by the music as the king and I were. She could not contain her enthusiasm and burbled about the songs and the scenery through the long carriage ride home. But by the next week, she was once again as cold as her sister to me.

They need to be gone and married—if only Prince Charles

could get rid of those awful Protestant Germans and reclaim the British throne! He would make a very suitable husband for Henriette. I push Louis to put his full support behind the Stuart venture but he is not fully committed. The French navy did help with a failed invasion in February, but he now insists that Austria must be our first priority.

Still, it would be very suitable if Henriette could go to England. A few years ago she was madly in love with the young Duc de Chartres, a relation of the king, but Fleury decided against their match—it would make the Orléans family too powerful. The duke was married off last year and Henriette has not stopped weeping since. Yes, Henriette to England, and then Adelaide could go to Sardinia or someplace even dirtier, for I have a particular dislike for her. But with four more sisters still to come, it will be a decade at least before they are all gone.

I murmur my approval of his plan to bring his daughters home and cover his chest with butterfly kisses. We are in bed together, tucked inside the most private of all rooms, safe at the top of the palace, above his private apartments, above the state apartments, above the enormous halls of the reception rooms. Louis had this small room, entirely decorated in shades of green and gold, designed especially for us; surrounding our nest is a buffer of empty rooms, cocooning us from the rest of the palace.

Very faintly we hear the sounds of Versailles at dawn rise up from below as the great palace stirs itself for another day: the clattering of iron grates; a clash of chains as the chandeliers are lowered to be lit; troops on gravel in the courtyard outside. The fresh smell of orange wax as it is rubbed on the floors wafts dreamily up. Soon I will slip back to my apartment and Louis will descend to the state bedroom for the formal *levée*.

"You could be my Warrior King." It doesn't take long to convince Louis of anything.

"Well, it would be an adventure, certainly. And the marshals assure us of victory; our presence could only further guarantee it."

Our presence? Does he mean "our" as in us, or is it just the royal "our"? I hadn't thought of going with him, but I wonder if I should.

"But, Princess"—his special name for me—"won't you miss me? Why is it that you are pushing me to war, to leave Versailles and to leave you?"

I run my fingers down his thigh and he sighs in pleasure. Far away we hear one valet berating another, telling him to be careful with the steaming irons. "I would sacrifice my own pleasure for the sake of the nation."

"I would miss you, Princess. Perhaps too much." He shifts and I tighten my hand around him.

"I would miss you too," I say, and I mean it. I'd have to talk with Richelieu, but why not accompany him? It would be good to get away from Versailles, and see more of France. I've never been anywhere except Burgundy. I suggest the idea to him but Louis only laughs and shakes his head.

"No, Princess, no: the front is no place for women. Ladies, at least." I murmur my acquiescence and continue working my hand, to bring him to a place where he will deny me nothing.

☙

Richelieu likes the idea, both of them.

"Yes," he says, "let's get the king out to the front and away from Maurepas. And I don't see why you shouldn't go as well; Louis XIV went to war with both Madame de La Vallière and Madame de Montespan, at the same time, and it didn't hurt anyone then."

So it is decided, though Louis still has to agree. And perhaps Diane should come as well?

Diane

Why do you think peasants smell?" We are in the carriage, rocking along the road at a quick clip. I really, really hate traveling—my back hurts the minute I step into a carriage. And oh! The odors. Simply frightful.

"Because they are peasants," says Aglaë helpfully. "It's what they do, they smell."

We are four in the carriage, heading to Metz and to the king and war: myself, Marie-Anne, and our friends Aglaë and Elisabeth. Behind us is a second carriage with our women and clothes.

"It's true; if we didn't wash for a month we still wouldn't smell as ripe as they do," says Elisabeth. "Look at our grooms. They are poor but they don't smell. Yet peasants? It must be in their blood."

"But why don't they wash? Water is free, isn't it? When it rains they should just stand naked under the sky and wash that smell away."

"I think charities should give less food and more scent to the poor—a good dousing of rose oil would go a long way to solve their stink." We all nod in agreement.

Our friends are both older ladies with scandalous pasts. Aglaë in particular is good company; she is the daughter of the old regent and sister of the notorious Duchesse de Berry. She used to live in Modena and has entertained us with many funny stories about Italians and the dull horror of the court there. The heat inside the carriage is intolerable and we wear loose, old clothes for comfort and carry masks to keep our identities hidden. Overnight we stop at inns and eat the gruesome food. In my pie this morning I found the crest of a cock! It actually wasn't as disgusting as I thought it might be; it tasted rather like chicken.

During these stops we hear the local people talking, hear the rumors and gossip of the country. It is no secret that no one loves Marie-Anne or myself, or that they say scandalous things about us. Some of the things they say, of course, are true; I try not to think too much about that dreadful night at Choisy.

"I've heard he lets them ride him as one would a horse."

"That youngest one's a Protestant, mark my words: everyone knows the Tournelles are Huguenot sympathizers."

"Ten days of hail? Nothing like it in a century. Why, even my mother, all eighty-eight years of her, has never seen the like! But that's what happens when a whore rules the world."

"Apparently incest is all the rage at Versailles now; even the *dauphin* and his sisters are getting involved."

At an inn past Reims a table of drunken oafs next to us complains that *la pute*—the whore—is on her way to Metz and that will only create problems. Women at war cause excessive rain, as well as the drooping of a man's anatomy; neither is good for the fighting spirit. One adds that the Châteauroux harlot is a witch who has blinded the king, and that France will only prosper again when she is dead and gone.

Marie-Anne smiles her sour smile to show she has heard but doesn't care. She spends the rest of the day staring sightlessly out the window and chewing her nails. She is worried: Louis did not give her permission for this trip and she told the queen she needed time away to attend a personal matter. I don't like to see her like this: it is not her habit to regret a decision. As we near our destination I wrap the tips of her fingers in ribbons so she cannot further destroy her nails. Louis is very fastidious about such things and I know that Marie-Anne wants nothing to mar our arrival.

After five long days, we are in Metz. Almost in Austria, or at least the Austrian Netherlands—it's all very confusing. They say Austrians have enormous hands and feet and eat rotten fish; they have no choice as they have no coast. I hope we shan't meet any.

No one greets us on arrival and this puts Marie-Anne in a bad mood. She snaps at the chambermaid who comes to wash her and slaps me when I drop her striped petticoat, one she was saving for this reunion, on the floor. We are lodged at the abbey in the center of town; Aglaë and Elisabeth are garrisoned—I like that word, we are really at war!—in another room. Marie-Anne orders me to join them there before the king arrives, but I am still in her room when he bursts in. He holds Marie-Anne for a long while and she snuggles in his arms. Finally he holds her away from him.

"Too long! Too long! I shall not stand to be away from you for this length of time again."

"Fifty-eight days, sire," says Marie-Anne shyly. "I counted every one."

Marie-Anne says she loves the king, but I am always confused by how silly and childish she acts when they are together. Not like herself at all. It's just an act, she says. I must pretend to be a little girl so he can be a man.

"Leave us now, Diane," she simpers, and the king fair pushes me out the door, giving me a resounding slap on my backside as he does. "You had best beware," he calls after me. "I have army manners now."

Later we join them for dinner and I see that all of Marie-Anne's nerves are quieted and she looks as radiant and happy as the king. We are an odd party—the king, us four ladies, and a smattering of stern-faced dukes and generals. We eat in a large mess hall that reminds me of the refectory at the convent, and the king regales us with tales of recent victories. He has been having a grand time and assures us that victory will be France's before too long.

"Is that not true, Noailles?" he cries, and his chief marshal inclines his head and says he could not agree more with His Majesty, though his words are accompanied by the unmistakable odor of displeasure. Noailles is a friend of Marie-Anne's, but it is clear he does not support our arrival.

I was afraid we would be served army food, gruel or dried cod or some such horrible thing, but instead we dine on spicy lamb stew, cheese-and-egg pie, and delicious apple breads. I have a sudden craving for apricot jam, eventually settled the next day at breakfast with some damson marmalade.

"Perhaps you're pregnant," says Aglaë shrewdly, sipping her chocolate, watching me pile my third bun high with jam.

"No, Diane always eats like that."

I consider, then grow excited and flush. "Oh! Perhaps I am."

Marie-Anne raises her eyebrows and the ghost of something sour flits across her face, then disappears as quick as a wisp of smoke. She gets up to hug me.

The king comes in and joins the hug before we can separate.

"What is the occasion, mesdames?" he inquires, releasing us, then takes a slice of cheese from the table. "No, no." He waves the footman away. "I will not sit to eat. We ride out early."

"Diane might be expecting." The three of us know from the timing that it is not the king's, but the flushed look on Aglaë's face shows she is avidly considering the possibility.

"Ah, Lauraguais will be delighted. A man can never have enough sons."

"Perhaps, sire, but my husband is so unfaithful, I am not even sure if the baby is his."

The king chokes with laughter and cheese spurts out of his nose. When everything is cleared away and the tears have dried in the king's eyes, he takes my hand and bows to me, still chuckling. "And that, madame, was perhaps my least regal moment ever. If these were not modern times, I would have had you clapped in the Bastille for treason."

❧

The king spends hours overseeing dispatches and huddled with the generals in a room we call the Camp. On a table in the center of the Camp there is a sizable map of the area, and nothing delights the king more than to show us the changing pins of blue (us) and yellow (the Austrians) as battles are fought and won. It is all very dull but we are ready with polite murmurings of interest and take pains to conceal our ennui. Once Aglaë convinces one of the generals to stop lecturing about the proficiency of their Prussian allies and instead explain the forward thrust to us. I can't stop giggling. Marie-Anne runs her hands up and down the king's arms in a manner that causes him to blush and stammer, and causes the generals' eyes to almost pop out of their face.

We are very much aware that we are not wanted here by anyone except the king. Of course, he is the only person that matters, not the generals or the disapproving Bishop of Soissons, but there is a harsh atmosphere here that curdles our days. Everyone looks at Marie-Anne as though they want to chew her to bits, then spit her out.

We ride in a borrowed carriage around the streets of Metz, but it is a little town, nothing like Paris. The fashions are dreadful and most of the women are stout and ugly, and it appears that rouge and powder are not essential here. "Austrians look like that, too," says Aglaë knowingly; she is very well traveled and has even been to Vienna. "They are *thick* people. Not in the head, so much, but in the arms and wrists and legs. Lips. Such places."

We are invited to the house of the governor for dinner and suffer through an interminable evening listening to the man's son, a smug little boy of ten with a quavering duck voice, sing all six of César's arias from the opera *Giulio Cesare*. If you know that opera, you will know that the arias are very long. When we are finally released and back at the abbey, Marie-Anne declares that any future social visits will take place in our apartments. "Let the peasants come to us," she says, falling on her bed.

"The governor is hardly a peasant," says Elisabeth stiffly. There is a distant family connection.

"You know what I mean," says Marie-Anne in irritation. "These provincials. My God, why did I come here?"

That night we all drink too much plum brandy. Louis is away in Lille and it is a stifling hot night. Our rooms are on the first floor but even the open windows can't coax in a breeze, so we strip down to our shifts and fan ourselves and squeeze lemons on our arms and necks against the needling mosquitoes. We throw the bits of lemon on the floor and soon the floor is a yellow carpet.

"We are farther south than Paris, so that is why it is so hot," I say knowledgeably. Pauline once told me that in Africa, it is so hot the natives cook meat without making a fire, just by setting it out under the sun.

"Not south, just west." Aglaë knows; she has lived everywhere.

Richelieu will soon be joining us at Metz, and Aglaë entertains us with stories about him. They were lovers in her youth and she declares him to be the most accomplished man she ever had the pleasure of attending in bed, and tells us he uses his fingers as skillfully as he plies his cock.

"I am not sure this is a very ladylike conversation," Marie-Anne says, though I can tell she is interested.

"But there are no ladies in the dark," replies Aglaë, and we all laugh.

We fall silent and I start thinking about Pauline. I've been thinking about her a lot lately; of that last hot summer when she was pregnant, as I am now. How she used to complain! I'd like to talk about her, but Marie-Anne never wants to. Marie-Anne never really knew her; they were sisters but like strangers. Strange sisters. I giggle.

Marie-Anne rolls over and spills some of her brandy. "Oops."

The last candle snuffles itself out in a pool of wax. The abbey is frugal with their light; once it is dark, it is time to sleep. After the sun is gone the only thing that moves are the dogs in the streets and all is silent until the bells toll for matins.

"When do you think we should leave?" I ask. Part of me wishes to go back; I am beginning to press against my clothes and it would be nice to be at Lauraguais's Paris house in August. Take a cool bath every day in that marble room and order everything I crave from the kitchen. Apricot jam, lots of it. A whole pie filled with it.

No one answers.

"Summer is the worst time to be pregnant," I announce to the darkness. From the hot blackness Aglaë murmurs in agreement; she has six living children. To be so hot, and so uncomfortable. Pauline generally complained about everything, but now I understand her better. I hope I don't die in childbirth, as she did.

"I don't know when we should leave." Marie-Anne's voice is far away and I wonder what she is thinking.

"But it's not like you not to know," says Elisabeth in surprise. She's lying beside Marie-Anne and I thought she was asleep.

"I don't know everything. I'm not a witch. Despite what those men at the inn said."

"You must wait until you're older to be a witch," I say. "When you're an old crone, you can be a witch. Witches aren't young and pretty."

Louise

PARIS

August 1744

All night long the bells rang, and in the morning I rise early and send Jacobs out for the news. She came back with an ashen face, and even before she falls to her knees to weep out the truth, I know. Louis. Our king.

The news came to Paris last night: the king lies sick in Metz. He was ill three days when the horses left for Paris and we do not know how his health fares on this day. We can only hope and pray that he still lives. All around the city, bells toll and the news is read to the masses from the church steps. People cry in the street and the pews are packed: the whole city is praying for their king. On the streets they call Marie-Anne an incestuous bitch, the cause of France's woes. When I hear those harsh words I don't even cover my ears or turn away. She deserves that name. Bitch.

The Comtesse de Toulouse heard from Noailles that Marie-Anne and Richelieu have barricaded themselves around the king and allow none but the doctors in, not even the generals, the princes of the blood, or the bishops. When I hear that I wail. How can Marie-Anne nurse him? She has not a bone of kindness in her body. I would have been a good nurse. Oh, how I wish I were an angel that I could fly from this room to be by his side!

≪≫

Hortense arrives from Versailles with more dreadful news: the king's confessors are urging him to take his final sacraments. I fall in a faint and Hortense calls my women to help me to my chair. There is shouting in the street as news of the latest tragedy spreads. The king sick unto death! For all we know, he may be dead already. The thought is unbearable.

"The queen plans to travel to Metz," Hortense says softly as my maid wipes my brow. "She must be there, if . . ." She does not finish her sentence but we both know what she means. "She thinks to leave tomorrow if there is no further news."

"And Marie-Anne?" I ask.

"She persistently refuses to leave."

Louis must renounce her before he takes the final sacrament; if he does not he will die in a state of sin.

"Please, please, reason with her, and make her leave! She must do it for his sake. She cannot imperil his soul!" I rail awhile and feel better for the release my anger gives me.

"This is her retribution," says Hortense. "For her sins. Do not fear; she will be banished. I pray she is not there when we arrive, but if she is, you can be sure I will do all in my power to reason with her and get her to leave. Not that she ever listens to me."

"She never listens to anyone." I hate Marie-Anne with a fierceness I am surprised to still possess; I thought I had long forgiven and purged my ill will for her. That the king might be denied Heaven because of her! It is unbearable.

Hortense holds my hands tightly. "I will write to you from Metz," she promises. "I have asked Mesnil to come daily for comfort. He is a good friend."

"*You* are a good friend." We hug fiercely, then Hortense leaves and I am left alone with my grief and my anger. I wish Marie-Anne would die. A shocking thought and a shocking hope. Bitch. Whore. I say the words out loud and they echo off the plain white walls. There is a line, a finite end to the goodness inside us, no matter how we may aspire to virtue. I have been good enough.

This is the end for her. If the king is as sick as they say he is, she must be banished before he can receive the sacraments. Then he will recover, for he *must* recover, but he cannot go back on a deathbed promise. He will be reformed and live the rest of his days in harmony with the queen.

But first, he must get better. I spend the day and the night on my knees in the crowded church and allow some small, vicious thoughts to creep through the piety of my prayers. Where shall Marie-Anne be sent? It should be far, very far. And very austere. Perhaps one of the orders that observes silence? It should be cold in winter and hot in summer and surrounded by a dark forest, thick with wolves. Yes, a cold, far convent, where even the nuns will hate her.

Marie-Anne

Louis was fine. He passed the afternoon inspecting the fortifications on the outskirts of town. Then a pleasant evening; the talk was of recent victories and the fireworks the governor promised. Later we made love and I noticed nothing amiss: it was but a night as any other. After we lay together, Louis traced his fingers along my belly and asked me when I was going to give him a child. "I'd like a little daughter," he mused. "With her mother's mouth. We'll call her Rose."

"Don't you have daughters enough already?" I say tartly. I have decided I only want sons, two at most. His face clouds and I know I have erred. Louis loves his daughters greatly; his devotion to them borders on the bourgeois.

"I jest," I say quickly. "One can never have daughters enough. I would like four at least, delightful girls with their father's character and their mother's face. We shall call the first two Rose and Anne."

Louis smiles, my blunder forgiven. He wants to be happy and it is not difficult to prod him back to cheer. I have noticed a change in him since he is here at Metz; he is more confident and less reserved. Amongst the generals and the men he is easy and relaxed, and some of his shyness, that once built such tall walls around him, is gradually disappearing.

That night before he slept he asked for water and I poured him a glass from the pitcher by the bed. He drank thirstily and I was going to call for more but he shook his head and fell back on the bed. He went to sleep quickly, then fell even quicker into sickness.

In the morning when he woke it was obvious he was very ill. His fever was high and his eyes already glassy. I felt a terror like I have rarely known, that things could turn so quickly. A stag alive one minute and pierced the next, but without the premonition of the chase. His ashen face and already wandering eyes told us this was no quick and easy fever, raging for a day then disappearing. This was serious.

☙

Richelieu barricades the bedchamber and allows only us ladies and a few doctors in. The generals and the ministers, the pompous dukes and princes grumble against us but we hold the doors fast. I tell them it is a brief fever, and that the king needs peace and quiet, not a crowd with stale odors and incessant chatter. Most of all I don't want their carping looks and quick calculations, the glee they would not try to hide as they size up the gravity of the situation. Maurepas is among them, having oozed his way to Metz over the summer.

Diane takes up duty on her knees by the bed, praying for hours. I am grateful to her. I feel a strong urge to pray myself but I want to give more practical help. I pester the doctors and hover while they administer their endless bleedings. Louis does not improve but continues to burn, and though we drench him with water and fan his body, he is as hot as the evening embers. I hold on to his hand, pressing, squeezing, exhorting him to listen to me and to become strong again. I forbid him to leave me. If he leaves, my world is over. I need him. And so it passes for six days and then I remember the folklore from Burgundy: five days in a fever. Beyond that, no cure.

Louis's mind wanders and his eyes run with a curious yellow liquid. The doctors bleed, then bleed again, as if the little leeches can slay this demon of a fever. They consult and confabulate and then bleed again. I call them the leech masters, and the chief doctor, Peyronie, snarls at me, as he would never have dared snarl before. Another doctor, a thin, swarthy man reputed to be from Turkey, pleads to be allowed to administer an emetic, but the others ignore him and order more jars of leeches. I keep Louis well sated with water and diluted wine, but the truth is that he has eaten nothing—nothing—for six days. His skin is stretched and he looks like an old man. A dying old man.

I succumb to terror and fall to my knees and implore and beseech God. "If not for me, then for France. Louis is too young to die. We cannot be parted." For one awful moment my imagination leads me to the scene of Louise being banished from Versailles. In a snap I know her pain as it hurtles toward me and knocks me off my knees. I am being punished, and I deserve it.

On the seventh day the generals, princes, and religious men force their way in, encouraged by the doctors who have turned against me. They shout at me to leave the room and to leave the king in peace, but I ignore their bluster and hold my ground. No one knows what to do; to foretell the death of a king is treason, yet the king may be dying. Only Maurepas, my sworn enemy, hisses that I shall be banished, once the king comes to his mind and takes the final sacrament.

"It's the end, girl, do you understand that?"

"You are a fool gambler, Maurepas." I muster as much odium as I can. "And you are gambling on the king's death. I say it *will not* come to that, so think what will happen to you, talking thus to me."

Maurepas sneers and waves a hand toward the bed. "He's dying and you know it as well as the rest. The time for his final confession is coming. And when it comes, girl, then you go."

The king's confessor, Perusseau, is that most unusual of creatures: a sympathetic and kindly priest. I demand of him if it is true that the Bishop of Soissons, who circles me like a vulture over carrion, will force me to leave.

"I do not know, madame," he says softly, looking everywhere but in my eyes. But I want to know. I want to know the worst, so I can be prepared. To fail to plan is to plan to fail. I must not fail.

"Tell me!"

"I cannot, madame, I cannot, for I do not know. The king . . ." Perusseau stands helplessly before me. Diane rubs my shoulders and my back and suddenly I whirl around as though demons are forcing me to turn.

"Well?" I shout, not caring who can hear or not. They all know what we are talking about. "Tell me, just tell me, or damn you!" I swear, not caring that I am in the abbey and surrounded by monks, brown-suited ghouls with centuries of censure clinging to their skirts. No one answers, for what if the king does not die? They know I will remember clearly everyone who said I should go, and everyone who wanted me to stay.

ⵥ

It's early morning, pale warm fog filling the sick chamber, eight days since it all began. Outside the bells toll and the masses gather, their prayers and cries piercing the thick stone walls of the abbey. At last Perusseau comes to tell me that the bishop is getting ready to administer the sacraments, and that I must go. If I do not, the king will die without sacraments. And the king is dying.

Richelieu looks at Perusseau as though he were a bug he could step on, but says nothing. Perusseau shuffles nervously and I know he agrees with the bishop. A wave of terror washes over me: something bad, very bad, is going to happen. I flash to the face of the fortune-teller Sybille, her tense mouth and strained smile. Black-stained fingers of death. The woman was humoring me; she saw something beyond what she told me.

I fight my way back to Louis's bed but he only grows worse, and by noon his breath is alarmingly shallow and his skin the color of ashes. He slips in and out of consciousness and once even thinks we are at Choisy. Oh, how I wish we *were* at Choisy!

"*Bijou, Bijou,*" he calls. I am sure he is calling for his jewels, and not for Louise. I listen intently but he never mentions me.

"Long enough!" roars the bishop, storming into the sickroom. "Get that whore out. The king must confess, and all must be readied for the sacraments."

Back in my room I sit numbly on my bed and close my eyes. The king has agreed to confess and take the last rites, and has agreed that I must leave. He said it himself. Louis said I must go. In delirium, but still, it was said. The dauphin and queen are to arrive within days. And I—and Diane and our friends—we must go. Banished by order of the king.

"When must I go?" I ask. I am a duchess. I thought I was immune, I thought I would never know insecurity or want again.

"Today," says Perusseau firmly. Maurepas comes in and repeats the news. I wish I could spit on him, but instead Diane does it for me. The spittle misses and lands on the ground near his boot. He steps back in surprise and disgust and suddenly we are laughing, hysterically. I point my finger at Maurepas. "This is not over, and I will remember what happened here, today."

He bows and doesn't even bother to smirk. "Madame, go. Now. Listen—outside."

We fall silent and hear the chanting of people outside, crying that the whore must be banished or they will kill her themselves, for the sake of their king. I blanch. Richelieu enters and he is all business; he will survive this, as he always survives.

"Go today, right now. Belle-Isle will give you his carriage and none need know it is you inside. Rest and recover and prepare for the future."

What future? I think numbly as the servants stuff our chests and gather our dresses. Already carpenters are outside in the laneway, pulling down the wooden bridge between our apartments and those of the king, to show the world that the hated harlot cannot reach him ever again. I realize I have not said good-bye to Louis. My heart stops and I double over in pain.

"What is it, sister?" Diane rushes to my side but I shake her off. There is no need to say good-bye, I tell myself, because I will see him again. I *will* see him again. And not in Heaven. I will see him again on this earth. I know it. And all those who hustled me out shall rot in Hell. Yet my legs wobble like jelly and inside I am not sure of the truth, not sure of anything.

❦

We close the curtains and the carriage rolls through the streets of Metz. We sit tensely in the fetid box, breathing easily only once we have cleared the town. Then we are out into the countryside, heading south to a château where Richelieu assures us we will be welcome. A man on horse passes us at a gallop and in the next village we are jeered at and pelted with rotten cabbages. They cry that we are dangerous whores who shall burn alive. I wait to be dragged from the carriage and murdered by the mob.

Surely this is not how it is going to end? Diane grasps my hands tightly and Aglaë thumbs her rosary with her eyes shut while Elisabeth cries into her hands. They must regret our friendship, I think. But we get through that village, and two more like it, and finally take the road through a thick pine forest to the small provincial château at Fleury—an ironic name. The forest is dark and close, and as night falls we hear wolves and other beasts of the black night baying around us.

"Those men, all of them, the bishops, the generals, the peasants—they were like wolves," I say, "howling for our blood." It is the first word any of us has said in more than an hour. I am glad when we are finally beneath the gates of the château that is our destination for the night; at least here there are friendly faces and a welcome meal. I am trembling inside, we all are, and I gulp at the wine that is offered. Without having to be asked, the young hostess orders brandy brought and we drink in silence.

Everything is over. I have lost. God has abandoned me. One does not have to be religious to see something biblical in my punishment.

Diane faints from exhaustion and is carried upstairs to her room. For the first time I remember her pregnancy and wonder if she will lose the child. Then I remember Louis running his hand lightly over my stomach and asking me when we would have a child. Almost the last words he ever said to me. I feel the abyss upon me, and in front of everyone I begin to cry with great big heaving sobs.

The next day we receive orders that we must remove ourselves even farther from Metz; apparently four leagues is not far enough for such as we. We decide to head back to Paris, as we have received no instructions that we may not. Outside Reims, we pass the queen's entourage, traveling quickly in the opposite direction. Hortense is probably with her. No one recognizes our carriage and when we pass we stare straight ahead.

We were in Metz for only a few months, but it seems an age ago that we set out from Paris, laughing, gay, nervous. Now it's the middle of August and the fields are swollen with wheat and rye and my senses rush with the smell of Burgundy just before the harvest. What if JB had never died? I would still be in Burgundy, and never would have met Louis, or become a duchess.

They can't take that from me, my title. Or perhaps they can. Mistresses may be adored while alive, but before the king's body is cold they become the worst of whores. Hated and despised.

"Why do they hate us so much?"

Diane starts to cry and says: "They tried to tear Pauline's arms off."

We are almost to Paris when our carriage is recognized and we are surrounded by a mob that screeches like an owl and pelts our windows with stones and soft turnips.

Diane

It is going to be another hard winter and already frost and snow as deep as knees blanket the city. I know that nothing will ever be the same again. Everything has changed and everything is worse. We are trapped in the house, and when I hear the bells of the Bastille ringing for its prisoners, it is as though they ring for us, the hollow sounds floating through the thin air to taunt us in our jail.

We are back in our childhood home, the house a present from the king to my sister. We are in my mother's gold-paneled bedroom, her bed now gone, but the dead can linger in so many ways. The servants weren't expecting us and our first few days were filled with dust beaten from the carpets and the curtains, making me cough and irritated. Marie-Anne looked at me with dull red eyes and even managed to smile: she said she had never seen me irritated.

"Well, how can I laugh with dust in my throat?" I said tensely.

We have been all alone these last months; no one comes to visit, or even writes. I can't blame them, for contact with us is as deadly as if we were stricken with the pox. Only Aglaë remains, though she frets about her daughter's upcoming marriage to the wealthiest little boy in France—will her prospects be damaged by this? Elisabeth slipped back to Versailles last month to see if she has been damaged beyond repair. I think I will miss Court but I am not sure. Perhaps I will be allowed back? But could I abandon Marie-Anne?

I think I could. If they send her to a convent, I really don't want to follow her there. I've done my time in a convent, I think, remembering the slow, steady life at Port-Royal. Then, it was enough for me. But now? Never. I decide if I can't go back to Versailles, I will stay in Paris.

Marie-Anne is defiant. She says even if they banish her to a convent in the middle of the Auvergne, she will escape and flee across the border where the king's justice can't find her, and then she will make her way to Martinique.

"I have money, I have jewels," she brags, and spends her days poring over the chests that Leone has managed to bring from Versailles, rescuing what she can before all is confiscated in the name of revenge or law.

Through it all—the tears and the flight, the king's miraculous recovery and our current plight—I feel my baby kicking inside me. No one cares about this child except for me. She—or he, though I think it will be a girl—will be mine completely. No one will be disappointed if it is a girl; Lauraguais says he is hoping for a son but he would not have married me if he needed them.

My husband comes to visit and inspects my belly and tells me I am more pregnant than any woman he has ever seen.

"What," I say sourly, "how many naked pregnant women have you seen? How many children have you sired?" I am so tired and my nerves are stretched so thin; I am in no mood for his bantering comments. I feel like hurting someone: I want to pull off his legs, like Marie-Anne used to do to spiders.

He surveys me and softens.

"Wherever they tell Marie-Anne to go, she must go, and you must let her. It's not a good time to be her sister, and you must distance yourself from her."

I cover my belly again and caress the big, lumpen egg. Yesterday, she was kicking as though clamoring to come out, but today all is quiet. She wants nothing of this world or of this life.

"The king will never give her up. He loves her too much." I

believe it; I have never known a man as infatuated as the king was with Marie-Anne. So utterly, utterly in love. Sometimes I wonder what that would be like, for I have never had that experience. I am sometimes with the king, but only when Marie-Anne is unwell. Suddenly I think: I am like one of Lauraguais's breast pillows. A chest coddle, something to offer comfort, but only when needed. The thought is not pleasing.

My husband shakes his head. "You're wrong. The king cannot go back now. He has received the final sacraments. He has made a vow in front of God." He points up to the ceiling, just in case I had any doubt as to where He lives. "All have read his printed confession. There is no love strong enough in the world to overcome that."

"You don't know what love is."

"Neither do you."

That may be. That may be. We look at each other in silence. But I think I will love this little baby as much as any little baby has ever been loved, and maybe she will truly love me in turn. Before he leaves, Lauraguais hugs me, strongly and fiercely, and I think in surprise: But I *am* loved. I remember Madame Lesdig holding me, so tightly, the day I learned that Pauline died; there is grace in this world, in those that surround us.

✍

Today the king returns from the border with Austria, all triumph and majesty. A string of victories: France's prestige is restored and now the streets are noisy with cheer. Marie-Anne was right to encourage the king to go to war. It was her undoing, but her efforts have made the king more popular than he was before. The cries are for *Louis the Well Beloved* and even the pigs in the streets seem to squeal in approval; Paris is infected with love. Marie-Anne paces nervously through the rooms and then up and down the stairs.

"He will love that name," she murmurs. "Louis the Well Beloved. He will be so pleased."

She slumps in a chair by the window, her cheek pressed against the icy glass. The courtyard below is the repository of all her hopes and dreams. A visit, a letter, a sign. But all is silent and empty, the snow a smooth white blanket over the cobblestones. There are no wheel marks; no one has come to see us in weeks.

Marie-Anne's woman, Leone, comes in, shaking off snow and bringing with her news from the street. "Such a crowd, such a crowd. I've never seen so many people in my life! And all drunk with happiness and love." She stops and looks timidly at her mistress. Today there was a service of Thanksgiving at Notre-Dame and all afternoon the streets were raucous. By fall of night the crowds have dimmed and the chanting is replaced by drunken singing and the crash of fights.

"I want the truth," snaps Marie-Anne. "I'm strong enough for it."

"They clamored for the king . . . oh, how they clamored for him. He appeared in a window—the crowd was such I couldn't see him myself. But my! The roar when they saw him. Louder than the bells of the Bastille; louder than the largest thunderclap. Something to hear, indeed, and something I will never forget. Such noise! Such joy!"

Marie-Anne stays by the cold window, refusing food and drink though I make sure she has a pot of something hot beside her at all times. I have a maid bring a heavy blanket from one of the bedrooms, but even wrapped in the sumptuous pelt, she looks frozen and sad. The window is nothing but a thin piece of black glass between her and the icy night. She is not looking well, drained like a sack of curds pressed of whey. Her face is gray and black circles rim under her eyes.

I can't bear to see her like this, so frightened and vulnerable. Louise was always the one who would comfort us in the nursery, sing us a song when we had a toothache, pat away our tears when our toys broke. We need her now. She lives near this house, just across the Seine, but it doesn't matter: she is as far away as if she were on the moon. I put the idea of inviting her firmly away, and pray it doesn't bubble up in my chatter. I caress my stomach.

"He's coming," she says. "I know it."

To dampen her hopes would be far too cruel. But it is as my husband said: what the king has done, he cannot undo. "Of course he will come, Marie-Anne," I say. "He loves you more than anyone, and cannot be apart from you."

The clocks chime eight and it is already well dark on this bitter winter night. Marie-Anne continues her vigil by the window and stares out into the black void of the courtyard, willing a carriage to appear. There has been no letter from him, only a short note from Richelieu saying that the king regrets all that happened. Even Richelieu does not visit us, though he too has returned to Paris. Marie-Anne says she understands and that in a similar circumstance she would not take the risk. "It wasn't friendship," she says dully. "Only ambition."

"You must come away. The drafts will kill you." I am seated by the fire, my arms outstretched in supplication to the flames. Even the ring of braziers can't fight the cold that comes in from the icy night. The clocks chime nine into cavernous silence. We are in the Gold Room, where my mother used to sleep, and her ghost hovers around us now. Perhaps Pauline is here too.

Then we hear the sound of the gates being drawn, sweeter than anything that Couperin ever composed. A carriage rolls into the courtyard, fighting through feet of snow, the horses neighing and trumpeting in the thin air. Marie-Anne puts her two hands straight onto the cold glass. "Diane, come here!"

In lantern light against the pale snow we see a man descend, wearing a vast old-fashioned wig under a tricorn hat. "It's him," she whispers. "He came. Only days in Paris and he comes. I knew he would. I knew he would not forsake me."

Marie-Anne's confidence is infectious. I hug her and laugh happily. "He comes! You were right, you are always right. This is not the end. He loves you too much. He loves you *so* much. Come, we must get you ready. You can't receive the king looking like this. Some rouge, the pink and silver gown. I will entertain him while Leone—"

"No," says Marie-Anne, pushing a strand of hair back into her cap. "I will greet him like this. I want him to see what they have done to me. What he has done to me."

A footman opens the door and announces that the doctor has arrived.

We are cured. Life can begin again.

Marie-Anne

EVERYWHERE AND NOWHERE

December 1744

All of them, the hated, the pernicious, the fence-sitters, the black vultures, they are all to go: the Duc de Bouillon, the Duc de Rochefoucauld, Balleroy, the hated Bishop of Soissons. Even the priest Perusseau, though a part of me regrets that one. Five *lettres de cachet* will heal my bruises quite a bit. Only one man will remain, and on this the king stands firm: Maurepas. He claims that with Fleury gone, only puerile Maurepas will do.

We reach a compromise: Maurepas will stay but it is he who will personally ask me to return to Court. Perhaps humiliation, rather than destruction, will prove the best revenge?

I allow the king to kiss me, and when he puts his arms around me my body responds like a flute to breath and I shiver in pleasure. I pull away even though I want nothing more than to melt into his arms and lie with him and erase all of this ugliness in passion and love.

"Go," I say to him. "I'll come to you at Versailles. Soon the butterflies will open their wings again."

The next day Maurepas arrives and I receive him in my bedroom. The last few months have been a nightmare but I have come through, and though I am once again in the sun, I am so very tired. Maurepas is brisk and his manner is confident, but in his eyes I see an interesting mixture of fear and defiance. Around us gifts lie strewn on the floor: pots of jams and oils, a goose pâté, a new chair, a box of coconuts from Saint-Domingue, a fine silk shawl. The news is that I am victorious, and suddenly the whole world is my friend again. Diane sits on the new chair and spoons herself a pot of raspberry jam, her eyes on Maurepas. Aglaë sits beside her, nervous and worried.

"I propose a truce, madame," says Maurepas in his oily voice. "It appears the king needs both of us."

"No." I am without hesitation, for I have thought long and hard of what I will say: "The king needs me, but the king only *thinks* he needs you."

Underneath his powder the man blanches slightly.

"You have something for me?" I ask imperiously.

He hands me a note and my hand brushes his bare fingers. I shudder.

It is the king's wish for you and Madame the Duchess your sister to return to Court and retake your places on Saturday next. He would be pleased if you did not refuse him this request.

I do not enjoy the moment as much as I had hoped. When Maurepas leaves I lie in bed and cry, though I am not sure why. I am so tired, so very tired. All I want to do is rest. I believe my soul is exhausted, more so than my body. It's freezing in the room— in the whole house. I find it intolerably cold. Diane and Aglaë fuss around me. I can't hear them properly but I don't really care, I'm so exhausted and speaking is more than I can manage. I must rest. When I took the letter from Maurepas's bare hand I felt as though evil entered me . . . Does the Devil work through men like Maurepas? I feel Diane's hand on my cheek but I pull away from her, and then there is a hard kicking in my stomach even though I am not pregnant.

But I will have a son, not a son like Maurepas, but a good son. My son will be a prince, a son of the king. I must go to the king, on Saturday I will go. I will wear my pink and silver dress, his favorite, and I will find a hothouse rose for my hair, even if it costs me a hundred *livres*. A hothouse, yet this house is so cold. Now there are more people around the bed, talking, talking. My head is starting to throb and their words are like little lances piercing my brain. I call to them that they must help me, but they don't help me and then I am wet with blood, and the blood reminds me of the jam that Diane was eating, and then suddenly, though I am not sure how this is possible—perhaps Richelieu will know, or a priest—I am in the garden at Tournelle, lush with roses and buzzing bees, and there is JB, which is strange because he is dead now and just a name carved in stone.

But look, Louis the king is here. My love is here. I think the bees are dead. They have drowned in honey, or red jam, but my insides are on fire and there are too many people in the room. I drink from a copper cup but the liquid burns my throat, and where is Louis? Why am I not at Versailles? Is it Saturday yet? I hear voices that I have not heard for a long time and I feel great waves of love coming from the crowd gathered round my bed. I hear Louise's voice and I want to tell her that I know, I know . . . but what is it that I know?

Now I am floating down a dark stream. Perhaps it is a canal— at last I am in Venice. Are the canals in Venice filled with black velvet? Hortense is holding my hand and I want to say to her, *Hortense, you are a hen but you are my sweet hen and I will love you forever.* I can't get the words out because the black velvet waters come rushing over me, and oh, how wonderful it is to drown in black velvet. Everything disappears in the dark and the last thing I see is Sybille, the witch from the rue Perdue, and she looks at me with all the sadness in the world and suddenly I understand why she could not tell me more of my future.

Louise

The house is shuttered against life and the cold, the gifts lie forlorn in the bedroom, and the servants creep around. The death of Marie-Anne, and of dreams and hopes. Hortense is as white as pain—will she ever be the same? Will any of us? We are all here in the house on the Quai des Théatins, our childhood home; we were estranged, but Marie-Anne's tragic death has brought us back together. I visit daily and we huddle in the comfort of the familiar.

Diane gave birth to her child just days after Marie-Anne died, and now she alternates between laughing and crying, as we all do. The child is small and crumpled; she was going to be named Pauline but now she is Marie-Anne.

"But Paris is not safe for children," says Hortense. We are silent, remembering our first memories, the vast bosom, the milky smell of the sheets, the manure and the peat fire of the house in Picardy.

Diane dips her finger in a honey jar and gives it to the baby. The child sucks blindly.

"Is honey good for a baby?" The two mothers ignore me.

"But the country—Madame d'Houdancourt's children did not thrive well there," protests Diane.

"Yes, but that was Brittany. So cold! Picardy is not the same, my little Freddie and his sister are doing just fine."

"No, I want her close by me. I want her here with me," says Diane stubbornly, wiping her finger on the child's cheek.

Diane's odious husband visits, but he is surprisingly tender with her and coos over his little baby daughter. He comes with his two children from his previous wife, a quiet little boy and a girl with pale, corn-colored hair and no eyelashes. At first they peer with solemn shyness at the little swaddled bundle, but soon they are treating the baby as their doll, playing with her in their innocence, unaware or uncaring of the great death that has just happened. Their smiles and giggles and the cries of the new little Marie-Anne are all reminders to us that life goes on, even in the midst of such sorrow. Madame Lesdig is here too, fussing and calling both Diane and the baby her little chicks, and all the visitors and the commotion help to dampen and bury the pain.

There is talk of poison, of Maurepas, but the words are hollow and it comes to nothing. The doctors found she died of an infected stomach, worn out, they said, by the rigors of the last few months.

The king does not visit. Will he come? The unasked question, unanswered as well, hangs in the nursery and covers the house with wishes and longing.

I hope he doesn't come. I'm not an old woman but I feel like one: though I should be beyond such cares, I still don't want him to see me like this. But the question, though unanswered, is clear, for I know he won't come. He always ran from anything unpleasant, like a mouse from the jaws of a cat.

"He won't come. I know him—he won't come." I remember him at Saint-Léger after the death of Pauline. He was torn asunder by her death, but too soon he was able to bury the pain deep inside him and then it was as though she had never even lived.

"He loved Marie-Anne so much," says Hortense. She is going back to Versailles today, back to her duties with the queen, back to her life that will continue on without Marie-Anne. The new *dauphine* arrives this month; Diane's husband will travel to escort her to France. Life, the great life of that palace, of that world, will continue in Marie-Anne's absence.

Hortense embraces me and promises to seek me out more

often when she is in Paris. "We must—*must*—stay closer. We can't let anything keep us apart. Not again." Hortense cries as she speaks and I know her words are sincere. She is right. Petty struggles, silly feuds, all of it, in the end, what does it matter? We were sisters; we should have loved each other.

Little Marie-Anne starts to cry and whimper at the world. I pick her up and carry her around the room, show her the snow outside in the winter streets, whisper to her of all the things that she will do and see in her life. I gaze into her wide, unseeing eyes. Her little fingers wrap around mine and I feel a pang for the unborn children that could have, should have, been mine. Only God knows why.

I hand her back to the nurse; Diane snores gently on the bed. I take my leave of the house—I'll visit often, and care for this child and nurture her as she grows. The carriage wheels heavily through the snowed streets. Tomorrow I will go to Saint-Sulpice and pray for Marie-Anne's soul, with none of the spite and hate of my previous prayers. I will pray for Marie-Anne, for my sister, for the woman who caused me the most pain of my life.

There are things in this world we cannot forgive, nor should we. But I can forgive her.

I can.

Hortense

PARIS

An VII (May 1799)

The two young women come in, tutting as they always do and ready to scold.

"But, Grandmama, why are you sitting alone in this darkness? Every time I tell that Sophie to pull back the curtains and yet every time we find you like this!" Elisabeth is the oldest and the bossiest of the two sisters, all twenty summers of her.

"It's so stuffy in here," echoes Claire, settling herself onto the sofa opposite my chair. "Really, Grandmama, I don't know how you stand it. Why must you insist on living in this darkness?" Claire has a dreadfully affected voice, speaking half with a common accent and half with a lilting lisp that reminds me a little of that woman . . . but I can't even remember her name now. She wore lavender. Now apparently this affected voice, with its connotations of the street and the common citizen, is all that is fashionable.

I say nothing; I rarely do these days. We have this conversation every time, and every time I cede to them, but only for as long as their visit lasts. In truth, I prefer darkness. I have seen all that I want to see in this life and now I prefer the shadows. I am not afraid; the only ghosts in this room are small wisps that my memory conjures, that dart and hide behind the sofas, harmless to an old woman such as myself.

Elisabeth pulls back the heavy curtains and recoils from the window, coughing and smoothing the dust off her rosy cotton shift. A broad shaft of light cuts through the middle of the room in a dusty tempest and illuminates a portrait of Diane that hangs above the mantel. She keeps me company in my solitude, one eyebrow raised, and even in darkness I know she is with me. It is hard to be too melancholy around Diane.

They come every week, these two young great-granddaughters of mine, thinking with the arrogance of youth that their presence pleases me, thinking to fill their virtue books with the charity of their visits. In truth, I do care not much for them; they are rude and thoughtless, with none of the grace that I remember from the women of my own youth. But I suppose I should be grateful, for they are all I have left of family.

My two children are long dead; my son, Frederick, died when he was only twenty-two, a grief that is still raw and tender within me. My daughter also died young, in childbirth like my sister Pauline, and then the baby girl that killed her—my only granddaughter—lived but to the age of twenty-four. Now her two daughters are all that are left me, but they have their father's name and so little of my own blood running in their veins.

They are dutiful, I will give them that, and perhaps eager to maintain the bonds of family, for they are orphans—their mother long dead and their father executed in the Terror.

"So, Grandmama," Elisabeth says, settling back on the sofa, the room now awash in light, "what news do you have for us?" Her wedding is planned for this summer, and I know she will only become more insufferable once she is a married woman.

I look to them sometimes for traces of my sisters, but I never catch enough to satisfy. The way the younger one, Claire, laughs and shakes her head sometimes reminds me of Diane, and when Elisabeth winds her curls around her finger, as she does when she is bored or distracted, I catch fleeting glimpses of Marie-Anne.

How long ago it all was, and how fast the time went.

I force a weak smile, all that my face will now allow. "I am well, thank you, my dears." In truth I am not; I am eighty-four years old and my whole body aches. I have outlived all I knew from my youth, and even those from my old age. People admire me for my great age, or pretend they do, but no one thinks of the pain: Why must I be the one to see everyone I love die, when that grief is spared so many others? Why do some pass through this world so quickly, while others tarry too long?

"And you, my dears, what news do you have?"

I listen with half-closed eyes as Elisabeth chatters on about her upcoming marriage and threatens to bring her young beau for a visit. Claire tells me about the dresses she has planned for summer, in the new slim style. They look like Romans, these young people, in their silly chemises pretending to be dresses. Suddenly I am far from this room, far from these prattling girls, back in the Marble Court at Versailles, shivering with cold and excitement, wearing a Roman dress. That magical night, the night that Marie-Anne first met the king, the night when everything went wrong.

"I was a Roman once," I think, then realize I have said it out loud.

Elisabeth leans over and pats my hand condescendingly, for she knows she will never grow old and foolish like me. She looks down at me with amused indulgence.

"There, there, Grandmama, don't be silly. You're not a Roman and I'm sure you never were. Are you feeling quite well? Have you been eating your fruit?"

My maid, Sophie, brings in coffee and a plate of tarts. The girls talk and eat as they do, drinking their coffee and clattering the cups as they place them back in their saucers. Dreadful. These days the world is impolite; sometimes it seems as though the laxness of dress and the laxness of the manners combine for all that is odious in this modernity.

I think of them so much these days. My sisters. My memories are more sweet than bitter, though frustrating in their evanescence. But it was all so long ago: I am thinking of a life so far gone I can't believe it was ever mine, and all I have left are the letters to remind me it all was real. Diane and I were closest, in our later years; we were together, longest living, after all the others had died. First Pauline, then Marie-Anne, both taken so young and so cruelly.

Louise . . . well, she died on her day of exile. Her actual death came not too much later, in 1751, after nine cruel years of solitude and prayer. I pray she died happy. When she passed they found a hair shirt under her simple gown, and we knew then that her piety was not a ruse but a deep conviction. She never saw the king again. He knew of her death, of course, but if he grieved it was in private. It was a cruel end for a woman who sincerely loved him, perhaps more than anyone ever loved him.

After Marie-Anne's death, the extraordinary story of Louis XV and the Mailly-Nesle sisters ended. Her memory—our memory—was quickly quashed beneath the torrent that was the lovely Madame d'Étioles, the bourgeois fish from the forest who became the Marquise de Pompadour, and whose place is well assured in the history books. She reigned for many years and Louis loved her to obsession. He wasn't faithful—no, not Louis, not the man he would become—and she had her share of fighting off rivals, including, curiously enough, another Marie-Anne de Mailly, a cousin of ours. But that one was just a pale imitation of the original, and she lasted no longer than a cheap-wicked tallow candle.

After Louise died, only Diane and I remained, both of us still at Court through all the changes that came and went. Diane's little girl—our new little Marie-Anne—died before she reached the age of five. Of all the tragedies and the heartaches that our family has suffered, this I feel was the cruelest. The death hit Diane hard and I grieved for her; she was one of the good ones, never a bone of artifice in her body, and she deserved her small share of happiness, which in the end was denied her.

And Versailles is no place to mourn.

Diane finally retired from Court and died in 1769, thirty years ago now but a time that passed in a blink of an eye. She died at the height of the *ancien régime*—even now we call it thus, though it was less than a generation ago. Our Louis was still on the throne then, and it was before the changes, before the Revolution, before the world stopped then started again. I am glad she did not live to see the world she loved with sincere abandon explode in such a horrid way. She died at the right time, and though only our Maker knows the hour of our death, sometimes I regret having lived so long.

I survived the Revolution that struck this country, that awful broom that swept the land and rid it of the dust and dirt accumulated over centuries. They say that change is the great constant, and even those like myself that lived in gilded cages knew it was coming, but why did it have to be so cruel and so bloodthirsty?

I was imprisoned during the Terror, and many that I knew and loved perished. When they arrested me I was seventy-eight years old—can you imagine? An aging widow, wearing black and passing her days listening to her maid read aloud from old letters, her eyes riddled with cataracts. What threat was I to anyone? What was my crime—had I bored the revolutionaries with long-winded stories of my youth?

But I was not killed like so many I knew; instead they released me, and so I live on.

"Grandmama! We have a surprise for you! We went to Versailles last week." I pretend I haven't heard Elisabeth; I don't want her to even say that word.

"Can you hear me, Grandmama? I said we went to *Versailles* last week. Béranger came with us—I can't wait for you to meet him. The gardens are in a dreadful state but it was of passable interest. We had the most divine blackberry ices, and for five centimes you could boat on the canals."

"We bought you this," says Claire shyly—only she has the feeling and the grace to be uncomfortable. She places a small piece of gilded iron in my hands, cold and heavy. "We bought it from one of the peddlers. He said it was from the gate to the Court of Honor."

My hand won't cooperate and I drop the piece of iron into my lap. Versailles as I knew it in my youth, in all its pestilence and its glory, will never be again. Now the great palace sits empty, desecrated and ravaged by the Revolution. I can't bear to think of it like that.

I myself left in 1776, along with so many others. A virtual exodus it was, all of us disgusted with the new queen and her peasant ways. Funny to think the worst among us used to compare the late Queen Marie to a peasant; no, her Polish manners were sometimes rough, but she was at heart a queen and her blood never betrayed her. But that Austrian girl—you would have thought she had been brought up by the gypsies, the way she was determined to flout all that everyone held dear and true.

Once I left, I never went back. And now . . . its great halls destroyed, but not my memories. With my good hand I thumb the piece of golden iron like a talisman, willing it to bring me back to that place and time, that will never, ever, come again. Gone, like a faith that has disappeared and never been reclaimed.

"Thank you, my dears," I say softly, and to my horror I realize I am crying.

"Oh, Grandmama, don't cry!" The girls are horrified and uncomfortable; they have not the manners to deal with the spectacle before them. The tears continue to roll down my cheeks as they take an awkward leave, promising to visit again next week when I am better. I am surprised at how my tears fall, for I didn't think there was this much left in my dried-up old body.

After they are gone my maid, Sophie, comes in and closes the curtains again. She doesn't chide or scold me, or treat me like a child, just presses a handkerchief on me then leaves me alone again in the dark. It is in darkness that my memories come, floating like feathers down through the years to settle at the bottom of my soul. I long for them, I live for them, for what else do I have left? In recent years my mind has played tricks on me and the memories and images of my childhood rise up brilliant and clear, as though they had happened yesterday; meanwhile what did happen yesterday is lost in shadows.

When I was younger I saw the world in black and white and

thought the Bible was best read as a guide for judging others. Now I know that the world is but a storm sky filled with infinite shades of gray, nuanced and deep, everyone striving through whatever sorry hand they have been dealt by God and fate.

My sisters are all gone and soon I will be too. What then is left of their story—our story—the story of the famous Nesle sisters? Lingering memories in the old-timers, a flicker of recognition in some when they hear our names. A tomb in Saint-Sulpice, a place in the gossipy *mémoires* of Court life "in the old times," in vogue in recent years as if people need to be reminded of all that they had worked so hard to erase.

They circulate Richelieu's memoirs, but I don't think he wrote them: he was everything scandalous but at base he was a discreet man. He died in 1788, his timing impeccable as always. He enjoyed the life that our world gave him immensely, and died before he had to pay the price.

I close my eyes and wait to see my sisters again. Soon, out of the darkness, a memory comes, blazing through the black, its colors vivid and bright, and there they are. I am back with my sisters in our nursery on the fourth floor of the Quai des Théatins, the one time we were ever truly together, before fate and circumstances and malice and greed separated us all. I see Louise, always so quiet and content; Pauline organizing treasure hunts but never hiding the treasure; Diane so funny and playful, laughing at everything and everyone, pretending to feed raisins to the wooden giraffes; and little Marie-Anne, so clever and so innocent then. I smile at them, and they smile back.

How I wish that were how the world would remember us, but I know that that is only the vain hope of a silly old woman.

May God have mercy on our souls.

A Note from the Author

The story of Louis XV of France and the Mailly-Nesle (pronounced *My-ee Nell*) sisters is stranger than fiction but all too true. When I first learned about their fascinating lives, I set out to write a nonfiction account. But as I dove into the research and writing, the voices of the sisters—strong, true, funny, sometimes imperious—kept insisting on a more intimate and vivid portrait, demands best met by a fictional retelling.

Researching and writing *The Sisters of Versailles* was an exhilarating, challenging, and frustrating experience. Apart from one biography written by the eminent Goncourt brothers in late nineteenth-century France, mainly focused on Marie-Anne, little has been written specifically about the sisters. To discover them and their lives, I drew heavily on contemporary autobiographies and memoirs of the day in which they appear as secondary characters. However, most if not all of these sources contradict each other, for each account is subject to the author's personal biases, the lapses of time (many were written years after the fact), and differing desires to titillate and exaggerate.

Generally, the sisters' lives were best documented when they were at or came into contact with Versailles (though subject to the contradictions outlined above), while their childhoods and early lives have remained fairly obscure. I have endeavored to be as faithful to the historical record (or what passes for it) as possible, with just a handful of deliberate changes for the sake of clarity or timing, including the date of Hortense's wedding changed by a year and the dates of the Duc de Richelieu's sojourn in Vienna extended. All of the primary and secondary characters (with the exception of Zélie, their childhood governess) are based on real persons, and as much as possible tertiary characters are as well.

Every person that has ever lived is so much more than just the collection of dates and the handful of anecdotes that the void of history may provide. I've filled in the broad brushstrokes of the sisters' lives and personalities with an array of foibles, quirks, and faults that we as humans all have. I like to imagine Louise, Pauline, Diane, Hortense, and Marie-Anne reading my book. Perhaps they would laugh and giggle, cry at the memories, raise their eyebrows at what I got right, frown where I missed the mark. My hope is that they would recognize at least a part of themselves and their fascinating lives in this book, my tribute to them.

Acknowledgments

Writing can be a very solitary pursuit, but many hands have helped to bring this book from initial concept to finished product. First, thanks have to go to my agent, Dan Lazar, at Writers House, and to my editor, Sarah Branham, at Atria, for all their wonderful work and ideas, as well as to Alison McCabe, who helped enormously with the first draft.

The research process for this book was very interesting and rewarding; thanks to the DILA in Paris for the informative tour of the Hôtel de Mailly-Nesle; to Deborah Anthony at French Travel Boutique and to Odile Caffin-Carcy for bringing me behind the scenes at Versailles; and to Google Books for making so many obscure eighteenth-century books available online and for free, an amazing boon to any researcher. And of course thanks to my family and friends for all their encouragement and support.